PRINCE OF CAHRAMAN

A RETELLING OF ALADDIN

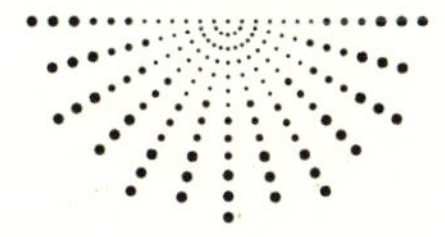

LUCY TEMPEST

FOLKSHORE

Ah, Love! could thou and I with Fate conspire
To grasp this sorry Scheme of Things entire,
Would not we shatter it to bits—
and then Re-mould it nearer to the Heart's Desire!

— THE RUBAIYAT, OMAR KHAYYAM

INTRODUCTION

Welcome to the magical world of Folkshore!

Fairytales of Folkshore is a series of interconnected fairytale retellings with unique twists on much-loved, enduring themes. It starts with the Cahraman Trilogy, a gender-swapped reimagining of Aladdin.

It is followed by the Rosemead duology, a retelling of Beauty & the Beast and *Princess of Midnight*, a Cinderella/Snow Queen crossover.

Join each heroine on emotional, thrilling adventures full of magic, mystery, friendship and romance where true love is found in the most unexpected places and the fates of kingdoms hang in the balance.

Coming retellings will be:

Sleeping Beauty, Hades & Persephone and The Little Mermaid!

MAP

Faerie
The Fair-Folk Ocean
ERICURA
THE NORTHLAND KINGDOMS
NIXIE
IDAFRO
AVONGART
LYONESSE
OPONA
ARMORICA
The Forbidden Ocean
UPPER CAMPANIA
ALMASKHAM
SILVER SEA
JALDOT
ARBORE
ROSAMIA
The Silent Ocean
EGLANTINE
ORESTIA
CAHRAMAN
ANBUR
LOWER CAMPANIA
DEEP RED SEA
SUNSTONE
THE GRANARY
AVESTA
GEMISHT
MERJAN

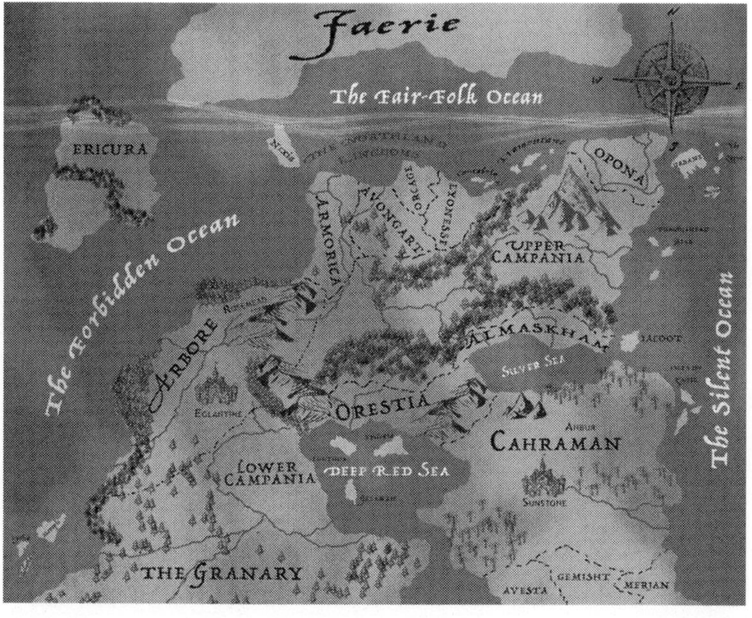

CHAPTER ONE

In the five years since my mother died, I'd become an expert in an assortment of petty crimes. Now I was about to graduate to a much more serious offense.

Arson.

The plan to start a fire had burst into my mind the moment the Final Five of the Bride Search competition had been announced—and I'd been chosen among them.

I'd been certain I'd be cut, that I'd survived elimination in two major tests in the past month by a combination of sheer luck and others' total incompetence.

My shock had been followed by relief. I'd thought this was a lifeline fate had thrown me, another chance to remain in the palace, to finally get to the gold lamp I was here to steal. The lamp I was to trade for the lives of my best friend and her father, and a portal back home to Ericura.

Then reality had sunk in like a rock tied to my foot, dragging me to the bottom of despair.

None of that would be possible if I stayed. Now the other girls and their entourages were leaving, without the divided attention they'd afforded me and without Cyrus to sneak me out of my quarters and around the palace….

My heart clenched painfully, as if it was shrinking, becoming a dried-out husk at the thought of him.

There was no Cyrus.

My Cyrus, the servant I'd thought was a fellow thief, the one I'd built all my hopes for the future around, was Cyaxares.

Cyrus was the Prince of Cahraman.

Every time my mind tried to wrap around this discovery it unraveled, spooled away into chaos. And if during my initial shock I'd fleetingly thought that I could use this fact, that I could continue the competition, and even win—win him—that notion had now joined the massive heap of hopes that had shattered with the blow of one realization.

I couldn't possibly win.

I didn't even know how I'd thought there was a chance I could.

Without Cyrus's help, I couldn't hope to get into the king's quarters, especially now with the heightened scrutiny that would come with only five of us left. I'd been invisible as one of fifty, but as one of five, I had no hope of escaping everyone's notice. I wouldn't be able to get the lamp, and Bonnie and Mr. Fairborn would be sacrificed to the Beast of Rosemead!

Being one of the Final Five wasn't a lifeline, it was a tightening noose.

Since I couldn't wait for it to choke the life out of me, I had to find another way to get the lamp. And it had to be *now*. While the crowd of far-more important people cluttered the palace, where I had one last chance to disappear.

But to get into the most guarded place in the whole kingdom, I had to create as destructive a diversion as I could.

Burning down the ballroom we were all in might be an extreme measure, but I was out of options. I was a cornered prey. To get out, I had to lash out.

I eyed the largest chandelier that hung over the now-empty dance floor, blazing with a thousand candles. Though no one was anywhere beneath it, and I calculated no one could get harmed, I was literally playing with fire. Fire was unpredictable, unstoppable, and the smallest spark could result in devastation. But I couldn't consider that now. This was my last chance to save the Fairborns.

Trembling with the enormity of what I was about to do, I picked a carving knife off the service table before retreating deeper into the ballroom. At its end, I ducked behind a column next to the thick, knotted rope that held up the chandelier.

Eyes darting around to make sure no one noticed me, I breathed as deep as my constricted lungs would allow. I let all my breath out in an explosive rush as I slashed the rope with a slicing blow—and only cut halfway through it.

Fright and frustration booming in my head, I gave my back to the room, trying to hide further behind the column, and frantically sawed through it. My heart seemed to have migrated to my arm, painfully throbbing in the hand that gripped the knife, threatening to loosen my cold, sweaty grip on the etched handle. I was sobbing by the time the rope finally snapped.

With my next heartbeat, the chandelier plummeted to the floor with a crash that shuddered beneath my feet like an earthquake.

All who stood within its vicinity scattered like the pearls of a snapping necklace, their shrill screams joining the cacophony of its shattering glass and distorting metal as the lush carpet instantly caught fire like it had been soaked with fuel.

With a blooming pillar of smoke, the ballroom descended into mayhem.

Shuddering, I tossed the knife back onto the table and dove into the crowd, hands over my head and screaming with the rest of them as they stampeded for the doors.

Guilt clanged within me before its echoes faded among the shouts and stomps surrounding me. I couldn't feel bad about my actions now. I had no worries to spare for anyone who wasn't in direct danger. I could only think of those whose lives depended on me. Whatever I did now, it was out of desperation to save the only family I had.

But that didn't stop me from being skewered with worry for my friends. For Cyrus.

I looked feverishly around, heart squeezing harder until I saw them. They were at the front of the panicked masses as all double-doors were flung open to accommodate the escaping herd. Cora was dragging Ariane by the hand behind her while lugging Cherine on her back like one of her massive bags. Master Farouk had lost his fez, his usually groomed hair falling around his eyes as he pushed as many people as he could towards the exit while bellowing, *"Loujaïne, Loujaïne, where are you?"*

Then I saw Cyrus.

He wasn't fleeing like everyone as the fire raged. He'd climbed atop a chair by one of the exits to tower above the crowd, the prince I now knew him to be shepherding his subjects and guests to safety.

His voice rang even over the din. "Slowly exit the room, so everyone can get out safely. Go left once you're out, then down the stairs to the entrance hall!"

Left and down. That was where all the guards would now be. I had to go right and up, far from witnessing eyes. It was also where I believed the king's quarters were. Where the lamp was.

Breathing through a layer of my skirt, I waited for the largest numbers to squeeze themselves through the doors. As I hung back, I couldn't help watching Cyrus, sun-streaked hair in disarray, sweating from the soaring heat as he continued to shout orders, somehow managing to control the panicked crowd. A born leader. More proof that the Cyrus I'd known had been an act. This—this was the real him.

My heart clenched harder when I noticed him looking around, searching for someone. Then his wild eyes met mine and their intensity made me gasp, inhaling a noxious lungful of smoke.

I had caused him this distress. I'd ruined the night he'd spent months planning. He'd looked so pleased with himself when he'd danced with me earlier tonight, so excited when he'd announced the names of the chosen to thunderous applause. To him, this night had been a successful step in his efforts to choose his own destiny.

Now I'd literally sent it up in flames.

Holding a hand over his mouth to block the smoke, he gestured with the other one vehemently for me to run, to get out. But he was staying behind, endangering himself to make sure everyone else got out first.

I wanted to stay and help him, then afterwards ask him to help me as he had before. But that wasn't possible anymore. I was going to further ruin all his efforts when I disappeared tonight. Just like he'd ruined mine when he'd told me who he was. But he'd done more than that. He'd shattered my plans for all our futures harder than I had that chandelier.

It was painful to look away from him, like peeling off a large scab, re-exposing my bleeding wound to the harsh air. This would be the last time I'd see him.

But I had to push all my warring feelings about him to the back of my mind and continue. Bonnie and Mr. Fairborn's very lives depended on me pulling off this last gamble.

I dove into the current of fleeing people the farthest away from him. Once outside, I broke away to the end of the hall. Around the first corner, I stopped. Taking in shuddering breaths and coughing out smoke, I tried to listen over the turmoil of my breathing and heartbeats for any approaching movement. When no guards rushed past and the pandemonium I had unleashed grew distant, I bunched up my skirt and sprinted up the nearest green-marble staircase.

At the top of every flight was a portrait of a former king, but there was not one of the king I was meant to rob. And now I knew why. Cyrus had hidden in plain sight, impersonating a servant to oversee the contestants himself. He couldn't risk any of us recognizing him, had needed to hide his resemblance to his father. The father who'd indirectly put me in this position. If he hadn't banished Nariman and taken her lamp, she wouldn't have kidnapped me and held my friends hostage to force me to retrieve it for her.

As I reached the top, now-deserted floor, sweat was drenching me, making me almost slip out of my shoes and lose my grip on the bannister. It wasn't just effort, but my dread doubling.

What if the king's guards hadn't left their post? What if they had, but I couldn't pick the lock? What if I did, but he kept the lamp in a hidden safe? Would I have time to search for it and unlock it? What if there was a magical ward on everything?

What if he was still in his quarters?

Caught in the storm of what-ifs, I stumbled over the final step and flew into the hallway. Swallowing a shrill shriek, I flailed and came to a staggering halt, right eye a few inches from a statue's spear.

After dodging so many dangers, I could have died the dumbest death, impaling myself right at my target's door.

Straightening up, heaving in difficult breaths, I scoped out the place.

This floor was less spacious than the ones below it, the layout more complicated. Decorations crowded every inch: mounted paintings, engravings, calligraphic art, platforms holding figurines, idols, vases and busts of both royals and gods.

From robbing a few lords' houses and a mansion or two, I recognized the pattern. Places like this were built to impress. Arranging one's belongings in ascending order of extravagance pointed to the best spot around, acted like the dotted-lines in treasure maps. When the king entertained dignitaries and other royals, they'd no doubt be taken down this hall, to see the best of his acquisitions, before they reached his private quarters.

It meant I was in the right place.

Feverish with fear, I felt like I was dragging my feet beneath a sweltering summer sun. The exhaustion that accompanied inescapable heat was growing as well, as if I was seconds away from fainting on a scalding road, like I once had when I'd been homeless.

I was close. I couldn't lose my wits now that I was this close.

I struggled to pull myself together, reminding myself that

this was my one chance to get the lamp and escape, to undo everything Nariman had done to the Fairborns and to me.

This time tomorrow, the three of us could be back home, with Cahraman and the people I'd met and befriended, or even loved, a faraway, fading dream…

A cooling shudder snapped me out of it. I had to focus on my task, on this moment. Nothing beyond either.

Just as I was about to turn the last corner, the towering double-doors at the end of the massive corridor creaked open.

I almost swallowed my tongue smothering my gasp as I jumped back and flattened myself against the wall as voices flowed out of the chamber. They rang against the walls in an ominous echo, still too far to be distinct but quickly growing closer.

I had to turn back!

As fast as I soundlessly could, I rushed back to the stairs. On the verge of hyperventilating, I barely resisted the urge to jump down entire flights. But that could end in yet another form of disaster.

As I reached the floor below, I heard multiple footsteps following me down steadily.

It was no good. I was too exposed. Once they reached the next bend, they'd see me fleeing and it would be as good as a guilty confession.

I had no choice but to turn and pretend to be ascending.

Stiff with dread, I met the last person I wanted to see halfway up the flight of stairs.

Princess Loujaïne—the king's sister, whom I'd belatedly realized was Cyrus's aunt—stared down at me coldly, slim brows pulled into a frown, grey eyes shining with irritation. "Lady Ada, what are you doing up here?"

"Your Highness!" I pretended to be relieved, avoiding her gaze and hoping she couldn't hear my teeth chattering. "I have been looking all over for you!"

Her frown deepened, shadowing her bright eyes. "Why would you be looking for me?"

"The ballroom caught fire!" I shuddered with the effort to keep from breaking down and weeping over the lost opportunity.

Her stiff expression shattered on a yell. "*Fire?*"

"Y-yes. Everyone ran out and headed down, but we couldn't find you," I stuttered, feeling my sweat grow cold, along with my blood. I could sense her disbelief setting in, see the probing interrogation about to follow in the hardening lines of her mouth. I quickly added, "Master Farouk is still looking for you."

With the mention of Farouk, I more than managed to distract her. The suspicion and disdain she'd been aiming my way at once melted into agitated concern. "I better let everyone know I'm fine then."

Before I could excuse myself, duck into a different direction to return when she left and try to salvage this mission, Loujaïne grabbed my arm and led me down the stairs. The staff members she'd been speaking with tailed us. "But first let's escort you back to your quarters, Lady Ada."

I had no choice but to let her take me back. If I resisted her, that would invite more questions. About why I of all people had been searching for her—and up here of all places— and why I wasn't eager to regroup with the girls in safety now that I'd found her. She might even ask about the fire.

All the stress had depleted me. Coming up with more plausible lies would be impossible tonight.

As she half dragged me behind her, despair descended on me, almost crushing me.

I'd set a ballroom on fire with hundreds of people inside it for nothing.

I'd wasted a month of never-ending trials and distress on *nothing*.

This had been my only chance to get the lamp and slip out of the palace with the departing contestants. And I'd lost it because of *her*. As dangerous a gamble as it had been, it had been by far the easier of my two options.

Now I had nothing left but the other choice. To continue as Lady Ada of Rose Isle, one of the Final Five competing for the hand of Prince Cyaxares of Cahraman.

But this time I needed to compete to win.

And it wasn't because I wanted to win Cyrus. I wasn't here for him and my desires didn't matter. I needed to win because only the winner of this competition, the one the prince would choose to become his future queen, would be invited into the king's quarters to receive some royal heirloom as congratulations. That was my remaining chance to get in there, to get the lamp.

Even if it seemed impossible, I *had* to win.

It was literally a matter of life or death.

CHAPTER TWO

"Can you believe it's down to us?" Cherine Nazaryan, second-cousin to the prince and my most unlikely friend cooed smugly. "Out of fifty girls, from all known corners of the world, and the Fates insisted we remain together."

All known corners except mine. This world either never knew Ericura existed, or had forgotten it ever did.

But it didn't matter if I was here by fate or force. I, like Cherine, was in Sunstone with only a week left to an uncertain future. But while she'd either go home disappointed or remain a princess, I'd either prevent a tragedy or meet a grisly end.

In other words, I was between a rock and a hard place. Except the rock felt more like a boulder balanced precariously above my head.

"No, I really can't," I sighed, hoping I sounded wistful rather than overwhelmed. "Guess it's going to take a little longer to sink in."

It had been less than ten hours since I'd ended the ball in

fiery mayhem. All attendees had since been accounted for, apologized to, and either escorted to rooms in the palace or to their homes. The aftershocks of my arson still reverberated through the palace, but my friends had seemingly shaken off the incident.

If anything, Cherine seemed more excited, as if the fire had only reignited her thrill in the competition. Now that I considered it, that scare couldn't compare to the heart-stopping fear she'd experienced when she'd been dangling from a gargoyle, one wrong move away from falling off the mountain.

Her reaction was a tiny relief. The fire had been a desperate diversion I'd believed wouldn't harm anyone. But just the thought it could have, froze my blood solid. I would have never put Cherine in danger, but if things had gone out of control, would it have mattered what I'd believed? Would I have been better than Fairuza, who'd pushed her over the palace wall?

The instant my mind wandered to Fairuza, my defeated, self-loathing mood flared into aggression. Now most of the competitors had been dismissed, I'd have more exposure to her. And to Loujaïne. Both would no doubt find new ways to undermine me.

On top of that, we were bidding our shared quarters good-bye. Our final week started with a move from one end of the palace to another, with each finalist in her own quarters. I, at least, hoped it would be somewhere closer to the one thing I was here for, so I could try to steal it again.

The stifling sadness of my failure and the upcoming separation from my friends turned the hopeful yellow of the new day to a murky, burnt grey. Like the fire I'd started, billowing a mile-high smoke pillar, blocking out the sun.

It had been a month since I'd last seen Bonnie and her father. Thirty whole days since the witch Nariman had arrived in Ericura and kidnapped us, bringing me here to do her bidding with the Fairborns' lives hanging in the balance. I was in this desert kingdom and they were all the way across the Folkshore with a beast that terrorized the woods of Rosemead. Until yesterday morning, her threats of sacrificing them to a monster had been just that, threats. I'd kept hoping she'd been exaggerating, lying even. But the glimpse she'd shown me, of a hulking shadow cornering a terrified Bonnie and her father…

I held back a sob. Now wasn't the time to drown in my own misery. I had one last week to prevent their situation from worsening. She'd said she'd hold back the beast until the winner was announced, implying that I should win, as my only remaining way of getting her the lamp.

If I were here for the competition itself, I would have agreed with Cherine. I would have thanked the Fates for turning things in my favor, securing me prestige and importance even if I lost. But she didn't realize the Fates had only given me more time to go mad with stress.

"Do you think it's one last test?" Cherine continued, blissfully unaware of my spiraling inner turmoil. "It was one test every ten days in the first month, but now we only have seven days. Will it be by the week's end if it's one?"

To escape answering, I pretended to check under my bed though I'd already gathered everything the night before. I'd been ready to split the palace the second they announced the Final Five, I'd told my *qarin*—a servant spirit Nariman had given me—to unbox itself and carry everything to the train leaving the kingdom.

But my papery helper had remained sleeping at the bottom of my trunk.

Seemed that it had known I wasn't going anywhere yet. To think I was more in the dark than it literally was.

There was also no escaping Cherine, who waited for my answer with crossed arms.

"Who knows what the prince has in store for us this time," I mumbled.

"Oh! I forgot to include *him* while thanking the Fates," Cherine exclaimed as she started putting pearl-tipped hair-pins in her dark-blonde hair.

"What about the judges?" I asked.

"*Pff*," Cherine huffed dismissively. "I would have thanked only the king, if he'd been involved in the competition. And though he might be in this last round, I'm sure it will be just a formality. This is for Cyaxares to pick his wife, and I'm sure the king only wants his son to be happy. The only one who partly matters beside him is the princess."

She was right. Most of the judges in the Bride Search were unremarkable, and I'd paid little attention to the ones I wasn't personally dealing with. But the ones I had dealt with had paid too much attention to me. Princess Loujaïne's pale eyes had always seemed to follow me, gaze fluctuating between dislike and suspicion.

I couldn't blame her. After all, I was suspicious. I was sent here by the witch her king of a brother had exiled from the kingdom. If she smelled trouble whenever I passed, then she was as sharp as a guard's hound.

But it wasn't her who had my insides tying themselves into elaborate knots right now. It was the other two I believed had chosen me. Master Farouk, who had clearly favored me, and the prince I'd failed to even suspect. The prince who'd masqueraded as a servant and thief, helped me countless times, made my time here exciting and made my heart flutter with hope and joy. Now my heart only shivered with worry and conflict, because I knew who he really was.

While Master Farouk had nearly given me a heart attack last night as we'd danced at the ball. He'd casually mentioned that no Bride Search invitations had been sent to the land I claimed to come from. I was almost certain he knew there was no Rose Isle in Arbore. Though I'd been too shocked to whip up an explanation, for some reason he hadn't exposed me on the spot. That had been all I'd needed since I'd expected to never see him again, and would leave before I ever saw the prince.

But now I'd see them both again, for a whole week, and anxiety was trickling back into me, like a melting block of ice.

Would Farouk tell Cyrus? Had he already told him?

If he had, then I wouldn't still be here. Right? But if he was keeping this information to himself, how long would he do that, and what would he do with it?

Cherine slammed her verdigris trunk shut, jolting me out of my daze. "Fates, judges, prince, princess or even king, what matters is that we all made it this far, right?"

"Shame it had to be *all* of us in the last five," said a cranky voice, bursting Cherine's flowery mood.

Cora, who had haphazardly stuffed her belongings in her bags, was still on her bed, hugging one of the four posters, one foot up and the other dangling idly. Or it would have dangled if she weren't so tall.

"I know," Cherine groaned, rolling her hazel eyes. "After all she's done, Fairuza still makes it to top consideration with us? This is an insult I will never forgive Cyaxares for once we're married."

I *had* to admire her confidence. From day one, Cherine had arrived believing, not hoping, that she'd marry the prince. I'd found that funny, back when the prince had been an afterthought, and I'd fantasized that Cyrus and I would run off together with a bag of treasure and the lamp.

But as the prince himself, Cyrus would not be going anywhere with me, but would most likely be choosing one of the two princesses.

"I was talking about me still being here." Cora snorted, lightening up a little. She was the only one, besides me, who never wanted to be here, who couldn't wait to go home. "But that works too."

"Careful, Cherine," I sighed. "Or she might try to off you again."

Cherine wiggled with fury. "She so much as breathes near me and I'll take out her eye."

"With what?" Cora grinned, malicious intrigue brightening her green eyes.

"With an ear of corn from your bag."

Cora threw back her head and laughed, unfurling her golden hair from its messy bun. "For a second I thought you'd said a unicorn horn."

Cherine pretended to consider it, tapping her lips thoughtfully. "If you have one of those, that will do too."

We exchanged one silent look then we all cracked up.

The intensity of our laughter fizzled out fast but soft huffs lingered as we finished up our room.

I was going to miss them. I really was.

I wished I could confide in them, tell them about my situation in full, not only the bits I'd told Cyrus and Ayman. I'd wanted to tell Cyrus who I was yesterday, before he'd told me first. That path was sealed off the second a crown materialized above his name.

Telling him anything now would be equivalent to confessing to treason.

But in my fantasies, it was still possible for me to do so. I could even dream that I wasn't here on a mission, and that my only worry for the future was to be Cyrus's choice, his everything—

Then reality reared its ugly head and reminded me that just like there wasn't an Ada of Rose Isle, there wasn't a Cyrus. With just a small tweak to our names, a distance was placed between us, one as vast as Sunstone's mountain, and more insurmountable.

Shaking those thoughts off, I checked my bag and trunk. The *qarin* had seamlessly tucked my loot under the dresses, what I'd planned to start a business on Ericura with, and have a whole new life with Cyrus and my friends.

Sudden, sharp knocks on the door almost had me flying out of my slippers.

"Set your luggage at the foot of your beds and head out," Loujaïne's muffled voice ordered from the other side.

With a groan, Cora got up and stretched her back. Cherine smoothed her hair and dress, looking between us excitedly. "Ready for the next stage, girls?"

I took in a deep, steadying breath. "As I'll ever be."

Outside, we found the dreaded Princess Loujaïne with the other elites, Mistress Asena, Master Farouk and Master Zuhaïr. Princess Ariane of Tritonia was behind Zuhaïr in a peach gingham gown that clashed with her auburn hair. She waved at me good-naturedly, offered Cora an uncertain smile then merely blinked at Cherine. I waved back tentatively. She, like Cherine, had offered to ship me off to her land to marry one of her brothers. She'd reasoned that I'd come here for a prince, and when I didn't get Cahraman's, I could have my pick of her brothers, save for the crown prince. An offer I would have taken if I were in her or Cherine's shoes, where any royal or nobleman would be all I needed in life.

Ariane knew that her only real competition was Fairuza, as both were already princesses. Cherine was still the highest possibility after them, with the advantage of being a native to this land. She knew the people, the culture, the expectations and the royal family. Fairuza might be the prince's first cousin but she'd never visited Cahraman before this competition, making her just as foreign as the rest of us. While Cora wasn't noble, she would still make an advantageous match since her mother was the head of biggest farming region.

Whereas I had nothing to offer—absolutely nothing. No title, no land, no allies or experience to put me in true consideration. But I was still here. I had to have been chosen for a reason, one that wasn't as obvious as Ariane and Fairuza's titles, Cora's connections or Cherine's nobility.

Maybe I was *his* personal choice?

Cherine sped past me to fall into step beside Loujaïne. "Where's our fifth? Tell me she was picked only as a courtesy. I know Cyaxares is kind enough to spare her public embarrassment. Did he send her home in private, away from prying eyes?"

Loujaïne glared at Cherine. "Fairuza requested that the prince himself escort her to her new chambers. You will rejoin both at breakfast."

My foolish thoughts of being the special one among them were siphoned into a drain of despondency. *Fairuza* was the one who got him to escort her to her new quarters. That was a fact worth a thousand words I never wanted to hear.

So *why* was I still here? After all the incriminating things I'd confessed to him? For his entertainment? Did he find toying with me funny? Was that why I'd won each round against many girls who would have made great wives and princesses?

I'd thought I'd known what Cyrus, the servant-slash-thief, had wanted from me. But what did Prince Cyaxares want? It surely wasn't pleasant company, or else he wouldn't be favoring Fairuza now.

I hated to sound bitter and jealous—but of course I was jealous of her! Aside from having his attention and a fifty-percent chance of becoming his princess, she was beautiful, noble and wealthy with incredible talents and no worries. I had too many of the latter and none of the former. I didn't even have his attention now.

I wished there was a way to turn back time. Back to the exact moment Bonnie and I were pulled into this mess. I wished none of the last month had happened.

Mostly, I wished I'd never met him.

I wanted to hate him for making everything so much harder, for twisting my feelings and scrambling my plans. But I couldn't. Not when I'd fallen in love with the side of him he'd shown me. What might not be real at all.

Conflicting emotions swirled within my head like the suffocating smoke from the fire as we reached a circular hallway with three doors along the curve of each half. To the right of each door was a veined, pink marble pedestal with the bust of a woman. Though made from the same monochrome material, from their features, it was clear all six women were from different lands.

Their names said as much: Helia of Orestia, Alysanne of

Arbore, Morgana I of Almaskham, Ethelstine of Orcage, Primavera of Campania—and Princess Zafira of Cahraman.

I remembered that last name. In *The Anthology of the Dunes* —the book Master Farouk had given me at our first test—the explorer Esfandiar of Gypsum had noted that he was sent into the desert to recover treasures by a Queen Zafira. Either this princess became that queen or she was her namesake.

Next moment, every rational thought fled my mind like steam from a boiling teapot. From the door by the bust of Alysanne of Arbore, came Fairuza. Her shiny dark hair was twisted up in a three-tiered bun, set by a peacock-shaped comb, with her jewels as if made to complement her bell-shaped, silver-satin dress. The epitome of calm perfection. It made me want to wring her by the neck and ruin both.

But Fairuza *was* uncharacteristically serene as she floated out to us, her handmaidens rushing to flank her sides like they were extensions of her. All three wore the same calm, smug expression like they had the peace of mind I so desperately wanted.

The black eye I had given her was healing well, too. It was now more easily covered up by makeup. I wanted to punch her other eye when Cyrus came out of her room last.

All my anger faded when I saw him clearly, and was immediately spellbound by his presence. He wore an open coat the color of his eyes over a white ensemble, a simple design but nevertheless it was complex in rich material and subtle embellishments. His thick mane of sun-streaked hair was styled as it had been last night, when he'd transformed from Cyrus to Cyaxares, with the fairer locks of his fringe smoothed to one side rather than in a natural part or a mess over his bright green eyes.

I had once noted the timeless beauty of his features,

compared it to the royal sculptures hidden in the vault, imagined him made of the same precious material with his skin smooth gold, his hair shining bronze and his eyes encrusted emeralds—the crown jewels of his magnificent face. That had been before I'd known that he was, in fact, the descendant of those royals.

But with that in mind, he did look like a different person. I didn't know whether this was my perception now I had to reconcile both aspects of him, or if he truly was different now that the act was over. Yet, regardless of what I thought, he dazzled me more than the glittering structures of Sunstone and all the treasure in the palace vault put together. He was their combined luxury in motion. He was the living embodiment of Cahraman's history and wealth, and it made him fantastic to behold and painfully unattainable.

Still, this was the man I needed to win. Not for my own desires, but because I had to. As the prince, he was no longer my prize, but a means to an end. Being chosen by him led to his father's quarters, to be gifted his ancestor's tiara. I'd only use the opportunity to steal the lamp and run, leaving him to settle for his runner-up. To marry Fairuza, as their aunt, Princess Loujaïne, clearly wanted from the start.

That would have been the unquestionable plan if I hadn't formed a relationship with him. It may have been based on us both lying about who we were, but the time we'd spent together, the words we'd spoken, the feelings we'd expressed had felt so genuine, still flowed in my blood and reverberated in my being. I couldn't yet stuff them in a dark corner of my mind among all the painful memories I stowed away so I could survive.

I didn't know which I wanted to do more, run my hands through his silky hair or punch Fairuza in the eye again. Or punch them both. What had he been doing in there anyway? Couldn't he at least have the decency of pretending he was giving the rest of us consideration?

I knew I had more important things to get riled up over, but that didn't even alleviate my irrational anger.

"Good morning, my ladies," he greeted us with a wide grin. It wasn't like any of the ones he'd given me in private, was as perfected and put-on as the rest of his outfit.

I couldn't help the snarky grumble that whistled through my clenched teeth. "Is it?"

None of our handlers looked pleased with my comment. Fairuza curled her lip at me in distaste. I mirrored her expression, no doubt looking far uglier doing it.

Cyrus's fake smile dulled slightly. "I take it you're still spooked by yesterday's incident? It's only natural if you are."

The correction of *I am more spooked by your aunt* died on my tongue as I held it back.

"Do we know what caused it?" Ariane asked, diverting his attention, softening his uneasy expression into a thoughtful one.

"The rope holding up the chandelier snapped under its weight," he said, like it was an answer he'd memorized, likely fed to him by his council. "It must have been too old or too weak for such a heavy piece—"

"Or it was cut on purpose," Loujaïne interrupted, lips in a grim line.

It was an effort to control any tells, to give my best wide-eyed look of confusion. "Why would anyone do such a thing?"

Cyrus gave his aunt a quick, cutting glance. "It is unlikely that someone did."

"It was fine and firm for decades," Loujaïne snapped. "Why would it snap yesterday when the room was full of nobility?"

"*Because* it hasn't been replaced in decades?" Cyrus suggested, his tone signaling that he was done with this conversation. "And that is what an accident is, Your Highness."

Loujaïne, nevertheless, persisted. "Rope that tears looks different than one that's cut. The Head of the Royal Guard said this was cut."

As Cyrus's posture stiffened and Farouk reached a hand for the princess's shoulder, Cora snuffed out the oncoming disagreement with an uninterested drawl. "Well, you did spurn twenty noblewomen yesterday. One of them was bound to set you on fire for that."

While I had to stifle my snort at Cora's comment, everyone, even Loujaïne faced her with stunned expressions.

Cora cocked her head at all of them, before rolling her eyes with a long-suffering sigh when no one seemed to catch on. "The last two times you sent girls home it was in a private setting." She turned to Cyrus. "Yesterday, you didn't even bother naming the eliminated or sheltering them from the embarrassment of being personally disqualified by you. You spurned them right in front of a roomful of their peers, publicly humiliating them by picking girls they no doubt think are inferior to them." She made a vague gesture at herself and me, making him more uncomfortable with each word. "Highborn girls probably see public rejection as grounds for retaliation."

"What Cora is saying is, maybe one or more wanted to take the place down on their way out," I joined in, following the path she'd paved me—whether purposefully or not—out from Loujaïne's scrutiny. "If it was to derail the competition or just express anger and exact vengeance, we'll never know."

"That…makes sense." Cyrus nodded, hand rubbing his jaw,

brilliant eyes narrowed in contemplation. "But most have already embarked on their travel home, so we neither have the means nor the time to conduct an investigation."

Loujaïne waved a hand, looking suddenly fed-up. "Perhaps it was an accident, perhaps it was one of the understandably upset noblewomen. There is no need to let such accusations follow them out the palace. And since there's no way to prove it either way, the last thing we need is to spark a feud with another land over unsubstantiated speculation."

I almost wanted to laugh at how quickly she'd conceded. But whatever relief I felt at throwing Loujaïne off my trail fizzled out when I noticed Cora's sideways glance and rosy lips quirked in a smirk.

What was going on in that golden head of hers?

Master Farouk coughed into his fist, getting our attention. "Can we please get back to the reason we are gathered here?"

Loujaïne nodded, tucking her hands in the flared sleeves of her floral emerald robe. "This hall is where the finalists of Cahraman's first Bride Search settled. It is believed that each room holds its own luck, so your destiny might reflect that of the girl who boarded there."

"There are six rooms, though," Cherine pointed out. "I don't remember there being a sixth suitor during Abraxas the First's Search."

"That's another part of the tradition," Cyrus said, not entirely looking at her. "With every Final Five is a female member of the prince's family. Supposedly to see the girls in a way he can't and decide who she thinks is the best."

Cora raised her eyebrows at him. "I thought you were the one picking?"

His eyes landed on me then, bright and hypnotic as ever. "I wish it were that simple."

CHAPTER THREE

$\mathcal{A}$s Cyrus's gaze bore into mine, it felt as if I'd forgotten how to breathe.

After what felt like an eternity, he tore his eyes away, and continued, his deep voice ringing off the marble floors and walls. "Varying factors went into choosing who left every Elimination Day, including opinions and impressions. Mine were among many."

Curiosity smothered my inner turmoil. What opinions did I inspire and what impressions did I invoke during our time together that made him choose me? Because I had surely done the opposite of everything expected of potential brides. He didn't even need the watchful eyes of his guards, judges and aunt to know that I wasn't princess-worthy, and that I was trouble. He'd experienced that firsthand.

"But you weren't even there," Cherine pointed out, pouting. "Did you just read reports on us?"

"He was there," said Cora, idly twisting one long lock of her wavy hair. "He helped me pull you and Ada up off the wall, remember?"

All eyes turned to him. Loujaïne and Fairuza wore matching expressions of stony-faced shock, though Loujaïne's had to be an act. She had known the entire time what he was up to. This explained her reaction every time she had seen him around me. She'd hadn't been annoyed with a random servant's misconduct, but disapproving of her nephew singling me out.

How had he convinced the whole palace to be in on his ruse? How did no one slip up and address him as their prince? How long had he planned and trained for this?

As the Prince of Cahraman he must have had all the time in the world to perfect his deception. While I got the fly-by-the-seat-of-my-pants option when Nariman tossed me into this kingdom and contest.

"Yes, I was, though I shouldn't have been," he admitted, that fake, reassuring smile back on his effortlessly handsome face. I didn't know how I had missed it before, how he held himself, gestured, walked, how regal his every move and expression was. He was every bit the storybook prince that fueled most folktales.

On the other hand, my perception of a real-life prince was too bogged down by the old, fat, drunkard merchant-lords I'd served in taverns throughout Ericura.

"The last time a prince of Cahraman needed a Bride Search was over a hundred years ago." He sighed mid-explanation, as if the subject now exhausted him. "The eliminations were conducted by his advisors and immediate family. He only got the final week to pick the one he agreed with the most out of the Final Five. Even then, his closest female relative provided him with the ultimate truth on his candidates."

I did not like where this was going.

I liked it even less when I caught Loujaïne staring at me,

her silver eyes flashing with a combination of disturbing feelings. Not those they'd held during the sabotaged chandelier argument, but a familiar concoction that had been brewing the whole month. Each time I'd caught her watching me, I'd found one of three intense emotions: suspicion, recognition and anger. It was like I reminded her of someone she hated. It was hard not to be on edge with her eyes on me, and it was harder still not to be curious about who I reminded her of.

My first night here, I'd spun up a story about safeguarding my jewelry as an excuse to get into the vault. Pretending they were all I had left of my mother had softened Loujaïne's hardness for a minute. Until I'd said my mother's name.

Apparently, the name *Dorreya* had an unshakeable impact on her the way it did on me. Not that it was possible she could have known my mother…

"You don't have a sister, do you?" Ariane asked Cyrus as he started pacing the hall.

He stopped by the bust of Morgana I of Almaskham, who I realized had the same brow-ridge and facial spacing as him, possibly the same deep-set eyes. "No, I don't. And my female cousins are competing for my hand, so neither can be the sixth lodger in this hall."

"What about your mother?" I asked, praying this wasn't going where I thought it was.

His false expression cracked, letting a real emotion slip through. Hurt. "She's not with us anymore."

The blood heating my face sank to my feet, numbing them and leaving me unsteady.

It had never occurred to me that he had no mother, mostly because he'd told me so little about himself. But that explained why we never heard of a queen. It was one crucial detail that tied my feelings to his once again.

I wanted to say I was sorry for bringing it up, tell him I knew the agony of being motherless, talk to him about my mother and hear about his. But I couldn't. I wouldn't. That was too personal, too intimate, and we weren't on these terms anymore. Relating to his loss didn't make me forgive the mind-boggling ruse that had me connecting with him in the first place.

"No sister, no mother, no cousins, which leaves…?" Cora counted on her fingers.

Loujaïne stepped forward. "Me."

I squeezed my burning eyes shut. Of course it had to be her. I wouldn't get away with anything under her watchful eyes.

"I'll be here if you need anything," Loujaïne said. "Questions and such. And to give each of you a good part of my day."

"That's not necessary," Cora said bluntly.

"But of course it is. For all intents and purposes, one of you will be my daughter-in-law." Loujaïne approached, soft, calculated steps clacking down the hall. "You will also spend time with one another. I see most of you are already friendly." Loujaïne paused to eye me. "Or at least friendly with one person." Her frosty gaze released me to move to Fairuza with a softer version of her disapproving glances. "So we'll shuffle the group dynamics a bit. If you're not with me, you're with the prince or with one another."

"What's the purpose of having tea time with the competition?" Fairuza asked, composure replaced with bothered impatience.

"To see how you interact with others in a one-on-one setting, especially competition," Cyrus said, stepping onto the center circle inlaid in the marble like a bull's eye. Fitting really, being the target of all this. "Beauty, talents, education and party planning are not all it takes to be a queen."

"What else is there apart from giving you heirs? Shouldn't you be checking if they're all fertile to begin with?" Fairuza butted in, impatience growing.

Cyrus inclined his head at her in acknowledgment. "This is precisely why the presence of a princess of the land is important. You would do whatever my dear aunt does as a princess, and even more the day you become queen."

"It's a job, girls," Loujaïne said. "If you're not up to it, you can always decline and make our search easier."

Predictably, Ariane, Cherine and Fairuza met this offer with a shouted "NO!"

Loujaïne's lips twisted at their overzealous response. "Good. The final week starts now, with the first test being your choice of room." She spread her arms. "Choose."

With a sweeping glare, Fairuza went back inside Alysanne of Arbore's room without another word.

Cherine beat Ariane to the room of Morgana of Almaskham leaving her to pick Helia of Orestia's room. I smoothed the sculpted bumps of Zafira's wavy hair to announce my choice.

That left Cora with either Ethelstine of Orcage or Primavera of Campania.

She shrugged and opened Primavera's room.

"Great. After you settle in, we will call you for lunch, then we can officially begin the personal tests," Cyrus announced, watching Loujaïne fling open Ethelstine's door.

After all doors closed, he paced towards me, hands behind him, a familiar ease in his smile and posture. "So, how was your night?"

"Stressful."

His breath hitched on a breathless laugh. "Not talking about the fire, are you?"

"No."

He lowered his head, loosening his hair from its side-part and back over his eyes, making him less stiff, less noble, more….mine. My Cyrus, not Fairuza's Prince Cyaxares.

Which version was the real one? I wanted it to be the one I knew, not the persona that had appeared since last night. But I suspected the one I faced now was neither.

"I thought you knew," he said quietly, coming closer, lifting his hand in an appeasing gesture, the rings on his fingers catching the sunlight streaming from the towering window at the end of the hall.

Those were not stolen from the vault as I'd thought, but his. A gold signet ring, beveled with his coat of arms—a sun. A decorative bronze ring, its sapphire stone set in a seat of claws. And a rose-gold one set with a silver pearl that stopped at the knuckle of his little finger.

Upon closer inspection, it couldn't be his ring. It was too small. A woman's ring.

His mother's?

At the thought of it, I was hit by a downpour of misery.

Before I'd resorted to stealing, I'd sold off everything my mother had left me, the last thing being her ring. The day I pawned it had been when I'd said goodbye to her forever.

Suddenly, all my anguish turned to anger. "How was I supposed to know? You were dressed like the rest of the staff, served us in between sneaking around. And you led me down through the tunnels and *into you family vault.*"

He came even closer, grazing his lower lip with his pearly teeth. "I somehow thought you'd worked out who I was. But it seems it was a better disguise than I thought."

Dragging my eyes away from his lips, I shook my head, insistent on making it clear how mad I was. "Yes, considering your own cousins didn't recognize you."

"I was banking on that," he admitted. "I've seen Cherine only once when we were children, and the rest of our 'friendship' was through correspondence."

"And Fay-Fay of Arbore?" I asked mockingly. I knew I had no leg to stand on, but I couldn't help letting how disappointed and bitter I felt spray out of my every pore.

He shook his head. "Never had any contact with her before last month. Heard plenty about her, though."

"How is it you communicated with your second-cousin and not your first?"

He slid Fairuza's door a sideways glance. "Because my father and her mother thought there was no need. They assumed that once she came of age they would send her here and I would marry her with no complaints."

Intrigue broke my resolve, softening my frown. "Why didn't you?"

His attention was back on me fully. "I told you down in the market, remember?"

There was something almost fearful in the way he said it. Like it would have hurt him if I had forgotten that day, or what he'd said.

Did that happen often? People not caring about or remembering what he had to say unless it was directly related to his status as a prince?

But I remembered everything he'd ever said to me, each word a block that built a lasting structure in my mind. Our conversation in the market was engraved there. About him wanting to go beyond what had been planned for him, so that even if he didn't find what he needed, and settled for what he already knew, he'd know he'd explored all his options. It had reminded me of my argument with Bonnie about her urge to venture beyond our island. But looking back with his new status in mind, his endeavor was far different from Bonnie's simple thirst for adventure.

He hadn't been talking about traveling, but about his rejection of Fairuza as his only option for a wife and holding the Bride Search to see if there could be someone else. That if he failed, he would have then married her knowing he hadn't surrendered to his destiny without trying to change it.

Was that why I remained here? Because, under the protection of anonymity, he'd shared too much about his true self with me? If *that* had been his true self at all.

Confusion squirmed in my stomach, felt like my intestines were trying to strangle each other. "I remember you messing with me," I mumbled.

His eyes widened. "Messing with you?"

"Don't *you* remember?" I crossed my arms over my chest to keep from trembling. "Pretending to enjoy my company, to be someone who'd help me grocery shopping and be all domestic and affectionate?"

"I wasn't pretending!" he yelled abruptly, only noticing the volume when it echoed back to him. He cleared his throat, lowered his voice to a gruff whisper. "I wasn't pretending."

I wanted to believe that was true, that our time together meant as much to him as it did to me, *so* much I wanted to smack myself. His feelings towards me ought to be the last thing I fixated on. Yet my intense feelings for him took up as much space in my conflicted being as those I held for the Fairborns' safety.

But he'd escorted Fairuza alone to her chambers. *That* still gnawed at my petty brain.

I hugged myself tighter. "Then what was the point of it all?"

"Hasn't it occurred to you our time together was honest?"

"It would have, if it had started honestly," I seethed.

Irony, thy name is Adelaide.

But maybe not. I'd been forced to impersonate a noble-woman for a noble cause: saving my new family. Cyrus had created a servile persona to spy on his prospective brides.

The worst thing wasn't that his charade was potentially dangerous for me. It was that he'd given me hope. Hope that I'd found someone like me, someone who yearned for a better life and could build that life with me. That hope that had filled my lungs like air now ate at me the same way the fire I'd started had eaten through that ballroom, turning everything to ashes.

He lowered his head until his eyes were inches from mine. "If I came up to you in all my primped and perfumed glory and introduced myself as Crown Prince Cyaxares of Cahraman, the one who sent for you and forty-nine others, would you have shown me that side of you?"

"Would *you*?"

He blinked as he unfolded upright. More hair fell over his forehead, casting shadowy tendrils over his brow and more contrast to his stunning eyes.

What felt like a lifetime ago, that ring I'd pawned had held a gem their color. That same lime-green that hid so many shades within its facets and shone brightest in daylight. My mother had called it an emerald her entire life, said it had been her aunt's. But the pawnbroker had said it was peridot, its less valuable counterpart.

It was the opposite with him. He'd turned out to be the prince, not the pauper.

Yet, looking deep into his hypnotic eyes, I could still see so many possibilities, ones I had already abandoned. For no matter how hard he might laugh at the girls who'd messed up their chance with him, how cocky he became now he was back in his born and bred status, his eyes had never been anything but kind.

Perhaps this wasn't a game to him.

He finally exhaled, a heavy, weary breath. "No. I believe I wouldn't have felt free to. Last night was supposed to be the first time any of you put a face to the name."

"Ruined my own surprise when I cornered you during that test, didn't I?"

"'Cornered'? You mean when you grabbed me by the collar and hassled me for information," he teased. "Though, most would say that gave you an advantage over the rest."

"Why? Because I got you to carry my groceries for me?" I batted my eyelashes at him in exaggerated innocence.

"Because you got to like me without the crown." He paused, hesitating. "At least, I hope you do."

If he was looking for assurance that, yes, I had liked him, too much, as he'd been with me, not as he presented himself now, then he was out of luck. The confession stuck in my throat among a jumble of molten emotions. And for him to be asking for reassurance, when I was the one who needed it, was as rich as he was.

As silence dragged past my usual response-time, he asked again, his voice a subdued rumble, "Do you?"

"Do I what?" I uncrossed my arms, sliding my silver bracelets down with a soft jingle.

Worry seemed to seep beneath his skin, tensing his form and twisting his features, making him a completely different person from his usual easygoing self.

He really cared what I thought about him?

"Why am I still here, Cyrus?"

He relaxed a bit, some humor resurfacing. "Still Cyrus, is it?"

"Would you prefer Your Majesty?" I injected as much pretentious air as possible into a stretched out *Your Majesty*, lifting one layer of my skirt in a pretend-curtsey.

"Highness," he corrected solemnly. "Call me Your Highness. Your Majesty is my father."

Alright. That was funny. I'd give him that.

His eyes crinkled adorably as he cocked his head at me. "Ah, got you to smile. Guess you're not too mad at me anymore."

"Don't push your luck, *Your Highness*." It came out angrier than I meant it to.

The smile fell off his face as he stepped back, hands raised in lighthearted surrender. "I believe that's my cue to leave."

I instantly felt bad. I reached out to him, fingers curled in uncertainty. "Cyrus…"

He only bowed his head. "I'll see you at lunch, my lady."

Before I could say anything more, he pivoted away smoothly, headed down the hall, hands clasped behind him, face turned up as if in distracted admiration of the ceiling art.

I watched him leave, feeling as if my heart was being dragged in his wake.

This hadn't gone well.

And I could only expect things to go downhill from here.

The moment I closed my new room's door, I slumped against it, the tension holding me up deflating.

Sighing raggedly, I took in the spacious room with its light coral curved walls and double-frame arched windows. Luxury items and polished wood furniture upholstered in matching deep pinkish-red spread throughout the whole space. The closest thing to me was a short wicker table with a silver tea set and crystal bowls full of sweets. But my gaze snagged on the lone queen-sized four-poster bed with its pomegranate-red, satin bedspread outlined with gold thread and dotted with sequins and crystal beads.

It would be another adjustment, being alone in this fancy room. If the girls were here, Cherine would be pouring us tea and scolding Cora for stuffing her cheeks like a squirrel.

Cora. Shrewd, watchful Cora who had long joined the list of people I wouldn't want to upset, not just because she could swing me across the room, but because, unlike Farouk and Loujaïne, she didn't suspect I was lying—she *knew*.

Strange thing was, she'd kept it to herself and had been feeding me ways out of tight spots since the day we'd first met. The questions of why would have to wait.

My trunk was at the foot of the bed, my dresses already in the hand-cut mahogany wardrobe across from it. There seemed to be a preset kind of magic working around the palace, what no one commented on or was so used to that they didn't notice it.

How did that magic work? Who worked it? Were people like Nariman born with it or did they learn it? All the old stories never clarified if witches were people who practiced witchcraft, or if they were an entirely different set of beings.

Was there a way to stop them beyond burning them at the stake?

Exhaling again, I straightened, and commenced a thorough search for ways out of the room. This time I started under the bed, but there was no hidden trapdoor this time, no false walls or any other exit that led to the bowels of this endless palace. There was no way for me to slip out of my room without tipping off the guards and in turn, Loujaïne.

The only other way out was the window. After my descent down the palace border wall to rescue Cherine, I certainly wasn't in a hurry to risk my neck like that again. Especially when I didn't have anyone to hold me up like Cyrus and Cora had that time—

"Aren't you a sad sight."

A calm, sardonic voice slithered through the silence, making me almost jump out of my skin with a strangled shout.

In the darkest corner, away from the downpour of daylight swathing half the room, was the flickering projection of Nariman.

Dark hair braided, with an ornamental snake tying its ends, and dark dress washed out to grey, she hovered by the cabinet, alive in its shadow, a waking nightmare with burning eyes.

"What's the matter?

Trembling with the aftershock of her arrival, my voice shook, breaking the furious façade I needed to reinforce my sarcasm. "*You're* the matter. You're the reason I'm in this mess."

"You wouldn't be in this mess if the king hadn't both robbed and banished me."

"You could have taken it out on his sister, not me," I blurted out the frustrated response.

Nariman chuckled, humorless, bitter. "Oh, I tried."

My brows shot up, practically bumping into my hairline.

She reached out a blurry hand, fingers twitching. Her entire form distorted as the curtains unfolded heavily from their hooks, blocking the sunlight.

At once appearing more solid in the dimness, she floated towards me.

While I knew she wasn't physically here, her clearer image flooded me with unreasoning fear, forcing me to stumble back raising an arm, ready to block any attacks from her staff.

Unconcerned by my state, Nariman's projection floated to the table, stared down at its mirrored surface as if something was written there. She wasn't reflected in it.

Moving out of cornered-animal mode, I swallowed the jagged lump in my throat. "What do you mean you tried?"

"Strange," she said calmly, still gazing down at the blank mirror. "After all that trouble to get me banished, I expected gossip about me to still be floating around the palace."

"Why? Why did you do?" I asked, emboldened by the intensity of my curiosity.

The corner of her mouth twitched in a cross between a smirk and a wobble. "In all your little talks, our dear prince has never mentioned me?"

"Why would he?"

She flashed her teeth in an unsettling smile. "Because I practically raised him."

Like a broken marionette, my jaw clattered open.

This was the last response I could have expected.

Nariman couldn't be older than thirty, probably less than ten years older than Cyrus, making her claim impossible.

Unless she was far older than she appeared to be.

I managed one trembling word, "H—How?"

"King Darius was too busy to do it himself." Her voice was loaded with venomous distaste.

"W-what happened to the queen? No one talks about her."

Her eyes rose to mine, raising my every hair on end. "There was no queen."

"How?"

Her brow furrowed as she raised her fist to cover her mouth, as if to hide a flare of emotion. "Cyrus's mother was the last princess consort. She killed herself before Darius succeeded his father as king."

I gaped at her.

That—that wasn't how it was supposed to be. Mothers died fighting fatal diseases or lost their lives to difficult births, giving their all so their child could have a chance at living. Or they died because of someone else's cruelty or thoughtlessness. What kind of suffering could drive a mother to end her own life and leave her child?

I now remembered the painful look on Cyrus's face when

he'd said his mother was dead. It hadn't occurred to me that he'd never gotten the chance to know her, to have her impact his life like mine had.

Suddenly, I almost doubled over as a horrific new thought swamped me.

I'd always believed my mother's death had been a tragic, senseless accident. I'd taken solace believing that if given a choice, she would have fought to stay with me, to spare me the last few years of my life. But—what if her sudden disappearance and death had been of her own choosing? Could she have been suffering an unbearable anguish that had driven her beyond endurance, beyond even considering me, and her one way to end it had been to end her life?

Though this possibility shook me to my soul, I couldn't consider it now. Whatever the reason she'd died, she had. And she'd left me. Like Cyrus's mother had left him. And it seemed his father had barely been there for him. Now, in choosing his bride, he wanted someone who wouldn't leave him.

I could be that someone. I wanted to be that one person for him. But I couldn't. I *had* to leave. Because of *her!*

Nariman now faced me with a strained face, daring to look moved, throat bobbing with a swallow. "Darius's wife was a...deeply troubled girl. It was hard, watching her go from a happy, healthy girl to the miserable, mindless thing she became at the end."

"You knew her?"

"Darling, I was her oldest friend."

This time I couldn't keep upright, sank where I stood by the tea table.

Nariman continued, "I, along with two others, accompanied her to Cahraman as her ladies-in-waiting when she came to marry the crown prince."

That revelation was almost as jarring as the two she'd already shared. But now suspicion was trickling among the shock, staining everything she said with disbelief.

Or—was it possible she wasn't lying, that she hadn't always been this evil?

I couldn't be certain either way. I needed to know more. If not about Cyrus then about her, so I could get a clear idea on what kind of person she was and how she thought. And with that, a possible way to reason with her, maybe even manipulate her into releasing the Fairborns.

I had to keep her talking. Anything I learned about her would help. Knowledge was my one weapon in this mess. And she always seemed willing to share information about herself when prompted. I hoped she'd continue to be forthcoming.

I sagged forward on the table. "Where did you come from?"

Nariman settled across from me, still faded and translucent but her voice disconcertingly clear. "The Princedom of Almaskham beyond the gulf of the Silver Sea. A beautiful land that will be a bastion of legend someday. I sent Cyrus there when he was younger, to be among his mother's family and to get an education he couldn't get here."

Cyrus *had* told me he'd lived elsewhere until recently. Now every word he'd ever said to me took on new meaning, felt like pieces of a puzzle falling into place.

"Do people learn magic there?" I asked, almost vibrating with urgency. Hopefully, she'd let another secret slip. Like when she'd intimated the lamp housed—something she needed.

"Yes, but you have to have the talent for it to begin with."

"Did his mother?"

"No, but the other ladies-in-waiting did, though none

close to my own power. That's why she developed such a dependence on potions. I never thought giving her a few drops of soother silk in her wine would escalate to that, but she wanted to be numb all the time…"

"Why did she hate it here so much?" I prodded, unable to contain my impatience.

Her expression grew grim, her hand closing around her serpent staff tightly. "Imagine being ripped from your home at your age to be sent to marry a man you've never met, all so both your fathers could sign trade deals and your husband can use you to incubate his heirs. We were packed up and sent here so she'd become the princess and myself and the other two to be married off to noblemen."

"Then what happened?"

"She married Darius. Hessa was engaged to a minister, but neither I nor our third married."

"Why?"

"Dorreya was the mistress of a prince in Almaskham, taken as a replacement after the prince's wife proved infertile."

I inhaled sharply. *Dorreya*. My mother's name.

I remembered when I'd first encountered Nariman in Ericura, how foreign she and her name had appeared, how she'd been the closest to my mother and myself I'd ever seen. How I'd thought we might even be related.

But that had been when I'd thought Nariman was from Ericura. That Ericura was the whole world.

But now I knew it wasn't, my mother's name was no longer an oddity. Dorreya was probably a common name around here, like Bree and Elenei were in the North and South of Ericura respectively. Nariman's Dorreya couldn't be my mother—that would be too much for me to bear. But that name still pointed to my mother, or at least her bloodline, originating from this side of the Folkshore.

There was also the fact that my namesake, the goddess 'Adalat, was nowhere to be found on the island.

If anyone had answers to any of this, it was Nariman, but I couldn't risk derailing the topic we were currently on.

"No one outside the three of us knew about Dorreya and her prince," Nariman continued soundlessly tapping long nails on the serpent head of her cane. "But the old king still ruined our prospects for good marriages."

"Why?" I asked again, pushing away the intrusive thought of Loujaïne, who too seemed to have known a Dorreya.

"King Xerxes was convinced that one of us was tampering with his heir's attempts to conceive with his new wife. That we put abortifacients in her tea, because he knew at least one of us was a witch and heard women from our land practiced petty magic on each other."

I swallowed, a heavy lump in my throat. "Do they?"

"They do, but we had no reason to. She was our princess, both here and in Almaskham, and more importantly, she was our friend. But Xerxes didn't see it that way."

I had a hard time imagining Nariman with friends. I couldn't see beyond the ruthless side of her.

"But they did conceive," I said.

"Yes. When the king had Hessa beheaded."

I choked on thin air and almost coughed my lungs out.

When I could finally breathe again, I croaked, "Why Hessa?"

"Xerxes only started with her, promised Dorreya and I we were next if Hessa proved not to be the culprit."

"Did she?" I asked in a small, strained voice.

Nariman shook her head in a *who-knows* gesture.

I couldn't help asking about the third witch, like I'd formed an attachment to her based only on her name. "What about Dorreya?"

"Dorreya vanished not long after, left me a note claiming that the prince who'd taken her as his mistress summoned her back to Almaskham. But since Cyrus was conceived after one witch's execution and his birth was followed by another's escape, Xerxes assumed that his plan had worked and let me live."

"Who do you think was the cause?"

Her amber eyes narrowed in contemplation. "It's hard to say. Witches tend to travel in threes, each with her expertise and level of power. Hessa was the weakest and youngest, specializing in small spells, while Dorreya was more practical, having a potion for every issue."

That wasn't an answer. It was as if she wanted me to reach my own conclusion based on the evidence. I only knew I couldn't blame the third witch for returning to that prince's bed. It was better than being at the mercy of a paranoid king or staying alongside Nariman.

Feeling a bit bolder, I pushed her for a better response. "Was it Hessa or not?"

"I don't want to consider it, but the coincidence was too suspect."

"But why would she do it?"

"She might have been asked to. Divorces are permitted if a marriage isn't fruitful. At least that was the case in Almaskham, as Prince Azal had his wife sent back to her land after she failed to give him children."

I processed this information to help flesh out this world for me, the ugliness of its reality making it feel less like an endless dream. "You think the princess asked her to stop her from getting pregnant?"

"I can think all I want, but I can never get an answer now they're all gone."

I couldn't imagine having to move to a new place with only three familiar faces then have two torn from my life while the third left me stuck there.

Wait. I didn't need to imagine. I was exactly in this situation. The two torn from me had their lives put at risk by the third who'd left me stuck here. The one currently worsening my wretchedness with her awful stories.

"You lost your best friends yet you hold mine hostage and threaten to kill her," I hissed, nails scraping the mirror, wishing it was her face. "You were basically a hostage yourself. How could you do to me what someone else did to you?"

She looked away. "Because I have no other choice."

"Yes, you do! You could have asked someone who works here to bring you the lamp!"

Her gaze returned to mine, lips curling in a vicious sneer. "Someone who works here and believes all the slander about me being an evil witch and would still risk stealing from his king you mean?"

"And when did someone's reluctance stop..." I stopped, realized. "Your magic doesn't work here! That's why you couldn't get anyone from here to work for you!"

"Yes, well, you see why it had to be you. Darius had the heads of magical regulation place wards around the city so only wizards who are native, or are invited in, can cross them. I'm a banished foreigner. It's why I'm here, actually. The wards have been strengthened, I won't be able to project myself anymore. This will be our last contact—until you bring me the lamp."

"Thanks so much for the visit," I grumbled. Then I realized I hadn't asked the most important question. "Why were you banished?"

Her eyes flared with that terrifying glow I'd first seen watching me in the Hornswoods, before she'd kidnapped and separated us. "I told you."

I shook my head, trying to hide how much she scared me. "No, not really."

Just like that, my attempt to glean something I could use, even leverage against her backfired.

Without another glance, she stood and floated towards the wall. "You have one week, remember?"

My insides tightened into a knot of panic as I scrambled to save the situation, lure her back into a talkative state. But every shaky word out my mouth only made things worse. " Why do you need that lamp so badly now? What's the rush?"

"The rush is that at the end of this week you will be sent home, and my last chance to retrieve something that is mine, that is priceless, will be gone."

"At least tell me why the king took it from you."

She stopped, facing the wall. "You should ask him when you meet him."

"Why do you say that when you know I have no chance of winning!"

"You don't?" she hummed in mock-intrigue. "To me, it looks like you have quite an edge over your rivals."

"I am completely out of my depth! I am cracking under the stress you've put me under and there is no way I'll make it to the end of this week intact or on top!" I rambled in a heated rush, muscles tightening, arms trembling. "If you really wanted me to win, you would have actually helped me, given me ways to cheat, rather than send me in blind."

"This competition is cheat-proof. I would know because I enchanted it to be so," she said matter-of-factly, twirling her staff. "Any tricks I could have armed you with would have caused your elimination or backfired as a hex. Besides, you're doing a lot better than I dared hope, and you *will* continue on that path."

That not-so-subtle threat only added to my climbing rage. None of my questions had gotten proper answers. She deflected the same way I did when someone interrogated me. You couldn't lie to a liar, not for long. Which meant she was hiding things. Things I could use against her if I found them out.

So what was she scared of? Could there be something that could scare her?

In my nerve-burning frustration, I tried again, forcing casual sweetness into my voice. "At least tell me what's in it?"

Nariman looked back at me over her shoulder. "In what?"

"The lamp." I grinned, my facial muscles wobbling out of control, no doubt turning my attempted smile into a manic grimace. "You said there was something in it."

"A week, Adelaide," she shouted abruptly. "You know what will happen if you don't come through."

She walked through the wall before my stampeding heart could stumble on its next beat.

Defeated, feeling even more trapped than before, I dropped my arms on the table and my head between them, thumping my hot, throbbing forehead onto the cool glass.

Another wasted opportunity. I just couldn't do anything right, could I?

Any shortcuts I tried only looped back to the same path— the long, treacherous route out of this situation.

The previous king had beheaded a woman for suspecting

she'd been tampering with his son's and daughter-in-law's fertility. What would the current one do if he caught me red-handed?

My stiff hand went to my neck where I could almost feel the slice of the executioner's blade.

After Nariman left, I didn't know how long I sat crumpled on the ground.

My mind replayed every word she and Cyrus had ever told me, matching them, cross-referencing them, and trying to come up with explanations for all that was left unanswered.

If she was even partially truthful about raising Cyrus, had her banishment had anything to do with him setting up the Bride Search?

Had she told him how his parents had married and why his mother had killed herself and he had wanted to avoid the same fate? Had he decided to choose his wife rather than have her be part of an arrangement that led to a life of misery that could include a premature death?

If that was the case, then maybe Fairuza wasn't such a shoe-in for Princess of Cahraman. At least, I hoped not. If he ended up with one of the other three girls it wouldn't hurt as much.

But I couldn't afford to dwell on anything beyond next

week, and what I'd do to get into the king's quarters, when I no longer had the luxury of being an insignificant.

Back when I was one of fifty, I had no other desires but to get in and get out unseen, save the Fairborns and get back home. And to be with Cyrus. No one had cared if I'd appeared shifty or disappeared for a few hours. They'd had others to worry about. Now I was one of five, and I had new things to worry about.

Among those, one idea insistently tapped me on the shoulder, whispering:

What if you have a real chance?

If I did, what would I do with it? Could I use winning his love to my advantage, manipulate him into giving me the lamp without telling him who I really was and why I was here from the start?

Even the fleeting consideration made me hunch over with gut-twisting shame. I couldn't do that to him. I guess I didn't have the self-serving soul most bluebloods and criminals appeared to share.

Bony knuckles rapped on the door in quick succession, followed by Cherine's muffled voice. "Come out already! I'm not walking there alone!"

Cora's drawl was equally muffled, infinitely bored. "What am I? A house plant?"

A chuckle burst through my turmoil at their exchange. Though I wanted nothing more than to curl up and wallow in self-pity, time with the girls, in whatever situation, never failed to lift my spirits.

I rose to my feet, but my blood didn't follow up as fast. I swayed for a moment, taking in deep breaths. Once steady, I smoothed my skirt and headed out.

I found Cherine and Cora blocking my door, squabbling about animals.

"Little dogs are not part fox," Cora stressed. "Foxes aren't even related to dogs."

"They're the cousins of the dogs," Cherine argued, making me wonder where her mansion-dwelling self could have seen a fox. "Just like wolves are."

"Maybe foxes are to dogs what cats are to lions?" I joined in, glad for the bit of distracting nonsense.

"No," Cora said firmly. "Also cats and big cats are like tree monkeys and apes, similar but not close enough to cross-breed, and definitely *not* like dogs and foxes."

Cherine waved a hand in Cora's face, regaining her attention. "What about dogs, wolves and desert wolves?"

"Isn't a desert wolf just a wolf?" I asked.

To my surprise, they agreed for once, snapping "No!" in perfect unison.

"Desert wolves are coyotes," Cora said. "Smaller than actual wolves, more like jackals."

I turned up my hands. "I don't know what either of those things are."

Cora shrugged, continued their argument. "You can cross-breed a wolf and a dog, you can't crossbreed a fox and a dog. If they can't bear offspring then they're too different and can't be counted in the same species."

"Wouldn't that make donkeys the dogs of horses? Since we get mules and wolfdogs?" Cherine babbled, raising her hands to different heights. "Also, if animals have to be closely-related to crossbreed then how do we get hybrids like simurghs and griffins?"

Cora briefly, hilariously, went cross-eyed. "What?"

"They're half bird and half big cat. How did they come about?"

Cora's confusion gave way into an uncharacteristic response. "...Magic?"

"You think so?" I said as seriously as I could, before I spluttered.

The girls exchanged a look then burst out laughing, too.

Our laughter was filling the circular hall as the other doors began opening.

Out first was Loujaïne. Without looking at any of us, she came to stand in the middle of the hall, seemingly caught in a staring contest with the bust of Morgana of Almaskham.

Though I hated to draw Loujaïne's attention, I needed information probably only she could provide. I also needed to try to endear myself to her.

Approaching her with caution, chest still bobbing with lingering laughter that had more than a touch of hysteria, I asked, "What happened to all these women?"

A startled inhalation rattled the clear aqua beads over-laying her grey, gossamer shawl as she whirled to face me. Composing herself, she smoothed imaginary stray hairs. "Simple. One of them became queen and the rest went home."

"But which one became queen?"

"I can't tell you that now," she said. "Each girl's choice of room is supposed to reflect the luck of the first girl who slept in it."

"Is that magic or superstition?"

Instead of an answer, she jabbed me with a question of her own, with the same unnerving scrutiny Nariman had subjected me to. "Tell me, Lady Ada, do you have any Almaskhami blood in your family?"

That threw me off.

After my first few lies to set up my false identity—with Cora's invaluable help—I hadn't thought I'd be asked for more details. Everyone liked to fill in the gaps for themselves with assumptions, ones I went along with. But this was a more specific question than the usual, one I couldn't give a vague answer to.

I went with the safest option. "I don't know."

But now that she'd asked, I wondered how the people of Almaskham differed from Cahraman. Though she was much fairer than Loujaïne, Fairuza's features seemed to favor her Cahramani side. Could I pass myself as being the same?

No, I would have already mentioned that. No backtracking on established lies, unless I got caught in one.

"Why?" I asked, trying to smother my nervousness in a smile.

"You remind me of someone from their extended royal family." She wagged a manicured finger at my face. The proximity of her hand and the subtle hostility rolling off her made me think that she was about to gouge out my eyes. "Your face, it's almost like…"

She trailed off, shaking her head and ending the conversation with a loud clap that made me jerk. "Girls! Time to go."

Fairuza was the last to exit her room, her shadows Meira and Agnë two steps behind her. Ariane must have taken a long nap as she joined us bleary-eyed and yawning. Cora and Cherine each hooked one of my arms and marched me after Loujaïne.

We left the chamber hall and headed down a wide, carpeted slope leading to the first flight of stairs.

As we walked, I was once again entranced by the sheer extravagance and artistry of this palace. I'd never get tired of admiring the walls and ceiling art with its block printing, mosaic paintings and plaster bas-reliefs of suns, stars, clouds and simurghs. The chiseling on the birds' chests and outstretched wings, etching three-dimensional feathers that looked as soft as ones, was mind-boggling.

Caught up in the details, I looked straight into the intense brightness of a turnip-shaped chandelier that briefly blinded me and jogged last night's memories free. Guilt-ridden what-ifs wormed their way into my head, along with grisly images of it falling and crushing us beneath it.

I was blinking back tears when the girls tugged me back before I slammed into Loujaïne.

She'd stopped before towering double doors painted a rose-red with the handles fashioned like flying simurghs.

The doors opened and two bearded guards in royal blue robes and brown pants bowed us in. The oval dining room was massive with soaring ceilings and an expansive set of arched windows that overlooked the edge of the mountain, with a view of a sparkling city in the distant horizon. From Cherine's accounts, it must be her city of Anbur.

A rectangular, black-marble table surrounded by twenty seats centered the room. The doorways to its left clearly led to the kitchens, since I could hear faint clunking of pots and pans.

Cyrus was sitting at the end of the table, toying with a fork and speaking to a guard standing next to him in a full suit of armor. Ayman, no doubt.

At our entrance, Cyrus stood and bowed his head. "Ladies, thank you for joining us."

Fairuza strode ahead and dropped into the seat to Cyrus's right, shooing her handmaidens out. My face grew warm at the sight of them close together, and I unthinkingly rushed for the seat to Cyrus' left. Cora took the seat before the biggest empty tray with Cherine between us. That left Ariane stuck debating which side she should sit on. She at last grudgingly sat beside Fairuza, so she wouldn't be too far from Cyrus.

Loujaïne took the seat to Cyrus's opposing end, where the king should be. Masters Farouk, Zuhair and Asena joined us, taking the seats close to Loujaïne.

Cyrus picked up a small silver bell but Fairuza gripped his arm, stopping him from ringing it. "Shouldn't we wait for your father?"

"We have waited for him," he said firmly. "He hasn't shown."

"We should still wait for him," Fairuza insisted.

He raised an eyebrow at her. "There are ten of us. Why should we wait for one person?"

"Because he's the king and it's respectful," she argued, tapping his hand coaxingly.

"How about we take a vote? Should we order lunch now or once Father arrives?" Cyrus searched each face around the table, giving me a quick wink.

So, he wasn't upset about earlier?

The elites and Loujaïne had begun to speak when Fairuza cut them off again. "You can't take a vote, this is a monarchy."

"Calm down, Fay-Fay. It's just food, not legislation," I said, picking up a knife and examining the fine craftsmanship of the gold-lined silver.

She still had her hand on his when she spat, "I didn't ask you."

"You didn't ask any of us." I flashed her a goading grin.

"Because this isn't up for debate," she retorted through stiff lips. "This is the king's palace and we wait for him."

I resisted rolling my eyes, twirling the knife as I pondered aloud. "Funny how you're the one giving the orders when you're a guest here."

Her glower heated. "I'm doing no such thing. But it must be hard for you to recognize that, since you don't understand courtesy."

"Wouldn't it be proper courtesy to not force your opinion on the prince?" I briefly locked eyes with Cyrus, found him watching me intently. A hot flush flew up to my ears, making them burn as I faced Fairuza. "Isn't he in charge when the king's absent?"

She shut her mouth so hard I heard her teeth collide.

I felt very smug.

Smiling tightly, Cyrus removed his hand from under hers and rang the bell.

As if they'd been waiting by the door, a queue of servants marched in carrying trays and pushing trolleys. Soon serving plates were set along the table and their lids were removed, flooding us with mouthwatering steam and potent spices.

My stomach rumbled like thunder as a silver serving plate with filigree edges was placed directly in front of me. It was heaped with golden rice topped with masses of raisins, squares of meat and fry-toasted hazelnuts, almonds and pine nuts. Next to it was a glazed roast turkey on a bed of couscous and chickpeas, and behind that, a huge soup bowl. Around the main dishes were colorful smaller ones filled with dips, sauces, salads and quarters of flatbread.

We were served the creamy, garlicky lentil soup first. My breath may be awful later but I was going to enjoy it nonetheless.

Cora and I slurped our bowls in record time while Cherine kept pouring more sour cream and Ariane swirled it curiously. Fairuza pushed it aside.

"You going to eat that?" I asked her.

She pretended she didn't hear me. I reached across the table, took her bowl and held it up to Ayman.

"What are you doing?" Fairuza snapped. "That's mine!"

"And you don't want it."

She fisted her hands on the table. "You can't give my things to the servants, especially without asking."

I smirked at her. "Would you have given it to me if I'd asked?"

"No."

"Point proven then." I shook the bowl at Ayman and he took it with a nod but made no move to start eating.

With his mouth covered by his ringed fingers, Cyrus cleared his throat. "You'll have to excuse him for not obliging you, Lady Ada. Guards can't eat on the job."

"I know, but since there's nothing to guard right now, there's no use in making him stand around and watch us eat. Especially since one of us isn't even touching her food."

"You're too kind." The warmth in his eyes intensified as our gazes locked. "You might need to learn when it's necessary to not be kind."

"I'm only nice to people who deserve it."

"What about those who don't?" he asked.

I wrinkled my nose in distaste. "You're looking at her right now."

Fairuza turned as red as Ariane's hair. "If your family is as crass and classless as you are, then it's no wonder they lost their money and social standing."

"Can't you come up with a cleverer insult?" I countered in a bored tone.

She raised her chin, nose in the air. "It's not an insult if it's true."

I flapped my napkin, making a show of dabbing my mouth clean. "Guess you'll have no problem with me calling you an unhinged murderer then."

She slammed her silver goblet on the table, sloshing its sour-smelling burgundy juice onto the tablecloth. "In which loony world you came from is that true?"

If only she knew.

But she made me remember the harrowing minutes when I'd climbed down a knotted curtain to save Cherine. We could have both plummeted to our deaths.

I leaned forwards, narrowing my eyes. "Let's see. You felt threatened by another girl, thought the best way to eliminate the competition was to push her to her death."

"I didn't push her!" Fairuza spluttered frustratedly.

Cherine backed me up, jabbing her finger in her direction angrily. "You did!"

Fairuza rose to set her hands on the table, hissing, "I did *not*!"

"So I threw myself over the wall?" Cherine asked caustically.

Cyrus rang the bell again, silencing us. "Can you discuss this on your own time?"

"There's no discussion. She provoked me, argued with me and waited until we were by the edge to push me." Cherine cried, pushing her chair back, shaking the table. "I almost died, Cyaxares! If not for Ada, I would have. If Fairuza were anyone else she would be on the chopping block. And yet she's still here!"

"The real wonder is why *you're* still here," Fairuza spat. "Why the *three* of you are still here. But I suppose the need to follow tradition is important, even if it's ceremonial. We all know that if he had it his way, Cyaxares would choose between myself and Ariane."

"Leave me out of this, please," Ariane begged, busying herself with a plate of oil-drenched eggplant slices.

Cyrus cut in, louder and tenser. "*Five* of you are here because it's not only myself that makes the decision."

"But you're the one marrying me," Fairuza exclaimed. "Your decision is the only one that matters."

"If it were that easy I would have made my choice weeks ago." He sounded fed up as he pushed aside his bowl.

Ayman set Fairuza's bowl down as well. He'd inhaled the soup while we weren't looking.

I tried to catch his eye but he remained looking ahead. Right at Loujaïne, in fact. Was he as wary of her as I was?

"But why the competition at all?" Ariane asked. "Marriage is always an arrangement between two families or kingdoms."

"Not this time." Cyrus frowned as he picked up his goblet. "And to win this competition, you need to win over several people, because they'll eventually be your people."

He clearly despised arrangements, like the marriage that had been brokered for his parents. What had ended with his miserable mother killing herself.

Even the pettiest part of me wouldn't wish such an ending on Fairuza.

As servants removed the soup bowls, Cyrus stood and brought the turkey closer, then unsheathed a long carving knife and two-pronged fork. "Call on which part you want."

"Leg," Cora answered immediately, the first thing she'd said since we got here.

Cherine cut off Fairuza, announcing, "I'll have the breast!"

Miffed, Fairuza sat back, crossing her arms, saying nothing.

When everyone had made their choices, I said, "Wings. I need to leave room for the other food."

"As you wish." Cyrus offered me the knife and fork with a secretive smile. "Would you like to do the honors?"

Static sparked between our fingertips as we exchanged the silverware.

It took a lot for me not to stutter, "What do *you* want?"

He sat down, linking his fingers and setting his chin on them. "Choose for me."

That request made me giddy. It was an easy sort of trust to hand over, having me choose for him.

But then again, I'd be serving him, like I'd served strangers as a waitress and barmaid.

Still, it hadn't been an order. I'd offered and he'd responded. As far as I could see we were on equal footing here. And he was letting me choose for him!

And I was making a sentimental mountain out of a vapid molehill.

After I distributed the requests, I gave him a chunk of breast. Fairuza made a sour face then accepted the leg I offered her. But every time she tried to cut a layer off the bone, the drumstick rolled away.

"Just eat it like this," Cora mumbled as she tore off another large bite.

Disgust was Fairuza's only response to that.

Idle chatter reigned until all main course dishes were removed and coffee and tea were served in the long-necked, beaked, silver pots. Then Fairuza took it upon herself to return the conversation to its uncomfortable state.

"How are we supposed to win over the public?" Fairuza asked Cyrus as he poured her tea. "And why do we need to?"

"Because one of you will one day be their queen," he said simply, setting the coffeepot down.

He'd poured for her and not for me. Why hadn't he even offered to pour for me?

"You needn't be so political with your answers," Fairuza said, blowing steam off her cup, looking at him from beneath the long lashes she batted.

"He does, as do you all," Loujaïne spoke up from her end of the table. "You will be meeting with elders, leaders and nobles in the coming days. Starting today, in fact."

"What?" Cora coughed through a mouthful of meat and rice.

"Today," Loujaïne repeated. "Your first test is this afternoon, on how you will deal with public issues. After tomorrow is your second, on dealing with another faction of our subjects, and two days after that you will each be charged with hosting a visitor to the palace."

"What do you mean by host exactly?" I asked, already stressed thinking about it. "We show them around? But we don't know the palace. Also, what's today's test?"

I needed to plot how I'd steal the lamp when invited into the king's quarters, not to spend most of the time outside the palace and the only day within it babysitting a politician's wife.

"Oh, I love hosting. I've done it many times for my father," Fairuza fawned giddily, holding her cup out to the side, expecting it to be filled. As it was. "I've been learning how to be a proper hostess since I was five."

Proper hostess? Was that the rich version of the attendant's mask, the peppy, accommodating persona we slipped on while serving customers?

I hoped it was. Otherwise I was doomed.

CHAPTER SIX

I'd always thought I'd only set foot in a courthouse if I were on trial for theft.

Yet here I was, in the capital's Palace of Justice, not to be sentenced for theft or deception, but to be judged in a bridal competition.

Judged on what, though? That remained to be seen.

By now I knew it was the rule for these tests to be vague and misleading. The palace elites in charge of the Bride Search had a nasty habit of keeping all relevant details to themselves until the very last minute.

"Do you know why we're here?" I asked Cherine, shielding my eyes from the declining sun as I looked up at the entrance.

Compared to the rest of the buildings I'd seen in Sunstone, the courthouse was disappointingly plain. It was a white-washed rectangular building with its protruding center pouring black marble stairs. Its pointed archway soared between two narrow walls, their facades emblazoned with the iron engravings of a winged woman. In the space above the arch itself was the same woman, now kneeling with her wings spread.

One would expect a bit more decorative effort from something referred to as a *palace*.

I chuckled inwardly at the thought of my new, heightened standards. Just one month ago I was on an island whose grandest architectural feats were limited to manors the size of Cahramani mausoleums. It wasn't my fault the majesty of Sunstone and its true palace had spoiled the simpler things for me.

Just like the Cyrus I'd gotten to know had spoiled the prince for me.

Cherine caught up with me, holding up the skirt of her yellow dress, its reflective gossamer layer shimmering brightly in the sun. "Today's test must involve Cahraman's legal system."

"*Ooof*, I hope not," Cora huffed, climbing the remaining steps in lunges, her golden hair held up in a messy bun, the stray hairs crowning her hairline sticking to her flushed, sweaty face. "Arguing about laws and amendments is mind-numbing. I'd rather use crocodiles as stepping stones to cross a rushing river than sit in another council meeting."

That was a funny, if a scary visual. "Oddly specific for a hypothetical preference."

Cora gave me a small, devilish grin. "Who said it's hypothetical?"

"What were you doing in council meetings?" Cherine fanned her face with little hands, the polished silver of her rings flashing in the sweltering sun.

Cora turned to her at the top of the stairs. "As the next Mistress of the Granary, I need to be prepared to run the largest farming region in Lower Campania. Aside from knowing how to barter, farm, store and trade everything our earth yields, I need to know how to deal with the political and legal side of things." Cora checked behind us impatiently. "Are they going to join us or what?"

I followed her gaze, hand angled low to shade my eyes. All three princesses remained at the bottom of the stairs, while Master Farouk and Cyrus talked to three men with dark, curly beards in flat-topped hats and two women in pewter robes with long red-tinted pigtails.

Seeing him as he was now, deep in serious discussion, wearing his royal garb, his hair combed and his expression neutral, I couldn't help comparing him to the servant that had accompanied me to the marketplace last week. The one who'd helped me shop, flirted with me, taken solace with me in the fact that we were both insignificant in this great big city, kissed my cheek…

I touched that cheek wistfully as I compared the prince's solemn face to that of the messy-haired, carefree thief. Yet, as much as my heart wanted to, my mind still couldn't reconcile both versions. I knew Cyrus and Cyaxares were the same person, but it was hard to accept when the difference was far beyond a change of clothes.

Everything from the way he spoke to the way he held himself had noticeably changed. I couldn't help noticing every little detail and latching onto the small differences, wondering just which part of the Cyrus I'd known had been genuine and which had been an act.

But if I felt this betrayed by his disguise, how would he feel about mine?

As much as I didn't want to admit it, him playing the part of a servant was nothing compared to my own deception.

My discomfort amplified now I knew the lamp wasn't just

a peculiar heirloom coveted by a wronged woman. By Nariman's own words, there was something nefarious about its existence besides an ugly waste of gold.

She'd said that something had been lured *in* it. It couldn't be a being like the *qarin* that slept at the bottom of my trunk, since she probably had dozens of magical "underlings" like it. I couldn't begin to guess what it could be, and this morning's attempts to gauge what she was up to had fallen flat harder than the chandelier I'd sabotaged last night.

To find out what it was and what she needed it for, I had to ask someone who either knew her personally or knew about witches in general. Loujaïne had taken her place as the king's right-hand, and the manager of the Bride Search. If anyone knew the details of Nariman's banishment, she did. But with the way Loujaïne looked at me, like she was itching for me to out myself as a fake, I couldn't risk validating her suspicions.

The next best person to ask would be Cyrus. But I could no longer ask him like I would have a servant for the gossip that echoed throughout the palace halls. I needed to be smart about how I brought her up. I had to find a way to use whatever today's test was as a conversation starter.

Hopefully, I could also find out *how* she'd been banished. Whatever had flung her out of the capital the first time could hopefully fling her further away once I had the Fairborns back.

With the same practiced smile he'd given us this morning, Cyrus shook hands with the judges then climbed the stairs with the armored Ayman following him closely.

Fairuza and her handmaidens weren't far behind. Her complex dress made climbing the broad steps a chore, needing all their hands to be lifted off her feet.

As luxurious and covetable as it was, she had the most

impractical wardrobe. Her dresses, all bell-shaped with multi-layered skirts, were made for gliding across marble floors rather than going up and down stairs. Along with sleeves, their shiny, heavily embellished materials seemed made to trap heat, must be stifling her now.

Knowing Arbore was right below my island of Ericura, her clothes were made for temperatures that fluctuated more than a cat's moods, from windy summers to frigid winters.

Maybe a part of her attitude could be blamed on the heat here. But her mother was a Cahramani princess, so she ought to have known better. In fact, most of her attitude might be blamed on her mother, if Queen Zomoroda was anything like her sister Loujaïne.

Once my mind wandered to our eldest princess, I noticed Master Farouk and Loujaïne bringing up the rear. Though their faces were blocked by Ariane's pink parasol, I saw their arms linking and Loujaïne setting her delicate fingers on Farouk's biceps.

Though I'd noted the clear rivalry between them in the management of this competition, I'd also noticed the instances when they'd displayed subtle interest in each other. This instance was so far from subtle it raised both of my eyebrows. Loujaïne, as far as I knew, was not married. There were no mention of Cyrus's cousins beyond Fairuza and her siblings and Cherine and her brother. None from Loujaïne.

The peculiar intimacy between the couple didn't last long. Once Fairuza and Ariane joined us atop the flight of stairs, they separated, pointedly averting their eyes from one another.

Curiosity surged within me like a fanned flame.

Why weren't they married? If they liked each other, loved each other even, and lived and worked in the same place for years, then naturally, they would marry and have children running around the palace. Farouk would then be Cyrus's uncle. Cyrus seemed quite friendly with him, friendlier than he was with his real relatives. I didn't blame him. I too would want a man like Farouk as my uncle.

If I married Cyrus then that could be a reality.

As the prince turned to face us, the whimsical idea of a string of weddings involving us, Bonnie and Ayman, and Farouk and Loujaïne fled my mind. Looking at him now, in his deep-blue, embroidered with gold thread kaftan, his hands clasped behind his back, his chin tilted up to survey us all, I was reminded of my predicament.

This wasn't my Cyrus. This was a wholly new version of him that filled me with intrigue and worry.

Taking in a deep breath, he loosened his shoulders and smiled. "Ladies, now that you're finalists, there will be a few changes." He paused, his eyes searching our faces, their color a bright, clear green, like sunlight through peridot. "Instead of a test every ninth day, you'll have one every other day until the weekend, when you'll have audience with the king and we'll review your results, and decide which of you shall be our future queen."

Loujaïne had introduced that concept at lunch, but it hadn't sunk in until now that they weren't going to be retreads of the first tests. Whatever leeway had been afforded in the preliminary rounds was no longer part of the deal.

"Today's test concerns governance," he continued, his eyes meeting Farouk's, who nodded encouragingly. "It's not only important for you to know the law, but how to deal with situations that require both knowledge and wisdom."

Cora raised her hand. Cyrus' expression became an

endearing cross of amusement and confusion. "Yes, Miss Greenshoot?"

"Are we going to debate on amending certain laws?"

"No, no amendments or debates, or any specific laws." He shook his head, briefly locking eyes with me. Tension trapped the air in my chest until he looked away. "You are going to pass judgment."

"We'll be the jury?" I remembered my mother and Mr. Fairborn being called to local courthouses to make up a jury in civil disputes.

"You will be the judges," said Loujaïne, moving to stand by Cyrus. I caught her resentful look at Ayman as he made way for her, and my fiery curiosity demanded to be fed. I knew how people here felt about those who looked like Ayman, with his moon-pale skin and purple eyes, but Loujaïne's reaction to him—and myself—felt…personal.

"You will be given a case to judge." Cyrus ushered us towards the entrance as the judges passed us. "You in turn will be judged on your decisions and their reasoning."

"A case?" I asked, just to be sure. "Just the one?"

The familiar twinkle in his eyes took me back to the first test. The first time I'd seen him in broad daylight, eavesdropping and reacting to our responses. "Just the one."

In my experience with assigned tasks, the lesser they were in number, the harder they were to complete. But I knew this was going to need a bit more concentration than thoroughly plucking a chicken or peeling a sack of potatoes for a tavern dinner.

"Erm, Your Highness?" Ariane followed him first, shutting her parasol. "If you don't mind me asking, what does this have to do with being your consort?"

He tutted amusedly. "Isn't it obvious?"

Fairuza, still holding up the front of her skirt with Agnë and Mcira holding the back, stuck her head between Ayman's and Cyrus's shoulders. "No. Isn't that what appointing lord judges is for?"

As the judges beat us into the shadowed depths of the building, Cyrus's answer echoed off the walls. "It is, but that's not the point of this test."

"Then what is?" Cherine asked as he rushed ahead. When he didn't stop, she roughly linked her arm with mine and dragged me behind her. I caught Cora's wrist, and we rushed through the paved hall in a line like schoolchildren.

Ariane tucked her parasol under her arm and laughingly latched onto Cora, joining the line.

"Looks like we picked up another passenger," I said, trying to stifle my giggles as I admired the high ceilings and the pillars of the hall.

"All aboard the Anbur Express!" Cherine announced, pumping her free arm in the air as she increased her speed and pull on me.

"Destination?" I asked her.

"A stuffy courtroom for an hour of contrived nonsense!"

"What does Cahramani legal nonsense entail?" Ariane asked, starting to pant. "Is it any different than Orestian law?"

Cherine gave her a perplexed look. "Aren't you from Tritonia?"

"Tritonia and its neighboring islands are considered to be a part of Orestia, and by extension, Lower Campania," Cora explained, the only one not even breathing faster. "And from what we've seen here so far, their legal nonsense is bound to be even sillier."

Cherine huffed, nose in the air. "Sillier than you barefoot farmers fighting over cattle?"

Cora and Ariane exchanged knowing looks, before Ariane laughed breathlessly. "What is it with these desert-dwellers thinking they're more advanced than us?"

"Likely because their nations are newer." Cora rolled her eyes with a sigh. "They think that compared to them we're old and backward."

I almost stumbled on my own feet trying to keep up with Cherine and listen to the girls. "Wait, how old is Cahraman?"

"The kingdom itself is less than six-hundred years old," Cherine explained distractedly. "Cahraman, and the princedoms of Almaskham, Merjan and Gemisht as well as the Kingdom of Avesta, are what remains of the Avestan Empire after its collapse."

Avesta was where the White Shadow from the *Anthology of the Dunes* claimed to be from, his story predating the empire's collapse. Sadly, people's attitudes towards albinos like him and Ayman hadn't changed since.

Before Cyrus's devastating revelation, I'd planned to take Ayman back to Ericura with us, where he wouldn't be feared or burned by the sun. I'd even had fantasies of recruiting him to help save Bonnie, and that they could be a modern version of the White Shadow and his wife Nesrine, whom he'd rescued from a demon-guarded tower.

"Could you even call Avesta a kingdom at this point?" Cora pointed out. "It's in a pitiful state. If I were you I'd petition the king to invade it and absorb its land."

Fairuza's voice crashed into our conversation. "Fancy yourself a conqueror?"

Cora leveled her with a hard, blank stare. "Yes."

It was such a blunt and unexpected answer, I found myself cracking up.

Before an argument could break out, our line came to a

halt at yet another pointed archway, open to reveal a hexagonal courtroom with dark, wooden furniture. The dais facing us loomed over the whole room ominously, and had my apprehension back in full force. One of the women in pewter ascended to the dais, and the other four each took a seat at the pews below her. Loujaïne and Farouk followed the lesser judges to their seats and Cyrus ushered us in, walking deeper into the room while Ayman stationed himself at the doors.

"You will be presented with a single case," the head judge addressed us. "You will each give your judgment one at a time. Once you give a verdict, it will be final. You cannot adjust it."

"Why not?" I asked thoughtlessly.

The judge squinted down at me. "Don't question the rules. You give only one verdict, so decide wisely."

The harsh finality of her statement set an intense mood as other judiciary members in grey entered the room, filling up every level along four of the six walls, surrounding us. This was the place I'd spent years roaming to avoid, where they decided if those like me were meant for imprisonment or execution. Being here, even as an observer, was riskier than rescuing Cherine.

Cyrus came up to Fairuza and I, offering each a hand. "Let's get you to your seats, shall we?"

Our elbows collided in our rush to be the first to take an offered hand. I stepped away from her warningly as she glowered at me, the fading bruise around her eye a clear reminder of the last time we'd been this close to each other.

Cyrus cleared his throat. "I suggest you put whatever issue you have aside for now. You'll need all your concentration."

She turned away first, giving him the biggest, brightest smile. "Of course."

I gritted my teeth as he seated us at the same pew as

Farouk. My friends sat by Loujaïne next to us. He sat with Ariane across the room.

His seating plan seemed focused on keeping Fairuza and I together, and keeping himself far away from me.

The hollow clang of a bell rang in my ears.

"Bring forth the subjects."

Two guards in similar garb to those who guarded our rooms at the palace marched in, gripping spears with scimitars hanging from leather belts at their hips, escorting two women with a toddler between them.

Each woman had a tight hold on one of the boy's hands, like they were afraid he'd slip away or be ripped from them. Waves of mutual hostility came off both as they stopped before us, enough to make Fairuza's and my distaste for one another seem like playground antics.

"Present your case."

One of the lesser judges, a stocky man with a greying curly beard stood up. "Your Honor, these here are the widows of Lord Elyas Maraash. Not long after their husband's death, an executor came to settle his will but couldn't settle the custody of the child."

"How is that possible?" the head judge asked. "Give the child to the one who birthed him."

"That is the issue, Your Honor. Both claim to be the mother of the child."

At that, I realized that this test wasn't going to be a simple case of declaring whether one was guilty or not guilty.

This must be Cyrus's personal test, like our first one with the metal boxes. Going by how that one had turned out—and the way he was sitting forwards in his seat, attentive, excited —we were in for some duplicitous task.

The judge began the session with a bang of her mallet as

she announced, "Swear before the eyes of your judge, your prince, and our supreme god and declare that you will not desecrate with lies and libel the Halls of 'Adalat."

'Adalat.

That name crashed into my mind, catapulting me into the past.

CHAPTER SEVEN

Within a blink, I saw myself sitting in a dingy kitchen, watching my mother prepare that night's cabbage and carrot stew.

I'd been pestering her about her past, and the family I never had. She'd dodged every question as usual. But this time she'd given me the smallest morsel of information to quiet me down.

"I wanted to call you *'Adalat*," she'd said while grating carrots, sweat pouring down her face. "But a friend said no one here would be able to pronounce it so I simplified it to Adelaide."

"What does it mean?" I'd asked, fascinated.

"It's the name of a local goddess in my region. In its old tongue it meant *justice*."

To my Ericuran ear, *'Adalat* began with a strange sound I could only compare to the throaty groan one makes on the verge of vomiting. A letter that didn't exist on our island.

But she'd said she'd come from Man's Reach, where she'd claimed to be a cousin of Bonnie's mother Belaina. It had been why I'd traveled to the northernmost part of Ericura, to search for relatives and answers. But I'd found no mention of 'Adalat across the North, and by the time I'd reached Aubenaire, Belaina had been long-dead. I'd almost left when Bonnie found me, and gave me a home with her and her father.

But now that I knew 'Adalat was a goddess here, Loujaïne's question of whether I was part Almaskhami joined the spinning wheel of doubts in my head, tangling over Nariman's mention of a Dorreya.

I'd always had my suspicions about my origins. Ones reinforced by Bonnie's insistence on leaving the island to explore beyond it and find the lands of our ancestors. She—and now I—had figured that those who populated the north of Ericura were the descendants of Arboreans, with the Southerners likely hailing from Cora's region of Lower Campania.

But could anyone in Ericura have been from here? I'd never seen anyone there who resembled me apart from my own mother. But there were certain features I didn't share even with her. The shape of my brows, my dark, hooded eyes, and larger, firmer bone structure.

Now that I thought about it, if anyone resembled me, regardless of color, it was Ayman. Looking beyond his impossibly fair skin, white hair and the bloodshot purple of his eyes, he had the same heavy eyelids, the thick, arching brows and the protruding lower lip that accentuated his mouth's downturned pout.

Ayman was from Almaskham, that much I knew. So was Nariman, who had the same skin tone as me, and they both had the square jaw I certainly didn't inherit from my mother.

Could my mother have been from one of the lands that

used to be the Avestan Empire? But how could she have gone to the other end of the Folkshore by herself?

A tight pinch on my thigh yanked me off the blurring wheel of conspiracy theories.

"Pay attention," Cora whispered. "We're just getting to the good part."

The good part in mention was the merchant's widows heatedly arguing.

Apart from the fact they'd both been married to the same man—something I hadn't thought possible—they were both relatively young, younger than Loujaïne. The one with the long, brown braid, hooked nose and sun-worn, freckled face was probably from a farming district, likely where Cahraman's extensive spices were grown. The other widow, younger by a few years judging by the pitch of her voice and the roundness of her tan face, had big, dark eyes, and hair the color of the persimmons I'd seen at the market.

"Quiet!" The head judge rang her bell, its cringe-inducing clangs making me scratch my nails over the polished wood of the table. "State your case in a civilized manner or we'll solve your dispute by giving the child to his father's closest relative."

At once, the widows stopped squabbling, both still gripping the toddler, who was sobbing inconsolably. I wanted to take him out of their grasp and put him far away where he wouldn't be fought over like a ragdoll.

"I am Soumaya, first wife of Elyas Maraash and the mother of his only son," said the older, dark-haired widow. "After years of sorrow, of losing my children before they could draw their first breath, of making pilgrimages to every fertility goddess in the land, I became pregnant with our son."

She stopped to wipe her reddening nose and wet eyes as her deep breaths escalated into dry sobs. "I couldn't risk losing another child, so I left Sunstone and spent the duration of my pregnancy in the care of the best midwives and temple priestesses my husband could afford. But I returned with our son to be faced with the humiliation of my husband marrying the servant girl."

Fairuza was the first among us to speak. "And why did he do that?"

Tears spilled out of Soumaya's furious grey eyes. "After my many failed pregnancies, he wanted to ensure the birth of his heirs by marrying a younger, healthier girl. He didn't even wait to see if my last pregnancy bore fruit. He replaced me while I was away, suffering." She pointed at the redhead accusingly. "And it wasn't enough for her to take my place, my husband and my home, now she wants to take my child!"

"She's lying!" the redhead interrupted, her voice shaking. "Why would I want to take a child that is not mine?"

"You planned this!" The other widow snapped. "You waited until I left to take everything away from me—"

"Yes, but why would she take the child?" Fairuza interrupted her, oddly engaged in this situation, arms firmly folded, grim expression with the undercurrent of threat, making her scarily like Loujaïne. "That's a fairy-like thing to do—kidnap babies, or curse them even." She looked to the redheaded widow, eyebrow quirked. "Are you a fairy of some sort...?"

"Marihan, Your Grace," the redhead stuttered, doe-like eyes darting from face to face, the fear in them shining like unshed tears. "I am not a beast of any sort. I swear it."

"Don't listen to her," Soumaya cried, trying to yank the toddler from Marihan's unyielding grip, making him cry out in pain. "Her voice might be bewitching you as she bewitched my late husband."

"You didn't answer her," I said to Soumaya, trying to suppress the urge to snatch the baby away from them. "Why would she steal a child?"

"Isn't it obvious?" Cherine spoke out, appalled. "She wanted the woman's husband, her home, and now the only way she can keep the late husband's house and money is through the child."

Soumaya nodded vigorously, shaking the tears further down her cheeks.

Marihan's jaw dropped, distress quickening her breathing. "No, I wouldn't...I didn't..."

"She has cheated me out of my own life!" Soumaya sobbed. "Now she wants to keep my child as hers, to take the inheritance meant for my husband's heir. Please, stop her. And evict her from my home, because she won't leave any other way."

Cherine, deeply moved by Soumaya's laments, was tearing up herself, hands folded over her heart. Ariane was in a similar state, holding a handkerchief to her mouth. Cora appeared uncertain, slouching in her seat and watching the women with a half-open mouth.

I didn't know what to make of this either. This young, ambitious servant girl could have offered her health and fertility to her rich employer in exchange for a leg-up in life, something a lot of women would do. But the man had died before she could cement her position with children and her only way to keep that luxurious life from slipping from her grasp was to claim the child was hers. The first wife's history of fertility problems conveniently supported her claim.

"What about your husband's family?" I asked Soumaya. "Shouldn't they know which wife bore him a son?"

Soumaya shook her head and her braid along with it. "They live in Gül, my lady, on the other side of the kingdom.

We haven't seen them since his sister's wedding four years ago."

"And he doesn't keep in touch with them?" Fairuza probed, arms still firmly crossed, tapping her long nails on sheer sleeves impatiently. "The birth of a firstborn didn't warrant a note home to mother? One that included the name of the woman who bore him an heir?"

"I'm not sure, Your Grace." Soumaya aimed a glare at the flustered Marihan. "I wouldn't be surprised if he gave it to her to send, and she instead threw it in the furnace."

"I would do no such thing!" Marihan's distress increased as she sought out any of our eyes, pleading. "She has always despised me, my lords and ladies, long before Elyas asked for my hand. She's doing all this to punish me, because he chose me and because I did what she never could—give him a son."

I understood Cora's uncertain expression now, felt it on a deeper level. This was one baffling situation. Neither seemed to be lying, both had serious reasons to be upset, to dislike one another and to fight over the boy.

If Cyrus had handpicked this case, as he'd written the poetic, snarky responses within the metal boxes in our first test, then this proved him to be far more calculating than I'd thought.

Just how much of his servant persona had been great acting and how much of it harbored his true personality?

"You see?" Soumaya jabbed her finger at Marihan accusingly, crying even harder, furious voice ringing off the walls. "She is using my past failings against me, to reinforce her lie that my sweet Armin is hers, so she can have everything for good, and punish me for once being her lady, and avenge her years of serving me."

Cyrus leaned forward, resting an elbow on his table and

his chin in his palm. "Ladies, do you have any more questions or have you made your verdict?"

"This one is the mother, she has to be," Cherine said, pointing to Soumaya, moved to tears herself.

Horrified, Marihan pressing baby Armin's face against her. "No! No, please! He's my baby, he's mine! I *swear* it."

"Is this your final verdict?" The judge asked Cherine, who nodded vigorously. "What fuels your belief?"

"Look at her!" said Cherine fervently. "The woman is a wreck at the possibility of being parted from her baby. Giving him to that ambitious serving girl will be a great injustice that sullies the halls of *Adalat*." She wrinkled her nose at Marihan. "This one has barely shed a tear! She isn't in the least bit invested in this child outside of the wealth and status he comes with."

Marihan's tan face paled to an unhealthy shade at Cherine's words. "But I…"

"Lady Cherine is right," Ariane cut her off, dabbing her eyes with her handkerchief. "Besides, look at the boy. He looks nothing like you."

Ariane had a point. If anything, the boy with his light brown hair and hazel eyes looked like he could be Cherine's younger brother.

But if this was the test Cyrus—*Cyaxares* had set up, it made me reexamine the first one with its three boxes. The most obvious option had been to pick the gold one, but he'd ridiculed those who'd picked it for being shallow. The silver, a median choice to appear humble—or in Cora's case, not invested—got a harsher assessment. But the biggest risk, the lead box I'd chosen, had gotten no response at all.

None written, that was. In hindsight, my choice, along

with my performance in the rest of that test's tasks, had spared me from elimination.

If I knew anything about either side of him, servant and prince, I knew he was doing the same thing now, if on a higher scale. I needed to treat this test as such, because the goal now wasn't to avoid elimination but to win.

I needed to read the rest of the room, measure the situation through everyone's responses. People had patterns of behavior, which meant Cyrus, and the other judges were probably following the pattern of the first test. I had to do what had worked for me then as well.

Judging by how immediate and final their responses were, I knew that Ariane and Cherine had once again chosen the gold box.

Cora went next, scratching her head as an uncertain precursor to her verdict. "I think if one of them won't stop lying, then maybe we should remove them both from the equation."

"Meaning?" Cyrus slowly nodded, prodding her.

Cora shrugged. "Like the judge said, the boy should be given to his father's closest relative. That's one certain way to know he'll be raised by family."

Both women's shouts of protest were so instantaneous, so desperate, I almost jumped out of my chair. Little Armin, at the brunt of their distress, broke out into frenzied screeching that made my heartbeat stutter. The lesser judges started weighing in on the situation. Cherine and Ariane jumped to reinforce their points.

"That's such a heartless thing to say!" Ariane protested.

"Yes!" Cherine elbowed Cora's midriff. "And it doesn't solve anything. That maintains the conflict between them, while depriving the baby of its mother."

While Cora had once again picked the silver box, what Cyrus had dubbed the coward's choice—not presumptuous enough to pick gold yet finding lead too much of a gamble—she did have a point. The baby needed to be removed from this toxic situation for his own good, at least temporarily.

I heaved up and my chair scraped across the old marble with a teeth-gnashing groan that silenced all dissent.

"Sit back down!" the head judge ordered.

I ignored her, moving to the center of the courtroom and scooping up Armin from both women's grips.

Marihan merely stared at me, while Soumaya instantly tried to snatch him back from me.

I retreated out of her reach towards my table, bouncing the baby lightly, shushing him, hoping I could briefly put him at ease.

"Miss…?" the head judge began impatiently.

"Ada," I answered distractedly, preoccupied with the heavy toddler whose loud cries had thankfully quieted into sad sniffles. I realized belatedly I hadn't told her to address me as 'Lady,' as a real noblewoman would have.

I didn't care. I was still a judge in this case, and by my namesake, I was going to resolve it.

I cooed to Armin, hoping he'd give me a sign who his mother was, maybe reach for her once he saw her from the vantage point of my arms, but no such luck.

Farouk came around the table, asking in a hushed voice, "Lady Ada, what are you doing?"

Since he'd mentioned he hadn't sent me an invitation to the competition, I'd been avoiding him. But I didn't feel any ill will or, bizarrely, any suspicion from him. He was looking at me with the same expectant interest as he had in all previous tests. Maybe he'd forgotten?

Unlikely. But I'd worry about that later.

"They were distressing him." I hopped on the table, resting my strained arms by setting Armin on my lap. "We weren't getting anywhere until he was out of their literal grasp."

Farouk gave both widows a disapproving side-glance before offering me an approving nod. "Very well. Have you made your verdict?"

Not yet, but I was still tinkering with my idea. I had chosen the lead box—the child in this situation—once again. But since it was as empty, with him giving me no leads to go on, I had to improvise. I had to do something that would give me a good answer, if not the right one.

I had to provoke them, but I didn't know how yet.

Buying myself time, I shrugged towards my left. "Let Her Highness go first."

The expected sneer from Fairuza didn't come. She was busy watching the widows with unwavering concentration, like they were a riddle she was determined to solve.

When she finally moved, it was a startling snap of movement, standing to point at the older widow accusingly. "She said it herself. Her story is suspect because of her history of failing to bear children to term. From my experience, the simplest answer is usually the truest one."

"Your Highness—" Soumaya began to protest, eyes refilling with tears.

"Besides, the redhead looks healthier and is younger, she could have easily had the boy, doing what your husband chose her for, and that infuriates you," continued Fairuza. "A lord only marries to have heirs, to leave his lands and business in trusted hands."

As Soumaya broke down, the room erupted with more dissent from both sides.

I could barely hear most of the arguments, the most I caught was Ariane reinforcing that Marihan didn't look like the boy with Fairuza snapping back at her, "Red hair is not easily inherited, it's why it's rare. *You* of all people should know that."

Though I hated to think it, I mostly agreed with Fairuza. Soumaya was being vindictive and her tears weren't ones of desperation. I would know.

In the first year without my mother I had found myself breaking down regularly. Running out of things to pawn for money ended with me being evicted from the house, then I was too old for an orphanage to take in, yet too young to hire for work. The worsening spiral of my life had only halted when I learned how to steal and pass myself off as an adult.

But I was very familiar with the specific nature of her crying fit. The heat that permeated her tearful shouting didn't stem from fear and fragility, but fury and frustration.

By the time the arguing had died down, it was my turn, and my plan was fully formed.

Farouk extended a hand to me, either an invitation to speak or for me to hand over the child, but I kept Armin with me. Safe from being physically fought over.

"I don't have a verdict as much as I have a solution, an adjustment to Cora's recommendation," I addressed them, searching each widow's face for one last impression. "Since you both want to be his mother so much, so be it. You both get to keep him."

The absurdity of my verdict struck both women silent.

It still warranted a shrill "*What?*" from Cherine.

Cora raised a finger, a pinch between her blonde brows. "I second that *What.*"

Farouk took off his fez, smoothing back his black hair as if to diffuse the trapped heat of conflict in this room. "Lady Ada, could you please explain what you mean?"

"I mean they can each move to one of their husband's properties, and that they can share the boy on an alternating schedule." I gently stroked his head, his fine hair soft as a cat's fur beneath my fingertips. "One day, Soumaya has him, and the next she turns him over to Marihan, and so on. That way, everyone is happy, and he still gets to have two parents, especially ones who love him so much they each want to keep him for herself."

I waited with bated breath while the women mulled over my words, like a fisherman on a quiet lake, patiently waiting for something to bite his bait.

"I agree," Soumaya finally said. "As much as I want her out of my life, and since I can't prove my words, this is an efficient solution—"

Marihan's shout cut her off. *"No!"*

"Beggars can't be choosers," Soumaya snapped at her, fists clenched, shoulders stiff with hostility. "But you must have forgotten that now you believe yourself my equal. Since I can't cut you out completely, I am willing to share him—"

"But I'm not," Marihan cried, finally emoting, eyes filling and voice tremulous. "We *can't* share him."

Eyes now dry, Soumaya's nostrils flared with impatience. "Why not?"

"Because we can't keep tossing him back and forth through our doors like a rubber ball. This would be an awful existence for a growing boy, to see one mother one day and a different one the next, for no reason other than pettiness." Marihan rubbed at her eyes, her dry sobs like hiccups. "He deserves love and a stable home."

Soumaya rounded on her, practically spitting. "I'm not conceding to you. Elyas let you have everything in his life, you're not getting it in his death, too."

Marihan dropped her head in defeat, her red curls casting shadows on her face as a single tear trailed down her face and dripped off her chin. "Then you can have him."

Soumaya shoved her out of the way, arms outstretched as she closed in on me, but I held out a hand, keeping her at bay.

"She conceded that the baby is mine," Soumaya burst out.

To my surprise, Fairuza pushed Soumaya hard enough to make her stumble a few feet back. "She said no such thing. And mind who you're talking to."

"She said I could have him!" Soumaya exclaimed, a manic edge to her eyes and voice.

"Because she doesn't want him to suffer a life of being torn between two women who hate each other. With you no doubt poisoning him against her and turning his daily life to a living hell," I said. "To spare him, she would have given him to you, who desperately wants a child. She put her child first, as a mother would. Something you clearly know nothing about."

"Being a mother means I gave birth to him!" Soumaya cried.

"Concern for your children and their future doesn't end with their birth," Fairuza gritted, like she had a personal grievance in this argument. "Being a mother means you would care about them more than you cared about the status and money they came with, or about your vendetta with your rival."

"And you would consider how your behavior affects them," I added, baffled by Fairuza's stance, trying hard not to gape at her. "A mother would do everything to keep her children safe and stable for as long as she lives."

I believed my mother had done that for me to the best of her abilities. Even if she'd never told me the truth, or if she'd truly ended her own life. I had to believe she'd had over-whelming reasons for either decision.

"Even if you were the one to bear him, you shouldn't be the one to raise him since you don't care at all for his wellbeing."

The head judge rang that abhorrent bell again. I covered the boy's ears, hoping to spare his little head from further headache. "Final verdict, from each of you. Who is the real mother?"

"Soumaya," Cherine sniffed.

"I agree," said Ariane.

"At this point, I don't know," admitted Cora.

Fairuza lifted her chin, draped in confidence, the kind that came from knowing that in most cases her word would be law. "Marihan."

I slipped off the table, stroking the baby's small, soft head one last time. "Marihan."

Farouk checked behind him, silently communicating with the judge and Cyrus.

Cyrus rose from his table, clapping slowly. "Congratulations, Princess Fairuza and Lady Ada. Through different means, you both reached the correct answer."

Relief flooded me, cooling my worries and redirecting my thoughts down a path of optimistic predictions for the rest of the week. But my gut stalled their flow down that easy route, because I had a feeling it wouldn't be that simple.

Cyrus strolled towards us, his face unreadable. "Though the princess's verdict mainly came from guesswork, and the lady's gauging the truth from their responses was clever, their methods still left a lot to be desired." He reached into his pocket and took out a piece of parchment, opening it along its fold-lines as he swept a glance at all five of us. "None of you asked to see if the child had a birth certificate, which he does. I tracked down the one made by the midwife who delivered him, which names Marihan as his mother."

The unspent anger at him from earlier rose, fueling my snap. "I stand by what I said."

Cyrus cocked his head at me. "Pardon?"

"That it doesn't matter if Soumaya gave birth to him," I said, watching him as he came closer and closer, feeling the heat of my conflicted feelings flaring under my skin. "Judging by her priorities and behavior, she would have been a terrible mother."

"But it wouldn't be just, to give him to the wrong woman,

only because she seems like a better choice," he argued, now close enough to look down at me, mouth curved in a cocky smile.

I was torn between wanting to pull him closer and kick him. "We could think that way, if this was an inheritance they were fighting over, or ownership of an object."

He inched even nearer, hands in pockets, a familiar ease seeping into his posture, a form of him I wished was reserved for me. "But?"

"But we're not here to settle *their* dispute. We're here for the *child*. The only one we need to do right by is him." I tried to emulate Fairuza's confidence. It was hard, as I wasn't a princess who'd grown up knowing my word was above all others. I was just someone tired of people like Nariman and Lady Dufreyne and now this Soumaya making other people suffer for their pursuit of selfish ends. "It wouldn't be just if we gave him to the woman who didn't put him before every-thing in the world, starting by herself, birth-mother or not."

Like a flame behind opaque glass, his eyes had gone from a soft flicker to the brightest thing in the room, ignited not by oil or candlewicks, but by my words and how they affected him.

As ambivalent as I was about the change in his personality since he'd resumed being Cyaxares, about the difference in his tone, carriage and style, his eyes were still the same.

And I never wanted them to look away from me.

CHAPTER NINE

Upon ruling that Marihan was the child's mother, she rushed across the floor and hugged me, kissing me once on one cheek and twice on the other as we exchanged Armin. When she moved to do the same to her other unlikely champion, Fairuza froze up against her but nonetheless accepted her kisses of gratitude.

Watching her tolerate this common woman invading her personal space, smiling slightly as she listened to her rambling thanks, I couldn't help wondering. Why had she made that verdict?

She no doubt believed in seniority, and hated being unseated from her assured spot as Cyrus's lone candidate for future queen, and having that consideration spread out among girls she saw as inferior. So why had she sided with Marihan—a usurper like all of us—and joined my argument against Soumaya? From the way she'd seemed invested in the boy's wellbeing, it must have reminded her of a personal issue. Perhaps her relationship with her own mother?

It struck me that I'd never considered what problems

someone like Fairuza could have. Aside from the rumors about her brother turning into a monster, she seemed to lead a charmed life. Like Cyrus, she was the product of a royal arranged marriage, like the one she was meant to have, a princess marrying a future king. But if Cyrus had called a Bride Search to escape a similar fate to his parents, then what was Fairuza's aim here? Was it possible her goal to be his queen had a different goal other than expectations and duty?

Whatever deeper look I wanted into her psyche, it would require either mindreading or a civil conversation between us. I couldn't tell which was more impossible.

Without exchanging a word or a look, Fairuza and I bid Marihan one last goodbye. Cyrus was fielding arguments from Soumaya, and questions from Cherine and Ariane about their evaluations.

He escaped them and headed in our direction, cracking an expectant grin. "Think you can maintain your standing in the next test?"

"Depends," I said. "Whose idea is it?"

Fairuza tapped manicured nails on the stones of her rings, an irritating, chipping noise. "And what's it about? Does it involve more squabbles over inheritance? I have yet to see what civil disputes have to do with being queen."

Loujaïne approached, bunching up the side of her deep-green, satin skirt, with Farouk in her wake. "It's testing how you'd deal with the issues of your people when you become one."

"Then shouldn't you be giving us a case on the scale we're likely to deal with?" I asked.

"Unfortunately, we're all out of national crises at the moment." Cyrus quipped, his humor tickling me, compelling the corners of my lips to twitch. "This was the best we could do on short notice."

Little moments like this reinvigorated me, made me rethink my stance on the prince.

My Cyrus was in there. How much of him, I wasn't sure, but I needed to find out.

But other answers, namely about Nariman, and when they'd leave us alone so I could plot to retrieve the lamp, took precedence.

The head judge announced the session officially over, thankfully without the jarring knell of her bell.

Cora stretched her arms as she dragged her feet towards me. "Let's go, Ada. The sooner we're back in the palace, the sooner I can eat."

I fell into step with her. "Is that all you think about?"

She huffed. "It's all I've got to look forward to here."

As we headed to the door, Fairuza met my eyes for the first time today. "It seems that only you and I have proven ourselves capable."

There was no venom in her comment, just cold observation. From the thoughtful way she was regarding me, it felt like she was rethinking her view of me as well.

I only nodded to her as we and Ayman followed Cyrus and Farouk out, tailed by Loujaïne, Asena and the girls.

Cherine—unsuspecting that she was walking beside the one who starred in her dreams *and* nightmares, as both white knight and ghoul—pursued Cyrus with renewed complaints.

"I *still* don't understand what the point of this was."

Ariane, on his other side, readied her parasol. "Yes, you never responded to what this precisely has to do with being your princess?"

"Or why we would ever bother with something this inane," Fairuza added, passing us with her handmaidens at her heels.

At the entrance, Cyrus rounded on them, a silhouette against the sunset and our glimpse of the city, with an oil-spill of a shadow reaching our feet. "If, after four tests you still can't understand what the aim of this competition is, then you need to reassess your presence here."

Fairuza dropped her skirt and entered his shadow, anger raising her voice. "I am here to be your queen and the mother of your heirs! As the daughter of a king, of a princess of Cahraman, I am the one best suited to fulfill those duties. What else is there to investigate?"

The neutrality of his formal tone faded only to be replaced by repressed anger that darkened his quiet question. "If that was all I needed, why would I have ever called this search?"

I didn't need to see her face to know she was glaring at him. "Perhaps you thought you could find better than the best."

He looked down at her, face grimly shadowed. "The best at what?"

"At everything! You've seen how I've performed in each ridiculous task you've set to see if there was someone better than me and there *isn't*." She inhaled sharply, as if on the verge of crying. "Why am I still not enough for you?"

"I'm not marrying a garden, Fairuza. I'm not looking for a pretty addition to my palace that will sprout heirs come next spring. I am looking for a *queen*."

A trace of vulnerability lined her statement. "A queen sits by her king's side as he rules and helps raise the next king."

"That is not all a queen does!" The intensity of his frustration sent a wave of shock through me, further chipping at my own previous impression of him and re-sculpting it into the powerful figure that cast his shadow over us all. "If that's all you've witnessed growing up with a queen for a mother then I pity King Florent for the hand fate dealt him."

Fairuza stepped back, a horrified hand over her heart. "Have you no respect for your aunt or myself?"

"This isn't disrespect, this is disappointment. And since you're all so determined to know the answer, I'll spell it out." His voice filled the hall. "The point of testing your judgment as a future consort was to see if you have the ability to rule. If I should fall ill or die, leaving you as regent to our children, and ruler of the land, what would you do?"

Fairuza took another step back, as if suddenly unsteady on her feet. "I…I don't know."

I gaped at her. That was literally the last thing I could have expected her to utter.

Cyrus shook his head at her. "If you're wondering why you went from being my sole choice to one of many, we both now have our answer."

Having Cyrus shatter Fairuza's illusions, pulling the rug out from under her, had been on the roster of fantasies that kept me going. But now it had come to pass, it didn't feel good.

Against all reason, in this moment, I somehow felt bad for her. She hadn't had a fraction of my experiences, from the insignificant ones to those that remained soul-shaking. But I recognized this moment as the first drop of the downpour that was reality crashing down on her.

It still rained for me, because I had no castle to shield me from the storm ravaging the land. But she did. She would always find shelter. If not with Cyrus, then with another prince.

Without another word, Fairuza rushed past him and down

to the carriages, barely giving her handmaidens time to climb in before she slammed the door shut.

Ariane and Cherine must have taken that scene as a sign to leave him alone and descended the steps quietly.

I wanted to take this moment to talk to him alone, but Cora remained half-leaning on me, and I couldn't ask someone as observant as her to carry on without me.

Unbuttoning his cuffs as if his formal attire was stifling him, Cyrus invited us to head down. "I'm sorry you had to listen to that."

"No worries." Cora shrugged and herded me down.

Cherine had climbed into Loujaïne's carriage. I could hear her interrogating the princess about her performance. Ariane, who'd arrived with Cyrus and Ayman, avoided any lingering anger by sitting in our carriage with Farouk.

This was my chance.

Cyrus beat us to the pavement, hands held out to help us down the last step. He offered a cold, impersonal touch, but the smile that shone through his eyes warmed me.

Caught up in the resurging feelings, I almost forgot how to speak. I managed to get my words in order before he could help me up to the carriage Ariane now occupied.

"Can we accompany you?" I said. "It seems our carriage is taken."

Ayman opened the prince's carriage for me before Cyrus could respond.

Giving him an amused sidelong glance, Cyrus bowed to me. "I would be delighted to have your company."

Cora only gave me a blank look as she pushed past Cyrus and climbed in first, ignoring protocol and shocking both driver and footman.

Cyrus didn't take offense to her entering before him, shook his head fondly. "Have to admire how hard her head is."

"Fairuza's head could crack geodes," I retorted.

"No, it really couldn't." He faced me, hand outstretched again to help me up.

I set my fingers on his palm, trying not to betray the feelings that scattered like pearls beneath my feet, making every step and thought a struggle for balance. I also had to rein back my anxiousness about the information I needed.

I hated to use whatever he might feel for me—especially if it went beyond simple affection. But if I won, and things went well, then he would have me wholly. It couldn't hurt to have his help, whether he knew he was providing it or not, could it?

"So, this test was to find someone to take on Princess Loujaïne's duties?" I asked, my heart spilling its beats in a hammering rush as he handed me up into the carriage.

"Among other things." He grinned as he looked at Cora, who'd thrown her head against the back of her seat and was softly snoring. He sat across from me, suddenly frowning. "Now that you mention it, Loujaïne has been acting as queen in more ways than one lately."

That was a rope he'd unknowingly thrown me. I had to grab it and pull myself closer, to know more about his life and about the witch who'd tossed me in it. "Just lately? Was there someone else before her?"

He blinked, an overt display of confusion, as if he'd suddenly realized something. "Yes, my father's previous advisor had most of Loujaïne's duties, even some of Farouk's. She was the one who supported my demand to hold the Bride Search, even helped me set it up."

So, that part of Nariman's story was true.

"What happened to her?"

"Lady Rostam, according to my aunt, was a witch who was conspiring against the crown, planning to overthrow the king." Discomfort melted his smile, sadness snuffing the light behind his eyes. "But according to my father, she wanted to marry him, to be his queen at any cost, even dark magic."

"She could have aimed to become his queen then depose him or dispose of him," I thought out aloud, thinking back to Nariman's claim that the king had promised to marry her, only to take the lamp before banishing her.

What if that lamp was used to banish her? What if she needed it to walk back in?

"What did he do once he found out?" I prompted, even if I hated the unease this subject clearly caused him, but I had to know. I *needed* to know.

"Though practice of black magic comes priced with public execution, my father only chose to banish her," he said, twisting his rings around his fingers one at a time, another sign of disquiet. "I still don't understand why, but it makes me question the accusations if she was spared that fate, as we don't tolerate any form of black magic nor treason in Cahraman."

I'd been right in believing I could never tell him the truth.

I tried not to gulp too visibly. "You don't believe that her goal was to replace him?"

He shook his head, his mouth twitching in a humorless smile. "If anything, I believe she just wanted to be queen, like the fifty girls she sent for did."

The mention of her saddened him, but not with an under-current of bitterness or anger, like one would remember someone who'd hurt them. His dejection plucked at my heart-strings. It was too familiar, it was what I felt whenever I thought of my mother.

As horrid as she was, Nariman might really be the closest thing he'd had to a mother.

But as worse as that made things, I didn't have the luxury of dwelling on his complicated relationship with Nariman. Extracting as much information about her from him was vital.

"If you don't mind me asking, how does one banish a witch?" I hoped I didn't sound too suspicious.

"Why?" he asked, lightening up a bit. "Angling for information that will help in your next test?"

Had he been still my Cyrus, I would have countered his teasing. But as the prince, I had to continue maneuvering him for the answers I needed. "Why? Are we fighting witches?"

"Close. But no, I wouldn't know how one banishes a witch. My grandfather forbade teaching me any witchcraft."

"It's a skill that could come in handy." A skill I wished I had to fix my problems. "You might as well learn now that the old king is gone."

"If you're that interested, perhaps we could learn it together."

I could barely contain my blush.

Our carriage ran over a bump, waking Cora with a start, and ending my interrogation.

I hadn't learned all I needed to know, but it was enough for now, to know more about Nariman as a person. And by his suggestion, I had a chance to know more in the next test, because if it involved witches, maybe I could learn how to repel one.

We spent the rest of the ride back to the train in idle, light-hearted chatter, broaching many subjects, none invasive or polarizing. It felt different than before, talking as prince and lady, in the company of others. A public sort of familiarity that wasn't as intimate as our time together in the tunnels and the vault or in the market, but was new and exciting nonetheless.

The shock of his real identity had at first made me hold on tighter to my impression of Cyrus, reject the possibility he could have anything in common with the Prince of Cahraman. Now I found that I wanted to really get to know Cyaxares. I could see myself loving that side of him as much, and as easily.

But that was a fantasy I couldn't entertain. I had to stick to the reality of my mission. I wasn't aiming to win him for myself, but for the chance to save my family.

But when no amount of logic could deter my fantasies from taking over, one thing did. The repulsive thought of Cyrus's and my future children calling Nariman *Nana*.

CHAPTER TEN

At the stroke of seven, Cherine burst into my room and hassled me out of bed. Groggy and confused, I got dressed as she complained that our second test had been advanced to today.

It took over a half-hour for all five of us to be rounded up for a quick breakfast with only Loujaïne. I supposed Cyrus and Farouk's absence had to do with the sudden shift in our schedule. Throughout the meal, Fairuza and Loujaïne traded whispers, likely discussing the test and how Fairuza was to pass it. Nariman may have made the competition cheat-proof, but that didn't mean Fairuza couldn't be coached by her aunt.

I kept an ear out for any information as I drank as many small cups of coffee as I could. I needed to be as alert and attentive as I could. Yesterday's success would become point-less if I flubbed today's test.

When the clock struck nine, a guard knocked and announced the arrival of our guests.

Like a coiled spring, Loujaïne bounced to her feet and clapped. "Time to go!'

Fairuza, Agnë and Meira passed us, one of the hand-maidens slamming a shoulder into Cherine.

Cherine made to chase her, but I caught her by the skirt. "Shhh, let it go. You can hide her shoes later when they're helping Fairuza bathe."

Her indignation subsided quickly, hazel eyes brightening. "That's not a bad idea."

"Of course not. None of my ideas are bad."

"You were going to give that child to both women," Cherine reminded with a wag of her finger.

"That was just a ploy to find out who the real mother was."

"That was irresponsible! Imagine if they'd both agreed!"

"But they didn't, that was what I was depending on."

"Yes, but what if they had?"

Cora leaned down, sticking her head between ours. "Doesn't matter. It didn't happen. Don't dwell on the past."

"Why not? We learn from the past," Cherine argued.

"Only if you let it pass, otherwise it becomes ever-present," said Cora.

That was a fact I needed to remember. My tendency to dwell on what happened and what-ifs kept me from moving forward. It didn't matter if everything could have gone differently, bad things had happened and now I had to make sure they got better.

Loujaïne turned to face us in the circular hallway. "If there's anything you will learn to do as a wife, not just a princess, it is to influence the views and positions of your husband's guests and allies." Her voice rang around the soaring walls and expansive, marble floor. "Today, those are three leaders from neighboring regions. The king, the prince and myself will hold audience with each of them. Your job is to receive and accommodate those who accompany them. You must find a way to convince them to influence their leaders to agree with our demands."

"Why?" Cherine asked, mouth full of pins, blindly fumbling around the back of her head to stabilize her chignon.

Loujaïne's silver eyes sliced an annoyed glare her way. "I just told you why."

"I didn't get it."

A deep huff slumped Loujaïne's shoulders, dropping her beaded shawl to the crooks of her arms with a soft rattle. "A merchant-prince of Lower Campania, a captain of the Deep Red Sea and the Crown Prince of Almaskham are visiting today for business negotiations. Each is bringing companions with them, be it a wife, a first mate or a son. Your job is to attend to their guests while we handle the dignitaries."

"But there's five of us," I pointed out.

"I believe one is bringing two companions, so two of you will have to entertain the same party." She moved to lead us out of the hall. "It should be a good exercise in court politics for you."

Picking up her skirt to hustle after her, Fairuza seemed a bit fazed. "How can we share one guest? We're competition!"

"I don't have to spoon-feed you everything," Loujaïne grumbled, volume rising with her thinning patience. "You're all women of marriageable age from noble families. You should know how to entertain guests in the presence of others."

"I do, but not while competing," Fairuza argued, distressed.

A muscle flickered in Loujaïne's cheek as her glare hardened.

Fairuza's lips trembled, but she said nothing. Neither did

anyone else as we continued our departure from the dining hall.

At the first turn, Cyrus appeared, with Master Farouk right by him, reading him something from a scroll as he listened and nodded.

His hair was combed back and arranged neatly off his face today, bringing out more of his bone structure, making him appear older, more intense, especially as he frowned in concentration.

Like at the courthouse, there was something wildly different about him in that moment, something mysterious and powerful. The way he held himself, the clipped words and straightforward tone, the commanding gestures.

This was the man who would be king.

This was something I would never get over. That he could be two people on opposite ends of the spectrum so convincingly. Even though he insisted that every part I'd seen was all him, it left me to wonder which was the version he would normally be on an everyday basis, Cyrus or Cyaxares. And which I wanted more.

The problem now wasn't that I'd seen him as two very different people. They'd since started to merge. I'd settled one side of the issue—recognizing him as the same person with many facets to his characters and still retained my intense feelings towards his whole person.

But the princely aspect of him didn't stop at his personality, but continued past him into the realms of expectations, responsibilities, duties and all that made the kingdom go round.

Cyrus noticed us as we approached, breaking out that wide, white smile to greet us. "Good morning, ladies. I hope you had a good night's rest. Have you been briefed on today's mission?"

I resisted a flinch at the word "mission," and the reminder of my real purpose here. That damned ugly lamp, and Bonnie's lifeline beginning to slip through my fingers.

"Not really," I admitted. "What are we supposed to convince the guests of your guests to do exactly?"

"Good question," he said, before going into a brief but comprehensive explanation of every guest's business here, and our role and test.

As discussion rose, he turned, beckoning us to follow. I caught up with him first, listening intently as he told us about one of our guests—a navy captain, and how he tied into Cahraman's need to build port cities along the Deep Red Sea.

He gestured as he spoke, his rings glinted softly, catching the morning light from the soaring windows. I wanted to ask about the silver pearl, about his mother, about what else he knew of Nariman, if he had known my mother. Ideas of telling him everything dangerously circled my head again like vultures.

I couldn't ask a man to rob his own father, his king, especially when he already had people out looking for the lamp. It would be beyond suspicious of me to tell him, *"By the way, it's most likely in your father's personal safe. Do you happen to have a spare key?"*

Unless I could convince him. Today we were supposed to convince people to do something for the crown. Plant the idea in their companions' heads so they could in turn influence them. I supposed we had to convince them of something they were resistant or at least ambivalent towards.

If I convinced him to do something he would never

normally do, he could help me with this, then help me with Bonnie then—

Cherine caught his arm, briefly unbalancing him and ending my foolish musings. "You better not be giving her tips on today's mission."

"I would do no such thing," he assured her in mock-seriousness, carefully removing his hand from mine.

I could almost feel the holes Fairuza's eyes were burning in the back of my head as she hustled closer, the materials of her skirt rustling menacingly. "What are our individual missions then?"

I almost slammed into the ceiling when Loujaïne spoke next to me. "Miss Greenshoot will attend to the merchant-prince's wife. Lady Cherine will accompany the merchant-prince's son. Princess Ariane will escort the captain's first mate, and Princess Fairuza will host the advisor to the prince of Almaskham."

She went on to describe the details of the guests' business in Cahraman and what the girls were supposed to do.

When she overtook me, I was forced to ask, "What about me?"

Loujaïne looked back at me with the usual contempt. "You will help Fairuza host the prince's advisor."

Fairuza's and my exclamations clashed together, an unintelligible warble of distressed noises that bounced off every surface of the mosaic-spread passage.

"I'm not working with her," Fairuza protested. "She has no experience, no formal training and no manners. She will ruin the negotiation for us."

"Those manners of yours are what would ruin anything," I snapped.

Fairuza's cheeks trembled as her eyes hardened, becoming

colder than the matching line of polished turquoise around her throat.

Just when I'd thought we'd reached some sort of understanding yesterday at the court. But Fairuza wasn't Cherine, who was here to compete but not alienate her competition, who could be upset at the tests rather than at those who made them. Fairuza would never be half the noblewoman Cherine was, or half the person I was…

The charged air between us was cleaved by Loujaïne blocking our view of one another.

"How you handle the situation will reflect on you," she said bluntly, effectively ending the conversation.

As we stepped apart, I found that I'd rather dangle off the mountain's edge again than be stuck a few hours with Fairuza.

CHAPTER ELEVEN

I was meant to co-host someone from Almaskham, a prince's advisor no less.

I'd heard so much about Cahraman's northern neighbor, but with Loujaïne's questioning if I had any Almaskhami blood, and my growing suspicions, the idea of meeting someone who represented the land had me buzzing with curiosity.

I only hoped they'd be less obnoxious than Fairuza.

Master Farouk bowed in the first party, announcing them as "Captain Baher Qursan, head of the Deep Red Sea Navy, and his First Mate Yorgho."

Captain Qursan had a rough, booming voice, a lined, tanned face as bloated as the rest of him, and a red, bushy beard that reached the middle of his massive chest. I suspected he was balding under his fancy sea-foam turban.

His first mate, on the other hand, was what I imagined a merman to look like. Tall, tan and built like a swimmer, he had wavy blond hair scattered with sun-streaks that passed his waist. He wore a necklace of seashells and wore no shoes or had taken them off, and I suspected both his hair and shirt were wet.

Just the sight of them made me miss the windy, humid city of Galba, and every coastal city I'd visited before settling in Aubenaire with Bonnie.

Loujaïne gracefully bowed her head and Ariane half-curtsied in a stumbling step. The captain held out a necklace of white pearls to Loujaïne, slipping it over her bowed head. Yorgho picked Ariane's hand and kissed it lingeringly, making her flush pink and giggle stupidly, earning her a raised eyebrow from Loujaïne.

Blushing deeper, Ariane held an arm out to Yorgho, and both she and Loujaïne led their guests out of the hall.

Captain Qursan's voice was still reverberating back to us long after they'd left our sight when Farouk announced, "The Lord Eukharistos, merchant-prince of Campania, and his lady wife Galena and son Rhodion."

The merchant-prince, a short, pot-bellied man, had a trimmed salt-and-pepper beard and a shock of the blackest hair. He wore a wine-red cloak over a beige tunic overlaid with a diamond-studded medallion. His wife, long-nosed, as plump as her husband, and with her tawny hair in a curly bun, offered Cora a glass jar of herbs and Cherine a transparent bag of shelled pecans. Her son, a bit younger than us, awkward and gangly, seemed to be terrified of Cherine.

Lady Galena followed Cora's reluctant shuffle out of the hall and Cherine took a hold of Rhodion and dragged him out, already talking his ear off, not being the least bit subtle about what she wanted out of him today.

Lord Eukharistos held out his pudgy hand to Cyrus. "I take it you'll be negotiating with me today, Your Highness?"

Cyrus gave him a firm yet friendly handshake, nodding. "I

will, but I hope you don't mind Master Farouk escorting you to my offices first. My father has been delayed this morning, so I need to greet Prince Miraz in his stead."

The man nodded understandingly, patting Cyrus's shoulder. Farouk, seemingly surprised, exchanged a glance with Cyrus before escorting Lord Eukharistos up the stairs without announcing the prince and his companion.

Prince Miraz walked in, a young man around the same age as Cyrus, but more baby-faced. His golden skin barely managed a light stubble, and his black hair parted down the middle, accentuating the emerging squareness of his jaw, and the doe-eyes radiating optimism. With the way his mouth curled into a lopsided grin and his hooded eyes were set into his long face, the prince looked a bit like Ayman. But his straight black hair, dark eyes and long legs reminded me of myself, adding more weight to Loujaïne's suspicions.

Prince Miraz passed the blinding daylight of the window, coming more into focus. He wore a heavily embroidered, white gold cotton kaftan that stopped past his knees with dark bronze satin pants and same colored curling shoes. His adornments were a heavy gold bracelet on one hand and a big diamond ring on the one he extended to Cyrus who met him halfway.

They greeted each other warmly, like they were old friends, clasping hands and moving into a hug.

"Miraz, it's so good to see you." Cyrus for once sounded honest and enthusiastic in his pleasantries. "I was expecting your uncle today. What's with the surprise?"

Miraz answered with all the rushed eagerness of a child. "I told Azal that, as the future leader of Almaskham, I need to learn how to handle diplomacy myself. And what better place for me to try my hand at it than at the home of a relative?"

"That way, if he makes a fool of himself, you will go easy on him and there will be no risk of war," an old woman walked in, surprising all of us, including Miraz, with her cutting remark.

My heart sank as I realized she was the one Fairuza and I would share.

She was a short, unamused woman in a verdigris silk gown with a downturned mouth and crows-feet framing her half-moon eyes. They were the same dark blue as the lapis lazuli that dangled from her ears, but their drooping eyelids shadowed them so much I'd first mistaken them for black. Her hair was long and graduating from pale silver in her crown roots to white-gold that tumbled past her shoulders in waves. The color of faded blonde hair, not the greying of brown or black.

From the style and shade of her hair, and her sun-kissed skin—with a warmer, rosier undertone than Miraz and my cool-toned olive and Cyrus's pale gold—she could have been Cora's grandmother.

Miraz panicked slightly, almost tripping as he bowed to introduce her. "Prince Cyaxares and lovely ladies, I present to you, my grandmother and advisor, the Dowager Princess Aurelia."

Aurelia raised a thin, curved eyebrow at us, hands on her whitewood cane, not making a move towards us herself.

The surprise she instilled in me soared. It had never occurred to me that someone could be a princess into old age. It was odd enough Loujaïne was in her thirties and still a princess. Then again the idea of a dowager one never crossed my mind to begin with.

While Fairuza, Ariane and Loujaïne did look the part of a king's daughter, in decorative clothes and priceless jewelry, the Dowager Princess Aurelia, mother of a reigning prince, and grandmother of the heir before us, was more like a fairy queen from Ericuran folktales. Old, somber, a bit unnerving but radiating power and confidence.

Clearly no run-of-the-mill grandmother. She seemed more likely to beat me over the head with her fancy cane than offer me sweets.

How was I supposed to convince this woman to do anything, let alone influence her to sway her grandson? As an advisor, she had to be well aware of how to manipulate people's opinions and shift their thoughts around. As a grandmother, she could just flat out tell him *no, we're not doing that*, and he'd have to listen.

Cora and Cherine were meant to help broker a tit-for-tat trade deal with produce rather than money—spices from Cahraman for rare fruit from Campania. Ariane was meant to ask for the freelance navy to work with Cahraman to expand its trade routes across the seas to island nations. Fairuza and I were meant to ask Almaskham to help us invest in both these ventures, with the argument that both nations would benefit.

How was I supposed to do that with such an uncompromising woman? While keeping Fairuza from derailing my efforts? She'd agreed with me yesterday, if for her own unknown reasons, as we'd reached the same verdict. I didn't expect anything would make her cooperate with me again today.

And then, if there was anything I'd learned from working in several service establishments, getting someone to invest in something, even if it made sense and sounded lucrative, was difficult. Investment in general was a gamble and gambles were, largely, unnecessary. Not to mention dangerous.

You could always maintain your business as-is and keep

your money. But if you try to multiply it by investing in something new—like Cyrus was investing in the Bride Search and Nariman was in me—it might bring you prosperity—or ruin you.

I wished him the first outcome, and her the second.

Cyrus bowed to Aurelia. "Your Grace."

Aurelia's beady eyes followed Cyrus as he continued with, "It's a great honor to have you here for the first time in years. The people of Cahraman have missed your presence," and other pretty, empty courtesies he was trained to spout.

She cut him off mid-sentence, "I don't see any of your mother in you."

I could almost hear the halting crash in his mind.

"*Taita*…" Miraz whined, embarrassed.

She cut him off too with a silencing gesture.

Unease trickled back into me when Fairuza stepped forward, curtseying and bowing low enough to not have her bejeweled tiara slip off her gleaming head.

In a sweet, accommodating voice I'd never heard she greeted, "Your Grace, I am Princess Fairuza of Arbore, and in all my years of duty as part of a royal house I have never heard of a woman as accomplished as yourself. My mother, Queen Zomoroda, always uses you as an example in efficiency and poise, and I hope that, in your brief time here, you can impart some of your wisdom on me."

That was perfect. Something I couldn't hope to match. Forget punching her in the eye. I now wanted to kick out her pearly teeth.

The urge deflated when Aurelia just tsked and said, "Why's that?"

Fairuza straightened, still holding the sides of her skirt, a hint of confusion furrowing her brows but not reaching her effortless smile. "So I can be the most supportive wife to a noble king."

"Support? Is that what you think you're here for?"

Unfazed, still smiling, Fairuza flawlessly replied, "Why, yes, of course. While a future king is mentored by his father and guided by his council, his unwavering support should come from his wife as not just the woman raising his heirs but as his confidante."

Somehow, Aurelia remained unimpressed. "Tell me, did you come up with that yourself or did your governess write it down for you?"

I held back a disbelieving laugh as Fairuza's resolve cracked.

"I'm not sure what you mean, Your Grace," she said innocently, her voice an octave higher.

"Do you actually believe what you are saying or are you just regurgitating the same bull your betrothed here has been force-fed since infancy?" Aurelia asked callously, barely lifting her hand to wag a finger between Fairuza and Cyrus disparagingly.

"Taita, *please!*" Miraz yelped, scandalized. "We're guests here!"

Cyrus moved in to correct her. "Your Grace, the princess is not my—"

She cut him off again. "What are you still doing here talking to me?"

Cyrus blinked at her. "I…pardon?"

"Don't you have that fat oligarch waiting for you, eating baklava in an office somewhere?" she said scathingly. "It's rude to keep him waiting, though I guess you wouldn't know since your oaf of a father is keeping my grandson waiting as well."

"My father is held-up with his council—"

"That's no excuse. We're not some envoys he can keep waiting. Not if he has any hope of having us loosen our purse strings for his harebrained schemes."

This woman didn't give anyone the chance to speak. How was I supposed to get a word in, let alone out of her? Why would she listen to me when she didn't listen to the prince who was second in power in the kingdom she was a guest in?

But then she wasn't here as a fellow blue-blood, but as someone with business to conduct. Cyrus had emphasized that the members of the Almaskhami ruling family were here to invest. As an investor, Aurelia was here to be impressed, not flattered.

She was a *customer*.

From experience, I knew that there were three types of customers. The first kind saw servers as an extension of the business, someone they could boss around and get mad at when something didn't go their way. The second were always insecure about their orders, ate a wrong order or drank a cold coffee or flat beer to avoid confrontation. Finally, the third who only wanted to get what they paid for, preferably with a few perks, friendly waitresses not included.

Though at first she seemed like the first kind of customer, I could tell that Aurelia was actually the third kind. The kind that wanted to be served exactly what they expected, or else surprised with the unexpected quality of their order. They didn't want to chitchat, to be told that swapping a part of their order was impossible or to haggle with their waiter. Not because they feared confrontation, but because the whole point of paying for a service was to give an order and having it carried out to their specifications without cajoling or argument.

Cyrus had started the unwanted chitchat, and being here instead of his father was the equivalent of replacing her potatoes with a salad without warning, then haggling with her to make her accept it. Fairuza was also the overfriendly waitress, the kind that could get cranky and lose her tip.

While I—I could handle this. I thought.

Aurelia turned her eyes on me. I immediately felt the scorching heat of her disapproving gaze searing my skin.

"And who are you?"

I didn't bow, I didn't curtsey, didn't do anything her title required because she knew all too well that it came before her as a person, and I didn't want to remind her of that.

I used my hostess voice, not too chipper, not too neutral, just in the middle, and unhurried. "I'm Ada."

She scowled at me. "Ada what?"

I shrugged. "Do you really care?"

Her penciled eyebrows shot up. "As a matter of fact, I don't."

I offered her my arm. "Good. Now, why don't we get you seated? Would you like to put your feet up? It must have been a rocky trip getting here."

Aurelia nodded, limping away from an aghast Miraz and a watchful Cyrus. "About time someone asked. From how long I've been left standing, you'd think I really didn't look as old as all the sycophants tell me."

She bumped past Fairuza, not even throwing a quick "Excuse me," over her shoulder. Fairuza audibly gasped in offense.

Linking her arm with mine, leaning half her weight on me, Aurelia motioned with the end of her cane. "You better not make me walk up the stairs."

I was meant to take her up to the ladies' common room,

where all female elites and heads of every post in the palace gathered to drink tea, gossip, snack and, occasionally, nap on the giant cushions.

But supposed to or not, the customer was always right and if she asked for wine instead of beer she was getting wine, on the same floor, with a view, too.

"But we'll have to walk a bit," I said. "So brace yourself."

"It had better not be too far, or else you'll have to carry me," she warned.

"As long as you don't mind being thrown over my shoulder like a sack of potatoes."

She made no reply to my comment, just eyed me briefly before facing ahead.

As we turned the corner, I saw Fairuza still standing back there, mouth half-open. I resisted the urge to wag my tongue out at her, to rub it in her face that I had won the opening round, whatever it entailed.

Released from his grandmother's intimidating presence, Prince Miraz jabbered excitedly next to Cyrus, who was intently watching us leave.

His full, sculpted lips finally cracked a true smile, one I hadn't seen since we'd been in the marketplace.

It was a genuine emotion that reached his eyes and shone through them like starlight. Meant for only me to see, straight from his heart to mine.

Then he mouthed, "You're doing great."

And the crazy urge to take all this seriously, to do everything in my power to win, came back with a vengeance.

CHAPTER TWELVE

After seating Aurelia on the porch overlooking the southern gardens, I pretended to go in search of a footstool.

I did find one but I mainly wanted to get what was set up to pamper her upstairs. A servant saw me carrying the tea tray and insisted on taking it down for me, while another carried the footstool and I threw a shawl over my arm.

After they set everything on the porch and left, she greeted me with an abrasive, "What took you so long?"

"The tea got cold during and I had to ask for a fresh pot," I answered, not entirely lying.

I set the tray on the polished bronze table between us, the footstool under her tiny feet, and offered her the shawl.

She squinted at it. "What's that for?"

"It gets breezy here. And it cools during the evening."

"It's still early noon."

"We could be here a good while," I reasoned. "That and you're old and dressed too lightly, and there's a risk of you catching a cold."

I was expecting a caustic retort to that, but she just nodded and snatched it from me. "Have you much experience with old people, girl?"

"A few."

"You're the youngest in your family?"

I poured her the tea in a flowery, gold-rimmed teacup, and fanned out ridged anise biscotti in a matching saucer. "That I know of."

"What? You can't quote your family tree by heart?" she sneered witheringly. "Can't tell me all about what relic spawned your line? Whose daughter, niece, and half-cousin thrice removed you are?"

I sat down across from her and pulled my chair in. There was another one meant for Fairuza, but she hadn't joined us so far. "To be honest, I'm lucky I even know who I'm named after."

"What did your father do?"

I had a feeling she wasn't asking about his occupation. "What do you mean?"

"Either your whole line has been wiped out or one of your parents did something to alienate the rest of the family." She dunked her biscotti into her tea, just like I liked to do. "So, which is it?"

"Both, I think?"

"How so?"

There was no way I could spin a whole family history without painting myself into a corner. I hadn't given myself a family name, as those were traceable and Fairuza likely knew every noble family in her kingdom.

I composed myself and took the easiest route in a soft interrogation. A variation of "I don't know" and letting *her* fill in the blanks as she saw fit.

Her deep blue eyes watched me from over the flared rim of her teacup, intrigued. "So, you have no family worth mentioning, no titles worth stating and I'm guessing no money. Another in-name-only noble trying her luck here for a better future, is that it?"

I nodded. "Pretty much."

"What future is that, may I ask?"

One where a vengeful witch wasn't going to make my best friend a monster's dinner. One where I could have my cake and eat it too—save the Fairborns and win the competition. Have it all. Have Mr. Fairborn walk me down the aisle, Bonnie meet Ayman, and all of Cyrus's pretty green-eyed children, and live happily ever after.

My wishful, sentimental streak aside, either or could happen. Or neither.

I sighed. "A future where I don't have to be so tired and stressed all the time."

"Do you think the life of a woman in a palace is relaxing?"

"No, but at least at the end of a nerve-wracking day I can sleep on a goose-feather pillow and eat food I didn't have to ration or scrounge for myself."

She set the cup down, empty, folded a hand on top of the other, showing me the biggest ring on her thin, wrinkled fingers. Bulky and platinum, it had diamonds studding the side patterns and a gold seat clutching a faceted, rectangular aquamarine stone. A smaller ring kept it from slipping off her finger. It was clear it wasn't hers. A man's. Her husband, the late prince's?

"Do you have any idea what it takes to be a prince's wife? A king's?"

"No, but I have a good idea, and I'm no stranger to the daily grind."

She scrutinized me. Not in the suspicious way Loujaïne did, but like she was checking for something she knew she was going to find. "Tell me, girl, if you hadn't been chosen to come here, what would you be doing?"

It was an answer I didn't have to modify, because it was the truth. "Living as a guest in a relative's home and working a job or two in the town."

"You have actually worked for other people?"

I nodded.

Surprise edged her crabby mood. "Is your family that disgraced?"

Years of loneliness suddenly weighed down on me and I felt their misery and stress creeping over my face. "They're all gone, Your Grace."

Dead or taken. And if I didn't win, the taken were as good as dead.

"What will you do if you don't get picked by the prince?"

"I don't expect to." I shrugged, releasing some tension by cracking down on the tough biscotti.

"So, once you're sent home you'll resume that pitiful existence you called a life?"

"Seems so."

She suddenly slammed her hands on the table, upturning her empty teacup and saucer and making me inhale dry crumbs. "For goodness sake, where is your ambition?"

"I'm sorry?" I coughed a throat-full of anise seeds and crumbled biscuit.

"This is a once-in-a-lifetime opportunity and you're fine with letting it pass you by?"

"I don't have a choice in that, do I?"

I expected a lot of things. But I would never have expected

this elderly, dignified princess to roll her eyes at me and go "Ugh!"

Then she leveled her disapproving glare on me. "You're a girl who's willing to work hard to survive, who's strong enough to do so with no one to help her out and who isn't stupid enough to try and play games with me. What use are all those qualities with no ambition?"

I gulped cold tea to soothe the burn in my throat. "I—I don't know?"

"Why don't you know? You obviously have the ability and the willingness to do the grueling job part of being a princess. I'd say you had a good chance, considering your competition, a girl with clear ambition to win but no drive to work, a girl who has no idea what it would take to rule a kingdom."

"But she was bred for it. Her parents are a king and queen."

"And? Mine weren't." She drummed tough, bony fingers, sending tremors through bronze table and rattling every item on it. "Do you want to know how I became who I am? It wasn't because my parents had planned for it or because I was one of few options for a future ruler."

"No?"

"I'm a miller's daughter from a fishing village."

Once again, the last thing I expected. The idea of a common woman becoming a princess only seemed to exist in folktales, never in real life.

Instantly fascinated, I forgot everything else as I sat forwards. "How did you get here then?"

She regarded me for a moment, as if gauging if I was worth a story.

As if coming to a decision, she sat back, harrumphed. "Our village was the halfway point between two warring kingdoms and that made trade, our only way to survive, ever harder.

Still, any man with a boat was better off than those without one. Then while trying to open up trade routes to the far south, my father and uncle encouraged a dozen girls to accompany them, to find husbands in the foreign lands."

"Why?"

"Because we were all poor. Our parents couldn't support us and no man had the means to build a home with us."

"And that's how you met the prince?"

"No." She started spinning her ring around her finger, the distracted caresses speaking volumes. "After a year sailing the oceans, we finally stopped at a port in the Deep Red Sea and disembarked. None of the grooms we were promised were there, but the slavers were."

I slowly set down my cup, heart pounding as if I was watching it all happen.

Aurelia looked out to the garden, watching the palace denizens putter around the hedges and stroll through the courtyard. "Apparently, a lot of men in the region were willing to pay good money for a blonde girl, because they believed they were the descendants of fairies and had magical powers."

"Did your father…?"

"No. Of course not." She gave a dramatic pause then added, "He did worse."

I slid to the edge of my seat, stunned.

"The grand-vizier came to pick a few girls for the palace, but asked first what kind of magic we could do. My father, the blithering goat, told him that none of them could work magic, but his own daughter could."

I gawked at her, horrified. "And he believed him?"

"He seemed to. He forked over enough money for me to buy all the other girls!"

"What happened after that?"

"Nothing, at first. Then the prince summoned me and demanded that I do tricks for him, like a witch would. I managed to use their complete ignorance about fairies and witches against them and told them that our magic needed a lot of focus, and privacy. "

She purposefully paused again, and my curiosity flared out of control. I couldn't help badgering her for more details. "What did he ask for?"

"Things my father claimed I could do, like turn coal into diamonds and straw into spun gold. If I didn't manage them then my father would give them the money back," she laughed. "By then, he was back on his boat and far into the ocean on his way home."

"Did they sell you to someone else when you didn't?"

"Oh, no. The alternative to getting their money back was for me to be beheaded."

I choked on another piece of biscotti. That hit too close to home, making a chopping block where I could meet my end float before my mind's eye.

She flicked her hand disdainfully. "I just did whatever ridiculous task they asked of me."

I coughed the debris from my windpipe, eyes watering. "H-how did you do that?"

She faced me, still toying with her ring. "I didn't spend a year on a trade ship preparing to be a good wife like the other girls. I learned how to barter for anything. I had information and favors to promise in return for the gems and gold I obtained. Once I managed that miracle enough times, they believed that I was magical."

"And then you married the prince?" I was getting excited now.

"No."

"Then what?" I whined. I couldn't wait for every detail to be laid out before me, not only to sate my curiosity, but also in hopes of finding what I could use in my own dilemma.

"They debated whether I should be kept around the palace as a resident enchantress or given to a temple to be trained as a priestess to appease their gods. If I stayed, I would have been asked to perform more miracles, and sooner or later, they'd ask something I couldn't barter or manipulate my way into obtaining, and if I left…well, it was one guess which kind of goddess I'd end up serving. And by all the fish in the oceans I was not going to be a temple courtesan."

I recoiled at the thought.

"Exactly," she said, tapping her teacup.

I poured her another cup. "Which option did you choose then?"

"Neither."

I paused, teapot poised over my cup. "What?"

"I made a third option."

"How?"

"Easy. Once people believe you have power, any kind of power, you can leverage that over them, even if you have nothing and they can crush you."

"But how do you do that?"

She raised one finger. "First, learn everything you can about the place you're in and its people." Another finger. "Second, learn the arts of misdirection—manipulation so subtle you'd make those you're steering believe they're acting on their own ideas."

"And then?"

"In between each maneuver to better your position, be observant, never speak first, never contradict yourself, make people talk about themselves instead of answering their questions, and tell useful truths at strategic moments. But most of all, give good advice, so when it works they never again doubt what you say." She sat back, huffing. "Safe to say, within a few weeks I had replaced the old bum who bought me, then I was the one whispering into our reigning moron's ear."

I jumped in my seat, clapping. "You became grand-vizier!"

She snorted dismissively. "Child, I became better than that. I became an *un*official confidante and advisor. Having a title that says you have the prince's ear puts a target on your back."

It finally clicked in my mind. That was what Nariman had been here.

She had risen to that position, hoping it would become a precursor to being queen. She had said the king had promised to marry her.

"I take it you didn't marry the prince you were advising?"

"As a matter of fact, I didn't." Her grouchy snap was less cutting than before. I could hear the smile in her voice even though it didn't reach her face.

"Who was he?"

Every stern line, in face and body, softened as a wistful gleam appeared in her eyes, a hint of sadness seeming to weigh her bony shoulders down. "The unlikely heir, his nephew, Prince Faisal."

"Unlikely how?"

"There were six others in line for the throne before him, so our marriage didn't cause too much of a stir like it would have had he been the heir."

I sighed, resting my cheek on my palm dreamily. "Did you love him?"

She held out her hand before her, catching the light on her

ring. "I did, and in that respect at least, we were extremely lucky."

"How come?"

"Love rarely has any place in a noble marriage, as they are beneficial first, political second, and personal last—if at all."

Those three reasons and their descending importance charred any rosy thoughts I had to ashes.

Unlike Aurelia's husband, Cyrus was first in line to the throne. If Cora and Cherine were beneficial and either princess was political, then I was personal.

But what priority did personal choices have in this world of thrones?

CHAPTER THIRTEEN

Fairuza suddenly spilled onto the porch, pink-cheeked and sweating, a few hairs out of place and tiara askew.

"What are you *doing* here?"

I gave her a flat stare. "Talking? Where have you been?"

"Looking for you!" she accused, shrill and angry. "I went up to the common room, where we should be, then looked everywhere. Why did you take her here?"

I dunked my biscotti into my tea, giving more attention to softening it than to her. "Fay-Fay, you can't expect me to walk our guest up two endless flights of stairs."

"Yes, I can, because those were your orders," she shouted, fists clenched, arms rigid at her sides.

I bit off the soggy end of the biscuit and chewed slowly, an excuse to ignore her.

"I'm talking to you!"

I popped the rest of the biscotti in my mouth and dusted my hands while smiling at her. "I don't work for you. No one here does. So you might want to ease up on the demands."

She glowered at me, her brilliant eyes the focus of her scrunched up, flushed face. "No, you don't work for me, because I would require my servants to have a modicum of common sense or class."

The skin of my face tightened, pulling at my tense features as I held back a frustrated growl. "Fairuza, I wouldn't work for you if you paid me all the gold in Cora's hair."

"And why's that?"

"Do you really have to wonder why I wouldn't want to help anyone who tried to murder my friend?"

"Stop saying that! I didn't do anything!"

She was so offended, I could have possibly believed her. But you couldn't lie to a liar. "My mistake, it was the wind that pushed a fully-grown girl over a stone wall."

She slammed her hands on the table hard enough to tilt it sideways. "You can't talk to me like that."

"I just did."

"I could have you thrown in the dungeon for insulting me. You're practically a peasant and I'm a princess, a future queen!"

I raised my hand, putting down a finger with each count. "One: no, you can't. This isn't your kingdom and the judge, jury and executioner don't work for you. Two: you're not engaged to Cyrus or any prince yet. And three—shut up."

To my shock, she did.

Deciding she'd had enough, Aurelia whacked her on the leg with her cane. "Sit down! I didn't travel all the way here to watch you two squabble like children."

Remembering Aurelia was there, Fairuza's entire demeanor flipped, becoming just as soft-spoken, sunny and courteous as she'd been earlier. "Your Grace, I'm so sorry to keep you waiting. If she hadn't spirited you away to this dusty patio, I could have given you a proper welcome. We had arranged for you to be hosted among more suitable company in the women's common room above—"

"I came here for one-on-one discussions while my grandson did the same. The last thing I need is to be stuffed into some perfumed henhouse."

Aurelia truly had a unique power of making people shut up. Did she always talk like that? Had she talked to her husband like that before they'd fallen in love and gotten married? Or was this something she'd developed from years and years of navigating court politics?

Either way, leaving people speechless was a mighty useful skill I wish I had, but wasn't yet fearless enough to cultivate. Probably would never be.

Fairuza moved to sit beside her, but Aurelia blocked her with her cane, pointing next to me. "In front of me. I can't converse with you if I can't see your face."

Fairuza obeyed, sitting next to me with no complaints. Yet.

"Now that you have finally joined us, we can get down to business." Aurelia flicked her fingers up toward us like she was shooing us. "Go on. Begin."

"Well, Your Grace, today we have other guests from other lands, and each is here to discuss a trade deal with Cahraman," Fairuza started at once, to beat me to it, but talked slowly, as if to someone slow. "Lord Eukharistos is from a very fertile land, with control and connections in many plantations in Campania, and we would like to arrange an exchange. His fresh and unique produce for our priceless spices. Captain Qursan —"

"I've figured all of that out for myself, thank you." Aurelia sighed, uninterested. "No need to talk to me like I'm senile yet."

"Captain Qursan is here to negotiate using a part of his navy for our trade," Fairuza continued like she hadn't been interrupted. "Travel by sea is much shorter than by land so the food from Campania would not spoil and the spices —"

"What did I just say?" Aurelia snapped. "I know why a merchant from a fruit valley and a navy captain are here, but do you know why I am?"

"Yes, Your Grace." Fairuza nodded.

"Then you shouldn't be wasting any more of my time, we already did enough of that waiting for you to show up."

Fairuza opened and closed her mouth like a fish. She'd been trained to host people, to flatter them, to entertain them, but not to deal with them outside rehearsed methods.

It seemed every time anyone interrupted her line of memorized thought, and she failed to retie it, it snapped. That was why her solution to every criticism, every retort from myself or Cherine was to lash out, and every interruption from Cyrus or Aurelia left her stuck.

She didn't know how to argue.

How was she expected to help influence the people in this palace and negotiate with people beyond it if she didn't know how to conduct an argument?

I guessed that was one downside to being born royal. Everyone had to do what you ordered them to and agree with what you said, so you had no idea what to do when people suddenly didn't do either.

I sort of felt bad for her. That this half-formed personality and abrasive behavior were the result of the way she'd been raised.

To earn myself more points and save us her inevitable outburst, I took over. "Almaskham is Cahraman's neighbor and it's fairly new, isn't it?"

Aurelia nodded. "Almaskham as a princedom has just celebrated its bicentennial."

"But it's quite wealthy, as much as Cahraman is?" I guessed.

"Wealthier." Aurelia raised her face proudly. "As expected from a nation born out of a fabled land of treasures—the *Diamond in the Rough*, the Avestans called it. Once we gained our independence from the empire, we kept the title, but in our own tongue."

"Diamond in the rough," I repeated wondrously.

That was what Almaskham meant.

I'd even been told that it had domes and towers built out of a magical material that shimmered like diamonds in the sun. "I take it the treasures take a lot of digging to find?"

"We have a lot of mines and are closer to the mountain range, so we export everything from fuel to stone to metal to diamonds," she said. "Though we have more bronze and silver than gold, more coal than oil and more marble than granite."

"Which you get from Cahraman?"

She nodded, eyes watchful. "Among other things."

"And I'm sure there's not much you can naturally grow in the desert. So, it would be good for you to enter the trade deal with us to open up your exports and imports."

She shot me a ridiculing glance. "Would it? If we had wanted produce in exchange for our marble, wouldn't we have arranged that ourselves by now?"

I shrugged. "I don't think so."

Both of them stared at me.

From my experience of roaming across Ericura, small or young places needed a lot more time to fill with people, businesses and necessities. I remembered one city in the South that had opened its first marketplace only ten years ago.

Before that they'd had to go on daytrips to nearby towns to bring back food.

I clarified. "If you're a new settlement you spend the first chunk of your lifespan just establishing the place itself, making it habitable and trying to get a routine going." That was all true of the small businesses I temporarily worked in.

Aurelia cocked a considering head at me. "And?"

"And by the time all that is done, you finally have time to think of the less immediate and vital things, like new business prospects that aren't about infrastructure or survival. That's why I don't think Almaskham had time to go into trade on its own—and now it shouldn't. It should join Cahraman, an older, more influential land, who has the far-reaching connections and long-established routes. By simply helping to fund its trading, you'd get a return on your investment while letting the more powerful kingdom do the heavy lifting. And while at it, you'd be enriching your land and letting people across the seas know that it exists."

"And that's a good thing why?"

"More trade options? More workers coming to live in your principality and diversifying your demographics and adding to your skill market? More tourism? More food? Who doesn't want more food? Especially if it's exotic?"

On that note, I was hungry. The biscotti had just managed to get my stomach working.

"So, you want us to expand?" Aurelia asked, more of a demand to elaborate than a genuine question.

"Yes."

"Why?"

Was nothing I said a good enough reason?

I wracked my brain, trying to find supporting arguments for saying yes, and for saying no.

They'd mentioned oil here, and so did she. That meant that, along with magic, trains, boats and assorted machines ran on oil. On Ericura, some riverboats had replaced coal with oil but it was rare there, and prohibitively expensive. Lands with lots of it were bound to become rich.

Cahraman could end up being the new Avesta, while Almaskham could turn into another land swallowed up by time.

"What if your principality collapses because of food shortages and the lands around you don't want any more marble? What if Cahraman's oil becomes more important than your coal and no one wants to import it anymore?"

She didn't answer me, just watched me, her eyes betraying nothing. But I could feel her uncertainty with how to proceed.

All of the sudden, she looked to the doorway.

I followed her gaze to find Cyrus casually leaning against the wall, his kaftan open, its sleeves rolled up, his arms crossed, the embodiment of vigor and effortless attractiveness.

He seemed more relaxed now. No part of him was rigid with formality and his eyes shone with mirth in the afternoon glow, while his mouth was quirked to one side in a soft smirk.

It was achingly familiar. Like I hadn't seen this side of him in ages, and I'd been pining away for it, for him, for years, when it had only a couple of days.

He lifted one hand in a small salute, winking. "Don't mind me, I'm just stopping by."

Taking in this change of behavior, he must have picked up on the same thing I had. That Aurelia did not want to be flattered in any shape or form.

The man standing there now wasn't the prince, but my thief.

Or what I had thought was mine, and a thief.

At this point, I had no problem taking the former, as long as I got him.

Aurelia beat me to asking, "How long have you been standing there?"

He rolled his shoulders, lips curling in a knowing smile. "Long enough."

"I take it your father bothered to show up?" Aurelia glowered at him. "And you are done with that oligarch that wants to sell all his funny fruits?"

"I am."

"And?"

"He's agreed to a trial period of supplying us with seasonal produce in exchange for our dried legumes and herbs. If we agree to continued trade, then they can have the spices."

Aurelia gave him a nod of approval. "And how is my grandson faring?"

Cyrus uncoiled away from the doorway, arms going behind his back. As he strolled closer, I inhaled sharply. He smelled woodsy with a hint of spice, a cologne he must have brought out for the occasion. But underneath it all was the unique scent branded on my senses. The scent of just him.

He stopped directly between us, his smile widening. "Father is going easy on him."

She tutted, her scowl deepening. "Everyone is going too easy on him. He'll end up a doughy head of state that way."

"Not with you around, I bet," he assured her . "Am I interrupting?"

"No," Aurelia kicked the stool from underneath her feet and stood up. "We're done here. One of you show me where I'm retiring for the night."

Fairuza jumped upright, so fast she could have flipped the table. "I'll do it!"

She extended her bent arm to Aurelia who ignored it and just limped right past her. "Lead the way, and it better not be upstairs."

Again, Fairuza didn't immediately follow.

She lingered by Cyrus, fists clenched and arms stiff by her sides as they were before, but this time with an insecure dent in her posture.

She stood there, looking at him with the desperation Cherine had when she'd been hanging off that wall. Like what she needed was close but not enough to help her.

Cyrus reached for her shoulder as if he, too, had sensed her agitation. "What is it?"

She stepped back, chest moving noticeably.

She looked close to hyperventilating.

I touched her arm, trying to snap her out of it. She jerked away hitting me in the chest.

I caught her by the upper arms, steadying her. "What's with you?"

She stumbled away from us, tears rising in her eyes.

"Are you going to keep me waiting all night?" Aurelia called from inside.

Fairuza rushed to her, wiping her eyes.

Cyrus moved to follow her, his hand outstretched, stopped, looked back at me.

"You humiliated her." I wasn't sure if his tone held disapproval or praise.

I shrugged. "I did my job. I hosted the guest, made her feel comfortable and discussed with her the subject you assigned to me. What does that have to do with Fairuza?"

"Just that she was supposed to do all of that." He bared his teeth, not in a smile but in a wincing loss for words. "Farouk paired her with Aurelia, the most important of the lot because out of all of you, Fairuza was supposed to be the most qualified to host her. She boasted endlessly about her skills at hosting but when she got the chance, she couldn't do it."

"There's a phrase for that where I'm from: don't talk the talk if you can't walk the walk."

"Funny way of putting it." His lips twitched in unwilling amusement, eyes twinkling with mischief. "Did you walk the walk?"

Pride and relief filled my chest like an air balloon rising with the hope that I had passed the second test, was now closer to fixing everything. "Compared to her, I sprinted."

Any remaining seriousness melted as he chuckled, shaking his head chidingly. "I know. I came here the minute I was done with Eukharistos. You made a good argument."

I immediately fished for assurance and praise, batting my lashes at him. "How good?"

"Good enough to convince me to invest in you." His smile warmed as he cupped my elbow, thumbing the sensitive crook of my arm.

I could swear my heart spun inside my chest.

It was remarkable how he spoke to me with the ease of a best friend, like I was someone he trusted, but touched me and looked at me like I was something more, something valuable. Something to cherish and gaze at in wonder.

"Every time I think I've figured out who you are, you surprise me."

"Who did you figure I was at first?" I asked innocently, still baiting for compliments.

"Just another pretty girl in a pretty dress, here for the crown and all its luxuries but none of the work, and certainly not for the person that comes with it," he admitted. "It didn't occur to me that all of that was the casing for something so…"

"Smart? Interesting? Funny?" I suggested jokingly.

"Rare," he said simply.

I was taken back. "How am I rare? There were literal dozens of me out there."

He reached up and tucked a lock of hair behind my ear, lowering his head so I could count each fleck of gold highlighting the green of his eyes "Believe me, there aren't. None of the fifty girls who came here had any of your qualities."

I put my hand over his, keeping it there. "Is that why you like me?"

"I like Cora and Cherine and Ariane just fine, but I don't want to spend more time with them than I need to. I want to be around you for no reason other than your company."

"Is that why I'm still here?" Heart now quivering in my chest, I tried to get a solid reassurance.

He moved back, eyes widening. "You really don't know why you're still here?"

"I failed the second test and I didn't get to know if I passed the third."

"Of course you passed the second test! You saved Cherine's life! I was there, I helped you, watched every thought going through your mind, every decision you made just as I had eyes and ears around watching the others."

"So, you let me stay on out of courtesy for saving her?"

"Courtesy?" He coughed an incredulous laugh. "The test was to show your worth as a person, and you risked your very life to save a girl who was your competition. All the others let her hang when she fell—"

"Fairuza *pushed* her."

He ignored my interjection. "—and none even considered

doing a thing to save her, let alone risk their lives. I bet some were content to let her die so they could have a better chance with me. But you, you did the right thing regardless of how it could have affected your future, or the risk to your very life. *That* was noble. That *is* your worth, your value to us, to *me* as a person. And that's why I—" He stopped abruptly.

Heart almost exploding with the need for him to go on, I prodded, voice shaking, "Cyrus?"

He exhaled heavily. "This is not the time or the place to have this conversation"

"Then when?"

"After the final test, after tomorrow." He let his fingers comb through my hair as he stepped back. "Wait for me by the statue of the simurgh in the western hall."

I nodded eagerly. "I will."

His eyes gleamed with something I hadn't seen there before as he leaned down and whispered right in my ear, "I will see you then, my lady."

I stood rooted, everything inside me clanging as he straightened, turned away with one last lingering glance then strode back inside.

I didn't have a full moment to myself to process because Cora poked her head out of the doorway where he'd just disappeared.

"Has he proposed yet? Can I go home now?"

CHAPTER FOURTEEN

I picked up the last piece of biscotti and threw it at her. "Oh, shut up!"

She ducked, laughing. "No, seriously, I think the only one who still thinks his choice is up in the air is Fairuza."

"Just her? What about Cherine?"

Cora's smile immediately dropped into a dull look of disdain. "The little brat ditched me."

"Ditched you how?"

She gestured for me to follow her. On our way back to our room, Cora detailed all the shenanigans I'd missed. The highlight was Captain Qursan's first mate Yorgho aggressively flirting with Ariane and asking her to come away with him to the island of Galantis. Then Cherine up and abandoned Cora mere minutes into their assignment.

I was in too much of a buoyant mood to share Cora's irritation, a halo of giddy rose petals and triumphant stars rotating over my head, offering nothing but positive imaginary outcomes for a change.

I had passed the second test! And with Aurelia's encouragement, I dared believe there was a chance to both save the Fairborns and marry Cyrus. It wasn't an either or scenario anymore. All I had to do was dig up a way to outsmart or overpower Nariman—

The moment I completed that thought, I crashed back to reality, my optimism scattering like shards of broken glass. Outsmart or overpower Nariman? So far it seemed easier for me to sprout wings.

After the rose petals and stars, now a clammy sense of foreboding slithered at my heels like a malicious serpent.

Cora aggressively exhaled, fluttering her lips like a horse. "It wasn't even five minutes before she spotted something outside and ran off. Literally."

"Where did she go?"

"Anywhere and everywhere." Her scowl deepened. "Minutes later I found her running back past us, yelling at the air to just talk to her."

The people passing us as we climbed up the stairs must have heard her as they gave us funny looks. Cora bared her teeth making them move away faster.

Cora grabbed a handful of peeled prickly pears from the tray of a passing servant and popped one in her mouth, talking around it. "She left me with the boy and his mom alone for *two hours*. The woman even napped."

I tried not to crack up at that last bit. "Aren't you from the same region? Couldn't you find a common topic to discuss, I don't know—what were you supposed to convince them of anyway?"

"To give Cahraman certain types of produce in exchange for the fancy spices that cost as much as gold. And what was the point? The prince was already negotiating that stuff with her husband. What was I supposed to do with his wife?"

"Host her?"

"Host her?" Cora laughed. "What is she, a parasite?"

I let out a howl of laughter, the volume surprising even myself as my voice bounced off the marble interior of the hall. Almaskhami imports no doubt.

"And I don't host!" She continued complaining, despite smiling at my reaction. "I work, so when I run things I tell people what to do with confidence that I know what I'm doing." She slouched, rubbing her eyes. "I'm just so tired of being here. I'm tired of doing those silly nothings, of wearing shoes and constricting dresses because my own clothes are 'ugly' or 'indecent.' I'm tired of all these walls and how dry the weather is. I want to go home!"

"Just a few more days and you can," I reminded her.

"The trip from here to Campania will take ages, though." She exhaled loudly, loosening up a little as we reached our hall.

All doors were closed but mine.

Lungs constricting I peeked through the crack.

On my bed was Cherine, sleeping with her head in our direction and a thick book open on her face.

Cora pushed me in, throwing open the door and yelling, "You left me!"

Cherine flipped over, hurling the book to the floor, fluffy dark blonde hair a mess. "Oh, there you two are."

Cora pounced. Cherine flew back with a scream, dodging her clawing hands, hopping off and running around the chamber.

Cora chased her with one of those itchy throw pillows yelling, "You were supposed to do all the talking! It's all you're good for after all! You left me there and I had to eat that tasteless mush they served us!"

Cherine stopped trying to evade her, looking indignant. "Is food all you think about?"

"YES! Especially when I'm hungry!"

"Can you two stop yelling?" I begged. "This room echoes and I have a headache."

"She started it!" Cherine yelled, pointing at Cora.

Cora shoved against me, reaching for Cherine. "You started it when you bolted off!"

Cherine hid behind me. "I didn't know it would take so long!"

"It was two hours! I ran out of things to say after two *minutes*! Where did you even go all that time?"

"I can explain—eek!" Cherine ducked as the pillow came flying towards her head and hit me in the chest instead, knocking the air out of me in a dry cough.

"Enough!" I shoved Cora back and bumped Cherine to widen the gap between them. "What did I say about the yelling?"

They mercifully stopped, but I stayed between them, arms out to hold them apart. "And speaking of food, why don't you order some here while I go freshen up?"

I left them to sort themselves out and headed for the bathroom, stayed there until I got myself firmly under control. I came out to find three servants entering with five trays of food.

I rushed to take one and set it on my coffee table. Once everything was arranged, we settled around it. Cora dug into her large river fish with bare hands and I took the entire bowl of nutty fried rice. Cherine picked at her kebabs unenthusiastically.

"So what was it?" I asked, spraying rice. "What sent you running off like that?"

Cherine's distaste with our eating habits fled as excitement filled her eyes. "Remember when I told you about my dreams?"

"Which ones?" was what I assumed Cora said through her mouthful of fish.

"About the prince with the silver hair, the one who rescued me from the ghoul and carried me around."

I almost inhaled the rice down the wrong pipe. I hadn't expected her to bring up Ayman. It was still weird to have her refer to him with both shaking terror and dreamy wistfulness. Now he was a silver prince.

"Uh-huh?" I prompted.

"*I found him.*"

"Sure you did," Cora snorted, picking fish bones out of her mouth.

"I did!" Cherine wiggled excitedly. "I saw him passing by when I was offering Rhodion tea. He was looking at me!" She leaned over to me, her elated eyes filling my vision. "He was watching me and rushed away when I noticed him."

"That couldn't have been him," Cora argued. "He exists only in your dream."

"It *was* him! *He's real!*" she exclaimed in agitated delight.

So…she'd spotted Ayman spying on her and chased him for hours?

Cora rolled her eyes. "It must have been an outdoor guard. Those wear white headdresses."

"It wasn't a guard! He was fair, that much I could see, fairer than Ariane."

"Then he must be a ghost then," Cora brushed off, reaching for the plate of couscous-stuffed zucchinis. "No one's fairer than Ariane."

"He was not!" Cherine protested. "He's real and he knew me. He was looking for me!"

"Then why did he run away?"

Cherine's eyes grew rounder, her cheeks blazing with color. "Maybe he had somewhere to be. If he's foreign and visiting for work then he must have had an appointment. But he'll find me again, I'm certain of it."

"Why do you care so much about him?" I asked her. "Aren't you here for Cyrus?"

"Who?"

Oh. I'd forgotten only those close to him referred to him by that name.

Cherine waved. "Oh, Cyaxares. I kind of forgot about him."

She'd forgotten the man she'd come here to win? Ayman carrying her and doting on her while she'd been barely conscious that night in the vault had really done a number on her psyche.

Cherine picked up my copy of *The Anthology of the Dunes*, the book she'd had over her face when we'd entered.

She flipped to an illustration, held the book out to us. "He looked just like *this!*"

It was a sideways depiction of the White Shadow of Avesta, an albino like Ayman, his long white hair flying in the wind as he raised his arm up to a giant simurgh.

Could I tell her about Ayman? He hid for a reason. Cherine herself had insisted he was a ghoul the first time she'd seen him sneaking around our room at night.

That question belonged on the list I had for Cyrus after the final test.

CHAPTER FIFTEEN

*L*oujaïne had found out exactly who I was.

She burst into my new room to drag me out by my hair, yelling at me as I desperately clawed at her fingers, trying to loosen her grip on my scalp. Though she claimed that she'd throw me in the dungeons, the door she threw me through was not that of a cell but a brightly lit ballroom. With my wrists and ankles shackled, I hobbled down the carpeted aisle to witness the joyless wedding of Cyrus and Fairuza. The seats were empty save for piles of gold and jewels.

Up on the altar Cyrus stood, a bronze statue, while Fairuza was an ice sculpture, melting slowly on the carpeted floor.

Cyrus' bejeweled eyes carried the same quiet misery as the sculpture of Jumana Morvarid in the vault, but Fairuza's dwindling ice sculpture had its mouth gaping wider on a silent scream as her features melted and a crack crept through her frozen stalk of a neck.

Conflicted emotions swirled within me. I couldn't help

either of them. Or understand if it was sorrow, despair or full-blown horror that cemented me to the encroaching darkness until it swallowed me.

I was back in the room we had taken our first exam in, at the back of the line waiting to be tested by Master Farouk. The light coming through the high windows before me was bright yet soft, washing out my surroundings and rendering the people around us into shades, faint remnants of what they used to be.

I tried to speak but my voice was a muted hum, like the echoing vibration of a plucked harp-string. Shocked, I looked down, expecting to see myself a faded echo, but I still retained my color. Only my outlines were fuzzy, like the edges of a rough yarn sweater.

The young women before me all wore summery clothes in a similar style. All from this region and its related cultures. The girl that stepped out of the line appeared very short, but once my eyes adjusted to the encompassing whiteness blaring from the windows I realized she had my proportions—only she carried her head under her arm, the stump of her neck still glistening with dark blood.

My lungs emptied in one shuddering gasp out as my horrified eyes followed her fading trail.

Thoughts frozen with the scarring sight of the beheaded woman, I barely noticed the young woman moving past me. Her dark hair parted down the middle and fell in waves to frame her sad, wide face. Her big drooping eyes glimmered like peridots as she faded, disappearing among the sea of featureless ghosts, leaving a trail of melancholy in her wake like smoke.

What came after siphoned all my morbid fascination with

the headless witch and the sad princess. Nariman, her amber eyes void of emotion, her red-tinted, dark hair appearing burgundy in the glare.

The most vivid thing in the room was no longer the light but the anger that sparked within me as I tried to grab her. But my hands went through her as if she was fog, and my movements were heavy and slow, like I was wading in quicksand.

Anger burned into frustration as I struggled to run after her, my yells for her to answer my questions leaving my mouth as smothered, incoherent noise.

The penultimate examinee put her hand on my shoulder as she left her spot. I jerked around to see how she was touching me, to ask if we could communicate.

All questions died when I recognized her.

My mother.

Different as she appeared, I knew it was her. *Felt* it was her.

Anguish seared through me as I tried lifting my arms, my frigid fingers aching to touch her face, grab onto her dress and pull myself closer. All I wanted was to cling to her, close my eyes and forget myself and the world in the safety of her arms.

"I miss you," I tried to say, the sound that vibrated past my lips a long, lamenting minor-key note released off the swipe of a rough bow on the strings of my soul.

Her hand moved from my shoulder to cup my cheek, a comforting touch I could barely feel. She appeared younger, with a fuller face and longer hair, soft light pulsing within her rather than bouncing off her, her blue-grey eyes the most precise color in the room.

Her lips moved but no sound emerged. I tried to read them. I only made out a few words.

Sorry. Left. Lead. Away. Find.

After *"Find"* she said one last word, and despite her slowly enunciating it, it didn't register with me. Like it was a foreign term beyond my grasp.

Before I could ask her to speak louder, clearer, beg her to stay, my mother began to fade before me. Panic surged like bile, burning my insides and melting my eyes as I reached harder for her. But she still disappeared, like mist in the midday sun.

Overwhelmed with helplessness, I curled in on myself and broke down in tearless sobs that shook me until I started coming apart.

I couldn't bear being like this anymore. Helpless in my situation, fragile in my mind, and desperate for solutions that kept eluding my grasp.

As my breakdown ran its course, a low, piercing whistle penetrated the muted state of the room, startling me back into focus.

Where my mother had stood was now a clear view of the table. It had many things on it, but there were no judges along its entire length.

Ada, a distant voice called.

I searched for its source, found no one left around as I waded towards the table.

In place of the cane, book, tea set and metal boxes from the first test were a folded, golden wedding dress, a ring with a glowing stone--and a gold lamp!

The voice called again, more urgent. *Ada!*

I ignored it. I couldn't bear to look away from what laid before me.

There it was, the thing I'd been risking my life to find the whole month.

I needed to grab the lamp and run out of the room, out of Cahraman. I had to give it to Nariman and end all this madness before it consumed us all.

But…a part of me hesitated, kept my hand stuck hovering above the table.

The wedding dress beckoned, toying with my priorities, appealing to my basest, most selfish yearnings for a secure life, forever bound with the man I wanted. And the ring, possibly the one Cyrus mentioned could grant wishes, was pulling on my desires like a magnet.

Did my situation need to go the way I dreaded it would? That I'd remain completely at Nariman's mercy, whether I found what I was sent here for or not? Or could I find a way around this mess, a way to outwit her?

ADA!

The voice blew through the room, a piercing shockwave shattering it to a million pieces as the table and its offerings fell into the darkness.

My scream splintered in my chest as I spiraled into nothingness. "NO!"

"ADA, WAKE UP!"

With a startled gasp, my eyes flew open to be met with searing brightness. Recognition of my surroundings seeped in from the edges, focusing my blurry view.

Cherine was leaning over me, her hair loose and messy, her slim brows almost meeting in a worried squint.

I struggled up on my elbows, in my new bed, found Cora on my left, hugging the bedpost, hand still on my shoulder.

"What happened?"

Cherine slumped down on the bed, lips quivering, voice unsteady. "You wouldn't wake up!"

Cora sat on my other side. "You gave us quite a scare."

Touched, I reached out my arms, pulling them both into a hug. "I'm alright."

Cora pressed her rough palm on my forehead, checking for a fever. "You sure?"

No, I wasn't. But by now I knew lying to Cora was pointless. Still, until I figured out some plan, I'd keep my strange dreams, that didn't feel like dreams, and the feelings they inspired, to myself.

A knock on my open door turned our heads.

"Is everyone decent?"

Cyrus, in a fitted cream shirt and grey pants stuffed in dark brown leather boots, stood in my doorway. His hair, while not messy, wasn't immaculately styled like before, had a rakish look to it, like he'd run his fingers through it. He looked different today, less refined but not at ease. His good-natured tone was at odds with the apprehension in his eyes.

"Good morning, ladies." He remained in the doorway, Ayman's armored figure hovering behind him, his purple eyes fixed on my right, on Cherine. "Breakfast will be a bit early this morning."

I sat up, my arms still around the girls. "Why? Did something happen?"

"You could say that circumstances have changed the nature of today's test," he said, checking behind him as Fairuza's door opened across the hall.

Cherine wiggled off the mattress, holding my arm across her collarbones, dragging me with her, and by extension, Cora. "Oooh! What's the theme today?"

His lips quirked at her enthusiasm. "You're going to like this."

"Like what?" I mumbled, numb legs dangling off the bed, sagging against Cora as she rested her cheek on my head.

"Arguing." He flashed us a teasing grin as he turned away from the door. "Today, you're going to bargain."

CHAPTER SIXTEEN

Our train trip was longer than any of us had anticipated. Somehow, going that far away from Sunstone unsettled me more with every passing mile.

Cora, Cherine and I were thankfully without royal company, and free to juggle as many topics and jokes as we liked without awkward pauses or glares of disapproval. But whenever they snagged on a disagreement and bickered, my focus drifted back to the nightmares that had held me in their chokehold until the girls had forcibly woken me.

They hadn't felt like my usual nebulous dreams or my fear-fueled nightmares. They'd had an—otherworldly quality to them. Remembering them still made my guts twist with the horror and helplessness I'd felt at Cyrus and Fairuza's gruesome wedding, and the impossible choice of the table of temptations.

But it was the part where I'd seen the younger version of my mother and the other three women that still gripped me by the throat.

My mind could have been trying to reconstruct Nariman's

story about her princess, fellow witches, and their tragic fates. It now swirled in my head like incense, something hard to breathe in, but not repulsive enough to reject.

At least some of her story had to be true. Cyrus had proved as much. That meant the girls being tested had to be the late princess and her ladies-in-waiting. The headless woman, the first to leave the line, must have been Hessa, the weakest witch who'd been blamed for the infertility of King Darius's wife and executed. The sad ghost of the princess had looked too much like the sculpture of Jumana Morvarid...

The realization formed at once, solid and undeniable.

Jumana was Cyrus's mother.

Once that conclusion lodged into my mind, more pieces of the puzzle I was trapped in crashed into place.

The first time I'd laid eyes on Cyrus, he'd been fleeing the vault. I'd never gotten a clear answer as to what he'd been doing there, but now it all made sense.

When he'd taken me down there again, he'd lit Jumana an incense bowl, set a rose at her sculpture's feet, and spoken about her with conflicted emotions. He'd intimated that she'd taken her own life, but had still empathized with her enough to visit her and honor her as one would a goddess. He'd been shocked to find her likeness gracing the sculpture of Anaïta, the goddess of love in the temple we'd visited before the third test. It all pointed to him mourning the mother he never knew.

Though that realization was momentous, I could only care about one fact now. That Jumana had been closely connected to Nariman.

To know more about Nariman I had to know more about the last girl to become the Princess of Cahraman, and why her story had ended so tragically.

I also needed to know if my mother had truly been involved in this situation, if she was from Almaskham like I suspected. Or if I was reconciling two separate Dorreyas based on circumstantial evidence.

My mother. I'd been trying to avoid focusing on the part where she'd appeared to try to talk to me. Whenever the memory touched my mind, pain choked me and threatened to pour down my face. And I wouldn't be able to justify my condition to anyone.

It's just that since she'd died, I hadn't once dreamed of her.

It had been one of the reasons I had been so bereft, had felt so alone, not even having comforting dreams of her.

Then my mind had finally let me see her, and it was far from comforting.

"I don't think so!" Cherine's squeak jerked me out of my melancholy. Grateful for the distraction, I turned to the girls.

Cora and Cherine were trading guesses about what issue we were going to settle today. As I listened, I realized that Cherine's suggestions were, for once, more realistic while Cora's got more outlandish by the suggestion.

The highlights included Cherine's "What if they found a new gold mine at our border with Gemisht and now we're facing claim issues?" and Cora's dry, mocking "What if a giant crab crawled out of your seashore and tap-danced over the villagers?"

"Giant crabs exist?" Cherine squawked.

"No, but giant squids do."

"Then why did you say giant crab?"

Cora paused gnawing on her dried fig to roll her eye towards me in a fed-up stare before closing them with a loud, long-suffering sigh. I tried not to giggle.

The comforting background noise of their chatter was

sadly cut short once our train reached our destination. We disembarked to find three carriages waiting for us, each pulled by reddish-brown horses with black manes and tails.

Cora beat us out the door, going straight for the nearest horse and throwing her arms around its neck.

The sound of Cyrus's laugh made me miss one of the steps off the train.

Before I made a short plummet to the sizzling platform, Cyrus lunged sideways and caught me. My feet remained on the steps but most of my weight impacted him. For a moment, half outside, half in the train, feeling his solid strength making me feel weightless, I forgot where we were as he beamed down at me. All I knew was that I was in his arms.

"It seems you have fallen for me."

His teasing whisper flashed me back to our first trip in the tunnels beneath the palace. The second time he'd caught me when I stumbled down the stairs he'd joked that I liked being picked up by him. I'd made it worse, babbling that I might actually be falling for him.

Coming back to myself, face blazing, I gripped his arms to balance myself until my feet touched ground. "Falling over you, more like."

He pouted dismissingly. "Semantics."

I pretended to dust my dress, trying to avoid his eyes. "Is it?"

He lowered his head to make me meet them, his brown hair casting ever-shifting shadows on his sculpted features as a breeze blew past us. In the harsh light of midday, sweat made his golden skin glisten and plastered his commoner's shirt and pants to his body, outlining his physique. Everything about him was captivating, but the flecks of ochre in his eyes, what made them intense green, without a hint of blue or grey, hypnotized me.

I wished I had the upbringing of a noble girl, not just for the safety and luxury, but so I could have an artistic skill or two, like those the contestants had displayed. I wished I could paint, so I could capture all the colors in his hair, eyes and skin, to give lasting form to what would only live in my memory. Even if I won, I would for a goal beyond him, beyond Cahraman's borders. I'd still lose. Lose him.

There was only one way I could see out of this. Magic. If I had it, I would make the fantasy I took solace in a reality. I'd win both him and our freedom and defeat Nariman.

As if my dark thoughts tainted his brightening mood, his eyes dulled to a turbulent jade, and his teasing tone was tinged with dejection. "I take it you're still upset with me."

"I don't know anymore at this point," I admitted, throat tight.

"What can I do to make it up to you?" He reached to take my hand, but I kept it by my side. I couldn't risk transferring Loujaïne's attention from Farouk and Ariane to us. Cyrus exhaled, frustration tainting his tone and expression. "You must know I did not mean to deceive you. I never planned for any of you to see me, to notice me in the role of a servant, but you did."

I couldn't argue that. There was no way he could have expected me to practically chase him down and demand his help, for us to become friendly and something a bit more. Something I still didn't have a name for.

"It's not that anymore." I wrapped my arms around myself, looking to where the girls were giggling and shouting as Cora struggled to seat Cherine on a steed.

Cyrus touched my elbow. "Then what is it?"

"It's the fact that I got to know you first as one thing then discovered you were another. Had I met you when I was supposed to, then there wouldn't be a problem but…"

"But?"

"I can't change how I feel—felt about you, no matter how much I want to."

He shifted closer, shielding me from the sun with his shadow. "And how do you feel about me?"

An overwhelming sensation washed over me, filling my chest and neck like sloshing seawater that burned my insides and threatened to spring from my eyes. "I wanted Cyrus."

His touch on my elbow became a soft hold on my arms, his thumbs stroking my skin soothingly as he whispered, "I *am* Cyrus."

"You are Prince Cyaxares."

"I can be both. I *am* both," he insisted, lowering his head so I had nowhere to look but at him. "You have the advantage of knowing the other side of me."

"Which part of your servant personality was false?"

"Only the uniform I wore."

Loujaïne's loud call to gather round shattered the intense moment.

Cyrus let go of me with an exasperated mutter and returned his hands behind his back. Before he left my side he whispered, "We'll talk later."

Frustrated and fearing that 'later' might become 'too late', I shuffled in his wake, my shoes scraping against the hot gravel.

Having had their buffoonery interrupted, Cherine ended up climbing down from the horse onto Cora's back. We reunited halfway to the gathering group.

I could barely hear Loujaïne over the station's noise. Judging by her straining face, she couldn't hear herself either as she shouted, "Two days ago you were tested on how you handled the disputes of our people. Today the Matriarch of Zhadugar awaits you. In her possession is a royal heirloom we lost two-hundred years ago."

Suddenly tired of always trying to avoid or appease her, I met her stare head on. "How did you lose it?"

She might have not heard me, but from the tightening of her expression, it felt like she ignored me. Letting her gaze skim by me, she raised her voice even more. "Today you will demonstrate how you would act on behalf of the Crown, and how you would handle diplomacy, even with subjects you reign over."

"I was told we were going to barter." Cora said. "What are we trading here?"

"It is not bartering," Loujaïne sniffed, sounding offended. "You are going to *negotiate* the return of Queen Zafira's necklace. What you offer in return is up to your own ingenuity and that is what you will be judged on."

Loujaïne hadn't said anything about this test involving witches, but Cyrus had. From what I understood, half the population of Cahraman used magic in some shape or form, but the people of Zhadugar had to be something else. If so, I'd finally meet a witch who wasn't Nariman.

Whatever the test was, I had to pass it and gather information about who Nariman was and the real reason why the king had banished her. Most importantly, *how* he had.

If I could figure how to do the same myself, and find out what she intended to do with that lamp, then I'd finally have an advantage.

I was tired of being the cowering prey. It was about time I bit back.

Our carriage finally stopped, but our exit and regrouping with the others did little to end Cora and Cherine's argument about fruit.

"How do you expect me to believe that pomegranates are harder to pick than dates?" Cherine flung her hands at the slim, towering palm trees that dotted the location. "Do you think climbing those is easy?"

Cora shrugged. "It's easy for me. And palm trees don't sit at the mouth of the Netherfield."

That caught my full attention. "The nether-what?"

Cora stretched her arms above her head as she yawned. "It's what we call the underworld in Lower Campania."

"Oh, here it's Duzakh." Cherine pronounced the last letters with a rough scratchy sound, a bit like a snort. "Ada, what do you call your underworld in Arbore?"

It had been a while since anyone asked me anything about the land I claimed to be from. Not having an answer, I strode ahead, pretending to be preoccupied by our surroundings and hoped her child-like attention span would set her on a new topic.

The city of Zhadugar was built in and around a partially green valley that was dotted with spiraling towers and lantern-shaped houses. Everything was made of shining stone that reflected the sun like polished steel. A magical, silver sibling of manmade, golden Sunstone.

The deeper we descended into Zhadugar, the colder the atmosphere got and the bigger the shining buildings appeared, the tips of their twisted spires scraping the cloudless sky.

It reminded me of the tiny, lead-painted city within Bonnie's favorite snow-globe her mother Belaina had made. I'd once asked why she favored the most monochrome one and her answer had been, "Because it looks like a silver city straight out of Fairyland."

Seemed she'd been right about a seemingly-silver city being magical. But this one wasn't inhabited by fairies. I really must learn to paint, so I could depict this and all the breath-taking sights of Cahraman for her.

But if I married Cyrus after saving her, I could give her a royal tour of the land…

That fluffy fantasy ended by a literal tug back to the present.

"Ada?" Cherine roughly linked her arm with mine. "What do you call your afterlife in Arbore? Here we have levels of hell, heaven and the in-between. What about you?"

There was no shaking her off, was there?

The afterlives in northern and southern Ericura were likely similar to those in Arbore and Campania, as the settlers of both ends had probably hailed from these lands respectively. In the South, they said our souls traveled beneath the earth to be led by the Traveller to the Court of the Hidden God, who decided whether we went to one of two paradises or were flung into the void. In the North, they said the dead went through Faerie to be judged by its kings and queens before being given passage to an orchard isle or be given to the Horned God to devour. Neither was a comforting promise.

But I couldn't tell for sure which of those beliefs were built on Arborean remnants, or venture to give specific names. With Fairuza right behind me, I wouldn't get away with any inconsistencies.

The best way to distract Cherine was to get *her* to talk. "What is Duzakh exactly?"

Cherine, always happy to display how much she knew, poured on, "It's not so much our underworld as it is our hell. It's this dark, endless, stinking well that you fall through while demons rip you apart bit by bit, forever devouring you, flesh and soul."

I flinched as the statue of the Horned God at the Hornswoods, where I'd first seen Nariman's glowing eyes, flashed behind my eyes. "Do any of these demons have horns and masks?"

Cherine shuddered like a duck shaking water off its feathers. "I wouldn't want to know what's in there or even in Barzakh."

"What's Bar—Baz..." I couldn't even begin to pronounce that snort-like letter at the end. "What's *that*?"

"It's our in-between state, where the lost souls go."

"Well, now I know about your underworlds, what are your paradises?" I asked them both, trying to extend the diversion until we reached our destination.

Cora fetched a wand of licorice from her brassiere and

began to gnaw on it. Snacking, it seemed, was her version of biting her nails. "In Campania, all souls sail through the underworld but most go to the Land of Eternal Twilight, the Grey Meadows by the Court of Ipsomnus on the foggy River Nesci. The worst are thrown into the Hell-Pit of Erevor, surrounded by a fiery river, and the best enter the Amaranthine Lands and the best of the best go west of the first paradise to the Sparkling Isles."

"Oooh, that's a lot. Very structured." Cherine's intrigue swayed her attention completely towards Cora. "Did you say court?"

"Yes, there are many courts, subsets of the main one, since the underworld is a realm and Orcus is its king."

I breathed a sigh of relief as Cherine became wholly invested in knowing about the courts of the Campanian underworld, likely the Orestian one as well. Our line finally slowed by a three-tiered fountain full of ink-blue water with gold coins floating along the surface. My hungry impulse to steal was back, gnawing at my mind, making my fingers twitch with the urge to scoop out all the money.

I bit the inside of my cheek, steeling myself against the urge as we entered the Matriarch's house, one of the more memorable buildings I'd seen in Cahraman.

A three-floored, octagonal building, each of its side was smooth and shiny like the facet of a giant, dark crystal. Words in the elegant, cursive Cahramani script were engraved along the lines of the half-moon doorway, probably a spell to ward off malevolent spirits or something even more sinister.

Inside I was hit with a heavy cloud of perfumed fog. The combination of jasmine oil, saffron and a sour-smelling herb I couldn't name assaulted my senses, ripping a few dry coughs from my throat. My eyes watered, blurring the dimly-lit hallway we waded through.

I could only make out prominent parts of the décor, like the nail-studded frames of calligraphic paintings we passed, and the tasseled, ornate red and grey carpets we treaded. The low-hanging, black-iron chandeliers that lit our way emitted a fuzzy, dusk-like glow, and combined with the perfume and trapped heat of the narrow hall, I felt myself growing drowsy.

I was mid-yawn when Cherine nudged me. "You didn't tell me what you call your underworld. Also, what does it look like?"

Cherine proved harder to shake than an old habit. I had run out of ways to evade her.

"Arboreans go right into Faerie, right?" Cora answered for me. "They go through there first and are judged by its kings and queens before they can go to the lands beyond the fairy courts. The good sail to the Isle of Apples and the wicked sail off the edge of the world, right, Ada?"

Stunned, all I could do was mumble "Uh-huh" mid-yawn.

"Oooh, fairies have courts too? Tell me about them!"

"I would." Cora pinched her nose, the latter half of her response becoming a nasal drone. "But I can't."

Indignant, Cherine demanded, "Why not?"

"Being alive and all, I can't pop in for a slight bit of tourism," Cora deadpanned.

Cherine scoffed, elbowing the handmaidens out of her way to loudly ask Fairuza if she knew what the fairy courts were. Fairuza's only response was wide-eyed horror before her face fell into a sour scowl, as if the mention of fairies gravely offended her.

What experience could have wrung that reaction from her? Had a fairy knight tried to kidnap her, like they always warned us in the north of Ericura? Or was it something worse?

The hall ended at a collection of rooms. Two guards, beardless, with pointed ears, greyish skin, ushered us one by one into the brightest room. The smell coming from within, while less pungent, was still overwhelming. Its source was the smoke rising from a rusting incense bowl.

As she stepped in last, Cora whispered, "Next time I might not have an answer for you."

My yawn turned into a gasped gulp of air. I pretended to cough modestly, hiding half my face until I could contain my shock.

I'd lost count of the times Cora had covered for me. She had more fuel for unsavory accusations than Loujaïne could hope for, but because she'd never called me out, I kept forgetting about it. But if she knew I'd been lying since the day we met, since I claimed to be from a nonexistent island in Arbore, why hadn't she confronted me about it?

Was she waiting for me to say something?

I'd wanted to confide in Cyrus the night he'd revealed himself so we could run away with the lamp and settle back in Aubenaire, gaining the Fairborns two new family members. But unlike his truth, mine came with the risk of beheading, especially now I knew Nariman had been accused of treason herself. If I was found to be working for her I wouldn't be banished or jailed, I'd be ripped apart by lions.

Which brought the question: Could I trust Cora?

I considered her my friend, like I did Cherine. But I'd be stupid to tell Cherine any secrets. Those in a nearby city would hear her reaction. Cora, on the other hand, had kept this lethal information to herself. So far. For some reason.

Even if I didn't tell her who I was, where I was from and why I was here, I had to at least talk to her about it.

But that was a concern for another time. Right now I trailed after her to the table at the center of the room, and sat by Cherine, rather than between them as I always did. Cyrus escorted the rest of the girls to the seats facing the door while Ayman disappeared into a shadowy corner.

Loujaine refused to be seated and caught Farouk in a trade of hushed whispers. I tried reading her lips, and unlike with my mother in the nightmare, I discerned enough to get the gist. It was lucky that Loujaine enunciated as much as she did, or else I wouldn't have been able to read her saying "It's not cruel," and "I hate looking at her."

Me. She was talking about me. I dreaded to know what she meant by the former, but I felt like I already knew what the latter meant.

I reminded her of someone. Possibly more than one person. That much had been clear since the first night I met her. She knew Nariman well, had strongly contributed to her banishment. But if Nariman's Dorreya was my mother, and Loujaïne had known her as well, that was before Cyrus's birth. I doubted she had reason to remember, let alone hate, the insignificant lady-in-waiting of her brother's late wife.

The doors swung open and two guards walked in escorting a single woman in a simple, sleeveless, red gown.

Once in the light, the woman lifted her face and my breath caught in my throat.

While Nariman, with her youthful beauty, had reshaped my expectations of what a witch would be like, this woman, with her waist-length white hair, blood-red eyes and sunken face, was the crone of folktales and legends.

Though she had the body and posture of a young woman,

her hands were gnarled and tipped with long blackened nails, and the wrinkles that pleated her weathered cheeks and thin mouth weren't from years of fieldwork or even just age.

I had a feeling her haggard condition was the toll of practicing dark magic.

"*A witch!*" Cherine burst out of her seat and staggered back to press herself against the wall.

Fairuza jerked in her seat, seemingly itching to do the same, but she stayed put, her hands fisted so tightly I could see blue veins popping up against her creamy skin. "And you brought it in here? With us?"

"I've been called a lot of things, but *'it'* has to be the funniest among them." said the witch gleefully. "But you're on my turf, girl, and you'll refer to me as Lady Marzeya."

"On what grounds are you a lady?" Fairuza hissed, posture tight with simmering hostility, looking like she wanted to launch herself at Marzeya and strangle her.

So, she not only had a problem with fairies, but witches as well?

"On the grounds that all witches in the kingdom defer to me, and that I am responsible for half the magic that guards and runs this land." Marzeya bared teeth I could easily picture ripping off chunks of flesh in a bone-chilling grin. "Is that enough to earn me the title of Lady, or do I need to end a few wars and raise the dead first?"

Fairuza sneered at her. "I'd rather you and all who serve you vanish off the Folkshore, or go back to the hell you all came from."

"Aw, dearie, I would, but I'm afraid the hell-pit that spat us out doesn't want us back." The calculating amusement of Marzeya's response made Fairuza's jabs sound like a dumb puppy, overestimating its size and trying to intimidate a hawk with its yipping barks.

This wasn't an old wise-woman. This was an ancient entity that channeled the most powerful magic, and there was nothing that scared her, not even the dark depths of Duzakh.

Fairuza opened her mouth to respond, but Loujaïne ordered, "Stop it!"

Marzeya turned her attention to Loujaïne, reaching her clawed hands to the princess's face. Loujaïne froze up, breathing in harshly but remaining perfectly still as Marzeya stroked her cheek with the back of her hand then clutched her jaw. "You both favor Queen Morgana greatly. Unfortunately, it's just in looks."

If Loujaïne didn't clearly fear offending this woman, she would have no doubt ordered her hands to be cut off. "You knew my mother?"

"And your grandmother, and your great-grandmother, and so on." Marzeya released Loujaïne, turning her attention to us. There was something unsettling about her gaze, and it wasn't just that it came from red eyes, but the viewpoint behind them as well. I had been looked down upon by better-off people my entire life, people who saw me as beneath them, not just in class or rank but in species. To them I'd been on par with chickens.

But regardless of status, we *were* beneath her. I could feel that ugly truth in my soul. In age, experience, wisdom, knowledge, and above all else, power. To Marzeya we weren't animals, we were bugs.

I hoped none of them prompted her to squash us.

She approached the table and all of us, including Cyrus and Cora, shifted in unease or fear. Cherine was still flat against the fall, Fairuza looked like she was on the verge of enraged, terrified tears and Ariane's sea-green eyes were glued to the painted ceiling, lips twitching as she soundlessly murmured a prayer.

Marzeya circled us, stopping to examine each face, dragging her nails along the backs of our reddish wooden chairs in a long, uninterrupted scrape that sent my blood rushing in my veins, turning the room's pleasant atmosphere into an oven.

She didn't say a word to Farouk, merely checked Loujaïne over her shoulder and hummed at him interestedly before moving on to Ariane, who was determined not to meet her eyes.

She leaned in closer, causing Ariane to pant in distress and bring her eyes down to her lap before she said, "Word of advice—if your father becomes madder than usual, feed him to your brother."

Ariane smothered a gasp, but couldn't help looking at Marzeya, who pinched her cheek before moving on to Cyrus.

Cyrus stood and bowed his head. "Your Grace."

"Aren't you a polite boy," she cooed, grabbing his face with both her hands. His arms jerked and Ayman emerged from the shadows, unsheathing his sword but Cyrus stopped him with a staying hand. Marzeya frowned curiously at Ayman, creating more facial wrinkles, then snapped her head towards Loujaïne. "Whatever happened to your husband again, dear?"

Loujaïne was sweating, her jaw clenched and her penciled brows tense. "He is where I left him."

I hadn't even realized that Loujaïne had a husband. Maybe that was what prevented her from marrying Farouk.

"Ah, yes, he put you aside for that witch," she said distractedly, still holding Cyrus. "I haven't heard from her in a while. Did you have her killed?"

"No," Loujaïne ground out. "She disappeared not long after he sent for her."

"What was her name again? Hessa? No, that was the one your nut of a father killed, and I know Lamia Rostam's daughter was the last of Jumana's ladies here." Marzeya counted, a dreamy mood overtaking her. "I know she had a pearl name, too, like Hessa and Jumana did."

Looking straight at me, Loujaïne bit out, "Dorreya."

I bit my tongue, hard, to anchor myself, to keep my face blank.

I had stupidly told Loujaïne my mother's name my first night in the palace, when I'd thought it would be a quick job to find the lamp and leave. When I was sure I had no ties to this land, or to these people. Even when the evidence to the contrary had piled as high as Sunstone's mountain, I'd clung to the possibility that Dorreya was a common name here, that it couldn't be her.

But there was no escaping the conclusions now.

My mother had been from here, and she'd once been Nariman's companion, maybe friend, had been Princess Jumana's —*Cyrus's mother's*—third lady-in-waiting.

And that wasn't even the end of it.

She'd been the mistress of Loujaïne's husband, too, it seemed.

If my mother had been a witch, then that could explain how she'd ended up on Ericura. The same way Nariman had. But why? Why would she go there of all places and for what reason? Had she been escaping something, or someone? Was it Loujaïne's attempts to kill her for perceived sabotage, like her father had killed Hessa?

An overwhelming combination of bewilderment and fury bubbled in my gut with enough intensity to rival this witch's cauldron.

How could my mother not tell me this? Any of this? Why leave me in the dark my entire life?

But she'd tried to tell me something in that nightmare. It had felt too real to dismiss as a mere dream. What if she'd sent me a message from beyond the grave? If she had magic in life then her soul ought to retain it in death.

If only I knew the last word she'd said! If I did, I might figure out what she'd meant.

"Dorreya, that was it! Hessa, Jumana and Dorreya, Almaskhamis and their pearls!" Marzeya laughed, patting Cyrus's face. "You have your mother's eyes, did you know?"

Cyrus attempted to smile at her. "I know."

"You better not share her fate. I'd hate for Hessa to have died for nothing."

Cyrus's grimace told me that he knew Nariman's story, about his grandfather executing one of Jumana's magical ladies-in-waiting for supposedly meddling with her fertility. It hadn't helped much. Jumana had still taken her own life not long after giving Xerxes his longed-for grandson.

Tears stung my eyes but I didn't dare let them fall. Hessa, Jumana and my mother were all gone, and all would have been alive and happy had they never left Almaskham for Cahraman. And the Fairborns and I would have been together in blissful ignorance had Nariman not been the sole survivor of that group.

I didn't know if I could attribute that to luck or her own cunning. Or her magic. The magic my mother supposedly had, and had never used to ease our lives. What she'd withheld from me along with my own family and history.

Family. I had moved to Aubenaire in search of my mother's relatives. But she'd lied about being from there. If she'd been from Almaskham then I was from there.

I could have family there.

I might have grandparents, possibly aunts, uncles, and cousins! Depending on when my mother had become pregnant with me, and when she'd opened a portal to Ericura, my father could either have been from Almaskham as well or from the North where she'd first settled in.

This was too much information for me to stomach. And none of it helped me in anyway. I had to focus on finding out what would.

After wishing him luck on finding his princess, Marzeya released Cyrus, passing Cherine's empty seat to press her nose against mine. I went from being anxious to becoming anxiety itself as her bloody eyes stared into mine and visions of her teeth biting off my face flipped through my head like the pages of a windblown book.

"Oh, you, you are interesting." Marzeya pulled back a bit, letting me breathe. "You look like your grandmother, your father's mother."

Leaving me in shock, she moved on to Cora, who snapped her teeth shut near the hand reaching for her.

"Beastly, this one is." Marzeya laughed, her rough, ruined husk of a voice like the caws of a raven. The warning bite didn't deter her from ruffling Cora's hair fondly. "No mere man will be able to handle you."

She ended her nerve-wracking trip around the table by Fairuza, who looked ready to hit her and damn the consequences. Marzeya walked her fingers along the back of Fairuza's chair, leaning in towards her, farther away than she had with the rest of us. "You don't have a lot of time left, that's what you get for leaving things to sort themselves out."

"I don't know what you're talking about, witch."

"Then you ought to have a chat with your brother about

how bad manners make beasts of us all." She returned to the front of the room, busying herself with a two-tiered trolley stacked with crystal bottles filled with colorful liquids. Choosing a blue one, she opened it, and the scent of water lilies wafted to my overworked nose. "Although the fault with you both lies with your mother."

Fairuza moved to stand, but Loujaïne forced her back down.

"Now, why don't we get started with why you're here," Marzeya said into her glass as she downed the blue liquor.

Fairuza spoke first, voice pinched with impatience. "Over two-hundred years ago, our family lost an heirloom to you."

Marzeya swirled the remaining contents of the glass, more intrigued by it than Fairuza. "I know, the small cost of Artaxes thinking it was a good idea to declare war on Zhadugar."

Fairuza goggled at her. "That was because you invaded our land!"

"Funny how stories wildly differ, even invert, depending on bias," Marzeya tutted, checking Cyrus out of the corner of her eye then Ayman, who remained still with his hand on his sword. "But it's not a faded tale passed down through history. I was there."

"No, you weren't," Fairuza insisted.

"Dearie, I was there when the Avestan Empire rose and I was there when it fell." Marzeya seemed to be losing her patience, a sharp edge to her otherwise easy-going tone. "Your ancestor declared war on us, because he wanted to expel us from our land and take it for himself. The idiot thought he could take our sacred wells as his new water source, grow his figs and prickly pears with Anaïta's lifeblood."

Fairuza had no more retorts, settled for channeling her vitriol through her turquoise eyes.

Cyrus stood again, addressing Marzeya, "My lady, I can best explain the reason for our visit today."

"Go on." Marzeya patted him on the back on her way to take Cherine's vacated seat between Cora and myself.

When she tucked her chair closer to the table, I couldn't help the way my joints locked, slamming my knees together and my arms to my side. It wasn't that she radiated hostility, it was the power that thrummed through her, so strong I could almost see it, like the reddest, hottest core of an iron furnace. Nariman, as much as she intimidated me, didn't feel anything like this.

Cyrus moved so he could face us all. "We are here to negotiate the return of my ancestor's necklace, but neither myself nor Princess Loujaïne will do the talking. Instead it will be these five ladies speaking on our behalf with you."

"Hmm, and the one that does the best job will be your queen?" Marzeya hummed interestedly.

Cyrus inclined his head respectfully. "Hopefully."

Marzeya's dark lips spread in a crocodile grin as she clapped. "Let's begin then."

CHAPTER NINETEEN

"Well?" Marzeya sat forwards, looking around at us all. "Convince me why I should give it back to you."

No one moved.

I didn't want to go first. I wanted to wait until at least two went forward so I could read the situation, and gauge Marzeya's methods and limits before testing them in an argument. Patient as she had been with Fairuza's aggression, there was no telling what could provoke her into turning me into a frog.

Marzeya snapped her fingers, releasing a whip-like crack that made us all jump or jerk. She pointed at Cherine. "You, little mouse, come sit down. Present your argument."

Cherine swallowed, visibly shaking as she circled the table and took Cyrus's vacated seat. She was too far for me to comfort her or whisper that she'd be all right.

Cherine opened her mouth but only a croak came out. "Uh…"

Speechless. The presence of a witch was what it took to finally render Cherine Nazaryan speechless.

"How compelling," Marzeya snorted, pointing to Ariane next. "How about you?"

Ariane looked as apprehensive as I felt. Her typically serene, closed-mouth smile fought to remain on her face as her eyes looked everywhere except directly at the witch, as if she feared the red eyes would burn out her own.

"My lady, as Prince Cyaxares said, we are here to negotiate the return of an important heirloom of the House of Shamash." Despite her put-on cheerful demeanor Ariane's voice still trembled, gaze now in Marzeya's general direction, but more towards my face than the witch's.

I gave her an awkward smile, the most I could do to encourage her.

"I'm aware of that." Marzeya sighed, her earlier amusement falling to displeasure, like she had been expecting a troop of exotic birds and found only a clutch of hens. "Start negotiating."

Letting out a shaky breath, Ariane fastened her smile on. "It's known the heirloom in mention was handed over in a pact of peace after the witches' war with King Abraxas—Artaxes!" Sweat now coated her fair skin, her peachy glow turning bright pink. "But since it was so long ago that this happened—not that I'm invalidating your memory of the war, or your experience of it—" she rushed to add, before spilling out the rest of her argument in an agitated rush. "—but you and your people have since been peaceful subjects to the royal family, giving Cahraman its magic wards and trains. There is no need to hold onto a useless piece of jewelry anymore."

Downing the remainder of her drink, almost hitting me in

the face with her elbow, Marzeya's breath fogged up the inside of the glass. "If it's so useless, why do you want it back?"

"It's not—but I'm not—" Ariane paused to curb her stuttering before continuing. "It's not useful in the practical sense, Your Grace, like a sword or shield, but it has a symbolic meaning to the House of Shamash. A ceremonial use in the Bride Search I am currently participating in."

"So, you've come here to bother me because you want to wear a necklace for five hours on your wedding day? Why not just commission a replica or wear any other piece of jewelry?"

"Your Grace, we don't mean to disrupt your day—" Ariane coughed, putting a hand on her throat. "I understand it might have meaning to you, too, as a symbol of the treaty between your people and the king's. But you have long-since been at peace, and if it offers some form of security, perhaps if we offer you a written decree?"

Though I felt like Ariane was on the right track, Marzeya struck her offer down. "A piece of paper in exchange for rare jewels? What a steal."

Ariane looked winded, but tried again. "Some privileges then? A place at court? Once I'm queen, we could employ a court magician—"

Loujaïne cut her off with a firm, furious, "No."

"Why not?" Ariane turned to her, her eager-to-please simpering gone. "It would be a good way to plan more magical improvements in the kingdom, and an advantage over any enemies. Having a grand wizard or witch at your disposal as a monarch is—"

"No," Loujaïne cut her off, even louder.

Baffled, Ariane gaped at her. "But why not?"

"Are you as stupid as you look?" Fairuza spat. "Putting one of those in court, right next to the royal family, where they can work their dark spells to control the king, kill his heirs and damn his wife and daughters?"

Ariane narrowed her eyes at her. "I believe you're over-thinking this."

Fairuza's eyes hardened. "I'm the only one giving this any thought. Promising this witch any favors is opening the door to a flood of disasters!"

Before their argument could escalate, Cyrus snapped, "That's enough!" Loujaïne opened her mouth but Cyrus raised a finger to her. "*Enough.*"

Loujaïne still protested, "She was inviting her to our court."

"Yes." Cyrus's voice was as tense as his stance. "Princess Ariane is doing what she was brought here for, negotiating."

"We are not letting any more witches enter the palace," Loujaïne insisted. "Or hold any kind of position in our court."

Cyrus's expression turned grim as he faced his aunt fully. "Fortunately, you don't get to decide any of that."

Offense blasted from Loujaïne, giving me a glimpse into how she might have behaved around Nariman or towards her. There was no doubt Loujaïne believed she had an impossibly higher rank than Nariman and that she should have prece-dence over her. There was no way that she and Nariman hadn't butted heads over not only having the king's ear, but over rearing Cyrus.

With Jumana gone, that had left a void they must have fought over. Judging by how Cyrus interacted with his aunt, Nariman had won long ago, and Loujaïne must have fiercely resented her for it. Cyrus had said that King Darius believed Nariman had only wanted to compel him to marry her, while Loujaïne had believed she wanted to usurp the entire House of Shamash and rule as queen instead.

Seeing as Nariman was just banished, rather than killed, and Cyrus missed her, it meant—

Loujaïne. Loujaïne was the source of all my problems.

If her lies had gotten Nariman ousted from her position as a de-facto queen and mother, then she was the root of all this. If she had never been banished, Nariman wouldn't have kidnapped me and thrown the Fairborns in Rosemead, Cyrus would have had his mother-figure by his side in this competition and…

I would have never met Cyrus.

While I couldn't say I would have preferred to have never met him, I would have wanted to meet him under better circumstances, maybe as a true competitor aiming to win his hand.

Theories and beliefs came together in a tide of probable combinations, ebbing and flowing.

From the information I had gathered, Loujaïne, like Fairuza and Ariane, had to have been sent to another land to marry into another royal family. Yet here she was, no husband in sight or any children, remaining in her brother's court, never to be anyone's queen or mother. Marzeya had also said that her husband had cast her aside for his mistress, Dorreya. Nariman had said as much, that a Prince Azal had replaced his infertile wife with the woman who was most probably my mother.

It would explain why she hated me.

It was also awfully suspicious that all the Almaskhami women had been picked off one after the other. Hessa beheaded, Jumana killing herself, Dorreya disappearing and even Nariman who'd held on the longest, ended up banished.

If Nariman had known my mother who'd known of Ericura, one good explanation was that my mother had told here where she was going to escape Loujaïne's far-reaching wrath. What if Nariman had been looking for my mother when she'd appeared in the Hornswoods? Those hovering eyes had been a searching projection, maybe seeking out an old friend and fellow witch to help her after her banishment.

But when she'd failed to find my mother, she'd settled for me. To get her the lamp, to use whatever resided in it.

If this were all true, and it seemed very likely it was, then I hoped Nariman unleashed a dragon on Loujaïne.

Red-faced, Loujaïne squared off with Cyrus. "I am the king's sister and advisor."

A curt nod acknowledged her claims. "But in this competition you are only fulfilling the duties my mother would have."

"We wouldn't be here," Loujaïne hissed. "Holding this competition, despite you having a princess to marry, if your mother hadn't arrived all those years ago with her witches."

Cyrus gritted his teeth, straightening up fully, towering over his aunt. "I believe you are taking this a bit too personally, considering that *this* test was your idea."

"It's point was to see how these girls would handle themselves against witches, not to establish a sub-court for them within ours!"

He breathed in, then out, calming himself, sparing her from the fury I so wished he would unleash on her. "Princess Loujaïne, if you don't mind I would like you to leave the room."

She gaped at him, scandalized. Then she blurted out, "I will do no such thing. This is my test and—"

"It will go on without you," Cyrus cut her off, showing me another side of him. The uncompromising prince, who could be intimidating when need be, who knew his almost limitless powers over everyone in this land and how and when to wield it. "Leave, please."

Farouk finally intervened, gently ushering the protesting Loujaïne out, his quiet murmurs absorbing her heated complaints until Cyrus shut the door behind them.

Cyrus ran a hand over his face and up to smooth his hair. He was distressed as well as angry and struggling not to display either emotion. I couldn't imagine having to deal with someone like her my entire life, someone who didn't love me but demanded my love and respect.

With this new insight into their relationship, I wondered if his refusal of Fairuza as his betrothed had to do with her being like Loujaïne—haughty, prejudiced, obsessive and cold.

Fairuza spared no time in proving me right as she rounded on Cyrus. "Are you being contrary for the sake of spiting your family? Is that it?"

Cyrus rested his back against the door, arms crossed. "Why would I do that?"

"That's all you've been doing, with this competition and now in dismissing your own aunt."

"What kind of a king will I be if I do everything I'm told regardless of common sense and outcome?"

The biting finality in his deceptively calm words silenced her.

Marzeya yawned loudly beside me, shattering the tense moment. "As entertaining as family disputes are, no, I won't give you the necklace in exchange for a seat at court. That is something I should already have."

Ariane slumped in her seat, giving up.

I hoped Marzeya didn't target me next. I needed a few more minutes to put away all thoughts of my mother and Cyrus's, of Loujaïne and Nariman.

I didn't want to let the idea of Loujaïne sabotaging the lives of Jumana and her friends solidify, or else I'd be compelled to hand her with the lamp over to Nariman and have *her* avenge us all.

Not that I would if I could. If there was the slightest chance that Nariman did want to unseat the royal family, that would be disastrous for Cyrus as well as the whole kingdom. Her anger might be warranted against Loujaïne but not to the extent that it swallows everyone else into the chasm split open by her earthshaking vengeance.

I still had to find a way to appease her. Then stop her.

Marzeya thankfully looked past me to Cora. "What about you, Lady Coralia?"

Cora, who'd spent this whole time slouching in her seat, almost dozing off, sat up, for once fully invested. "How do you know who that is?"

"I'm old." Marzeya laughed, reaching a hand over Cora's golden hair.

Cora only displayed annoyance with the witch rather than the flat out fear I would have.

"Lady Coralia with flowers in her hair, Greenery and rivers following her everywhere, Mistress of the earth and all that it yields, 'Til what lies beneath pulls her to nether fields." Marzeya sang dreamily, inspiring the closest I'd ever seen to panic on Cora's steady face. "Is that how it goes? I can't seem to remember."

"Close," Cora muttered, watching Marzeya warily, like she was ready to jump and fight her off.

"Now, what's your argument?"

"I don't have one." Cora shrugged, leaning on her elbow and casually away from Marzeya. "I don't see why an old necklace is important unless it has magical properties. Does it?"

"Not much besides its beauty."

"Then why do you keep it if you don't wear it?"

"Because why not?"

Stomping over Cora's turn, Fairuza set her hands on the table, rattling it. "You won't trade it for a place at court and you won't wear it. What would it take to give it to us?"

Marzeya clucked her tongue. "Isn't it your job to figure that out?"

"I'm not going to waste my time with your inane games, witch. I see through you," Fairuza spat with far more vitriol than Loujaïne could have mustered.

If Loujaïne's issue with witches was the men in her life preferring them to her, what fueled Fairuza's personal anger?

"You don't see anything, little bluebird, " Marzeya scoffed.

"I do," Fairuza said in a heated rush. "I know your kind, you ruin people's lives for the worst reasons. You go around looking for excuses to validate your cruelty to those weaker than you and you are angling to do that now. I am not playing into your trap."

"There is no trap, dearie." Marzeya suddenly bared her horrific teeth. "And you are starting to anger me."

Fairuza eyed Marzeya with a mixture of disgust and loathing. "There is always a trap with your kind, and I am not walking into it. I am not begging you for anything just so you can give us a cursed replacement or turn us into beasts. You will give us the necklace as an apology and we won't prosecute you."

"Prosecute me for what?"

"Nothing." Cyrus moved to step in. "She's just exaggerating."

"Not you." Marzeya flicked her hand and Cyrus flew back to slam into the door. My airways tightened as he was pinned there by the same invisible force that held Ayman back, fighting thin air. "I am talking to her." She beckoned Fairuza with her bony, taloned fingers. "What do you hope to prosecute me for?"

Fairuza's teeth chattered, her mouth wobbling, but I felt it wasn't with fear like the rest of us, but searing anger, the kind I now felt at my mother's lies and omissions, at Loujaïne for getting Nariman banished and at Nariman for extorting me and endangering all of us.

I felt the magic radiate off Marzeya, a silent threat, waiting to lash out. "Well, Princess? Answer me."

"The accusation of tampering with us is enough to land your neck on the chopping block!"

This wasn't going to end well. I had to step in before the witch lost her temper.

Looking at Cyrus and Ayman, making sure they were just held back but unharmed, I tapped her on the shoulder. "Is it my turn?"

Marzeya turned crimson eyes on me, wrinkled, sunken face still contorted with offense. "What could you have left to say?"

"Not much," I admitted. "You said you didn't want a place at court, neither will you trade other jewelry for it or wear it yourself. I take it that you won't sell it to us either?"

"Not for any currency in your coin pouch or the king's vaults."

"Alright, if you're not using it for yourself, and you won't use it for leverage now that you have us technically at your mercy, then it's not power or money you're after."

Marzeya shook her head. "I have enough of my own."

"Then I have to ask. What do you want?"

Marzeya looked me over, her long black nails tapping on

the table, each third tap from her longest fingernail making me flinch. "What can you offer me?"

That was a good question. What could I give an ancient, powerful witch?

Witches could get any normal thing themselves, that's why Nariman's desire for the gold lamp had seemed so odd, until I realized that within it was something beyond her power.

The only thing a witch could want from me was to perform a task that was risky or impossible for her, because of who she was, but easy for someone like me.

"Not my eternal servitude, that's for sure," I said. "But I can offer you a service."

Marzeya's laugh broke over me, scratching at my nerves. "Really?"

"Is there something you want us to get for you, something you can't obtain but need for your magic? I don't know… maybe glowing grass from the Granary? Luminous fish from the Deep Red Sea? Silver lilies from Arbore?"

"How about a lock of your hair?"

Her suggestion shot through me with a thousand paranoid worries.

A lock of my hair could be an ingredient to spin a personal curse, or a way to control me.

But all Nariman had needed to control me was her magic snake staff. Marzeya, being far more powerful, wouldn't need my hair to do that.

Besides, most of this hair wasn't mine, anyway. It was Nariman's enchanted effort. Or so I thought.

I still wanted to refuse her demand, but I couldn't risk failing this competition or angering her. I needed to win at any cost so I could save the Fairborns. If in doing so I did something detrimental to myself, then so be it.

Steeling myself, I reached back to unbind my hair.

In a spark of glittering light, a silver knife materialized in Marzeya's hand.

As she picked out a lock to cut, Fairuza shouted, "You idiot! Did you listen to a word I said? This is a trap and you're playing right into her hands!"

"Be quiet already." Marzeya gnashed her teeth, red eyes glowing like hot coals.

Fairuza rushed in front of me. "No, I will not! Your kind always pulls these evil tricks."

I stood, speaking through clenched teeth, "Fairuza, stop it. We're almost done here."

Fairuza lunged, grabbed hold of my arms. "You can't give her a part of you! She'll use it against you."

"Since when do you care? It'd be good news for you if I dropped dead tomorrow."

That strangely seemed to rattle her as she stumbled a step back, releasing me. "I don't want you dead! I just want you to go back where you came from."

I huffed. "That's one thing we have in common."

"If you want to make it home safe, don't give anything to her!" Fairuza insisted.

A part of me couldn't believe there was no ulterior motive to her fervor. "You're just trying to get me to fail this test, aren't you?"

"No, she just has an unhinged hate for all magic." Marzeya rose to face Fairuza, who was far more courageous than I'd ever given her credit for. "Don't you, dearie?

"You deserve all my hate." Fairuza faced Marzeya, refusing to be intimidated. "Things like you wait for someone to come to you in desperation then take parts of them as payment, their blood, their hair, their bones, their souls, all to fuel your demonic rituals and suck that person dry."

Marzeya threw out her arm in an arc, drawing a sparking circle that matched her glowing eyes in midair, tearing a hole through the wall next to Fairuza, a doorway into bright, spinning depths. "I think it's time for you to go."

It was a portal, just like the one Nariman had opened in the Hornswoods to transport me and the Fairborns out of Ericura.

Fairuza stood gaping as the portal reversed its spin, sucking the air and turning off the lights around us. As I felt my feet leave the floor, I knew what would come next. If I didn't act quickly, Fairuza would be hurled wherever this portal led.

Before I could grab hold of something, and lunge for Fairuza, she grabbed a handful of my dress and pulled me along to be swallowed into another maw of the unknown.

CHAPTER TWENTY

$\mathcal{I}$ was spat out onto a cold, craggy ground.

But the impact that would cause me a hundred bruises and knocked the air out of my lungs was Fairuza's as she landed on top of me.

And she had the nerve to groan in pain . If I were Bonnie or Cherine, I'd be crushed right now.

I shoved her off me as I rolled up onto my hands and knees.

Where was here?

It was as dim as dusk, with rough-hewn walls and a ceiling that grew wider and higher the further I looked. A shudder spread through me, raising every hair on my body and tightening my guts.

We'd landed in a *cave*.

I hadn't been inside one since I'd been fourteen and desperate for shelter in the wettest part of Ericura. I hadn't slept in one since, taking my risks with empty houses in lively neighborhoods or the sheds of occupied homes.

But here I was, in a dry, desert cave who-knows-where, not of my own need or choosing, but because of Fairuza.

This was all her fault. She'd done her best to provoke Marzeya, and she'd taken me with her—wherever this was.

Bile scalded my insides, sloshing upwards as I stood, foot poised to kick her—and torches burst to life along the cave walls, bathing it in a warm, rusty light.

In the firelight, I could see a small spill of sunlight on the left side of the cave wall. A cave mouth!

My urge to bury my foot in Fairuza's stomach subsided.

I grabbed her upper arm instead, dragging her up and behind me. "Move."

She tried prying my fingers off as she stumbled to her feet. "Let go!"

I yanked her forwards with all my strength, almost dislocating my shoulder. "Walk ahead of me then."

She didn't protest, lifted the front of her massive skirt and cautiously led the way.

From the back, the multi-hued gems in the peacock comb atop her updo gleamed bewitchingly. I wanted to rip it out of her head. She didn't deserve such pretty, expensive things. She was a vile, troublesome brat just like her aunt. Only lucky to be born to royalty, knowing her family, its lineage and importance. Given everything—riches, security, praise, and beauty — on a silver platter. Excused of all transgressions that would get peasants like myself jailed or executed.

It had taken her aggravating a witch-queen to finally get her thrown in a punishment corner. But she'd dragged me there with her, along with sabotaging my efforts. I'd been about to win!

I just hoped it wouldn't take long to find our way back to Marzeya's house. With any luck fate owed me, I might still trade a lock of hair for the necklace, and an apology—for accidentally casting me out with Fairuza—for information.

That was if Marzeya hadn't tossed us too far away. If my mother and Nariman could open doors that bridged the distance between Cahraman and Ericura, then Marzeya could have very well flung us across the Silent Ocean.

Relief soothed my seething fury once we reached the mouth of the cave. It was still the afternoon and the unique cityscape of Zhadugar was shimmering in the distance. A few hours' worth of travel, but still within a day's reach.

Fairuza was trying to beat me to the opening, skirts rustling loudly in her rush. I bunched my skirt to mid-thigh and sprinted, determined to be the first one out and not waste daylight.

My foot was barely at the threshold when a wall of smooth, reddish sandstone slammed down before me, barely missing my foot, blasting a deafening blow through my bones, before echoing endlessly through the cave.

I stumbled backwards, shock still expanding as scratchy, smug laughter bounced off the walls, coming from no discernable direction.

"Did you think it would be that easy?"

"No…" I rasped, struggling to regain my balance. "No, please."

"Let us out!" Fairuza screamed. "Let us out now, witch!"

"Or what?"

"Or you will face the wrath of my father, my uncle, and both their kingdoms!" she threatened viciously. "Let us out and they might spare you!"

"You have already threatened me in my own home, Princess." Marzeya's disembodied voice was as tranquil and cold as a

graveyard chill. *"Your kind ought to know better than to disrespect your hosts."*

"You can't disrespect those who aren't respectable!"

Marzeya laughed harder, making me feel the cave shrink around me. I could almost hear the thousand legs of squirming, venomous bugs, and see the giant spiders above stirring in their webs.

I wanted out of this place now, and Fairuza further insulting the witch wasn't going to do that.

"Fairuza. Stop. Talking." I shoved her aside, turning my head up to address the witch. "Lady Marzeya, please, if you mean to punish her, you can at least let me out. I wasn't supposed to be here."

"No, you weren't," Marzeya said softly. *"For your agreeableness, I have left you Zafira's necklace. If you find it, I will let you out."*

I felt lightheaded, queasy. "But why?"

"You offered to perform a task for me, dearie, remember?" she said sleepily, her voice fading. *"That's it. I advise you don't waste time. And remember—don't touch anything but the necklace."*

"But Lady Marzeya—where do I look? Just give me a clue!"

She didn't answer.

She was gone.

Gone.

$\mathcal{I}$ didn't know how long I stood gaping at the seamless stone where the cavern mouth had been.

It had happened again. A witch had saddled me with a task, given me no hints or guidance, with failure coming at a fatal price.

But instead of being sent to a palace where I'd found friends, I was trapped in a cave with *her*.

Remembering Fairuza finally burned through the ice of shock. I whirled around, found her staring at our sealed exit, her face the image of stunned disbelief.

Couldn't believe she didn't get away with it this time, huh?

I couldn't bear the sight of her right now.

Looking away, taking in steadying breaths, I began to think. Marzeya was only being spiteful, but she didn't mean *me* any harm, so her task had to be easier than Nariman's. Unlike the palace, that necklace would stick out like a sore thumb in this dusty cave.

Composing myself, I started exploring, and realized three

things. The cave was the root of a mountain, it had been inhabited at one point—and magic ran through it.

I ascended a steep slope leading deeper into the cave, and candles blew to life as I passed beneath their ancient chandeliers. The ceiling soared higher and higher above me, the firelight revealing carved walls and elaborate decorations, all cobwebbed and rusted save for the rare gleam of gold.

The slope ended in a platform that gave me a plunging display of the ground below. More torches came to life, illuminating mounted staircases that spread up from the platform like wings, leading up to higher passages extending deep into the mountain.

As amazing as these feats of architecture were—hewn out of the mountain rather than built—I was in no state to admire them. The more the structures revealed themselves, the more lost I became, torn which way to go.

Fairuza caught up with me, huffing and puffing and loudly struggling with her skirt. "You could have waited for me."

I didn't answer her. I was too livid to speak.

Fairuza tapped my shoulder. "I asked you a question."

My response was to tie my skirt into a big knot before taking the staircase to my left, pressing myself against the wall.

Fairuza didn't follow me, which was a wise choice. Climbing the courthouse steps with such a bell-shaped, multi-layered contraption had appeared to be a grueling task. Climbing these would be a death-wish.

By the time I reached the first 'floor' I was coated in sweat and had wiped half the dust off the walls and was coated with it.

I found many open doorways to chambers filled with

broken furniture. At the third level, I found a locked door. Anything locked had to be guarding something valuable.

I unstuck myself from the wall, fetched a few pins from my hair and went to work.

The lock proved trickier than its basic appearance suggested, with a complex interlocking mechanism inside. The door itself was a block of solid wood no battering ram could have barged through. This had to be guarding the necklace! .

I finally opened the lock and braced my feet against the gravely ground to push the heavy, partially stuck door. Once open enough to slip through, I looked inside and—a shout exploded in my chest.

I jerked back violently, nearly tipping myself off the edge. I barely stopped, flew forwards, broke my nails on the stone as I pulled myself back. I trembled all over with shock and fright as I peeked back inside the chamber.

Where three corpses sat.

Browned bones, skeletal jaws clenched or gaping to one side, and empty sockets like holes into the void, the fleshless bodies still had hair, as long and as red as Ariane's.

Young women. Girls. All in their nightgowns. One in a rocking chair with a book on her lap, another on the bed, a comb in her hand, and the third propped against the wall, like they'd been having a night-in, when something had killed them where they sat.

I remained frozen by the doorway, unable to look away.

What did this to them?

Whatever it was, it could still be here!

I choked on nothing, gagging on my own tongue. Marzeya might have left the necklace on one of them, or somewhere in their room.

I had to go in and search them.

Gritting my teeth to keep from retching, I went inside and searched with only my eyes. Since she'd insisted that I touched nothing, the necklace had to be unmissable.

Finding nothing, I rushed out to lean on the wall, gasping for air that didn't taste of ancient death.

I forced myself off the wall and continued my search through every locked room I found on this level. Behind every door was the same macabre scene.

All the chambers were filled with families forever stuck in their last moment, their deaths a surprise that had ambushed them before they could even sense the danger.

There wasn't a word for what I was feeling as I went back down. Or I was feeling too many things at once. Sadness. Pity. Confusion. Dread. Horror.

"What did you find?" Fairuza asked when I rejoined her.

She looked concerned, not by our situation, but by however I looked now. I forgot why I was so angry at her.

Those girls up there, in their room, reminded me of all of us two weeks ago. Girls in nightgowns in one big room, part of a vast, beautiful palace, a court that housed hundreds like this mountain could have.

And they were still up there, decades past rotting. Forgotten.

We would be too if we didn't find the necklace. And so would Bonnie if I didn't find that lamp. All our lives hinged on a disjointed scavenger hunt.

Somewhere, up there, the gods of every land were looking down at me and laughing.

"What is it?" she repeated, softer than I expected.

"This place was inhabited…" I whispered gravely, my throat tight.

"I can tell. This must have been a court of some ancient king."

"No, I mean the bodies are still here."

"So, it's a graveyard?"

I swallowed. "It's the remains of a curse."

Fairuza flinched. I couldn't blame her.

But now I'd searched the upper levels, where I thought the necklace would be, as people usually hid their valuables in the highest places possible, that meant she had to have hidden it in a trickier spot.

The temperature dropped the further we descended into the bowels of the cave, so I couldn't tell if my shudders were from the cold or the sights I'd witnessed above, and their implications. I forced my focus back on the mission as I swept through the interconnected spaces, searching for a hint of sapphire.

Mind whirling with conflicting thoughts, I at one point found myself between the statues of a longhaired, bearded man gripping a really massive hammer with both hands, and a woman with a peacock crown holding a water lily.

I recognized them as Ataxsh and Anaïta, Cahramani gods whose shrines I had visited with Cyrus in search of the gold lamp. They were crudely made, not as life-like as the sculptures around the palace and Sunstone. They had to have been made by a more primitive people. A civilization that predated Cahraman, possibly even the Avestan Empire.

I wished I knew about these lands and their history. I wished my mother had told me where we came from, who her family and my father were, instead of leaving me ignorant and alone forever.

But Fairuza fully knew her ties to this land, and to the one that claimed her as its princess. And if not Cyrus, another prince would marry her and her children would be taught everything from birth about their family trees and culture.

But the only man for me was Cyrus, and the only family I knew were my mother and the Fairborns.

Giving up on this area, I turned to find Fairuza bowing before a heavily pregnant goddess who carried a child in one arm and a scepter in another.

I stopped by her side. "Who is this?"

"I believe she is Queen of Heaven, goddess of the moon, women and fertility," she said, head still bowed, eyes closed, a pinch of concentration on her face.

I exhaled as I searched another area. "Does she have a name?"

Ending her prayer, she straightened. "It differs in each land. The Gemishti call her Hat-Hür, the Merjani Athirat, and in both Avesta and Cahraman her name is 'Asherah."

"What about in Almaskham?"

"Ellat."

My heart fluttered. "Sounds like 'Adalat."

"My mother says 'Adalat was an Almaskhami import. Before her, justice was one of the many jobs of the head sun god, Xorsham."

At the mention of her mother, her eyes opened into a glare. She remained like that, staring menacingly at nothing in particular, until I nudged her. "Let's go."

Fairuza pressed two fingers to her mouth then to the cheek of the goddess. "Shouldn't we be searching in different places to cover more ground?"

"It's better if we stick together."

She crossed her arms. "Why? The first one of us to find the necklace wins."

"This isn't about the test anymore."

"Yes, it is."

"No, it isn't, and you made sure of that!" I snapped, my prior anger resurging. "Now because of you all we can hope for is getting out of here."

Fairuza turned her face away but remained in step with me as we entered another hall.

We emerged on the other side and fire basins mounted on basalt columns burst to life in lieu of torches. In their fiery light, the first thing that caught my eye was a glimmer of gold at the very end of the deep, uneven space.

It was two opposing statues of crowned kings, each with a golden hand raised. Beyond them was another slope that led up to a wider space.

Eyeing the curved, wooden doors, I tentatively reached for the nearest ring-handle then stopped, the sight of the three dried up girls flashing before my eyes.

I turned to her. "Why don't you check inside and I'll check out here?"

She didn't look at me. I grabbed her shoulder and turned her around. "Did you hear me?"

She looked up, eyes swimming with tears that tracked down her cheeks. "Yes, I heard you."

Half of me wanted to yell at her, for having the nerve to cry when I—someone who had plenty of reasons to—didn't. The other half wanted to ask her what was wrong.

The latter half won. "Are you scared of the dark? Or are you finally experiencing the peasant emotion that is 'guilt'?"

Instead of a snappy retort, she sniveled, a sad, wet, undignified noise. "Not exactly."

"Then what is it?"

"Why do you care?" she blubbered, indelicately wiping her eyes with her sleeve.

"I don't. I just want to know what reasons someone like you has to be upset."

"How about the fact that I'm going to die?"

"You're not going to die here."

She shook her head, crying harder, nose and lips bright red in the firelight. "I am."

"This is the first time you've ever been lost, isn't it?" A cross between a snort and a bitter laugh escaped me. "I'm taking that as a yes."

"How many times have *you* been lost?"

"Plenty. I was lost for years." I looked around, wondering if anyone had the chance to escape the attack that had ended all life here. "I still am lost."

Her gaze grew contemplative as she wiped her eyes again. "You don't believe you'll die here?"

"I'd rather not believe it."

"How does not believing it help?"

What an odd, reflective mood she was suddenly in. All this because this was her first brush with danger? Or was it something else?

"It's not that I don't believe I won't die," I said. "I will. Eventually. It's that I can't let that happen now. I have a lot to do before I go."

"I don't."

She didn't follow up that comment with anything else as we continued searching. We found chambers with signs of previous life, with belongings ranging from rusty swords to harpsichords to cots.

By the statues that towered over the end of the hall, Fairuza screamed.

I rushed to her side, hands fisted. "What?"

She pointed a shaky finger towards a chamber ahead.

It was filled with the dead. But these weren't like the ones above, frozen in time. These were ravaged remains, bodies torn apart, pieces littering the ground, their mummified flesh picked almost clean off bones. Something had devoured their dead bodies after *that* had killed them.

But this was an ancient place and those people could have been dead for centuries. Whatever scavenger that had been, I hoped it had long died out..

"We're going to die here." She backed away from the sight, arm shielding her eyes, hiccupping between each word "We're —going—to—die—here."

I reached for her, feeling just as overwhelmed, but I couldn't afford a breakdown right now. We had to get out.

I tried to drag her away. "I told you. We're not."

"It's all my fault." She stumbled out of my reach, stepping on her own skirt and grabbed the gold hand of the stone king to steady herself.

A groan of muted thunder rumbled through the mountain. It reverberated beneath our feet and up the walls like a subtle earthquake, raining dust and silt down upon us.

As the tremor persisted, I began to hear other sounds. The boiling rise of a thousand maddening whispers followed by the cacophony of rousing and rushing within the walls.

Something had woken up and was burrowing and clawing through the catacombs.

A clang of terror went through my chest, rattling my ribs and vibrating my organs. I didn't have to envision the worst anymore. It spared me the effort and came swarming out.

Corpse-pale, eyeless, hairless beasts with slit nostrils, their jaws kept apart by protruding fangs, and sharp claws curling out of knuckle-deep nailbeds.

Ghouls!

CHAPTER TWENTY-TWO

Dread felt like wet cement pouring over my body, drying to rock in a fractured heartbeat.

Then Fairuza shrieked and the paralyzing layer cracked and fell into rubble at my numb feet. I gripped her wrist and bolted up the slope.

I only dared to look over my shoulder when we crossed the doorway into the wider passage. Heart in my ears and throat, breath shearing through my lungs, I caught a glimpse of the ghouls crashing behind us in a frothing wave of demonic horror.

They began gnawing out each other's throats, gashes spraying black on their pale, nightmarish faces. Fighting among themselves over who would get the chance to eat us.

I tightened my grip on Fairuza, pulling hard enough to dislocate her arm as I dragged her up a steep, ladder-like staircase. Sobbing, she stumbled in my wake, struggling to bend the arm in my grasp to lift her skirt off her feet, slipping many times and almost dragging me down with her.

The moment we reached the platform, I panted, "For the love of Ellat, Fairuza, take that dress *off*!"

"I can't reach the buttons!" she gasped,

"How do you put it on if you can't take it off?"

"I don't! My handmaidens do all that!"

"Are you a toddler?" I yelled. "Why would you need help putting on a dress?"

"It's not a simple slip like yours. I can't just pull it over my head," she panted. "It's stiff, heavy—has so many requirements. Agnë threads the corset and buttons—while Meira sorts out—the skirts and train!"

Now was the worst time to criticize her impractical wardrobe. But the weight of that skirt could topple us off that ladder. There was also the issue of her shoes and—

"Are you wearing a corset right now?"

"Yes," she wheezed.

That explained why she was so out of breath. Her lungs literally couldn't expand. I had to rip it off her or else she'd soon faint mid-run and become an easy meal to the ghouls. I also couldn't carry her like I had Cherine. Heavy skirts aside, she was almost my size, and I could barely carry myself at the moment.

We still had two more levels to climb, each connected to the next by a stone ladder at its center. The last led up to a huge, circular hole in the mountain wall. The sounds of sloshing echoed from within, like waves on a shore. I would have expected any water within here to be stagnant, a spring or a lake, but if it were a river…

We could ride the current out of the mountain!

The tiny splash of relief evaporated as the slam of a hundred bodies exploded below us in a writhing, reeking mass, before they splintered, overflowing wall-to-wall, all converging to the same spot. To us.

Like a swarm of giant ants, they rushed at us, claws scraping stone in a hair-raising chorus. Any one ghoul that got closest to the ladder was dragged back and brutally ripped apart, not to be feasted on but to eliminate competition. But if even one of them escaped…

"We're going to die," Fairuza said solemnly, no sobs left despite the unending tears as she looked down at the swarm that broke into further competitive bloodshed. "We will be ripped apart and devoured and left like those people, nothing but bone and hair." She hiccupped harshly. "I always knew I'd die—but I thought it'd be in my own bed, in my home, where I'd be mourned and buried."

"I always thought I'd die on a dark road," I mumbled weakly. "That I'd be attacked or freeze while lost, only to be eaten by vultures and dogs before the worms joined them."

Fairuza raised a hand to her mouth, eyes puffy, red and wet and still fixed at the fight below. "How did this happen? Where did they come from?"

Broken sounds escaped me, huffs of exhausted, manic laughter. "Prior to our visit? Hell, most likely."

"And during it?"

"They must have been sleeping underground, and we've woken them up. Maybe our scent…" I stopped, realization hitting me, the accompanying horror of the situation finally sinking in. "The witch said not to touch anything. You touched the statue's golden hand before they appeared."

The hand over her mouth shook as the tempo of her breathing climbed into hyperventilation. "I-I'm sorry."

"I—"

She threw herself at me, hugging me clumsily, sobbing, gasping in my ear. "I'm sorry. I'm so sorry. I'm so sorry, I swear. I swear this was the last thing I thought would happen. I didn't mean to touch it, I didn't. I didn't know this would happen, I'm so sorry—" She broke into harsher crying.

I didn't know what to think or feel. Shock was intensifying, dampening my feelings, making it easier to run from them rather than remain in their path.

I wasn't mad at her. I couldn't afford to expend any thoughts or energy on judging or blaming her for our situation, which was entirely of her making. I couldn't burn any of what fueled both my mind and spirit on anything but thoughts of survival.

We could sort this out later. Now we needed to ensure there would be a later.

"An apology isn't what I need from you right now." I pushed her off me, digging my fingers in her shoulders. "I need you to stop crying, can you do that?"

"No!" She shook her head wildly, sending tears flying off her face to splatter mine. "I c-can't stop. I can't think, c-can't breathe, can't—can't—"

My palm landed across her face in a loud smack.

Her hand flew to her cheek, eyes wide and brimming with tears but chest calming and mouth closing, breathing through her nose.

"You hit me," she said slowly, the shock I'd aimed for sinking in, steadying her. "You hit me much harder last time."

"Last time I wanted to knock you out, this time I need you to shut up and run." I pointed to the next set of stairs "They won't be preoccupied like that much longer."

Nodding, she staggered there, tried to climb and slipped again as a handful of ghouls began crawling up the platform beneath us.

I went up after her. "Take off the dress. Take it off now!"

"And what? Carry it around everywhere?"

"Leave it here!" I yelled.

"Leave it? Are you mad? This dress cost more than your house. I can't leave it."

"Fairuza, you were just talking about us being eaten alive," I hissed. "Do you want to be buried in one piece in your castle's catacombs or do you want to be eaten in this dress?"

"My mother will kill me if I don't return with it."

"Loujaïne can reimburse Zomoroda. It's her fault we came here in the first place."

Reluctant, she turned and I unbuttoned her dress and tried to pull it down quickly.

"No, you're supposed to take it off over my head."

"It doesn't matter if it rips!"

"It matters because I'm wearing a hoop skirt! I can't just step out of it, the waist is too small and to rip something this thick would need those beasts' claws!"

I got to work lifting the dress, bouncing in place, trying to ignore the noise of the ascending yet still warring ghouls. "What in the world is a hoop skirt?"

"You'll find out—now!" She huffed as I lifted off her gorgeous monstrosity of a dress.

It wasn't just a corset and a slip underneath, but a petticoat over what looked like a steel birdcage that began from her waist and stopped a bit below her knees.

"No wonder you can't run," I grumbled, lifting the hoop skirt up and off her. It hit the floor with a hollow rattle and the petticoat followed it. "What is all this stuff?"

"You think the skirt looks like this by itself?"

"With all the effort, material and money that went into it, it should have. It should *walk* by itself!"

I'd started unlacing her corset when a ghoul broke through

the struggle. It crawled over the fighting mass, using them as leverage, and reached the top of the stairs.

Up close, its thin, colorless skin, featureless face and blackened teeth blew apart the steadying numbness and stabbed the fear of the Horned God back into my heart.

Here it was, the beast that fueled nightmares, that prowled in the night, that carried the wanderers and loners away and devoured them, flesh and soul.

Its eyeless face aimed at me, it kicked those that tried to pull it away, unhinged its jaw wide and lunged at my leg.

I jumped back with a throat-ripping shriek and kicked its head with all my strength, knocking it aside. When it rose back on all fours I pulled back my throbbing foot and kicked again. And again. Over and over in a frenzy, channeling all my hatred and fury into each kick as I screamed every conceivable insult.

With a final collision, the ghoul's head caved in, tar-like blood oozing out of its horrid face and onto the floor.

Fire coursing through my veins, I whirled around, found Fairuza with one foot on the bottom of the staircase, staring at me in a mix of terror and awe.

"What?" I panted, bending over to feel my toes. A simple squeeze sparked a rush of scalding pain.

The awe fled her face on a horrified shout. "Watch out!"

I was tackled to the floor before I could straighten.

I hit the rough ground with a bruising, scraping slam, screaming and struggling, as another ghoul pinned me with claws dug into my wrists.

Like a fish ripped from water, I heaved madly on the ground, feeling air flee my lungs as I screamed and kicked, trying to push out from beneath it. My struggles ceased when twin cuts slit through my skin like an asps' fangs. It had released my arms in favor of my neck, razor thumbnails pressed against the tender spots under my jaw. Panic pounded in my throat as I felt the burn of the cuts and the blood trickling down my skin.

I couldn't struggle without slicing my own throat.

Now that it had me trapped, it took its time opening its dripping mouth, the stench of its hot, fetid breath choking me and forcing scalding tears from my eyes.

The pale face of death with its snapping jaws grew closer with every breath, counting down to my last one.

I closed my eyes, bracing for the ripping of my skin, the heart-stopping pain—

A deafening clang and rattle ripped my eyes open.

Fairuza's hoop skirt had smashed into the ghoul's head, then again and again until its grip on my throat loosened.

Heaving for breath, I squirmed out from under it as Fairuza backed away, still swinging at its head, face frozen in fury and horror, but the force of surprise was gone. It left me to follow her in a slow, menacing crawl.

I grabbed Fairuza's dress, ran after them and jumped on the ghoul's back. It reared to throw me off, shrieking, and I shoved the end of the skirt into its gaping mouth, filling the span of its spread jaws. It lurched wildly beneath me and I wound my legs around it tighter, almost cramming my whole hand down its maw, choking it with more cloth.

Fairuza screamed and hit it even harder than before in a frenzy, until she irreparably dented her hoop-skirt and cracked its skull.

As the ghoul slumped beneath me, I could barely retrieve my hand from its closing fangs before rising on wobbling legs, heart stampeding, breath shearing in my chest and stared at Fairuza.

Two dead ghouls lay sprawled on the stone floor, at our feet.

But our victories barely had time to register before I noticed something off.

The struggle below us had gone unnervingly quiet.

Could they have all killed each other?

Hesitantly, I peeked over the edge.

The pile of dismembered bodies wasn't big enough to be all of them.

Before my heart could fire one more fractured beat, I heard the muted sounds of an approaching stampede, the scrape of a thousand claws, and the cacophony of hungry shrieks growing closer. I felt the floor shake before the ghouls burst through the opening to our left, crawling on all fours and climbing over each other.

Wrists bleeding, right foot shrieking, blood roaring in my ears, I bolted for Fairuza's outstretched hand and I urged her ahead up the ladder leading to the opening in the wall where I heard water.

Hope rode me until the sight of the cavern had my fervor dropping to match the temperature. There was no river. Just a pool where the water constantly rippled and lapped the edges.

The ghouls followed us, with less infighting than before, spreading out along the floor.

I backed away, pushing Fairuza behind me, trembling arms outstretched, fingers clenching and unclenching, desperate to find anything to fight them off with.

But there was nothing to use as a weapon and no way out of here.

This was the end of the line.

The ghouls crawled closer, slower, the confident prowls of

predators knowing they finally had their prey backed into a corner.

"What are they doing?" Fairuza pulled me back by the shoulders, her whisper a rough, shaky rasp. "Why aren't they attacking?"

The same question looped around my mind like a whirlpool.

Whirlpool. Water. The smell of the water. It had to be diluting our scent.

"They can't see us." My throat loosened with the realization. "And with all the water, they're having a hard time pinpointing our location."

But that didn't mean they wouldn't keep advancing until they found us.

As I dreaded, they began to move closer, sniffing, open jaws dripping expectant saliva. They knew they were closer, a lunge away from having an arm or a kidney each.

There was nowhere to run. That left only one thing to do.

When the first ghoul pounced in our direction, I turned and tackled Fairuza off her feet—and into the deep, dark water.

CHAPTER TWENTY-THREE

*H*itting the cold water felt like breaking through concrete, the bruising shock turning my world black.

Awareness came with a flash of blue. My eyes were open and there was water and bubbles all around me. Bright spots littered the walls of the pool, just like the tunnels under the palace, shimmering white light through the murkiness.

For quiet moments I sank, weightless, my hair floating above me, in liquid, encompassing tranquility. I couldn't even remember if I'd ever known such peace.

Then the air inside me slowly slipped past my lips in a stream of bubbles and a voice inside my head began to scream. *Swim. Swim up or you'll drown.*

My body didn't respond until my lungs began to burn and desperation shoved peace aside, then I was thrashing and kicking up. The whole world and our grisly situation crashed back into me the moment I broke the water surface.

I swam to the nearest wall, the water wobbling loudly

around me, spotted Fairuza struggling, barely making a wave in her efforts to remain afloat.

It hadn't occurred to me that she couldn't swim. It didn't look like she was going to get the gist of it any time soon.

I kicked towards her, the water feeling thick and restricting, every movement met with thickening resistance, like I was trudging through honey. I belatedly realized it was my dress. It hadn't been near as hampering as Fairuza's on land, but soaked with water, it could drown me, at least keep me from saving Fairuza.

Struggling out of it had my muscles aching and the burn in my lungs spreading. But I finally kicked it off and struck out towards the floundering and bobbing Fairuza.

When I reached her, and before I could grab her in the way I'd once seen a lifeguard save a drowning man at Galba, she latched onto me so rabidly we both went under.

Pressure waned as we sank, squeezing my eyeballs and sinuses and almost bursting my head. Any further down and my heart might burst in its cage.

Desperate, I kicked, propelling us back up to our initial spot, by the greenest glowing opal embedded in the wall. But it was too much. Everything hurt. I was almost out of reserve air, and soon I would faint and we'd both drown.

The only way we'd float back up was when our corpses became bloated and buoyed themselves back up to the surface.

At the last moment before I gave up, we hit the wall and she traded me for it as anchor. As the last wisps of precious air deserted me, I pointed up at the rippling surface and grabbed at the wall, using its steadiness and the water's weightless effect to propel myself upwards, vertically crawling on all fours. Fairuza followed my lead.

My lungs were about to pop when a sudden up-thrust sucked us up to the surface.

I broke through the water with a shrieking gasp. Fairuza emerged the same way then broke into harsh coughs.

Heaving and trembling, she finally choked, "What did you do that for?"

"Why do you think?" I gasped, jerking my head in the direction of the ghouls, who hadn't given up and gone, but remained by the edge of the water, waiting. "They can't smell us in here."

"But they can hear us."

"Yes, but they can't swim. It was either this or get eaten."

"So we go from almost dying on land to drowning in water?"

"It's not my fault you can't swim!" My shout interrupted my deep breaths, launching my own fit of coughs. Head turned up for better, deeper breaths, I noticed the stalactites melting from the ceiling above us.

"Where would I learn to swim?"

"Anywhere! Don't you have room-sized baths in your castles? Giant pools fit for a king or his whole court?" I swam away until I reached the pool's edge. Fairuza followed me, clinging to the wall until she reached my side. "And that's not the only problem here, it's that you have no sense of self-preservation. It's a wonder you've lived this long." I slapped the water, splashing it her way. "We're here because you couldn't hold your tongue long enough for us to leave the witch's home. You had to keep deliberately offending her, all because you couldn't just let me win one round."

She returned my splash, a weak slosh that barely reached my arm. "You think this was about the test?"

"What else could it be? I was about to win back the necklace and you had to stop it at all costs."

"That's not why I tried to stop you," she said, folding her forearms on the ground, not daring to look behind us. "Witches, fairies, mermaids, any of these things that resemble us only on the surface all want nothing but the worst for us. They use their promise of magic to manipulate us, are nice to us until they get what they want. And once we stop being useful they curse and torture us!"

"Is this one of your ridiculous beliefs or do you have proof that Marzeya was going to harm me?" I said snidely. "I find it hard to believe you'd care for my wellbeing."

"Do I have to like you to not want you to become her thrall?"

"No, but you have to have common decency, goodwill towards fellow man and whatnot, which was evidently not on your tutors' teaching plan."

"Would you stop acting like I'm an unfeeling evil fairy?"

"Then stop acting like one," I snapped. "I'm not buying your answer. Why *did* you antagonize Marzeya?"

"Believe it or not, I didn't want to risk her cursing any of us, that's why I didn't want to participate in this test to begin with." She wiped her face, smoothed back her plastered hair, its soaked state rendering it as black as mine. "And I told you, just because I want you out of the competition, doesn't mean I want you to die."

"Why not? You already tried it before with Cherine."

"How many times do I have to say she fell? Do you think I would have remained here if I did truly try to murder her?"

"Yes. You could do literally anything and remain because the judges want you here. *Loujaïne* wants you here. You're a princess and immune to the laws and punishments we're all dealt with." All my resentments spilled back, filling me like hot, acidic bile, doubling my nausea. "It's not like you can be fired from your title."

She scowled at me, droplets rolling down her face like sweat. "What do you think being a princess is exactly?"

"Exactly what you are, a pampered, guarded, prized and privileged girl who has nothing to fear and not much expected from you. All you have to do is be all wrapped up in what your life affords you."

"I'm pampered so I wouldn't complain about being valued only because I'm to be bargained away to whatever kingdom we need to strengthen ties with. And I'm guarded so no one kills me to start a war or prevent an alliance. Does that sound lovely to you?"

"It does."

She goggled at me. "Why?"

"I've been on enough strange and suspect roads to wish I had the paved path you're on, to follow it to a true and tried destination. One I don't have to worry about or doubt, where I am safe regardless of the reason, all because I am important to many people. That sounds incredibly lovely to me."

"How could it?

"You really have no sense of perspective, do you? Try thinking about it from my position." I removed one hand from the stone floor to count. "Someone who is poor, has no family, no connections or ancestral goodwill to fall back on when I'm in need. No good man has any reason to marry me, take me into his family and land because I have nothing and know no one to offer. I barely even know who I am." Water dripped from my hairline and down my cheeks, in place of the frustrated tears I couldn't muster. "So, yes, a life where everything is done for me, planned for me, every skill is afforded to me, where all I need to know are things that are useless, where I'm free to *be useless*."

"I am not useless!"

"You are! You have no qualities or skills that would help you survive beyond your castle's walls." I sniffled loudly, nose starting to run. "And from what I see you don't even have the skills needed to survive within them. You can't negotiate with or befriend people—are you even capable of being nice? Or pretending to be so? If all you expect to do is push out heirs and host your husband's guests, you could wind up alienating your children and starting a war because of how nasty you are."

She hunched, neck and shoulders re-entering the water as she looked up at me. "That doesn't seem to bother my mother. She's quite content being a friendless queen."

"You don't sound like you want that for yourself, why not act different than her?"

"For what reason? This is a competition, we're here to battle for the chance to win his hand—a hand that was always mine and should have only been extended to welcome me here as his betrothed." Fairuza turned her face up at the stalactites hanging above us, like she wished one would fall and impale her. "For all that importance I'm supposed to have, I was unimportant enough to have our since-birth betrothal easily discarded. And negligible enough to be called here as one of fifty, all beneath me in rank, breeding and country, and put through inane tests to narrow his choices." She looked down at the water rippling around us. "Being here, with you, someone who has nothing to offer, with Ariane, who is from a small, emerging island nation, with Cherine, who is a mere noble, and Cora, who isn't even titled, it says I am equal to you."

"You're not," I said. "We're here because the prince and his council believe we have something to offer him, and as you said, all you have to offer is your tiara."

It might have been the cold water or exhaustion, but her glare had no anger behind it anymore. "Luckily, all a princess needs is a tiara from a kingdom her betrothed can enjoy trade and peace with. That is the purpose of a king's daughter, to solidify treaties and alliances."

"Weren't you just complaining about your lot in life a minute ago?"

"Just because it's true, doesn't mean I have to like it."

I rubbed at my nose, starting to shudder. "Then what would you have done apart from this? What else is there for you to do? What more would you even want with every hobby, tutor and servant afforded to you?"

"I don't know," she admitted in a small voice. "And I'll never know, because we won't leave this cave, and I'll die here."

"You *won't* die here."

That was a bold promise considering I was beginning to lose the feeling in my legs and was growing drowsier by the minute in a pool surrounded by ghouls.

But at least we were safe for now, and I could catch my breath and think. But no matter how hard I did, there was only one way to fulfill my promise.

Finding Zafira's necklace.

I could see now why people hated witches. And to think my mother was one...

The crack almost didn't register at first. Breath trembling in my chest, my head snapped up in time to see a stalactite breaking off and hurtling down to cleave the water with a violent splash. A massive wave slammed us into the edge before it sank.

Gasping, I found only half of the ghouls by the doorway. The rest were crawling up from the walls and to the ceiling like giant spiders, some climbing down the stalactites, chipping at their bases until they cracked.

They'd found a way to fish us out of the water.

Another stalactite crashed dangerously close to us, the resulting wave almost rolling us back underwater but splashing the ghoul, scaring it off.

I swallowed water, Fairuza's weight making me sink beneath the surface. I kicked up, tried swimming back to the edge so she could hold onto it instead of me but more ghouls crawled down the wall, shrieking monstrously, their shouts of anticipation and hunger echoing off the cavern walls, increasing my shudders.

Even if we managed to evade the stalactites, we couldn't stay in the water forever, we were bound to fall asleep or faint, and drown.

I shook so hard I almost sank us both, not just from the water, but from the reality that I absorbed along with the cold.

No matter what we did now, it would end with us dead.

"We're trapped." I wheezed, chest too tight, losing the will to stay afloat.

I would drown before I let myself be eaten, and Fairuza couldn't stay afloat without me. We would die before I got the chance to find out who my mother truly was or seek out her family in Almaskham. Before I could win Cyrus along with the competition and find the lamp, and Bonnie would still die a brutal death thousands of miles away from home, away from me.

"Fairuza, you were right," I rasped, voice tearing as I wept. "We're going to die here."

"No." I felt her shaking her head behind me. "No, you promised me. You said that you weren't done with life yet, that you had things to do."

"So?" I cried, blubbering, hopes now at the unfathomable depths of this pool.

"So, do what needs to be done to get out, to do whatever you have left to do," she said, trembling against me. "And if I'm going to die, it's not going to be here, it will be at home with my sister and my brothers."

"It's nice that you're choosing to be optimistic, but now's the worst time to do it." I shut my eyes tightly, squeezing out tears. "You were right, witches do nothing but hurt us. Marzeya lied just to torture us for her own entertainment."

"She is torturing us but she didn't lie."

"What makes you say that?"

"Because I think I found the necklace."

I spun in the water, facing her, holding her up rather than having her draped on my back. "Where?"

Fairuza jerked her head to the flat wall to our right. "When the rocks fell and the water went up, I saw something blue there. Either there is another cave beneath the water or it's floating there."

That was where I'd been facing when I'd thrown us into the water, where I'd seen the blue flash.

Hope expanded within me, siphoning the ink of despair in my insides like a sponge. Our way out finally had a location. It was another obstacle to overcome. But that was better than nothing. I could swim down there and search for it, but Fairuza had nothing to hold onto anymore. I couldn't leave her.

"You can stay on my back while I swim down there," I said.

"If you do we'll both die."

"Most outcomes of this situation end with our blue, bloated corpses floating like logs," I agreed. "Can you stay afloat?"

She swallowed. "I'll try. But you'll need to hurry."

Not wasting another moment, I dove into the dim depths.

I was a dozen feet down when I saw the flash of blue again.

Going back up for air, I gulped the deepest breath I'd ever drawn, and dove back down towards the beckoning blue.

It was harder than swimming up in every conceivable way. Instead of gladly helping me sink further down the water resisted my downward strokes, and the earlier pressure I had felt against my eyeballs and heart was back, worsening the lower I forced myself to go.

Every muscle ached as the resistance grew and my force weakened. It was painful to keep the air in my lungs and my head tightened until I felt it would burst.

I was too close to fainting.

But I knew if I went back up for air I wouldn't be able to come back down.

Ignoring the tightening pressure in my chest, I continued my taxing dive down, eyes as open as the pain would allow.

A few feet down, the blue flash spread into five separate spots. The sapphires.

The certainty reignited my fight, numbing the stress on my heart and muscles but it wasn't enough to delude my lungs.

I needed to breathe.

Just a few more feet...just a bit more and I could finally breathe...

The sapphires were distinct now, neither in a cave or in an aimless float.

Standing on a giant rose quartz lily pad, the petals of the lotus flared behind her like the peacock tail of her crown, was Anaïta. Around her pale pink neck was the sapphire necklace.

This wasn't an underground lake, but a flooded shrine to the goddess of the waters.

Head on the verge of bursting, I floated before Anaïta's smooth, pink statue and unclasped the necklace from her neck with shaking fingers. Taking more time to clasp it around my own neck was potentially fatal. But I couldn't risk fainting and having it slip through my grasp.

I missed its hook clasp again and a frustrated scream rang within me, escaping my lips in bubbles. When it finally took, I blacked out.

Everything went dark, my body went limp and my jaw slacked. Water flowed into my mouth, wiping out whatever precious air I had left, filling my nose, my throat.

I was drowning.

Light came back, but everything was faint and silent. The resistance that had fought me on the way down was not pushing me up now. It had abandoned me, leaving me to float up only a few feet before the statue and remain there, caught in Anaïta's unfeeling gaze.

Please, I begged her, begged Marzeya, begged anyone. *Please. I didn't come all the way here to die. I can't die, not yet.*

Nothingness kept threatening to consume me, lasting longer with each blink, becoming harder to fight with each brush with darkness. I fought to keep my eyes open, but my vision dimmed, its edges blurring into the void.

Somebody please save me.

The world around me throbbed, as if the mountain shook,

and the thousand opals around me closed and reopened as glowing blue eyes.

I felt myself floating up, weightlessly soaring back towards the surface and before my vision finally flickered out, I saw Anaïta smile.

~

I CAME TO WITH A VIOLENT LURCH.

I was still in the pool, being held up by Fairuza.

My swollen eyes slid around. We were in the cavern, surrounded by ghouls.

We were still here. Why were we still here?

"But the necklace…" I slurred, head pounding. "Why—why hasn't she—" I couldn't find any words to complete that thought.

Fairuza, kicking to keep us afloat, held on tighter. "I felt the mountain shake. The door has likely reopened."

I didn't understand the point she was making, could barely manage breathing let alone speaking.

"What?" I managed, one eye drooping shut.

"She gave us a way out," she sobbed. "But we can't reach it."

Oh.

More air flooded my lungs and spread up to my head. Aware, but exhausted beyond words, I understood just how much worse our situation had gotten.

Freedom was now tangible, and we knew where it was. Just out of our reach.

"This…" Fairuza's teeth clattered. "…is why we burn witches."

Between one blink and the next, the mountain shook and we bobbed heavily in the water. Within another blink the ghouls were rearing up, sniffing the air, and by the time we turned, the ones blocking the entrance were running, fighting to beat each other out.

Someone else was here!

Yells echoed up, deep, discordant notes too vague to discern. The ghouls' collective screeches were unmistakable sounds of attack.

Horrifying bellows detonated, accompanied by the wet, nauseating sounds of bodies being crushed against rock, followed by the sickening rupture of skin, hacking of flesh and the thunder cracking of bones.

I tried not to imagine those claws viciously slicing through necks and ribs. I didn't want to accept that whatever poor souls had wandered in here had met their end between those monstrous jaws. And that we'd be next.

The ghouls over the walls and stalactites stampeded back to the opening as something—likely their comrades now smothered in human blood—approached.

Heavy footfalls stomped up the steps, then a pale, clawless hand gripped the edge of the entrance, fingertips dripping with dark blood.

*B*odies bent like bows, the ghouls appeared as anxious as I was as a man pulled himself in, armor coated in thick, black blood, hands clutching a scimitar.

"Apologies for the delay, my ladies," said Ayman, running a fingertip over the curved side of his blade as he eyed the clustering ghouls. "I would have come sooner, but *someone* insisted on coming along."

"You're damn right I did!" Cyrus appeared at the top of the stairs, jacket discarded, a sleeve torn, a bite-mark on his forearm still beading with blood, his hair a mess and plastered to one side with the blood-splatter that masked half his face.

Ayman. *Cyrus.*

They'd come for us.

It was too good to be true. But good things didn't happen to me. It made me wonder if I was still at the bottom of the pool, drowning, and this was a departing daydream.

Hallucination or not, they were quite the pair. Ayman, a calm and simmering threat with his intricate armor and vicious sword, and Cyrus, a half-wild mess in his stained and ruined clothes, brandishing an axe ripped from a war god's statue, bright eyes flashing in the firelight like a lightning-crack in a night sky.

He surveyed the beasts with violent disgust and the confident focus of a hunter, as if he was not to be their prey, but they were his. Ayman, without his gauntlets and his faceplate open, glowered at the encroaching mass with contempt, as if the sight of them personally offended him. Whatever both men's reasons were, they weren't afraid. And they were here to save us!

Suddenly the soaring hope was shot down by dread. There was no way they could go through all these ghouls!

Before I could beg them to leave, to save themselves from being cornered like us, Cyrus ordered, "Get out of the water, quick! A carriage is waiting outside!"

"We *can't*," Fairuza gasped, clinging tighter to me, shaking all over. "They'll attack us."

"I promise you they won't," he said in his commanding, princely tone. "Go!"

The effect of his composure on me was immediate. Gone was all the lethargy and disorientation as I made Fairuza hold on to an arm while I launched into a taxing mix of one-armed strokes and splashing kicks. It didn't matter how heavy and worn out I was by the effects of near-drowning. Cyrus was here, Ayman was here, and I was determined to reach them. If anything, I'd fight alongside them. I wouldn't cower in the water while they faced the monstrous horde alone.

When we reached land and began to climb out, a few ghouls rounded on us, salivating and hissing hungrily and Cyrus's axe came down on the neck of the one closest to us. As its severed head hit the floor, the three remained focused on us while over two dozen ghouls swarmed him and Ayman.

My heart lodged in my throat as I forgot the ghouls before me, desperately looking past them, to see how Cyrus and Ayman were faring.

They were back-to-back, swinging their weapons at the beasts, scoring precise swipes and cutting blows that lopped off hands and cleaved necks. They moved in a practiced, unhurried ease, not with the urgency of a cornered animal that I'd been brimming with earlier. It was like they'd done this before.

I'd never thought I'd ever see Ayman use his guard's sword, thought it purely for ceremony and precaution. What had been even less feasible was seeing Cyrus brutally swinging a heavy axe and bellowing the foulest curses as he cut down one beast after another.

They weren't merely standing their ground, they were winning.

Cyrus's blade cut through the air with a whoosh, cleaving into a ghoul's spine. "Go on! Have a bite! I dare you!"

"Don't goad them, one already nipped you." Ayman heaved, slashing an attacking ghoul's throat. "It better not scar. I'd hate to explain that to your father."

"Oh, why not? It would be a fun story to tell the grand-children."

"Keep following me into places like this and you won't have grandchildren."

Cyrus ducked as he buried his drenched-in-black-blood axe in a ghoul's midsection, stepping on two others' ribs and neck as he attacked the ones before us, crushing the skull of the biggest one. "Out! Out now!"

I flopped up onto the ground as our remaining ghouls jumped on him. Fairuza grabbed hold of my leg and I heaved her out as I got to my feet. Legs shaking, I stumbled around

Ayman and his determined handful with Fairuza clinging to me.

"Get out, *now!*" Cyrus's bellow made me stumble to the entrance, but I still looked back, unable to bear leaving them. I caught the instant Cyrus and Ayman swung their blades at once, Ayman beheading a ghoul and Cyrus cutting off both its legs in one brutal swing.

It was a jarring thing to behold. These two palace-bred boys whom I'd been to luxurious halls, treasure vaults, temples and courtrooms with, unleashing their bloodthirst and violence, destroying these man-like creatures with such intensity. It was yet another part of Cyrus I'd never considered, never thought could exist. I didn't know why I never had. Warfare was part of a future king's education. At least that was what the folktales of a king and his knights claimed.

When I became certain they had the upper hand, were in no danger, I tore my eyes away from Cyrus's viciously excited face, from the glint of savagery in Ayman's eyes, and ran.

Water poured from my hair and clothes, my slippery feet drying against the dusty ground as I dragged Fairuza with me down all levels, where nothing but the two ghouls we'd killed remained.

The entry hall was littered with bodies, some ripped apart from their initial fight against one another, others fatally stabbed or beheaded with precision, while others showed signs of struggle, multiple stab wounds and crushed heads and necks. Only one was an intact body, its neck simply broken.

I didn't know why the body of a strangled ghoul struck me as the most terrifying. The bruising on its greying throat didn't look like the imprint of Ayman's gauntlets, neither were they big enough to be Cyrus's hands.

The last thing I needed to consider was the presence of another kind of monster.

"Are they all dead?" Fairuza shuddered, rubbing her hands up and down her arms.

"Seems so," I slurred, my exertion catching up with me as my legs wobbled and the world swayed. The coppery stench of blood mixing with the dust made my waterlogged head swim with nausea.

Urgency subsiding, I slowed my pace, allowing myself to be sluggish, unsteady and exhausted.

Suddenly, something cold and heavy slammed me into a wall. I heard a deafening crack inside my head. My sight flickered like a dying fire as my knees hit the ground.

I couldn't get back up, couldn't lift my eyelids to see what was bearing down on me. But I didn't need to see it. I felt its breath, heard its teeth separating. My drained body had had enough and refused to move away. It started the fainting process before my mind could join it.

I couldn't even call for Cyrus.

Its teeth neared my bruised cheek as I sagged against the wall, ready to be claimed by the darkness, to be dead to the world before it killed me. But an enraged shout followed by the sound of sprinting dropped a fleck of wakefulness into me.

Twitching lids cracking open, I saw a woman charge a long-haired ghoul with a pole blocking its swiping claws. The ghoul ripped it from her and she only reared back and rammed her forehead into its own.

Cora!

Fairuza dropped to my side, pulling at me, begging me to get up, but my eyes fell shut again.

Pain sparked through my face, rousing me as the stinging remains of a slap buzzed under my bruised cheek.

"Wake up!"

At Fairuza's shout, I somehow made it onto my knees, and with my hands on her shoulders, I got back to my feet. The wave of disorientation that hit me as I stood threatened to knock me back down.

"What happened?" I slurred, knees buckling, head too heavy for my neck.

"Sh-she just attacked it with a shovel," Fairuza stuttered, struggling to keep both of us upright. "Then she head-butted it—like a bull!"

I let out a delirious giggle, "Bullheaded."

Deciding that she was too much trouble, the ghoul turned from Cora and threw itself back at us. Cora thwacked its head with the shovel and it fell at our feet as we stumbled against the wall. It clawed at my dress, but Cora landed knees-first on its back and gripped its neck.

It flailed pathetically in her grip as she heaved and growled, strangling it with a force that darkened its face to murky grey.

A brief crack filled the air then it went limp in her hands.

I didn't realize I'd slid off the wall until Cora caught me, her embrace lifting me to my toes. I sagged against her, body heavy like a vat of mead, and exhaled with relief, though my heart still rattled me with its mad pounding.

I could only choke, "Thank you."

Cora only gave me a tight squeeze I couldn't return, then swung me over the dead body as Cyrus and Ayman arrived.

Ayman's silver armor had been completely painted black, and Cyrus' hair and shirt had been plastered to him with sticky blood, the dried splatters on his face framing his features, like they had been purposefully painted on him. With the way it contrasted with his skin and outlined his jaw, it made me think how regal he'd look with a short beard.

Nearly drowning had certainly jumbled my priorities, because his appearance ought to be the last thing on my mind right now. But even smeared in all the evidence of a true bloodbath, the sight of him filled me with wonder and soothed the pounding in my head and chest.

Cyrus rushed over, dripping axe in one hand, the other bloody and outstretched towards us. "Miss Greenshoot, we told you to stay back."

Cora just held out a hand to his axe. They traded, Cyrus handing her his weapon and holding out his arms to me. I stumbled towards him, reaching up to steady myself on his shoulders, but he bent down and scooped me up.

Screaming foot blissfully off the floor, I sagged in his strong hold, not caring that he reeked of blood and sweat and finally let myself feel safe.

"Are you hurt?" His eyes searched my face, etched with worry. "Did they scratch you? Bite you?"

"No," I said dazedly, the smoking tendrils of sleep curling in my head, behind my heavy eyes. "I'm…I'm…"

"Safe," he promised. "I have you now. I'll take care of everything. You can rest now."

And for the first time in ages, I did feel safe, cared for.

Delirious with relief, I finally let go and everything went dark.

CHAPTER TWENTY-FIVE

The world rocked and rumbled beneath me to a steady beat. An incessant gallop of hooves and a chafing spin of wheels.

But what had dragged me from the depths of darkness was the cacophony of voices arguing. My head on someone's lap and my feet on another's.

Groaning, I shifted, opening my eyes to be met with the head of a long-haired ghoul. My heart rammed against my ribs hard enough to bruise both, but I couldn't move yet, couldn't even lurch.

Then I realized what I was looking at, the setting before me slowly making sense, and I no longer needed to.

The ghoul's head sat by Ayman, and had Fairuza pressed against the end of their seat. The russet sunset cast a dramatic light and shadows into the carriage as it circled the base of the mountain, leaving it behind.

It was a conical purple mountain, smaller than I'd thought when I'd been lost inside. On its plateau wasn't a palace like Sunstone, but what looked like a giant bird's nest.

I realized that my head was in Cyrus's lap while my feet lay in Cora's.

I couldn't understand what they were saying. It required effort and I had no more to expend. But I got the idea when Cora reached over and punched Fairuza in the chest, right between her breasts.

That very spot between my own ribs spasmed, and I felt the urge to cough along with her. Knowing Cora, this had to be a weak point exploited by fighters, and today she had proved to be far stronger than I'd imagined. Maybe Cora's mother hadn't lied about her being fathered by a god. Anaïta smiling at me as I floated away from her underwater shrine proved that gods existed.

Having nearly died three or four times in the span of a few hours kept me stunned silent, unable to even tell them I was awake. I just lay there, reeling, my eyes aimed at either Cyrus's jaw or the end of the carriage, where the girls' seated stand-off looked less like a livid princess and a furious farm girl locking horns, and more like a rabbit trying to intimidate a mountain lion.

It took me back to our talk in the water. Even while admitting she had little influence and would only be traded in alliances, she still had riches and kings in her family, and power by extension. But in sheer, immediate power, Cora's rough hands trumped Fairuza's tiara. I had no power in any form.

"Not even pigs would eat you!" Cora spat venomously, fist poised for another hit.

Cyrus gripped her shoulder, pulling her back. "That's enough."

Cora pried his fingers off her, eyes flashing with outrage. "Enough is when she bleeds."

Fairuza coughed, fists protectively covering the spot Cora had hit. "You lay one more finger on me and I'll destroy you."

Cora bared her teeth in an intimidating snarl. "I'd like to see you try."

Fairuza slid a fearful look at the ghoul's head, the one Cora had killed with her bare hands.

Gulping, Fairuza tried her best to sneer. "I'd do far worse than hit you. I'd have all your mother's exports boycotted, and bankrupt your entire region."

Cora let out a big, mocking laugh that made both Ayman and Fairuza jerk. "And when will you issue this order? When you become Queen of Cahraman in thirty years? Or when you go back home and nag your uncle into refusing food from the most fertile region in the Folkshore, so he can starve your people and cripple your economy?"

"We'll farm our own crops!" Fairuza seemed back to her prideful self, each threat returning my sour opinion of her and making Cora's shoulders shake with silent laughter. "This will create a surplus in your produce that will devalue your currencies. And when your land falls we'll invade."

Cora snorted, settling back and crossing her long legs. "Farm your crops in what new land? Will you magically change your soil? Stop growing your own native fruits and exports? End your wine industry because you decide to grow wheat and sugar canes instead of grapes and berries? And will you also import people from Lower Campania to farm them for you? And if you don't and your crops fail and your people starve, they'll revolt and overthrow your family and the most powerful duke will ascend as your new king, reinstate trade with us, and stabilize your land. Oh, and one kingdom 'boycotting' our exports won't cause a surplus, it will merely lower the prices of some produce or we'll reschedule their trade during the colder months." She massaged her fingers, saving the first crack of her knuckles for dramatic effect to make Fairuza jump. "You don't understand anything about how lands are run, do you?"

"I understand what I need to know."

"Which is evidently nothing." Cora continued cracking her knuckles, making my own knuckles itch to be popped. "If you had an ounce of common sense, you would have known if you wanted to rule a land, you'd need to understand its native magic and be on good terms with whoever wields it. But you don't care, do you? Throwing around threats about your power to a woman who could dry out this land's lakes, wells and only river?" Cora popped her wrists, squeezing them, as if channeling her urge to throttle Fairuza. "Do you even understand that arid lands like Cahraman and Orestia need magic to support their populations? Did that cross your mind at all when we entered that witch-city to negotiate with their queen? Do you even know what negotiating is?"

"I'll do—"

"Nothing. Because you can't do anything," Cora cut her off coldly. "Except cause problems for the rest of us!"

Fairuza looked faint, but she still persisted, "If you're so confident that assaulting me will have no repercussions and you could run your land in your sleep, how did my being punished by the witch affect you?"

"Because you took my friend with you, you writhing larva!" Cora yelled, intimidating in her anger. "She nearly *died!*"

Warmth lit up within me. Cora had been worried about me, had strong-armed her way into the rescue mission. What surged deep in my soul was a different kind of gratefulness, a softer blossom of affection than the one I felt towards Cyrus.

Instead of sending Ayman and palace guards, they'd both insisted on braving any danger to save me themselves. Cyrus fearlessly massacring his way through monsters to reach me and carrying me out to safety would forever be a perfumed, precious moment in my life, worthy of an epic romantic poem among tales of chivalry.

But Cora killing just my attacker with her bare hands was a grim reminder, an embodiment of my feelings for Bonnie. I'd do anything to keep the beast away from her, to keep her safe. Cora had done for me what I had yet to do for Bonnie.

Cora had also irrevocably earned my trust. I had to tell her everything.

She deserved to know.

Fairuza pressed against the door in an insecure hunch. "I didn't mean for any of that to happen. She knows that."

"Whether you're an arsonist or an idiot, breaking a lantern on a haystack still burns down the barn." Cora set her hands on my legs, palms burning against my clammy skin. "Meant it or not, you still caused it."

Looking more cornered by the second, Fairuza choked, "Never did I expect to be educated on manners by someone who can't use a knife and fork."

"Never did I expect a princess to not know the difference between manners and morals," Cora said snidely. "I may eat with my hands, but I haven't tried to do away with my competition. Twice."

Fairuza burned red, then she seemed to give up and turned to stiffly face her window.

I looked up at Cyrus, who had his elbow perched on the window and his face in his palm, staring thoughtfully out the window as we approached Zhadugar.

"This feels like one of the many arguments my aunt and Lady Rostam had, doesn't it?"

I thought he was speaking to me, until Ayman grumbled, "Their tiffs were at least entertaining. The effort they went through to insult each other indirectly was a sport in itself."

Cyrus chuckled tiredly, rubbing his forehead, smearing it further. "Do you think any of this would have happened if Lady Rostam was still here?"

"No," Ayman said at once. "Knowing her, the magic test would have been something benign like having them look in an enchanted mirror or trying to trap a *jann*."

Benign? Nariman was capable of being benign?

"Trapping a *jann!*" Cyrus exclaimed. "Why didn't we have that option? That would have been far safer than putting them in a room with Marzeya."

Ayman tsked, the click echoing through his helmet. "Too late for that. Besides, what would you do with a lesser genie?"

Cyrus shrugged. "Have it grant menial wishes?"

I finally found my voice. "Didn't you say there was a ring that granted wishes?"

Everyone jumped in their seats.

Cyrus and Cora helped me sit up. My world swayed, like there was still water that sloshed through my head. Gripping both to steady myself, I surveyed the carriage from the new perspective, reading their faces.

Fairuza remained in her corner, hands still curled over her chest, which rose and fell heavily, betraying her blank expression. Ayman, covered in his blood-blackened armor, only inclined his head at me. I turned to face Cyrus first, who was unbothered by his sticky, filthy state but emanating concern for me, his dark brows lowered, his clear eyes searching my face.

"How are you feeling?" he asked, tenderly touching the side of my temple, like he was feeling for my mind's pulse. At his soft touch, my heartbeat slowed to a quiet ebb and flow of warm blood, which spread under my skin in a flushing wave, melting away the icy fear that had turned my ribcage to an icebox.

He cared for me, he truly did.

Unable to withstand the intensity of my conflicted feelings now, I turned to Cora, who had set a hand on my shoulder, her fair brows and full mouth tight with worry.

She already knew enough, I just had to fill the gaps for her, and see what she thought of my situation, because out of anyone here she was the most world-weary. If she thought I could tell him, I would. If not...

I didn't know if I could risk it. Risk the Fairborns' safety for my own desire to be honest with him.

"Ada?" Cora pressed the back of her hand against my forehead. "You feel warm."

"I feel like I need to sleep for a hundred years," I mumbled, groggy and tired.

Fairuza let out a small cough.

We watched each other, all that we'd gone through in the mountain flipping through my memory like the windblown pages of a picture book. I wondered if her horrified gaze meant that she was reliving some of those moments.

The carriage came to a stop as I reached for the sapphire necklace still resting on my collarbones. Ayman jumped down first, opening the door for us. Cyrus got out, hand held up for me. I took his hand, but I couldn't get up. I was stuck to my seat like there was an iron trunk on my lap. Fairuza broke our staring contest by getting up. But she was cowed back by Cora, who stuck her hands under my arms and lifted me up.

Practically handing me to Cyrus, Cora then snatched up the ghoul's head and stepped down. Fairuza was the last one out.

Cyrus attempted to steady me, but my leaden legs tugged the rest of me down with them. He caught me before my knees could hit the dunes and all I wanted was to drop my face into his shoulder and fall back asleep.

Pressing an arm against my back, he started to scoop me up. I eagerly awaited another embrace to happily fall asleep in, but Ayman blocked him.

"We have company now. Wouldn't want anyone to accuse you of favoritism at this delicate stage." Ayman extended his arms. "Not to mention, after swinging about that war-axe for an hour, you could throw out your back."

Cyrus threw a look in the other carriages' direction. "Are you implying that I'm weak or that she's too heavy for me?"

"To be fair, she is quite tall."

"Cora is taller," Cyrus argued.

"Cora's a horse."

Cyrus snorted dismissively, but stepped aside, allowing Ayman to pick me up.

It was a rough, quick sweep that made me yelp, and the press of his cold armor against my back and the backs of my knees and thighs bit through my still damp clothes.

I still gave him my best appreciative smile. He wanted to avoid problems for both of us. I also didn't want to be forced to walk and I didn't want Cyrus hunched with an aching back tomorrow.

"You joining us?" Cyrus asked Fairuza, who remained standing, looking right at me.

I touched the necklace, felt the smooth oval stones and the bands of gold that linked them, and turned away from her. I had nothing to say to her, nothing either I or Cora hadn't already thrown at her.

The three of us caught up with Cora at the top of the Zhadugar valley, where the sunset glow had given way to dozens of giant lanterns that made the city a glittering pit. In front of the other carriages were Farouk, Loujaïne, Ariane and shooting towards us, arms outstretched and kicking up a sandstorm was Cherine.

"ADAAA!" She nearly tripped over her skirt as she slammed herself into Ayman to get to me in his arms. Wincing at how he must feel at this, I removed my arm from around his neck, almost tipping myself out of his hold, to hug her back.

"What happened? Where did you go? Are you hurt?" Cherine pulled back, her face shining with wetness, wrinkling her nose. "You all smell like death! Did you nap in a butcher shop?"

Cora raised the ghoul's head. "Close."

Cherine reared back with a screech of horror. The rest of our group closed in, their demands no different than hers.

"Apparently, the thing in our old quarters wasn't a ghoul," I said, patting Ayman's shoulder. Even beneath the hard armor, I could feel him stiffen against me.

"What do you mean?" Cherine shook violently avoided the ghoul's head.

"You said it was a man with red eyes," I said. "These things have no eyes, noses or anything to say they are men or women."

"Then what was it?"

"A lost palace guard maybe?"

"With white hair?" she shouted, still horrified by the head

or the mention of the 'ghoul' that had given her a few bedtime scares.

"Some people are very, very blond?"

I heard Ayman mumble, "What are you doing?"

I patted his armor, which rang loud enough to conceal my response. "Doing you a favor."

Cherine moved to Ayman's left, linking her arm with his, to walk alongside us while facing away from Cora's morbid trophy. "You found the necklace! Where was it?"

My exhaustion doubled at the question. "Literally the last place I wanted to look. Finding it was a nightmare."

"Tell me all about it on the way back to Sunstone. It looks like you've had quite the adventure," she babbled excitedly. "We could commission a poet to commemorate it in a dramatic fashion and distribute it at court."

My focus made a jarring swerve when Loujaïne gripped Cyrus by the shoulders. "What were you thinking?"

"What was *I* thinking?" he huffed mirthlessly. "You're the one who brought them here, knowing how witches respond to slights."

"They came to do one simple thing. The thing they will do as princess and queen when they speak on your behalf—be courteous and accommodating to butter up negotiations. That it went so far out of control is not my fault."

"You're the one who accused me of having no foresight by calling this search." He raised his voice, brimming with anger. "Where was your foresight in this situation?"

"That is not the issue here. You're the crown prince, our *only* prince, and you put yourself in danger, and for what? The guards would have gotten them later." She advanced to cup his face and stroke his hair, like an anxious mother fussing over her wayward child as she scolded him.

But Cyrus hadn't run down the stairs or pulled a wild dog's tail, he had charged into a lethal situation with only one guard to back him up.

"*Ameti*, we couldn't afford to wait. They were close to dying by the time we reached them." Cyrus didn't dodge her fussing, tried to soothe her with far more familiarity than usual. "We had an idea where they were and knew what lived there. You couldn't have expected me to wait for next morning to bring piles of guardsmen." He touched her hands before carefully removing them. "If we waited we would have been holding a funeral for two empty coffins."

"He's safe." Farouk laid a comforting hand on her shoulders, turning her away from Cyrus. "They're all safe, and that's all that matters."

Ayman came to stand behind him. Loujaïne's eyes went to Ayman first, then to me, or my throat more likely. But if she had initially opened her mouth to comment on the necklace, she put it aside to ask what had been on my mind. "Where were they exactly and how did you know of it?"

Cyrus only said, "Mount Alborz, near the Gulf."

Both Loujaïne and Farouk stiffened, but it felt for different reasons. Farouk's was a more general cringe, like he had only heard of it. Loujaïne appeared to be reliving a haunting memory.

I repeated a variation of his aunt's question. "How did you know to find us in that place?"

Cyrus and Ayman shared a quick look. Cyrus tapped his fingers on his axe's blade. "We may or may not have been there before."

Loujaïne's unease seemed to turn to nausea, her olive skin tinged with green in the lights of the city and carriage lanterns. "Do I want to know how or why?"

"The 'how' part isn't important." Cyrus shrugged. "As for the 'why'—we were looking for something."

"When was that?" she pressed.

"When we were still in Almaskham. Prince Salman's wife had told us about a simurgh that built its nest above that mountain, and all about how special it was in all our old tales, so, we had to see it. When Marzeya said she'd thrown them into a mountain of forgotten nightmares, I knew it had to be that one, and thankfully, I was right."

"And what did you see the first time and this time as well?" Loujaïne persisted, anger climbing.

"This." Cora swung the ghoul's head at Loujaïne, ripping a petrified scream from her.

Guffaws blew across the dunes and Marzeya appeared with a flash, white hair braided with a silk, black scarf, red eyes like hot coals. "You girls have proven to be far more entertaining than I thought you'd be."

Farouk stepped before Loujaïne and Ariane, arms out to shield them as Marzeya approached, humming joyously, red skirt and sleeves fluttering in the nighttime breeze.

"You though," she said to Ariane. "Proved to be quite silly and tame. Shame, I always thought redheads to be vivacious and adventurous." She stopped before us, addressing Cora first. "You, on the other hand, I have to wonder, what would it take to scare something like you?"

If she had objected to being referred to as *something*, Cora didn't show it. She gave the witch her usual bland expression and drawled, "Can't you tell? I thought you saw right through all of us."

"Second sight has its limitations, dearie," Marzeya said fondly. "These boys knew of the mountain and what slumbered within it, but did you?"

Cora shrugged. "What does it matter?"

Marzeya bared her sharp teeth in a knowing grin. "Not now, but as with all choices, it will matter later."

Looking annoyed, Cora cocked her head. "Meaning?"

Marzeya blinked slowly and her pupils constricted, like a snake's. "When War shakes the heavens and the Wind uproots you from fields to shores to aeries, follow the poppy trail beneath the earth. And when you embrace the darkness, your iron will be forged as your crown."

Cora crossed her arms, holding the head like a lantern, the only shift to her expression a raised eyebrow. "I thought only fairies spoke in riddles."

"It's not a riddle, dearie. It's a promise."

Though I wanted my own answers from Marzeya, I started when she snapped her head in my direction. "I see you found the necklace."

"No thanks to you," I said, sounding a lot braver than I felt. "You said you would leave it for me."

"And I did. I also said you would perform a task to obtain it, as you offered to do." The witch held the biggest sapphire, tilting it to watch the starburst crossing the stone. "Don't look so glum, I've done you a favor."

"A favor? How is making me almost drown myself to get out alive a favor?"

Marzeya gave me a smug smirk. "In the future many of your problems will look manageable, or even easy, in comparison to what you experienced today." She checked behind me. "As for the princess, I just wanted to teach her a lesson."

"If anything you reinforced her beliefs about you," I hissed, the heat not just from my climbing fever, but from my frustration with her.

"Good. It will teach her to be more diplomatic with things

like me. No good ever comes from attacking those more powerful than you." At that, she met my eyes in an intent stare, playing with the ring on her finger. "You first need to reach their level through new means, so you can surprise them before defeating them."

She was right in a sense. Dealing with her and her wrath, a far older and stronger witch, made Nariman less scary to me.

As for the last thing she'd said, it solidified the idea that I must try to overpower Nariman. To do that, I had to have something to give me the power I lacked. Something Nariman wouldn't expect. Which wouldn't be the lamp. If the king had used it against her, it was likely she now knew how to resist or deflect its magic.

It brought me back to the choices presented to me in the dream. If it were real, I would choose the ring, and have it bring me the lamp—and the dress.

There was still so much I wanted to ask Marzeya. About opening a portal to Arbore for me to find the Fairborns. About Nariman, about my mother—about myself. If my mother had been a witch, did that mean I could do magic?

But all those questions would betray my lies.

Forgoing my burning questions, I asked, "Where would one find that kind of power?"

"Finding power isn't the issue. It's learning *how* to use it."

I held back a groan. Vague answers were worse than none. But she wasn't going to make this easy for me.

To avoid Marzeya, Loujaïne, Farouk, Cherine and Ariane were now huddled by the carriages, and Cyrus had gone to them. They were talking. Arguing. The ones close enough to hear me were Cora and Ayman, I now didn't mind Cora knowing everything, but Ayman would tell Cyrus.

"Did you tell Cora her future?" I asked.

"In a way." Marzeya smirked, eyes glowing in the falling darkness. Cora curled her lip in a quiet snarl. "Would you like to hear yours?"

"Yes."

She tilted her head and stared, not at me but through me, eyes pulsating like twin red-hot coals in a bed of ashes. "You'll find all the answers you seek, but not before you cross the wastes into the realm of a thousand doors. No matter what you find beyond each door, do not leave the path beneath the peaks. Only through appeasing your foe will you know peace."

What could any of that mean? It sounded like pure nonsense to me.

"You can't be more specific, can you?"

"Now where is the fun in that?" Her eyes flit to Ayman. "How about you, the prince's pale shadow? Your distant past is more intriguing than your near future."

"Why is that?" he asked, neutral, quiet.

A humorous glimmer fluttered the heat in her eyes. "Let's just say that you'll come to a standstill."

He didn't comment on or question her claim. When she flicked her hand, dismissing us, he just nodded once and carried me past her. I watched her and Zhadugar shrink from over his shoulder.

Marzeya lazily turned to wave at me. "Goodbye, and remember, don't go through any of the doors."

The only way she could make sense was if she was talking about what I had just gone through. That I had crossed the wasteland that was the mountain, and the realm of a thousand doors had to be Sunstone, or even its palace. Appeasing my foe to know peace—I hadn't appeased Fairuza, I'd only kept her alive. Which left Nariman.

If—when—I found the lamp, I had to give it to her. But

there was no way I wasn't going to try to stop her from using it. That didn't sound so appeasing.

When Ayman set me inside the carriage, Cyrus came to see me off and I caught his arm. "Thank you, for coming for us. You didn't need to, but you did."

"I couldn't lose you." He put a hand over mine. "If it were up to me, you'd outlive me in our old age."

Had I wanted to smother my smile, I couldn't have. Brimming with adoration it spilled out into a dreamy, croaking laugh. "I didn't know you liked having me around that much."

"Ada." He gripped my hand with both of his, shaking them, making a passionate point that traveled down my arm and flared up to my tight throat. "You came into my life like a summer storm, upended my expectations and scattered them to the four winds. But by the gods, you'll stay through the winds of all the seasons of my life."

The passion he expressed had me overcome with joyous disbelief. It was all I wanted, too, to be with him ever after.

But Nariman taking me through the portal felt like I'd been whisked off to Cahraman on the east wind. Half of me still wanted to land back where I'd been.

"What if I leave with the west wind?" I whispered.

"Then I'll chase you like a madman at sea."

My laugh came out more of a sob this time. "How do you chase the winds?"

"With magic, I suppose." He let go of my hand, jumping off the carriage steps. "This is likely the worst time to ask, but how goes the search for your ridiculous gold lamp?"

I gaped at him. "You remember!"

"You think I'd forget the very reason we met?"

"When you put it that way…"

He chuckled, waving it off. "Don't worry, I have people looking for it."

Gratitude and concern butted heads within me. "You do?"

"I'm close to finding that ring too, or I think I am."

"Cyrus, how can I ever thank you?"

"By spending all of tomorrow resting, then meeting me the day after."

I wanted to drag him back, embrace and kiss him. But I couldn't yet, not without causing problems we could both do without.

I wanted nothing to rock the boat now I had options. If he found me the ring, I might have the means to overpower Nariman. If he also found me the lamp, I'd save the Fairborns and have him, no need to choose. If he didn't, and I still won, I would be welcomed by the king into his quarters, where I'd swipe the lamp and carry out my original plan.

Options were a luxury I hadn't dreamed of minutes ago, even if each came with mountains of uncertainty and risk.

But so what? Nothing could be worse than the catastrophe Fairuza had pulled me into.

CHAPTER TWENTY-SIX

The ghouls were chasing Bonnie, Fairuza and I
through the Hornswoods.

We didn't get far before Marzeya's black-nailed hands
broke through the earth and dragged us back to the mountain.

I watched in horror as Cyrus and Ayman failed their
rescue and were ripped apart before me. Ayman's head landed
before me in the water, only to be picked back by its long,
white hair and swayed like a lantern. Through the sideways
swings of his head, blood splattered everywhere and his face
blurred, skin, eyes and hair darkening, morphing from his to
mine. My head broke its own jaw with the power of its morti-
fied scream.

I woke up, struggling, not screaming but wheezing as I
cried, hands around my own neck. I only felt the thin
bandages for the cuts below my jaw bunching up. All the
bruises I'd sustained pulsated with searing pain, and I felt hot
needles were being stabbed into every bone of my right foot.

Staring at the canopy of my bed, I inhaled and exhaled,

hoping to calm my heart and suppress the traumatizing events and the nightmares they spawned.

I forced myself to think of the better parts of the trip to Zhadugar. Fairuza and I had gotten out alive, with no lasting injuries, Cyrus had insisted on coming for us himself, had known where to look and had come just in time, and neither he nor Ayman were harmed.

We were all safe and far, far away from Marzeya and the ghouls. We had avoided the fate of the people who had lived within the mountain.

One memory poked its ugly head above the surface. The mummified corpses of the three girls in their room.

Breath shuddering past my trembling lips, insides quivering with dread, I sat up, shutting my eyes, drowning all thoughts of the harrowing event in the memory of those moments in the flooded shrine. Calm waves spread through my mind as I reimagined the cool, quiet weightlessness of the pool, along with the rose quartz sculpture of Anaïta.

The meditative breathing and calmness ended abruptly as someone kicked my door open.

Cora stood in the doorway, hair in a long braid that sat over her shoulder, a basket balanced over her head, and a tray on her arm. The smell of roasted corn wafted over with the breeze from the open window. But the smell that resettled my calmness was from that tray, that pot.

Coffee. Not the Almaskhami spicy, yellow coffee, but actual black, freshly-brewed coffee.

"Morning." She greeted tiredly, kicking the door shut. "Care for an ear?"

I let out the breath my startled chest had trapped, relieved it was just her. "We're going to have breakfast later."

"The breakfast here is disgusting." She dropped the basket

on the table before setting the tray. "Beans, boiled eggs and weird, tiny, delicacy fishes."

"You're not wrong." I untangled myself from the bed covers, only to trip when my bound foot touched the floor and the stove-flame pain flared within it. I dove for the floor, arms up to shield my face, but Cora caught me by the back of my nightgown.

Effortlessly, she hauled me to the squat, wooden table. I smothered a brief alarm at her strength. She'd snapped the ghoul's neck with nothing but her weight and aggravation.

She dropped down to the carpet, bringing me down with her. "How's your foot?"

"Feels like it has been run over by a cart laden with mead barrels." I leaned back cautiously on a red and yellow-tasseled cushion, foot propped on its twin. In yesterday's spiraling storm of turmoil, I hadn't paid any attention to the escalating pain from my toes. Only when I had been turned over to the palace physician and his nurses to bathe and treat did I realize how hard I had kicked the ghoul. Crushing its skull had pulverized all my toenails—resulting in them being pulled out —and three toes. The physician, Master Wasim, said it was a wonder I hadn't broken every bone in my foot.

"And everything else?"

I shrugged as I rubbed my brow and lids. Though not yet harsh, the early morning light still felt like pinpricks to my eyeballs. "Better than it could have been."

Humming, she poured me a cup. "I'm not going to bother asking if you slept well."

"Wise choice." I piled sugar into it, stirring quickly to taste and add small splashes of milk. "Where did you find this?"

"I bought it when we went down to the market," she said distractedly, handing me an ear of corn. "They get good imports here. A lot directly from my family's farmlands. I always knew most of our sunflower seeds went to the east but I never thought they'd all end up in piles here."

Content with her being my only company, I bit rows off my cob, relishing the freedom of talking with my mouth full with no Cherine to reprimand me. "What's it like, living on a farm?"

Cora did the same, some of the stray fibers from the corn's peel coming out with her mouthful. "Busy. You get up early to feed the animals and make sure everyone else is doing their jobs. There's fresh eggs to be picked from the henhouse and cows to milk and stalls to clean and water to replenish. And depending on the season, you plow the earth or plant seeds or pick the fresh batches from their soil. We've started growing watermelons the past couple of years. They're a weird fruit." She paused to swallow. "Anyway, your day starts before dawn and ends way past sunset and you get dirty and sweaty hauling stuff or scrubbing or shoveling. Generally doing something with your hands, something physical and grueling."

And she loved it because it was. She could easily be the storybook princess if she wanted, but she was against taking the easy way out, which had chased her through multiple eliminations.

Though if she had wanted to win, she'd reinvent what it meant to be a queen. No king would fear leaving the kingdom to Cora. Apart from all the eclectic and vital things she knew, from how lands were run to how people behaved, she would scare any ambitious ministers or enemies into groveling submission and personally swing the axe at traitors' executions.

I shuddered at the thought. "You know, until you I didn't know anyone can be so against becoming a princess."

As I said that, I thought of Cyrus' mother and both of his aunts and their apparently unhappy marriages to princes. Nariman's story was too hard to ignore or even discount as a rare case. As for what Fairuza said in the mountain, that she had nothing to look forward to, that her entire life hinged upon a prince marrying her—it made me reconsider my escapist fantasy. The one I reserved for brief moments of peace, where I was in Fairuza's place with her lineage, family, dresses and confidence.

Cora set her bare cob down, took another. "A born princess? Maybe. A princess consort? Certainly not."

I exhaled. "What's the difference?"

"Power." She chomped another mouthful. "Precisely power over your own life."

"How so?"

"If you were born into a royal family and raised knowing your powers and limitations, you have a huge advantage over any clueless girl who marries into your family. You have power of your own stemming from your birthright not from your marriage, and you know the place, people, culture and family and how to deal with them all. It's why royals marry their relatives so often. It makes things easier when both sides know what to expect."

Though in Marzeya's house my assumptions about Cyrus' mother and aunt had swung from branch to branch up a tree of interconnected theories, Cora now made me consider the difference between them.

As a king's daughter, did Loujaïne have power over Jumana, a mere princess consort? Had she abused that power? If so, what would she do to the girl Cyrus picked, if she wasn't her choice?

Not wanting to dwell on that, I asked, "How do you know

so much about this?"

"My aunt Junia married a merchant-prince in one of Campania's oligarchies."

I leaned in, thinking back to Lord Dufreyne, the only merchant-prince I knew, the one whose house I'd robbed the day Nariman found me. "And?"

"And she was stupid to do so," Cora said venomously. "She didn't even know him! He saw her at a wedding and proposed to her on the spot. She agreed and left with him to his city. Now not a month goes by without her running back, and her visits are depressing. She complains all the time about how much she hates him, how his mistress, who is from his king-dom, and their bastards get better treatment than her and my cousins and how she can't stand living in the city."

That was not helping my conflicted feelings. In fact, it tangled them up even more.

"Then what will you do when you go home?"

"What I've been doing till now. Work. I have chores with the others, activities with my friends, festivals to set up, then I'll see if I can find a man who has no issue being outranked by me so I can do what all the women in my line have done."

"Which is?"

"Have a girl or two and later succeed my mother as Mistress of the Granary."

I regarded her, trying to picture her future. "That's what you want to do?"

"It's what I was born for, brought up in and trained to do."

"Is that any different than most of the girls whose expecta-tions are set for them from birth, who came here to marry...him?"

Her scrunched-up expression plainly said *Are you stupid?*

Then she put it into words, emphasizing each one. "Of

course, it's different. I'll be in charge of a place I know, with people I know, who will answer to me and respect me. Whereas the alternative is my family getting rid of me and benefitting from marrying me off to a stranger in a foreign land where I have no respect, power or experience. Where I'll have to learn everything from scratch and forever remain an outsider. There's just no comparison." She wiped her mouth on the back of her hand. "I don't want to be trapped in a strange place, with people I don't know, who don't care about me, and will be in control of me because they've been here longer. And that's why I want to leave."

"Then why didn't you take Loujaïne's offer to leave at the start?"

"Because I'm really here on business, for trade between our regions," she said. "I'll be selling them my exports and buying theirs for a good price later. So I wanted them to disqualify me, and owe me for it. I couldn't say I quit and burn bridges on my way out."

"You swung a ghoul head at Loujaïne."

She snorted a laugh, waving off my point. "What's she going to do about it? Tell everyone in the kingdom and beyond that she knowingly sent us into a volatile area rife with witches and that two of her charges were almost ripped apart by monsters because of it?"

I shuddered, gulping the last mouthful of coffee. "How are you so sure of everything? How do you not worry about things going wrong?"

"I'm not, and I do."

"You sure seem unsurprised by every situation."

"That's my face." She stared at me with a grim expression.

For a moment, I thought I'd upset her, something only Fairuza had managed so far. But she just cracked a wry smile.

"I'm joking. Nothing here surprises me because I've seen it before or heard many similar accounts, all the same throughout history with the same results. And it's not the first or even twelfth time a noble threatened me. The novelty wore off by the time I understood how much influence most actually hold."

"Ever been threatened by a witch or magical creature though? You held your ground quite well yesterday."

"The Granary is full of magical oddities and people, and both ends of Campania are rife with magic. I've travelled around all of them since I could toddle and asked as many questions as I could." She paused to pick kernel coats out of her teeth with her fingernails. "As for nobles, mages, and monsters, I've learned about which I'll likely deal with in my life and how to exploit their flaws and limits."

"So, you've dealt with ghouls before?"

"Not exactly. But lamiae aren't too different, more reptilian but still toothy and eyeless and dumb. They have a habit of stealing our goats and draining them of blood when they can't find children to eat." She talked as if about a common pest rather than a man-eating monster. "Usually I behead them with shovels, but when worse comes to worst, you can smother or strangle them."

"You're not afraid they'd bite your arm off?"

Deadly serious, her green eyes narrowed with contempt. "The last one that tried to do that got my entire arm shoved down its throat. It choked before it could chomp it off."

I couldn't help gaping at her, awe and disbelief swirling in my head like smoke on still water. No matter how experienced and confident she was, it didn't seem like she experienced fear the same way I did.

I'd thought Fairuza was inferior to me as a self-reliant

person. But Cora was the true superior being among us.

"What are you?" left my mouth before I could hold my tongue.

"A homesick farmer who has no care to spare, especially for the idle rich."

The corners of my mouth curled with fondness. "But if it's about establishing trade relationships, did it have to be you? Aren't there other daughters of merchant-princes and oligarchs that could have represented Lower Campania?"

"My mother is the closest thing to a queen in our area. If I said no and sent someone else's daughter in my place we could have lost allies or potential trade deals." Cora considered a thought then snorted humorously. "Imagine if we sent my cousin Chloë!"

"Chloë is your Aunt Junia's daughter, right? Or was that Cassia?"

She raised her brows at me, pleased. "Nice to know you listen to everything I say. But it's Chloë. She's what nobles would call third-in-line for the title of Mistress of the Granary." When I just stared at her, she huffed. "You know what a line of succession is, right?"

"Sort of?" I sounded as uncertain as I was.

"In a family with hereditary titles, if one heir dies, they have an ordered line of relatives that should follow as new leader. Sometimes it gets complicated, if there are no direct relatives like the Shamash family."

My attention locked onto her words. "What do you mean?"

"I mean the king has only one son and no brothers, so, if something happens to Cyrus before he has children, there are too many relatives who could qualify as his next in line, and you'll have a divided kingdom on your hands. That's how the Avestan Empire fell."

Before I could process this piece of momentous informa-tion, she gave me an expectant look with brows raised, a handless nudge. "You?"

All of the sudden, I found the inside of my empty cup interesting. I stared into it, unfocused, mulling over all that I heard from her now, from Fairuza yesterday, and from Nariman at the beginning of the week.

"Ada."

"You already know," I mumbled.

"I know you're not who you say you are, not from where you claim to be and barely know what you're doing." She scrutinized me for a minute, an intrigued smirk pulling at her lips. "You're a spy, aren't you?"

I jolted, finding "spy" even worse than "thief."

But now that I considered it, that must be the specific suspicious vibe I'd been giving off to her and possibly Loujaïne. "You're not wrong about the first part, but no…" I sighed heavily. "…that's not what I'm here for."

"Then what are you here for?" Cora set her chin in her palm, surveying me with serene amusement. "Because it's not for him."

"It used to be that way." I admitted quietly. "What are you going to do with that head?"

"Get it embalmed. And don't change the subject. Let's start with where you're really from."

"Ericura, it's—"

"You mean Hericeurra?" She asked, astounded, an expres-sion I didn't think her capable of. "That place exists?"

"You know of it?"

"In myths and legends, yes. They say it's a land that drifted far from our world and into the fairies' realm, but few believe it to be real."

"It's real, and I'm from there." She whistled in wonder. After a moment of letting her digest that, I had to ask her what I'd been wondering about since day one. "You've been covering for me since we first met, basically feeding me lies that got me out of many tight spots. Why?"

She simply shrugged. "Honestly, I just thought you'd be good fun."

I gaped at her. "What?"

"You were shifty yet inexperienced in whatever you were sent here to do, so you were going to bring a lot of excitement to this stuffy competition." She laughed slightly. "And you did, but not how I expected you to."

"How so?"

"You did the opposite of all operatives I've come across. You didn't sabotage anyone's chances or harm anyone, you've gotten more attention than anyone, both good and bad, but you didn't use that to manipulate anyone. All that made your presence here even more puzzling."

"You kept my secret because I *entertained* you?"

"There's that, then there's the fact that I liked you on sight, which is rare." She patted my shoulder. "So, I started sort of helping, to make sure you'd stick around longer."

I couldn't help returning her smile, a warm fondness unwinding my tension. "I don't know if I should be touched or concerned by your priorities."

She winked at me playfully. "Both. Both are good."

I giggled tiredly, scratching at my itching bandages. "Thank you, for everything."

"Anytime." She handed me another ear of corn, boiled and buttered this time. "So, what are you really here for?"

I took a deep breath then told her everything.

When Cora left, I found a green box of sweets by the door.

The note on top instructed me to *"Have a sweet after each dose of medicine."*

The elegant handwriting was the same as the poetic responses in the metal boxes.

Cyrus's handwriting.

As told, I cleaned my tongue with the sticky sweets in between cups of pungent pain-numbing draughts and soothing teas. Their combined effect kept knocking me off the dock of wakefulness and into more turbulent depths with only one exception. An ambiguous dream involving bird feathers, a floating carpet and a fountain.

It was interrupted by Cherine barging in, hassling me up and out of bed.

Supplied with more bitter concoctions, and a cane to limp on, I was too drowsy to remember how I got dressed or got to the dining room for lunch.

It was an awkward affair. Cyrus and Ayman were missing.

Miraz must have been with them, as Aurelia showed up alone, ate in silence as she watched us, then left without saying a word to anyone.

I faded in and out of focus, catching wisps of the small-talk Cora and Ariane made about Orestian and Campanian culture with Cherine's interruptions. Farouk and Loujaïne whispered among themselves while Fairuza stared at the wooden clock on the wall.

She watched every swing of the pendulum with an empty, pale face. A haunted air hung about her like she was counting down the minutes to a dreaded event. It was like she expected the swarm of ghouls to burst through the walls like they had in the mountain.

I wanted to talk to her about it, because she was now the only person I could relate to in that ordeal, but I didn't have the capacity to do so. I couldn't even find the words to offer her some of the numbing solutions Master Wisam had prescribed me.

Drowsiness amplified with the medicines coursing through my bloodstream, the hour set for lunch dragged on for what felt like a week. In between one trip into dazed distraction and the next, Cora spoon-fed me cream barley and fig jam. My return to the present began when I began digesting, the food soaking in my painkilling solutions.

The nightmare about the Hornswoods loomed back into view, replaying every instant of Bonnie's terror as we fled the ghouls. My mind was trying to tell me something, remind me of my duty to her. It wasn't like I could forget my deadline. It was all I could think about…

No. I hadn't thought about it as much as I should have this week.

It wasn't that I'd forgotten what I was here for. That wasn't even possible. But I'd been too caught up with life here, with the girls and the tests. With Cyrus. With my feelings for him, what he meant to me.

But I had two days left, and I still hadn't figured out a contingency plan if I didn't win and managed to steal the lamp while being congratulated by the king.

Which brought me back to the same old question: how was I supposed to do that?

That question had raked tracks in my brain by now, with no feasible answer in sight. How would I be able to steal a conspicuous object like the lamp, in such lofty and dangerous company only to get past all the guards and disappear from the palace?

I'd give anything now to be able to turn into a ghost or a shadow and slip past people and through walls without being spotted—

Ayman.

Ayman, when not masquerading as Cyrus's personal guard in full armor, had mastered the art of sneaking around unseen and used the tunnels to pop in and out all over the place. If there was a trap door that led to the king's quarters, he'd know it.

I'd wanted him and Cyrus to take me through there the night the Final Five had been pronounced. Then it had become impossible to tell Cyrus, and I hadn't thought I could ask Ayman without it getting back to him. But—now I felt I might be able to ask him to keep it a secret.

Though I was dying to tell Cyrus the truth.

The urge to come clean was a dagger slowly sinking deeper into my chest by the second.

But I'd asked myself this a thousand times: Would his feelings for me survive the truth? It wasn't a mere hypothetical question anymore, but would soon be put to the test.

No. I couldn't tell him anything. Not now. I couldn't afford the distraction or the upheaval if things went wrong with him. Not until I got back the Fairborns.

One gamble at a time.

Until then, I had to continue playing the role of Lady Ada of Rose Isle.

I had to continue deceiving him.

CHAPTER TWENTY-EIGHT

*N*ext morning was notable for two things. I had a rendezvous with Cyrus. And Fairuza didn't come to breakfast

Prince Miraz sat in her vacated spot, on Cyrus's right, and I'd given Aurelia my seat on his left. They were the only two who still stayed from our second test guests.

"Where is she?" Cherine asked, mixing heavy cream and apricot jam in her bowl.

Cora paused her open-mouthed chewing. "Probably hiding in shame."

"Did she finally realize she's a horrible person?" Cherine suggested amusedly.

"More like she finally realized she isn't the best thing since horseless carriages." Cora snuck a spoon of Cherine's mix for her bread. "Imagine, after all that money and all those years of training, you find out you're completely useless."

"What do you mean?" Cherine asked, now very interested.

Cora aimed her spoon at me, splattering me with sticky droplets. "Ada embarrassed the pearls off of her twice in a row. She did all the talking and negotiating with Aurelia and Marzeya. It doesn't help that she now owes Ada her life."

I was about to point out that we had saved each other but Cherine interrupted me, giggling excitedly. "Ooh, it must burn, being a princess and being showed up by a poor, backwater girl who has no experience or finesse—no offense, darling."

"None taken. But seriously, we owe each other, she saved me as much as I saved her. She killed a ghoul with her hoopskirt! It not for her this—" I pointed to my bandaged neck. "—would have been the end for me."

Both girls stared at me, Cora considering my statement, Cherine stubbornly dismissing it with a "Pfft!"

At the head of the table, Cyrus gave me a warm, approving smile, before continuing to talk to Aurelia and Miraz.

Looking pointedly at Ayman who stood beside him, I nudged Cherine. "What would you do if you found the silver prince of your dreams?"

Her eyes grew dreamy at once. "I would ask him so many questions. Where he came from, what he's doing here, who he is, if it's true that people with silvery hair have magical powers and if he is, in fact, a prince."

"What if he's not?"

"Then he must be some kind of ambassador if he's here," she reasoned. "Members of the royal family can be ambassadors. Miraz might end up being that someday."

"Aside from asking all these questions, what would you do if you met him?"

"I'd make him stay with me." Her answer was unhesitating, instantaneous.

"For what?"

"I don't know, I just want him to stay. I mean, we had to

meet at some point, why else would I dream of him if it wasn't a sign from the gods?"

I decided to test the waters. "What if I found him for you?"

Cherine slowly turned her head towards me, spoonful of cream still in her mouth.

Cora peeked over her head. "How would you find her imaginary suitor?"

"I think I saw him last week."

"Could you? Could you really?" Cherine jumped in her seat, spoon falling out of her mouth.

"I think I could."

She squealed and hugged me, catching the attention of everyone at the table.

When Cyrus turned to give me another smile, I felt even worse than ever that I'd be going behind his back.

AFTER WE WERE DISMISSED. I WHISPERED TO CORA TO DISTRACT Cherine then limped towards Cyrus who'd stopped by the door last, Ayman right behind him.

"I believe we'll meet again shortly?" Cyrus set his hand on my arm. The cool metal of his rings pressed lightly against my hot skin, filling my head with steam that I felt coming out my ears, deflating my anxious tension. I barely felt the ground beneath my feet.

I thudded back to earth when I remembered what I was about to do.

"Oh, about that. Turns out I don't know where that simurgh statue is," I said as innocently as possible, feeling terrible to be lying to him. "Think Ayman can lead me there?"

Cyrus looked to Ayman, who nodded and moved to follow me out.

Cyrus pressed a quick kiss to my hand before retreating. "Meet you there?"

I resisted the urge to do the same, and gulped, "Yes."

I waited until he was out of earshot then turned to Ayman. "You heard my little conversation with Cherine, didn't you?"

His deep voice was muffled by his helmet. "Bits and pieces."

"You like her, don't you?"

Ayman avoided my gaze bashfully. "I don't know her."

"I think you do. You've been creeping around her since we arrived."

"Sorry about that. I was just checking who was in each room that first night. I didn't know she was a light sleeper."

"And every night after that?"

He took his time answering me. "I—wanted to see if I could talk to her. Explain that I wasn't…"

"A nightmare?"

"Evil." He said with a sad finality.

"She knows that now."

"No, she doesn't."

"You heard her, she wants to meet you."

"She wants to meet the version she put together in her head."

"That's because she knows nothing about you. You want her to know who you really are, don't you?"

He again hesitated, exhaled, his breath echoing in the confines of his armor. "I do."

"But?"

"But she won't. No one wants to get to know me after they see me."

I stopped by the stairway railing, arms out to my sides. "I'm no one, then?"

I couldn't see anything but his peculiar purple eyes, but I didn't need to. They projected how he felt clearly enough.

It was a very familiar kind of disbelief, a disheartened quality I'd carried for years until I'd found the Fairborns, a belief that no one would ever care.

It became especially heartrending when he carefully asked, "Why do you want to know me?"

"We're friends, right?"

He didn't answer me.

"You like talking to me, don't you?"

"I don't talk to anyone but Cyrus, so, yes."

"Why?"

"They don't answer me if I do."

"Even the ones who know you here?"

He considered his answer. "Only some of the staff, those on a lower-tier. The ones who run things avoid me."

"Why?" I asked again.

"I scare them," he said sadly.

"All because you're as pale as alabaster?"

"Because they think I'm evil."

"I still don't get that."

He pointed to the spiraling stairs, telling me to move. I climbed down slowly, as each step tapered on one end and flared to a five-foot width on the other.

"People believe that my appearance is the cause of a curse, or that I myself am a demon," he explained. "They only think Cyrus somehow has me in check."

"Seriously?"

"Yes. On the southernmost part of the continent, whenever someone like me is born, their families either kill or hide them, or else others will hunt and dismember them."

I missed a step, stumbling with a squeak and clinging onto the railing for dear life. "What? Why?"

"They sell their limbs and organs to those who practice witchcraft. A man from the mountains of Opona took a trade ship down there once, to buy ivory, and they believed he was like me because he was so fair and had light yellow hair. They cut off one of his fingers before his crew saved him." The detachment in his voice seared me with his quiet misery. "In other lands across the Silent Ocean, they shun the colorless, believing that contact with them will bring bad luck or death. And on another island in the Silent Ocean, they sacrifice them to appease angry mountains."

"Angry mountain gods, you mean?"

His hands acted out something flaring up into the sky. "No. Angry mountains. The ones that crack open their summits and spew fire."

"Volcanoes?" I already felt sick to my stomach, but the word 'sacrifice' made me want to dry-heave.

"Is that what they call them?" He seemed intrigued before shaking it off and continuing down after me. "I don't know if those even exist in the north."

Not on Ericura, at least. I only knew of them from Bonnie's books. But while she was safe from being thrown into hot molten rock, any day now the people of Rosemead could switch their sacrifices from animals to girls.

"What about here?"

With bright daylight pouring from a stairwell window, his eyes looked more red than purple. Unlike Marzeya's dreadful red, his eyes had an ethereal quality to them. "In Cahraman?

They won't sell my arms on the black market or sacrifice me to the evil god Angramain. But they still fear and hate me."

"What about your parents? What did they think?"

"I don't know, but I can make a very good guess."

We reached the top of the last flight of stairs. I faced him, trying to show him I saw him for what he was: a great friend not just to Cyrus, but to me as well.

When he didn't look back at me, I exhaled. "Where are they?"

"I don't know that either. I know my mother lived here in the palace, and my father—" he stopped, looking down the stairs behind me.

Standing at the bottom, watching us with her arms tightly at her sides and fists clenched, was Loujaïne. When she noticed we were watching her back, she pretended not to see us and floated away.

I sighed. "She hates me."

"It's not you," he said with certainty. "She thinks I bring bad luck to the palace. Wanted to have me thrown out the day Cyrus returned with me."

"Returned with you? I thought you were born here."

He shook his head and I heard his hair scraping the inside of the helmet. "My mother was from Sunstone, my father was from Almaskham. I was born there. My father believed that I was a blight on his house, sent my mother back to her family and left me."

"Left you where?"

Ayman walked down past me and headed straight for a painting hanging on the wall of a white sand desert at the bottom of a purple mountain's craggy terrain where humanoid creatures were painted with faint, flickering strokes to give off the impression that they were made of flames.

"Here."

"Where is this?"

"Where you and the princess were, Mount Alborz in Gül, right across the Gulf from Almaskham. It's the, lowest hottest part of the desert, where it's said only the genies can withstand the temperature."

Horror shook me to the core. "They left you to die of exposure." He nodded and moved past the painting. I chased after him. "Why? Why would he do that?"

"Weren't you listening? Everywhere in the world, people like me are abhorred and feared."

"I got that, but your parents had to be better educated than the rest. It doesn't make sense for them to do that."

"What would you know?"

He was getting angry. I wasn't helping. "Sorry."

"Why are you sorry?"

"For upsetting you."

Helmet or not, I could tell he was looking at me like I was crazy. "Why?"

"I just am."

He reached up and pulled the faceplate, baring the bottom half of his face. He had a strong jaw, a flat chin, just like mine, and a wide mouth that was curved in the smallest of smiles. "Don't be. I can't get angry at you for being nice to me for whatever reason."

Guilt stabbed me like an arrow.

But I *wasn't* being nice to him to get him to help me.

I was genuinely interested and concerned, curious to know him as himself and as the man Cyrus trusted the most. I would segue into trading a meeting with Cherine for guidance through the tunnels to the king's chambers, but I *wasn't* using him. I was just making a good trade, and I was, in fact, his friend.

So why was I drowning in guilt?

Ignoring the sickening squirm in my guts, I patted his arm, returning the comfort. "Can I ask how you met?"

"It was less of a meeting and more of an ambush," he said fondly. "It was when he was sent to his relatives in Almaskham as a child. I hid in that palace like I did in this one. He went down to the kitchens after curfew one night and saw me stealing a meat pie." A chuckle echoed out of his armor. "Then he followed me and asked if I was the White Shadow of Avesta and if I could show him my pet simurgh."

"People can have pet simurghs?"

He shook his head. "They'd have to find one first. I've never met anyone else who saw one."

"Else? You've seen a simurgh?" I gasped, my dormant fascination with this land resurging.

"I…well, yes. I knew one. It's actually the reason I'm here," he responded awkwardly, like he wasn't sure if he should have told me. "Not here in Cahraman, but the reason I didn't die as an infant."

"It saved you?"

He nodded, rattling his helmet. "It kept me with it until I could fend for myself, then it dropped me off in Almaskham, and the rest is as you know it."

I had heard of people being raised by wolves, but this was a more fantastical and sorrowful tale, where instead of gaining the ability to shapeshift into a wolfman, he was abandoned yet again, lost, alone and unwanted—until Cyrus had latched onto him.

It hadn't occurred to me that their lives and their friendship could mirror mine and Bonnie's so much. I just hoped that nothing and no one ever separated them like Nariman had done to us.

"So, no, you can't have a simurgh," he continued. "But you can have a saber-toothed cat."

I couldn't hold back my amazed shout. "Where?"

"Some nobles in Almaskham kept it as an exotic pet."

"Amazing! Any other magical creatures? Are there dragons?"

He pondered that question for a second. "In the northeast, I believe."

"What about phoenixes?"

"What? Don't you have magical wildlife in Arbore? I could have sworn you had a few weird things in your woods, saber-toothed deer and horned horses."

"Unicorns," I corrected, thinking of the Hornswoods. "I've yet to spot one myself though." Putting aside my fascination with the Folkshore for now, I nudged him. "What happened after he found you?"

"He immediately decided we were friends. And when he found out that I couldn't read, he dragged me to the court of his uncle and demanded I join him during his and his cousins' lessons and be trained by the guards." He tapped his helmet. "The princely family were not happy, especially the reigning prince's nephew, Azal. He hated me more than Loujaïne does, and if it weren't for Cyrus he would have had me killed." Despite the awfulness of his recounts, he softened up towards the end. "I didn't know it at the time, but Cyrus had a whole plan figured out for our future."

It was the most human I had heard him sound.

Unbearably saddened, my eyes watered. "How so?"

"According to him, the moment he found me he knew he

was taking me home with him, and the only way that could happen was if I was the son of a nobleman or titled," he said. "Like how the ladies-in-waiting of a princess are actually titled 'lady.'"

Like Nariman was to the Princess of Cahraman.

But—if one had to be titled to accompany a princess, that meant that, not only had my mother been a witch, but she'd been a true lady.

It was becoming uncomfortably evident that I hadn't known my own mother at all. And in turn didn't know myself.

"How did he manage that?"

We had crossed into an empty, darker hall and he removed his helmet, shaking out his long white hair so it fell to the middle of his back. He raised the helmet, presenting it as part of his answer. "His argument was that I had good potential to be his personal guard, that my ability to go about unseen and even scare people out of their wits was very valuable. He also threatened to not attend his father's coronation if I wasn't allowed to return with him."

Even though I was on the verge of tears, I couldn't help grinning at that. At Ayman's poignant story and unique friendship with Cyrus. And at the mounting pain in my foot.

The bottom floor of the palace seemed to stretch on for miles, an endless expanse of multicolored marble forming swathes of images and patterns, each section with a different theme.

After a few twists and turns, we saw the simurgh statue in the distance. The fact that the hall wasn't empty became instantly clear.

Fairuza was by the other side of the statue, leaning a hand on the bird's wing as if to steady herself. Her hair wasn't perfectly coiffed and styled for once and her dress was a simple make, no embroidery, no layers. Practically a nightgown.

On second thought, that *was* a nightgown.

She looked like she'd sleepwalked here.

"Cyrus didn't ask her to meet him too, did he?" I asked, both concerned and jealous.

Ayman frowned at the sight of her. "No. Last I heard she was refusing to leave her room."

Intrigued and unsettled, I limped into the hall slowly. Ayman didn't follow.

Though Fairuza was in my focus, I couldn't help taking in the high ceilings, the cylindrical walls sculpted into bas-reliefs depicting sections of a sequential story, just like the secret passageway behind the vault. All the light came from the four curved rectangular windows behind the statue that looked out onto a section of the gardens.

Closing in on Fairuza, I touched her lightly. "Are you alright?"

She jumped around, hands raised, as if to ward off a blow. I stepped back quickly, nearly tripping over the edge of the simurgh's platform.

"Easy," I gasped, pain flaring in my foot. "It's just me."

Awareness seeped back into her eyes, replacing the primal fear as she let her hands down. Tears were silently pouring from her almost swollen-shut eyes. She looked—desolate.

Before I could say anything, she sagged into a heap at my feet and wept, "You."

CHAPTER TWENTY-NINE

$\mathcal{I}$ stared down at the girl who'd been my rival, the one I'd hated from the start for her perfection and privileges, and almost didn't recognize her in her grief.

What happened to her?

I stood almost on one foot, the pain in the other a searing reminder of what we'd both suffered, and was lost for words.

I'd wanted to talk to Fairuza about our shared ordeal, known she'd be the only one who'd fully understand. I'd thought I'd been shaken and changed forever by the experience. But looking at her now, it felt as if she'd been *destroyed*.

Chest tight, I held out my hand, not knowing how else I could comfort her.

Something thin and sharp stung my arm. It took a second to register the pain, and one too long to react, to face the source. I found myself confronted by what should have been a silly sight, but instead found it unsettling.

Fairuza's handmaidens, looked nothing like their usual pretty, lightweight selves. Meira had a long, sharp hairpin held in her hand like a dagger, and Agnë had a long silver chain held like a whip. Next moment Agnë lashed out at me again, this time almost slashing my face.

Flinging myself backwards, dropping my cane and flattening myself against the giant bird, I shouted, "What is the matter with you?"

"Get away from the princess!" Agnë hissed, face distorting as she lashed out again.

"What did you do to her?" Meira advanced, just as changed, weapon held over her head. "She was weeping at night and saying you were put in this world to make her suffer."

"What are you talking about? Are you crazy?"

Agnë's answer was an aggravated growl and another swipe at my head with the chain. I ducked out of her range, hurled myself behind the bird. They chased me, Agnë cutting the air in all possible angles with frustrated grunts, Meira stabbing it.

I worried more about the pin than the chain, fearing for my veins and eyes. It would be laughably tragic if I'd survived a horde of ghouls only to be stabbed to death by a berserk handmaiden.

"She was supposed to be the only one," Meira cried. "It was a promise made years ago, that he would be the one to save her. This was the year he was supposed to marry her. She was the only choice, the perfect choice."

"When he asked for dozens of other girls, it didn't matter," Agnë hissed. "She thought to let him play, let him see her worth. She was sure they'd all fail miserably in every way compared to her and be sent home. But *you* stayed."

I was caught between my survival instinct telling me to hobble away and the morbid curiosity to find out what they meant by "save her."

"Have you considered it has nothing to do with me?" I gasped as I parried. "That he just doesn't like her?"

"Why wouldn't he?" Agnë lashed out again as she babbled. "She's accomplished, noble, healthy, beautiful, has a the most important royal connection to this land and to another, speaks several languages, studied history and art, can sing like a nightingale, paint and dance. What more could a prince want?"

"Someone who's not a massive child that throws dangerous tantrums?"

A shriek preceded Meira's most accurate attempt to stab me. Fight or flight response kicked in. I chose fight.

I ducked and caught Meira around the waist, backing her up into the statue hard enough to jolt the air from her lungs. Holding her stabbing hand, above her head, I reached back as Agnë came to the rescue, caught the chain, rolled it around my forearm and tugged, making her stumble closer. Taking a leaf from Cora's book, I head-butted her. She stumbled back, chain slipping from her grasp as she hit the floor.

I turned to Meira, catching her by the throat and slamming her hand against the wall to make her drop the pin.

I squeezed her neck, shredding words between gritted teeth, "I've had the month from hell and I never had an easy life to begin with. I am under so much stress a pampered fool like her, and you, can never imagine, and you maniacs attack me—"

"Enough—enough, please."

Our struggle ended as we looked down at Fairuza. She was leaning weakly on the simurgh's platform, her beautiful cyan eyes dry, yet red.

"Leave her, Meira, Agnë."

"But she attacked you!" Agnë cried out.

"She didn't," Fairuza said, voice hoarse and subdued. "I gave you your orders, so go carry them out."

Reverting to their accommodating selves, they adjusted their clothes and paired up to walk soundlessly away.

Once they were gone, Fairuza finally whispered, "I didn't mean to." She shuddered and her voice shook. "I didn't mean for her to fall over that wall."

I narrowed my eyes at her, disbelief unwavering.

"We were arguing, she pushed me first and I pushed her even harder. But I didn't think that the wall behind her was low enough for her to go over it. I just wanted to knock her down, get her dress dirty, maybe even rip it."

"Then why didn't you try helping me rescue her? Why did you act like it never happened?"

"What could I have done to help? I can't climb walls, and the guards were there and did nothing." She started breathing loudly. "I-I was horrified, but I couldn't do anything. Then you saved her and-and no matter how many times I deny it, everyone still won't believe me."

For the first time, I found myself believing her. "You could have at least apologized."

"Cherine wouldn't have accepted it. She hates me."

"Most of us do—did. Can't you guess why?"

Closing her eyes, she didn't answer. Perfect spherical droplets clung to her lashes.

"I-I've been told I have a larger-than-life personality," she quoted miserably. "And it is too much for most people to handle."

"You have a *difficult* personality."

"You have an uncouth personality," she sniffed loudly. "Yet everyone likes you."

"Uncouth, but still better than your polished arrogance."

Meeting each other's eyes, we exchanged a tremulous smile. I put a hand on her arm gently. "So what was this all about? Apart from your handmaiden's bumbling attempt to maim and murder me, what's this about Cyrus saving you?"

Fairuza put a hand on mine, not to remove it, but just to touch me. She looked as forlorn as I felt.

She finally whimpered, "If he doesn't marry me, I'm going to die."

I gave it a good minute to filter through my mind. Her claim made no sense.

"Are we talking figuratively here? Did your mother send you here and tell you she'd kill you if you failed his tests?"

Her mouth wobbled as she sniffled, "I can't tell you."

"Oh, no, you can't just drop something like that and not explain it. You're telling me." She stayed silent. I shook her. "Come on. Tell me!"

"I'M CURSED!"

Her outburst seemed to siphon all her power. She slumped in my hold and sobbed, her breath ratting in heaves.

I tried straightening her, heart pounding in my ears. "You mean *literally* cursed?"

She nodded against my chest. "A fairy cursed me, then she cursed my brother."

"How? Why?"

She pushed away to slouch against the wall, her face an undignified mess of tears and snot. "When I was born, a celebration was held. My parents invited everyone, noble or magical, among them members of the Seelie Court."

A wave of memories rolled into my mind, of Mr. Fairborn talking about fairy rings in the backyard, how iron horseshoes and wind-chimes outside the house were meant to deter whatever might come through the Hornswoods.

"Seelies as in fairies, right?"

She nodded, sniffling. "Seven fairies. The first six came to give me a magical gift—the gifts of dance, song, grace, beauty, health and wealth. The seventh didn't have anything more to give me. Then someone else arrived late."

"Who?"

"A fairy queen. She arrived, unannounced, to ask where her invitation was, and my father said that his foreign wife couldn't deal with more than one type of fairy in her castle. My mother is Cahramani and to her fairies are the same as djinn—genies…" She hiccupped so hard I felt it might tear something inside her. "She hates magical beings, fears them, forbade my siblings and I from any magical part of Arbore."

"Even where there are unicorns?"

"Yes. But I got a unicorn filly for my sixth birthday from a minor lord who'd been courting my father's favor. He caught her for me in the grasslands by the Summer Court and she is beautiful," she gushed, startlingly happy for a second there. It had to be the most genuine expression I'd ever seen her wear.

"What's she called? What color is she?"

"Her name is Mabily and she's pearly white, even has a pearl-like sheen to her hair."

"Oh, I envy you so much right now."

"Not as much as I envy you," she said honestly.

In that moment, we both realized just how much our situations had shifted, how everything we'd felt about each other had changed.

She was a completely different person right now than she was last week, all haughty confidence, venomous sneers and disaffected beauty nowhere to be found. In her place was a sad, messy girl who was giving in to despair right before my eyes.

"What did the fairy queen do?" I asked, my own voice choked.

"The queen was offended that my mother didn't want her there. So, she gave each of my mother's children a 'gift' she deemed appropriate." She wrapped her arms around her middle, hugging herself. "My older brother's curse needed a catalyst, and it struck a few years ago, damning him."

"What happened to him?"

She shook her head, refusing to say, seeming ashamed even.

"And you?"

Her shoulders slumped further with a depressed sigh. *"Beautiful and wondrous she shall be, with a voice to bring any man to his knee. But on her eighteenth year's eve, all for her will grieve."* She let out a shuddering breath. "That's the fairy queen's curse."

Horrified though still suspicious, I asked, "What does this curse have to do with Cyrus?"

"The seventh fairy, who had nothing more to give, used her power to change the curse to give me a chance." She waved a hand around the hall. "This was my chance."

"I still don't get it."

"'At the dawn of her eighteenth year, death will leave her to his brother sleep. Unless the most noble of men proves his love for her true and deep, she will remain forever near-death's to keep.'"

I gaped at her. "The fairy altered the curse only enough to make you sleep—forever? How's that better than dying? That's the best she could do?"

"Yes. It had to be done before the curse took effect, and she gave me a way to break the curse," Fairuza said. "Have the most noble of men prove his love for me."

"And how is that man Cyrus?"

"He's a crown prince, will be a king, making him the most noble of men. And by marrying me he declares his love to be true."

"Fairuza, that's not what love is. And that amendment to the curse didn't say Cyrus specifically. How are you so sure it's him?"

She shrugged. "Who else could it be?"

"Aren't there other princes? Ones you know personally enough for them to like you, maybe even love you?"

"I don't know. I have been betrothed to him for as long as I can remember, I didn't think of finding other options," she admitted. "Now it's too late to search and he has rejected me twice. Once by setting up the Bride Search and the second by favoring you."

So this was my fault? Great.

"I tried to be all things a prince should want to love, but I've failed," she said quietly. "This Bride Search has opened my eyes to my—true worth. I'm now seventeen and a half. In two seasons' time, I will be as good as dead, all because my mother got on a fairy's bad side years ago."

Everything about her behavior towards Marzeya suddenly made sense. She hadn't been irrational, and she hadn't been trying to sabotage me. She'd been genuinely scared of magic and the prospect that the witch would curse me. Like she had been cursed along with her brother.

That also meant the rumors about her brother had been true.

My insides twisting at her fate, I leaned over her, touching her shoulder anxiously. "What do you want me to do? Is there anything else that can be done?"

She only pushed off the statue and rose to unsteady feet.

"Where are you going?" I called after her.

"To help Meira and Agnë pack," she said with defeated finality. "It takes a good three weeks to travel from here to Arbore. I want to spend whatever time I have left with my younger siblings, perhaps convince my parents to let me see my older brother."

"Wait, so that's it? After all that, now you give up?"

Fairuza picked up my fallen cane and held it out to me, handle-first. "I never thanked you. If it weren't for you, I would have died sooner and far away from home. At least now I get to have more time with my family."

Taking the offered cane, I was at a loss for words, lips stuttering over breathless, half-formed protests as she walked away. "Fairuza, wait…"

She stopped by the darkened entrance and gave me a melancholy smile from over her shoulder. "I guess I never truly believed he would break my curse but I had to try my best." Her voice cracked. "If accepting your losses and your failure makes you a better person, then I hope the gods will be kinder to me in the afterlife."

Any possible protest died on my tongue, for what could I say now?

I had no ideas to offer, no experience with fairies to fall back on and I barely knew what to do with my witch. Marzeya wasn't entirely right about our harrowing experience at her hands making everything seem simpler in comparison. Now I felt more twisted up than before.

I stood trembling, watching Fairuza fade into the darkened depths of the hallway, shoulders hunched, bare feet shuffling across the floor. In the end, the beauty, the family, the riches and the castles didn't matter. Her life would be brief and its end was going to be as meaningless as anyone else's.

I felt overwhelming pity I had never thought possible. Pity

for someone I'd thought I hated, as well as disappointment in myself, that I couldn't help.

But there had to be a way I could help her.

Ayman appeared like a ghost by my side. "That was interesting."

I kicked his leg with my good foot.

He raised a thick, white eyebrow. "What was that for?"

"Some guard you are! Her handmaidens attacked me and you didn't do anything."

"You handled yourself pretty well."

I kicked him again.

CYRUS ARRIVED NOT LONG AFTER FAIRUZA HAD LEFT.

I was sitting on the platform of the simurgh statue, twirling the cane, dark thoughts eddying in my mind. Ayman was pacing the hall.

"I hope I didn't leave you waiting long." Cyrus strode towards me, hand held out.

I forced a big smile on my face, hoping I didn't appear as shaken as I felt. "A little."

"Forgive me, I will make it up to you."

"You better." Especially since I nearly got lashed and stabbed for getting here before him.

He helped me up, linking our arms as he led us outside.

When we emerged I stood rooted. Before us stretched consecutive cascades whose downpour ended in a central fountain, ensconced in mirroring sets of hanging gardens, each level reached by fan-like staircases. If the architecture inside the mountain had been impressive, this feat of beauty and symmetry was literally breathtaking.

In the center of the fountain stood the same figure as in Anaïta's temple in Sunstone and the same as the hidden statue of Jumana Morvarid down in the vault.

Cyrus led me down to the bottom of the hanging gardens, beneath the waterfalls and to the base of the fountain and the feet of the statue. Her wavy hair tumbled past her shoulders and was adorned by a crown of conical rays, just like Jumana's. But unlike Jumana she smiled, a serene face with downturned eyes and full, youthful cheeks. A bittersweet version of the melancholic one in the vault.

Cyrus turned to me, my cane beneath his arm, holding both my hands, his eyes smoldering with an unknown intensity as he said, "Ada of Rose Isle, I would like you meet Jumana of Almaskham—my mother."

CHAPTER THIRTY

Responses fled my mind like residents abandoning a burning building, leaving me with nothing but an impulse exclamation.

"What's your relationship exactly to Aurelia?"

He laughed disbelievingly at my sideways jump in logic, shaking his head with an indulgent grin. "She's my great-aunt. Aurelia and Prince Faisal had only sons. My mother was their niece through Prince Miraj. The only girl left in the family at that time."

That explained her first words to him. *You look nothing like your mother.*

It wasn't out of her general spite, it was disappointment. Disappointment that she couldn't see what was left of her only niece in his face.

He held out his hand for mine and helped me step down the encircling steps of the fountain so we were directly below the marble version of Jumana. There were shells in the water, some open, displaying silvery pearls in their cores, like the smallest ring on Cyrus' hand. Marzeya had said Jumana meant *pearl*. And so did Hessa—and Dorreya.

There truly was little of her in her son. He didn't have her sad eyes, her soft bone structure, her dainty nose or even anything as minor as the shape of her fingers.

I couldn't tell if it was better that way, that he didn't see her in the mirror the way I saw parts of my mother in my wide smile and black hair. Marzeya had said that I looked more like my father's mother, neither of which I knew. A man and a woman I would never know, just as Cyrus would never know Jumana.

"You said her statue was in the vault so no one could visit her or pay her their respects."

"It was." He nodded, softly thumbing my knuckles. "Father apparently managed to both respect palace rules and find a way around them. When I asked him about her likeness in the temple, he said he didn't want people to forget her face or forget what she meant to him. Now all modern versions of Anaïta bear her face."

As touching as that effort was, it threw me off the sentimental path and into a skeptical ditch. From what Nariman had told me Darius and Jumana were not happy together. Certainly not to warrant this level of yearning and tribute from Darius. Even if Nariman had bent the truth, happily married new mothers did not take their own lives.

Unless his view of her had grown rosier with absence, leading to him immortalizing her the way he wanted to remember her.

"This is her grave." He announced, his hand moved underneath mine, sliding our palms across each other soothingly. "I had no idea it was until I talked to my father about the temple of Anaïta. If she had died any other way, she would be in the crypts with the rest of our dead, in a tomb, with her statue on the main floor. But once again, my father found a loophole to our rules by placing it here, pretending it's the goddess, yet burying her in her favorite place."

"Was it?" I asked, hoping this really was a place that made her happy.

"It was a wedding gift, this place. Father had begun its construction when their betrothal was arranged and took her here after they were married. She loved it here, I'm told." His voice deepened and softened with an inextricable mixture of sadness and tenderness.

The way he spoke of his father, despite my own conclusions, didn't add up, just like his parents' relationship. Unless Darius had happily accepted Jumana as his wife and, unbeknownst to him, she'd never returned his affection. If so, that made their situation a lot sadder than I thought possible.

I stepped closer to him, lowering our linked hands to hold onto his arms. He moved closer as well until I set my head on his shoulder and he rested his head on mine.

Being affectionate came so easily with him, like we had been in each other's personal space for years and didn't need to think about it anymore. That we had already passed the awkward stage, the part where we would figure out what was okay and what wasn't, and jumped straight to this.

This. Comfortable, comforting ease and intimacy. It was something his parents had never had. A side effect of most, if not all, arranged marriages that he wanted to avoid. His choice to reject Fairuza not once, but twice, made more sense now. He didn't want to doom them both to a trapped marriage or risk his children losing their mother.

But now I'd learned that his rejection could be what doomed Fairuza to a fate worse than death.

Choking on the thought, I said, "Tell me about her."

His chest moved beneath my cheek as he exhaled raggedly. "She was the only girl left in House of Morvarid, which made her targeted by all nearby kingdoms and princedoms who wanted wives for their heirs. She got so many offers she took a whole year to decide which one she'd accept." He sounded detached all of a sudden, like he was reciting an old folktale. "After a lot of thought, she was going to remain in Almaskham and marry one of her second-cousins, Prince Azal."

This was maybe the fifth or sixth time I had heard about Prince Azal, and judging by what Ayman told me, he was a colossal jerk.

"Why didn't she?" I asked.

"The ruling prince at the time, Aurelia's husband, decided against it. My mother was the only girl and they were a small princedom. They needed alliances especially to their closest neighbors. So, my mother chose my father and Azal was married to Loujaïne."

"Loujaïne?" I exclaimed, shocked that I hadn't considered her husband's identity before, even when Marzeya had taunted her with my mother.

So that's the prince who'd taken my mother as a mistress? Was *he* the reason she'd escaped to Ericura?

This was another piece of the puzzle of my incomplete history.

"Is Loujaïne still married to him?" I barely held back the question. "If not, why hasn't she married Farouk?"

He shrugged, moving our tangled arms up.

"So what happened?"

He made another noncommittal move, feigning ignorance.

"That wasn't something you were supposed to tell me, was it?"

"It was not." He pulled back slightly, an uneasy smile flitting over his sculpted lips. "But, you ought to know now anyway."

"Why's that?"

"Can't you guess yet?"

Heart doing another series of summersaults, I rose on my toes to bring my eyes closer to his, my voice a tremulous sigh as I whispered, "Looks like you're going to have to spell it out for me."

Slowly, he lowered his face to mine, bringing us nose to nose so I could see nothing but the shimmering waves of the summer sea in his eyes.

Then with one shared breath, he pressed his lips to mine.

CHAPTER THIRTY-ONE

The never-ending buzz that has plagued my head for years was instantly gone.

Empty and quiet, it was like I was floating in the aether, finally free of the world and its worries. The only thing in my sight, taking all my attention, engulfing all of me, was the sun. Warm, golden and powerful enough to pull me into its center. The sun that was Cyrus.

This was the peace I had been searching for my whole life.

Time stopped and the world no longer existed—until Cyrus broke off the kiss.

He pressed his forehead to mine, hands gently settling on my upper arms to hold me steady. "Do you understand now?"

"Mmm, I think you're going to need to explain it a few more times for the fact to stick," I said dazedly, leaning my spinning head against his chest.

His chuckle reverberated deeply under my ear. "What are you thinking?"

I hummed, feeling as if I'd drunk too much wine. "I'm thinking if you end up choosing Ariane after this, I will fill your pillowcases with eggshells and your mattress with fish heads."

His laugh boomed, his chest shaking beneath my cheek. "Oddly specific, and innocuous. Wouldn't poison in my wine be a more appropriate threat?"

I gawked up at him. "I would never hurt you! I'd do anything to keep you from harm, no matter what." I smothered my face again, harder in his chest. "I only wished you'd choose me, for every possible reason, but I still never thought I'd win, not when the others are so much better than me."

"If that's what you think after all this, then my wedding gift to you will be a roomful of silver mirrors."

"The mirrors are unnecessary because my self-esteem is bad enough as it is," I said sarcastically, before rethinking his words and everything stopped.

My jaw dropped and I could swear I felt it hit the ground.

I gaped up at him for what felt like an hour.

Then from an unending tunnel I heard my voice, pitchy as scratches on a blackboard. "Did you say wedding gift?"

I thought he'd brought me here to tell me I'd won, but he still needed to discuss with his judges and the king. But a wedding gift went beyond being his personal choice, or the uncertain status a winner would have before unanimous approval could bless his proposal. He'd made his decision regardless, and it meant everything to me.

I felt totally numb as I watched Cyrus nod, his gorgeous face beaming down at me with the most exquisite smile I'd ever seen. "Two days from now is the final day, the day I announce my choice to the kingdom. Tomorrow is the day my father meets all of you for himself."

That inadequate feeling rose back up like bile when he mentioned his father.

That dreaded lamp and all it entailed was too heavy a thought to brush aside.

"Does he have to approve your choice?"

"Of course, his approval does matter, especially regarding how people will respect you. But he's agreed to the Bride Search, said that he wouldn't approve anyone who didn't pass all our tests. That was why it was vital for you to. Now that you have won, even he can't contest my choice." He suddenly gave me a sly wink. "But don't tell anyone else that yet."

The way I was feeling, I might never tell anyone anything ever again. I could barely remember how to speak.

He moved back enough to dig through his coat pocket. He pulled out something small. "This isn't what I wanted to use, but for now please accept it as a placeholder. It doesn't look like much, but it should throw off any suspicion until the announcement."

It was a small, crude brass ring set with a brownish red stone—not jasper but something close. A carnelian maybe. It looked like an antique, very old compared to the heirloom rings I'd seen every woman in this place wearing. It seemed made before they mined enough gold and before rubies were plenty. Or made as a poorer approximation to gold and ruby rings.

But he was giving it to me. The fact that he thought of giving me something was enough, but if it was this specific piece rather than any of the prettier options in the vault, then it must mean something to him.

It finally hit me that he was giving me a placeholder for an engagement ring.

"You're *proposing* to me?" I spluttered, unable to get a grip on my mouth or voice, or any other part of me. "Aren't you— isn't this—"

"Early? Presumptuous? Not on one knee?" he offered cheekily. "But no, I'm not. Yet. I will, officially, at the final ceremony. I just found it impossible not to tell you, so, consider this a pre-engagement ring."

I shook my head, wanting to say so much, but all words deserted me. What could I say to something so unbelievable?

All I could say was, "Why?"

He caressed my cheek. "Ada, I almost lost you before I could get to call you mine. We both came so close to death in that mountain, and we would have died not just before I could choose you but on distant terms. We never know when the Fates might tear us apart, so I wanted to mend our bond and establish a new one as soon as possible. I would have proposed right after we left the mountain, but I wanted to have the ring first." He held out the ring to me, asking for my hand. "What do you say?"

Too overwhelmed to speak, I let out a cross between a sob and a laugh, and held out my trembling hand.

He held it, steadying it, and slipped the ring on my finger.

A shiver ran through me the instant the cold metal settled on my skin.

I half-turned to hold my hand up in the light, to see it from some distance. "Is there any significance to this ring?"

He came up behind me, a hand on my shoulder and the other around mine, moving it side to side, watching the stone catch the light. "You asked for the ring that could grant wishes. Ayman and I have made many trips back down to the vault to try on each ring we could find and make demands of it. None worked but I believe this might have some magic to it."

"What did you wish for?"

"Ayman wished for a darker complexion and I wished for

random things like pink snow or for all statues of simurghs to come to life."

"Clearly none of those happened, so what tipped you off about this one?"

He moved his hand up against mine, threading our fingers with our arms outstretched before us. "I had an ache in my back from killing all those ghouls and wished for it to stop, then this morning it did."

Which could be the effect of a good night's sleep.

So, was this ring wish-fulfillment or wishful-thinking?

A flash gleamed across the stone, darkening its color just a bit, like a layer of dust had been blown off it, intensifying its shine and shade. At once, another shudder coursed through me, this time infused with elation and foreboding.

Was this my answer, or was that what every girl felt when the man she loved slipped a ring around her finger?

CHAPTER THIRTY-TWO

$\mathcal{C}$yrus and I walked back inside, our hands still clasped until we reached a point where we could be seen. I hadn't been ready to let go.

It was still unbelievable, that Cyrus wanted to marry me, that he took me to his mother's grave and told me all I had left to be his bride was to meet his father. The father who would invite me into his quarters.

I was really doing this? I was going to be all Aurelia said I could be? I was going to be his partner, his princess, his everything? I didn't have to choose between my future with him and the safety of the Fairborns anymore?

This development, this path to a happy ending he had put me on was so—*surreal*.

My head ought to have been in the clouds, light with happiness, but worry for Fairuza anchored me to earth. Even though I knew that her fate wasn't my fault, and that stepping aside would not save her, I still felt like I destroyed her spirit, that her will to fight for her life had been snuffed out like a candle.

Cyrus waved Ayman out of the shadowy hall, turned to face me, holding my hand between us. "I must leave you now. Ayman will accompany you back to your room."

I tiptoed to whisper in his ear, "Will Ayman attend the celebration?"

"He should, if he doesn't find an excuse to hide in the corners and slip away."

"We could dye his hair, maybe get him tinted glasses."

His eyes softened, a look of heart-aching tenderness and affection I would never get tired of. "You are very thoughtful. Why do you ask, though?"

"He is your best friend, right? And I was asking because maybe if he has a companion he'll stick around the whole day."

"A companion? How would you manage that if I couldn't?"

"You tried setting him up?"

"A few times with girls who've caught his attention." He heaved out a heavy sigh. "He refuses to show up."

"I think I can manage. "

"And you still wonder why I chose you." With that he pecked my cheek then my hand, giving me one last glance filled with excitement and promise before walking away.

Ayman approached bunching up his hair to settle it under his helmet. "Let's go."

"Have you given my offer a thought?"

Sliding on his helmet, he murmured, "I don't think it's a good idea."

"Why?" I whined. "She's interested. Aggressively interested, and so are you. Why are you letting this chance pass you by?"

He just put his hand on my back and pushed me forward.

"You need a nap before dinner and you're wasting your sleep time."

"Hey!" I tried digging my heels in but my foot hurt too much and he was too strong. He had me gliding all the way to the stairs, catching baffled looks from passers-by.

The stairs, which I'd thought would be a good place to stop and argue, proved to be no problem for him, as he picked me up, set me on the fourth step, pushing me up the rest.

I leaned my weight back to slow him down. "Would you just consider it?"

"I have. My answer is no."

"She's not going to chase you like an idiot forever, she's a noblewoman, she'll have lords circling her like hawks the second Cyrus announces his pick." I clapped to emphasize the urgency of the matter. "You better act now."

He didn't answer. I took it as him mulling it over.

At the top of the stairs, he once again pushed me to my room like I was a cart. He was close to shoving me inside and tucking me in for my mandated nap when I swerved and knocked on Cherine's door.

She opened at once. As Ayman turned to leave, I stomped my good foot on his, pinning him in place as Cherine bounced to the tune of her own excited babbling.

"Ada, did you find him? The silver prince? I know I need to focus on the competition but how can I think of Cyaxares when he's around? And I doubt I will win. But I've made it to the Final Five, which guarantees me great prestige and a good marriage to a great man." She jumped again. "Do you think I can ask for him, whoever he is? What do you think he is? A real prince? An ambassador?"

"Would it matter if he's not either of those? I mean, if he

works here then you'll live in the palace with him either way, right?" I asked Ayman more than her.

She tapped a finger on her chin. "Hmmm, we'll see. I just need to get him when he doesn't have to rush anywhere. You said you could find him for me, didn't you?"

With all my nerves flailing, it was harder than ever trying not to grin. "I did."

Cherine took my hands in her hers and shook my arms with every begging hop. "Please, please, please!"

"I'll try my best."

She squealed excitedly and rushed back into her room, slamming the door.

I turned to Ayman who already had his helmet in his hands, teeth worrying his lower lip.

"I figured you needed to see just how much she wants to meet you."

"I'll do it."

"If that's how you feel then—what?'

"I'll do it," he said firmly, glancing at her door. "I'll show up at whatever place and time you pick."

"And you won't chicken out at the very last second? Because there's no use in getting her hopes up only for you to slink off into the shadows."

"I won't." He spread his big gauntleted hand over his heart with a slight bow of his head, as if in a pledge.

I held out my hand. "Shake on it?"

Briefly hesitating again, he took off his gauntlet and lightly grasped my hand.

As he moved to let go, I gripped his hand a bit tighter, leaning in. "Now that that's dealt with, I need a favor."

"Anything," he said immediately. "What do you need?"

My heart squeezed with guilt at his ready answer. At what I had to do.

No matter how I tried to work it, my original plan to steal the lamp when the king invited me to his quarters was unfeasible. It could be what unraveled all my efforts and got me killed. I would have relied on the ring, but for now I saw no proof of its magic.

With that in mind, I'd determined there were only two ways of getting that lamp, and they both hinged on Ayman sneaking me into the king's quarters through the tunnels. Then I'd either get in and steal the lamp before the celebration, or I'd find out where the lamp was once the king invited me into his quarters, then come back for it later.

Then I'd need the tunnels to escape the palace once my mission was complete.

I finally exhaled. "But you can't tell Cyrus."

CHAPTER THIRTY-THREE

Once in the privacy of my room, I lifted my aching foot on the bed and studied the ring.

Whatever it could or couldn't do, I'd find out nothing without trying it myself.

"I wish I had Nariman's lamp," I said to it.

As expected, the lamp didn't magically appear in my hand.

"I wish Bonnie and her father were here," I tried again, less of a true wish and more of a sad sigh.

No tiny, bookish girl and absent-minded smith materialized before me.

"I wish I knew the truth about this stupid lamp," I huffed in defeat.

Nothing happened again.

I gave up and stood to change my clothes—and noticed *The Anthology of the Dunes* open on the other side of the bed.

That was neither the place nor the page I'd left it on.

After an initial fright, thinking someone had been in my room, I closed in and found it open at the first story I'd read back during our first test, *The Silent City of Alabasta,* where

Esfandiar of Gypsum had to answer three riddles to be allowed out by the guardian beast, once again, a simurgh.

"I wish I knew what moved and opened you so I could get a good nap," I grumbled to the book as I picked it up.

Like a wet soap bar, the book slipped from my hands and landed flat open again. Esfandiar, a dark-haired man in an open kaftan stood in the dusty, stone-paved ruins of an open temple. His hair and clothes blew in the wind as he gazed up at a fiery creature with clawed hands whose bottom half was a windstorm spiraling out the mouth of the bottle he held.

Was that what was inside my ring? A genie? Had it just answered me?

And had it answered both questions? If genies didn't have to be in bottles, could they be in rings and lamps, too? Was that the thing Nariman had trapped inside hers? It seemed very likely. If only I could be sure.

"I wish I knew if you, or the lamp, hold genies."

Waiting for an answer, I held out my hand but the carnelian stone only gleamed innocently.

EITHER WISHFUL THINKING WAS TOYING WITH MY SANITY OR this *was* wish fulfillment.

To a minor extent.

Some wishes were answered, I thought—reheating my tea, fading a stain from my dress or locating things I couldn't find. On others, it did nothing at all. Any request that had anything to do with transportation went ignored. No matter how I phrased the wish, the Fairborns did not appear and I did not end up in the king's personal vault.

It was early light by the time I'd given up and turned on my side, my last thought being of Cyrus's proposal.

What felt like minutes later, I awoke to Cora kicking open my door with our breakfast balanced atop her head.

Groaning, dead tired and sore all over, I swung my legs off the bed. I only remembered my broken toes when I took a step towards the table and it was like I'd stepped on lightning. My foot flared with searing, cramping pain that collapsed my leg beneath me.

Missing the bedpost, I fell flat on my face before Cora could catch me, hitting the woolen carpet with a stinging, scraping slam.

Pain flooded my entire body. I landed in a twisted angle that had the floor collide with the fading bruise on my cheek. I could already feel it growing bigger and bluer than it had been before.

Cora peeled me off the floor, lifting me upright and keeping my feet at a hover. "You alright?"

"No." I yelped, feeling my toes spasm again. "I hate this."

"It will heal."

"Not just my foot, everything else. I have been in nonstop stress for years and it got worse last month, and every time I think I can enjoy a moment of peace, life finds a way to kick me in the teeth. I am just so *tired.*" I sobbed in between frustrated heaves, clutching her shoulders. "I just wish everything would stop hurting and—"

Like dust blown away in the wind, the pain all over my body instantly disappeared, only fragments of it remaining in the air to tell that it was once there.

I waited for a few seconds, in case my mind had tricked me into ignoring it, then I moved my weight off Cora and onto my feet.

Nothing. There was nothing but a faint, negligible sting, a quick-fleeting, irritating numbness that accompanied waking in a bad angle.

The ring's red stone gleamed with a passing flash, too bright to be reflecting the light.

Clenching and unclenching my toes, feeling the firm nails that weren't there a minute ago, I stared at the ring with slow-settling shock.

It *healed* me!

"That's an ugly ring," Cora commented, offering me a plate as she chewed her dried fig, the seeds crunching between her teeth like sand.

"What would you know?" Distracted by the ring once again, I sat on the floor by the table, trying to figure out how it worked. "The only jewelry you have are coral beads and woven arm bands."

"Just because I don't own any gems doesn't mean I can't tell which are pretty. I would have all the jewels if I could." She nudged the bowl of yoghurt my way. "Quick, the heat here spoils everything fast."

Obliging her, I spoke through a mouthful. "What's the difference between a genius and a genie again?"

She slowed her chewing. "Genii are the living essence of every object. It's like being haunted but not really, since it isn't someone else's soul tied to it, just a kind of consciousness in the object. Sometimes it can project a human-like form that talks to us. I've only ever seen field genii. They keep us updated on how the soil is doing."

"And genies?"

"Genies are more like nymphs in a sense, fairy-like, magical and mischievous, made from a certain element and you can catch them or they can possess you."

I swallowed my food before fully chewing it. It scraped my throat as it slipped down, roughening my squeak to a croak. "Possess us?"

"Mm. Or was that an ifrit?" She cupped her chin, squishing her mouth up thoughtfully. "I can't tell the difference. Ifrits and genies' domains stop at Almaskham as far as my end is concerned. I don't know. I think people trap them in bottles or lanterns."

I leaned in. "How do you trap a genie?"

She shrugged. "I just know that's where you can find them."

So, either this ring had its own sentience in the form of a genius, or it was a genie trapped in the ring. The same went for the lamp.

But since a genius didn't sound formidable enough, I'd bet on a genie. Especially since it picked and chose what it would do for me, like it had moods.

But now the ring had proved its great power. For the first time since I'd been dragged into Cahraman, I felt confident that I had a plan. A plan that could actually work. I could keep my promise to the Fairborns to save them, and to Cyrus to be with him forever.

But for now, I had another promise I needed to keep.

Right on time, a knock on the door had me rushing out on a newly mended foot to open the door for Ayman.

I told Cora a brief explanation and headed over to Cherine's room. She and Ayman followed me.

As soon as Cherine opened her door, I entered, leaving them outside. "He's here."

With an excited squeal, Cherine giddily clapped her hands. "How did you convince him to come? Are we sure he's not going to run away? He better not run again because I am tired of chasing after him! Ladies are supposed to be chased not do the chasing themselves."

I peeked out of the room. Ayman was hiding behind a column. I motioned for him to come over. When he didn't move, Cora pushed him, knocking him out of hiding.

As he approached, Cherine immediately recognized his armor.

Her level of excitement plummeted as she pointed at him accusingly, "You? You're *him*? Cyaxares's personal guard?"

Ayman remained still and silent, if it weren't for the heavy breathing one would think it was an empty suit of armor.

"It's definitely him," I assured her.

Cherine came closer, hands clasped up under her chin, eyes shining up at him wondrously. "I've been looking for you."

"I know," he responded gruffly.

"Why do you keep hiding from me?"

"I didn't want to scare you off." The aching vocal crack that splintered his words hit me like an arrow.

"Scare me? Why would you scare me?"

He looked at his feet.

"Take off your helmet," Cherine ordered. "I need to finally see the man I've been dreaming of for weeks."

He looked at me first, sighed then carefully started removing it.

She raised her arms to hurry him up, too short to reach his shoulders, let alone his head. He bowed to her and she carefully removed it, letting his long white hair fall out past his shoulders and gleam in the morning light pouring in through the mounted windows.

With a final fidget of hesitation, he raised his head, revealing his face.

Her smile vanished before her mouth fell open.

Before I could breathe, Cherine let out a blood-curdling scream. *"The ghoul!"*

Then she bolted to her bedroom and locked herself inside.

I was a bigger idiot than I ever thought I was.

A huge part of me had feared this might happen. I had still been stupid enough to hope it wouldn't.

Cora strolled in, idly swinging her arms. "She's still going on about that ghoul?"

Ayman turned to face her, shoulders hunched insecurely.

Cora stopped, looking from his face to the helmet beneath his arm. "I assume you're the 'ghoul'?"

"It would appear so," he said quietly.

"Huh." Was her only response.

How I wished Cherine could have reacted this nonchalantly. But, as the witch-queen had said, not much scared Cora.

Cora approached Ayman, scrutinizing his appearance. "Was your mother a dryad—a white poplar nymph?"

He watched her every step with nervous eyes, backing away. "No, she isn't."

"You sure? Their hair tends to be the same color as their leaves, and you fit the look."

He shook his head as he pushed back his hair. "I am no nymph, genie, ifrit, or ghoul. I'm just a man unfortunate enough to be mistaken for one."

I found my voice, approaching him carefully, hand reaching for his shoulder. "Ayman, I'm so sorry. I didn't think she'd react that way."

He raised his hand, blocking mine. "I did. I told you she would."

"I'm sorry," I repeated, finding no words to do my regret justice.

"It doesn't matter. We tried. I'm never trying again."

"Ayman…"

He just put back his helmet then walked out.

The moment he was gone, Cherine was out, yelling and screaming accusations that I'd brought her the ghoul to her room.

I didn't have time for this.

The bottle corking my emotions didn't pop, it shattered. "I wish you would shut up and forget all about that stupid ghoul idea already!"

Cherine's mouth slammed shut with an audible clack of her teeth.

Her eyes glazed over for a second in a distracted, daydreaming pause, then she snapped out of it with a shake of her head. "What were we saying? I got lost in thought for a minute there."

Cora let out a raspy "Ha!"

Cherine touched her forehead lightly. "Did I hit my head? I seem to have forgotten what I was about to say."

Cherine wasn't kidding. She had forgotten what she'd been saying.

Just like I'd asked for her to.

Cherine walked out in a trance and reentered her bedroom.

After a moment of stunned silence, I hurried back to my room. Cora followed me there with stuttering nostril puffs of tight-lipped laughter.

The moment we were inside, she said, "So, should I guess how you performed the miracle of shutting Cherine up, or are you going to tell me?"

I raised my hand. The stone obliged and gave her a brilliant flash.

She squinted at it for a minute then hummed, "Did Cyrus give it to you?"

I nodded, still dazed.

She nodded, impressed. "So when's the announcement? Today or tomorrow?"

There was no hiding anything from her, was there? I sighed. "Tomorrow."

Whatever was hiding in this stone, it did grant wishes. It ignored some commands, but the ones it answered were indeed major.

But maybe it didn't ignore me. What if I was just making wrong commands and there was a method to getting it to respond consistently?

At that thought, I needed to test something.

I took it off, handed it to her. "Try it. Wish for something."

Eyebrows raised, she took it, placed it on her little finger, the one where it fit, cleared her throat. "I wish I had a tray of baklava."

I huffed a laugh. Of course that was what she'd ask for.

When nothing happened, I said, "It doesn't seem to work that way. Wish for something in your own body. I wished that I stopped hurting, and it answered that wish."

"I wish my hair was darker," she said at once.

Nothing. Her hair remained as golden as her wheatfields.

I told her to ask for things that had worked for me. They didn't work for her.

She started to take off the ring and I rushed to add, "Make *me* do something."

Quirking an eyebrow, she said, "I wish Ada clucked like a chicken."

I felt no compulsion to obey her.

She finally handed it back. "Seems like this thing has your name on it."

I took it from her and walked to the window, heart racing as fast as my thoughts.

I held the ring up against the rays converging through the glass and watched it catch the light in an unremarkable shine.

If what Cora said was true, if it only answered my wishes, then it was more incredible than I'd thought. Not only power, but power that was all mine.

Every inch of me tingled as I remembered Marzeya's words. This was how I could level up to Nariman, how I could surprise and defeat her.

But first, I had to learn how to wield it.

The mood in the royal dining room this morning was the heaviest it had been.

I didn't know how much of that was my perception and how much was genuine tension.

I watched everyone around me, trying to read the room.

Ayman wouldn't meet my gaze as he stood on Cyrus's side, farthest from Cherine, who still had no recollection of their meeting or what I'd done to her. Cora entertained herself by picking the hardest pears and carving patterns into them.

Fairuza had skipped breakfast again, further cementing how much she had given up and making me feel even worse. Loujaïne had beaten Ariane to her seat.

Any other day, I would have been uncomfortable about her directly facing me. But it wasn't Loujaïne who worried me today. It was Cyrus.

He was on-edge for some reason, not touching his food and twisting the silver pearl ring around his finger as he stared ahead at the empty seat at his end of the table.

"What is it?" I asked, setting a hand on his under the table.

Cyrus checked the winged clock behind me, his brows twitching in a brief frown at Ayman. "Any minute now."

"Any minute for what?"

He squeezed my hand, eyes hard as they returned to the door. "Your final test."

The doors opened and Cyrus stood, followed by everyone but Aurelia. I pushed out of my chair, dusting any crumbs or creases on my dress.

Two guards entered, followed by a stony-faced Master Farouk, who bowed in a man in a white suit with a printed gold pattern.

"His Majesty, King Darius of Cahraman."

There truly was none of Jumana Morvarid in Cyrus. Everything from the golden skin, bowed lips, prominent cheekbones and thick, brown hair was all passed down from the king. The only difference aside from the laughter lines and the strands of grey scattered throughout his father's brown hair and beard, were the eyes. Cyrus's eyes were the bright green of northern lights while Darius's were the same cutting silver as his sister's.

I found myself not looking at the king, but at my future.

If everything went as happily as I planned, then within thirty years this would be Cyrus.

The king strode into the room, stopping behind his chair at the head of the table with arms open out to his sides, smile broad, but not reaching his eyes.

He greeted us with a rough voice heavy with age and smoke. "The Final Five, it is a great pleasure to finally see you for myself." He stopped, doing a quick headcount while avoiding looking at Aurelia. "Final Four then. Please, introduce yourselves."

Normally, the first person to bump us out of the way to

present herself would have been Fairuza. The uninterrupted silence from her absence was jarring.

Ariane took over for her by leading the introductions. "Your Majesty, I am Princess Ariane of Tritonia."

Darius nodded at her. "House Labraudos, great lineage. I believe your mother, the queen, is a descendant of one of your gods?"

"Mother is the demigod daughter of our sea god, Your Majesty," Ariane said proudly, which piqued Cora's interest. All Mistresses of the Granary claimed to be the daughters of gods, including Cora's mother, who claimed Cora was a field god's daughter.

Not that I would put this possibility past either of them. If my clunky ring was housing a genie, then Cora and Ariane could well be the blood of the gods.

"And you?" Darius asked Cora, his expression steady as she arranged her ornately carved pears.

She smiled tightly. "Cora Greenshoot, my mother's Mistress of the Granary."

Offering Cora a respectful nod, the king then shot his sister a judgmental expression, most likely wondering why Cora of all the real noblewomen remained among the Final Five.

"No need to ask who you are," Darius said to Cherine as she proudly curtsied. "But I'm afraid I'm not familiar with the one next to you."

I opened my mouth and the words froze in my mouth.

"Father, this is Ada of Rose Isle," Cyrus answered for me.

Darius sat in his chair, setting his hands atop the table. "Is she mute?"

I snapped out of it, shaking my head.

The king eyed me blankly for a second then forgot about

me in favor of Aurelia, who was giving him the harshest glare I had ever seen. Jumana had been her only niece, the only girl in her family, and she'd died here, possibly because of him.

Cyrus hadn't mentioned much about his mother yesterday. He'd only told me who she was but not what had happened to her. I again had to wonder how much he knew, and how much of it was true.

"The good impression starts now," Cyrus whispered tensely. "My proposal means nothing if not sanctioned by our reigning king."

His words struck me like a lightning bolt.

All I could utter was, "You said we just needed his blessing."

"That's what I thought. The rules of the competition state that the king and council would have to accept my choice as long she passed all the tests. But this morning I discovered that the result of the Bride Search still falls under royal marriage law, where the king's approval remains the decisive factor."

I was at a loss for words as the terrible reality finally hit me.

This man, this dead-eyed king, had managed to banish a powerful witch and, years before that, had made Jumana so miserable she'd ended her own life.

How was I supposed to endear myself to such a man?

Suddenly, all I could think about was Nariman. Not her threats, her crazy demands or her magic as a witch, but her life as a foreign lady-in-waiting, advisor, and surrogate mother to Cyrus, all of which had been ripped from her by this man and his father before him. That much of her story was true, and the conflicting claims of her trying to bewitch or usurp the king didn't help me pick a side to stand on.

The sway King Xerxes had held over the lives of Jumana and her witches was now held over me by Darius. His whims now dictated the outcome of my life the same way Nariman's did.

I had failed to rob him at the start of the week, and now I'd hurt Ayman, I could no longer count on him. I must cross the final hurdle to win on my own. Win that harsh man, and be invited into his quarters. Once near the lamp, the ring would obey my practiced commands and bring it to me.

But my plans had been broken and sealed back together so many times over the past week, and now, with the way Darius looked at me, they felt poised to shatter beyond reassembly.

This wasn't the desperation I'd suffered in the mountain, as I'd faced the ghouls, as I'd drowned, but it was just as overwhelming.

Controlling my breathing, I surveyed the room. The king had already gotten a general conversation circulating around the table, no doubt a ploy to fish for more impressions. Cherine and Ariane had eagerly joined in, both seemingly remembering Prince Miraz's status as another crown prince. Aurelia didn't converse as much as she nudged them all with pointed comments and biting remarks. The ones on the receiving end of her scalding temperament were not only Darius but Loujaïne as well.

I was convinced that without guests to give a pristine performance to, Loujaïne would have been openly horrible to me. It reinforced my deduction that she could have been one of the driving factors that had made Jumana's life in Cahraman hell. She could have been what my mother had gone to the ends of the known world to escape.

I'd agonized over all external factors that could stop me from being with Cyrus, but I hadn't given proper consideration to the internal ones: his family. When and if I saved the Fairborns and married him, what would they do to me?

I would be no different than all the foreign princesses who'd been shipped off to another land to marry a man they'd barely known. I'd be in an even worse situation having no ladies-in-waiting to keep me company and stave off my homesickness. Not unless I wanted to doom Bonnie to a life of glamorous imprisonment here as my roommate.

"What do *you* think?" The king aimed his fork in my direction.

I froze up with a flare of panic. "About what?"

"Your Majesty," Cyrus whispered.

"About what, Your Majesty?" I corrected nervously.

"So, she does speak," the king sneered. "But can she listen?"

"Father —" Cyrus began.

"It's terrible manners to ignore the words of your elders and superiors, especially in the presence of someone whose every word holds great importance," Darius cut him off. "Even more now that this meal is political, the hosts and guests all being noble in nature."

Realizing I wasn't going to answer, Darius aimed his cold eyes on his son. "Where's your cousin?"

"Fairuza has been feeling ill lately," Cyrus said, sending me a concerned glance. "The experience in the mountain has been hard on her."

Darius swept me in another bone-chilling glance. "Shame. *She* would have made such good company, and respectfully contributed to the conversation."

Cyrus tapped his utensils on the table as he gritted, *"Father."*

Darius disregarded him, flung the hand holding his knife out in an arc that encompassed the guests before him. "Is this really the best you could do? Fifty girls you demanded, five weeks you wasted weeding through them just to end with our initial choice, and four unnecessary others?"

"They were the best out of the fifty," Cyrus said, shoulders tense, fists clenched.

"I know for a fact that they are not, I oversaw them and their results. There were two dozen more suitable, talented, trained and respectable candidates with not only good lineage but the possibility to add vital alliances to this kingdom." The king accentuated each point with a screeching scrape of his knife as he sliced his meat. "Instead you send them home, keeping an insignificant island's princess, your pen pal, a field mouse and *this*." He gestured towards me. "Whatever this is. Grouping them all with the only real choice, embarrassing her by comparing her to them. No wonder she refuses to attend your mealtimes. It's offensive."

His words felt like I had been hit in the face with the silver jug before me. Repeatedly. Ariane let out a choking squeak and coughed. Loujaïne made no move to pat her on the back or even acknowledge her distress. Cherine crossed her arms disapprovingly and turned her nose up and looked away from the king, but gave me worried eyes when she faced me.

With a dismissive snort, Cora took her goblet and continued drinking.

I wished I could afford to have Cora's attitude. She didn't want or need to impress anyone here. She knew where she wanted to be and that everyone probably needed her more than she needed them.

"That was uncalled for." Cyrus had become steely-eyed, seething with rising anger.

The king regarded him with harsh disappointment. "What is uncalled for is typically necessary, something you should know as a future king. But this whole arrangement proves that this lesson hasn't stuck yet."

"What's necessary is for me to find a wife before my next birthday. I will announce my choice tomorrow, as promised."

"And it better be the right choice, because you have embarrassed us enough in the eyes of many elites and nobles."

"What is that supposed to mean?" Cyrus gritted between clenched teeth.

"It means that because of your stubbornness, all our current and possible allies had been given hope their daughters could one day become queen of this land through you, that Fairuza's fate as your queen wasn't set in stone. And had you chosen someone more suitable than her, it would have been understandable. But as I said, your choices beyond the princess herself are insultingly inferior." Frustration deepened the king's voice and sharpened his speech. "It would be an affront to all who participated and your entire family as well if you, at the end of all this, did not prove that Fairuza was the best choice all along."

His father didn't approve and he wouldn't. And I had known it all along. It had been partly why I'd been so reluctant to give in to Cyaxares the prince.

The meal ended abruptly when the king stood and strode out the room, acknowledging no one, even Aurelia who sent him off with a disparaging tsk.

Loujaïne and Farouk followed him, arguing quietly but heatedly among themselves. Cyrus gripped my wrist and pulled me after him.

He chased his father with wide, determined strides, making me run alongside him. I tried to struggle, wanting to run away from any further embarrassment but stopped when I realized where we were going.

The massive, double-door entrance of the king's quarters loomed closer. It was bordered by embroidered canvases depicting a scene with swooping winged men with guards below bracing spears.

We approached Loujaïne and Farouk and I could now hear him hissing, "The expected choice is not always the best one! We need some new blood, new possibilities—new dynamics. That was the point of the Bride Search this time."

"You're just covering for your failure," Loujaïne retorted. "You indulged the boy with this idea, helped set up his tests. You made us all play by your rules for a change and we still got the same result."

"We did not," Farouk bit off. "*She* was counted among the Final Five only because we knew leaving the princess out would cause problems within her family."

"That is a lie!" Loujaïne refuted, red-faced. "Fairuza is a true princess, has been trained to handle anything thrown her way since birth, and she passed every test."

Cyrus closed in on them, interrupting his aunt, "She did *not*. Despite her failures, her behavior and her shortcomings, I let Fairuza remain only out of respect for her family, the same reason Cherine stayed."

Darius stormed back to us, pushed Farouk and Loujaïne apart to square off with Cyrus. "Convenient, isn't it? That the one we had all chosen for you, the only one fit to be your wife, fails all of your pointless tests in the search you had no reason to hold?"

Cyrus lifted his chin in defiance, his grip tightening on my arm. "Call it what you want. It was proof she would be a terrible match for me."

"You are being extremely tiresome with your excuses." An undercurrent of threat entered Darius's lowered tone.

"We've played along long enough, now go arrange for tomorrow's party and be ready to give Fairuza your mother's ring."

"No."

The king took a menacing step closer, silver eyes bulging. "What was that?"

"No, I won't propose to Fairuza," Cyrus said, just as grim.

Darius' eyes flitted to me for a knee-knocking second before nodding once. "How's this then? If you don't marry her, you don't get married at all."

"Father, be reasonable. I have made my choice and Farouk can tell you why in great detail, so can I if you just *listen*."

"I've listened, Cyaxares. I've listened for months since the first time you rejected Fairuza. I gave you the freedom to explore your options so you could see that there was never another option." Darius stepped back, smoothing a hand down his gilded clothes. "Now save us all the trouble and send the rest of the girls home."

Cyrus took an urgent step toward him, his grip on me becoming painful. "Why won't you try to see my side of things, see all the merits Ada has—ask any of the staff, ask Princess Aurelia. Or just ask *me*."

"Because I won't risk another great mistake like what happened with your mother!" Darius boomed, his shout ringing off every surface and echoing in my head.

Cyrus dropped my arm, horror spreading through his eyes like ink in water.

"I don't know what foreign witchcraft this no-name noble did to grip you, but I'm not letting it happen. Not after your mother. I won't let another irreversible tragedy strike our house and our kingdom ever again." Darius choked up towards the end before his eyes hardened to flint, slicing through his son. "Marry her, and I'll have no choice but to disinherit you."

No.

This couldn't be happening. I couldn't cause this.

"You're dismissed." The king's shout reverberated off the walls as he swung around and yanked the doors to his quarters open.

He left them wide open for Loujaine to follow, and I finally got a full look into his quarters.

In the depths of the expansive chamber, by the massive bed stood a table with ornately carved wooden legs painted gold.

Sitting brazenly on top of its shimmering green marble surface was the spark that had set my whole life aflame.

The gold lamp.

CHAPTER THIRTY-FIVE

I had barely glimpsed the lamp when the doors were slammed in my face.

I'd never dreamed it would be out in the open like that. But at least now I knew where it was for certain. I had to go back for it, today, even if my only way in would be an even riskier gamble. One with possible fatal consequences. One I had to make.

"Don't let anything he said get to you."

I lurched out of my fugue at Cyrus's soft assurance.

I realized he was walking me down towards my room.

"We'll find a way around this. I just have to find an old law that can override his threats. It won't take long, then I'll..."

"He's right, you know," I cut him off, my voice trembling.

He stopped walking, turning to face me, blocking my path, stunning face ablaze with concern. "How can you say that?"

It physically hurt to say it, my throat constricting, my face burning with a numbing flush, but I had to respond. "With a clear mind. Something I haven't had for a while."

He shook his head, messing up his styled hair into the disarrayed state I loved so much on him.

"Marrying me would be a stupid idea," I insisted. "If you were literally anyone else it might have worked. But you're *the* Prince of Cahraman."

"It wasn't a problem before."

"I've only known this for less than a week." I paused as I choked up. "Last month you were someone else, and in a sense, so was I."

Frustration started to seep into his every line. "You came into this competition to appease a goddess and marry a prince. Why is it suddenly a problem?"

I burned to tell him why. I'd planned on telling him there was no goddess, just a witch with hostages, back when I'd had no idea who Prince Cyaxares was. Back when I'd thought us both the same, insignificant in the grand scheme of things, where we could run off together, to live as we wanted wherever we wanted.

But he was bound to this palace and I was bound to leave it.

If I told him the truth now, it would only make things worse, for myself and more importantly for him. He'd chosen the worst possible girl, one who didn't even exist. He'd proposed to Ada of Rose Isle, and even *she* would never be approved by his family and king. And it didn't matter if the real me was truly all of the things he wanted, if I could be the princess he needed. Unlike his act, which had only conflicted my priorities, my deception could ruin his life. It could cost him his crown.

And it wouldn't stop there.

As Cora had said, Cyrus had no one to take over as heir.

His disinheritance would lead to a war of succession and throw the kingdom into chaos.

I'd never let that happen to him, his family and the people they ruled.

"We'll talk to the high priest," he continued arguing. "I'll explain everything to him, and why I can't marry Fairuza."

I shook my head. "You can."

"But I don't want to. I want to marry *you*."

"What you want would cause turmoil for the whole kingdom," I said, more to myself than to him.

"No, no, don't take anything my father said seriously." He held my arms, looked me in the eyes, thumbs softly stroking my skin, a touch that had become achingly familiar and terribly needed.

He made it even worse, bowing his head to touch our foreheads. A sweet comfort, a loving intimacy that soothed the soul, what he couldn't have with Fairuza or anyone else. I knew, because I'd never have it with any other either.

But that was too small an issue in the grand scheme of things.

"We'll get married without telling anyone. Once it's done, no one can do anything but deal with that fact." He slid his hands down my arms to hold my own, raising them between us, pressing them between our hearts. "What do you say?"

Sorrow rose up within me like a giant wave, the splash of searing sadness flowing from my eyes as I made my decision.

"No."

CHAPTER THIRTY-SIX

*H*iding in my room didn't make things easier.

The barrier between us wasn't just the wooden door, but everything I had already thought through a thousand times.

He was a prince. This wasn't a fairytale. This had all been a means to an end for me. Love and happy endings were never part of the deal.

But thinking about it logically didn't make it any more bearable.

"Ada, talk to me!" He begged from the other side of my bedroom door. He tried the handle again before banging on the door. "Please, say something."

The air that fled my mouth as I spoke felt like shards in my lungs. "I already said all that I could. Your father and Loujaïne are right. Fairuza is the best choice for you as a future king."

That threw him for a moment, before he continued, growing more frustrated. "Fairuza will marry someone else, someone who wants her. And no one will matter when I am king."

"Which is in, what? Thirty, forty years? Your father could reign into old age, and until then, we'd be at his mercy."

That silenced him for a long moment. It was evident Cyrus hadn't considered the limitations of his own power as a crown prince until his father had denied him his choice. But if even that title was stripped from him, he, and the kingdom, would find themselves in a situation as precarious as mine.

I felt him lean against the door, heard his heavy sigh as he dropped his forehead on the wood. "Then we'll leave. We'll do what many others did before us until their time to succeed came, we'll move from the castle and govern a city."

His desperation to work things out, all out of love for me, sent burning tears flooding down my face. If it weren't for me, he would have never been put in this situation. This was all my fault.

"You know they won't let that happen, especially if you pick me."

He tried to offer up another solution that wouldn't change a thing but I couldn't bear listening to him sounding as desperate as I felt.

"You love your people, don't you?" I cut him off.

"Of course I do, why do you think I went to such lengths to find the perfect princess for them?" Cyrus' voice cracked towards the end, deepening the fissure splitting my breaking heart. "I didn't expect to find the one who was all I needed as well."

This was all I had ever wanted to hear, but not like this. This was too much to bear.

"Step by step, we'll figure things out. We'll turn them around. What kind of a king will I be if I can't make a stand for the most important things? For what I believe in? I believe in you, Ada. I believe in the great future we can have together, one I can't have without you." He paused to draw a difficult breath then added. "I love you, Ada."

My heart splintered into a million pieces.

"Ada, what do you say?"

I took a shuddering breath. "I say that neither of us can afford to think of ourselves. You have a responsibility to your people, and I have one to mine."

"Ada—"

"They need you, your family needs you, and Fairuza really, really *needs* you."

"What are you talking about?"

"Fairuza is cursed, and only by earning the love of the most noble of men can she break the curse."

But if he married her and but couldn't love her, she would die. Another dead princess in the House of Shamash. A repeat of Jumana's tragedy.

But at least with me gone, with Cyrus giving up on his dream of us, with Fairuza changed, he might love her, might save her…

"Ada. Ada, please," he begged, pounding on the door with each word, desperation now filling his voice. "I can't love anyone else. It's beyond my control. I would be no good to her. She must find the man to love her to save her before it's too late. We can both help her find him. But you have to stay with me. To do this and everything else with me. You can't leave me, Ada, not after all this. You can't do this to us."

This wasn't working. He wouldn't go away, wouldn't give up on me.

I raised my hand, watching my magic ring catch the afternoon light from my window and exhaled my anguish. "There is no us."

"But there will be, if you just listen to me and trust me to find a way to fix this I promise you my father won't be able to interfere. I—"

"I wish you would understand I'm doing what's best for all of us," I whispered to the ring with a heavy heart. "I wish you'd give up and leave."

Cyrus stopped talking and moved off the door. I heard him walk away from my room and leave the hall, his fading footsteps as steady and as heavy as my heartbeats.

It was over.

I sagged down against the door, heaped on the ground and let go of my last shred of control.

I didn't know how long I wept. All I knew was that I'd wasted enough time being a daydreaming, self-pitying fool.

But at least I had saved Cyrus from making a grave mistake. I might have also saved Fairuza. Now I had to save the Fairborns.

Now I was almost certain that Nariman needed the lamp for a terrible purpose, one involving Cahraman and its royal family. How could I possibly give it to her?

I had to do it. I at least had to show her the lamp, have her see that I'd kept my part of the bargain.

With no other options, and no one left to count on, it was all down to me.

CHAPTER THIRTY-SEVEN

My plan was set. As was its backup.

The first was easier but depending partially on luck, while the second was harder, but built around my knowledge of Nariman, and revolved around the ring. Around the symbol of our brief, tragic betrothal.

If it worked, Cyrus's love for me might still end up saving us all.

Now was the ultimate test for the ring and my ability to wield it, a final run before I faced Nariman.

Opening the door, I raised the ring to my mouth and whispered, "I wish every guard on duty would fall into a trance."

I peeked outside my room. None of the guards showed signs of being affected.

There wasn't anything else I could do. I had to leave, unseen or not.

Chest tight, I exited my room.

The guards remained looking ahead as I passed, but as I approached the third guard, my tension began to ebb. They all had the same unfocused gaze, seemed unaware of my presence, or anything else.

It had worked!

More confident of my plan, I disguised myself with a shawl and headed back up to the king's room, every step fueled with determination and dread.

I stopped at the corner before the king's quarters.

The doors were closed and the entrance guards now stood in a stupor outside. But I couldn't tell if the king was inside or not.

It felt like it had been ages since I had last staked out a target. I'd always had time to study the place and its people to know the first's layout and the latter's schedule and habits. Long enough to chart the perfect plan's ins, outs, and contingencies. But I had no time for that now.

The idea that I could influence him, too, make him approve of me or give me the lamp, flashed like a tempting gleam of gold.

I quickly snapped out of it. Influencing others for their own good was one thing, doing it for my own gain was another. But to rob the king of his will, for the rest of his life, would be far worse than anything Nariman did to me. To hold that kind of power over someone's life would be corrupting, dangerous.

I wouldn't do it. I couldn't go down that road.

I only wished for him to leave his quarters as soon as possible and waited. My target was on his bedside table of all places. It would have been better if it had been in a safe, something not in plain sight and hard for him to immediately notice its absence.

In my perfect world, I would have confronted Nariman, gotten the Fairborns back, and returned to Cyrus. The one good part to this heartrending change in my plans was that this was going to be a theft like any other, a break-in arranged on the day I skipped town, never to look back or be tracked down.

Minutes passed with me crouching against the wall, my head swimming with too many emotions. I was so distracted I almost blacked out with fright at the first sign of movement. Two councilmen in maroon robes arriving to knock on the doors. The king opened and headed out with them.

I heard them coming my way and hurried to hide behind a statue of Xerxes II. As they passed, I caught some of what Darius was saying.

"I should have never let myself agree to this," he grumbled to his silent companions as they headed down the staircase. "He had a bride and other suitable options in case anything happened to her. I shouldn't have trusted him to choose his own bride to begin with. I chose my own and look what that got me."

He *chose* Jumana? I thought they were like Cyrus and Fairuza, forced together once they were old enough to be married.

That just made their story a lot worse than I thought it was.

It also made his reaction to me a bit more understandable.

Once they were out of my earshot, I rushed past the entranced guards and entered.

The king's quarters were the size of our hall. The gigantic space was neatly arranged with gilded furniture, and his bed —predictably, king-sized—sprawled on a platform above the rest of the room. The bedside table was, to my surprise, cluttered, with the only personal touches I'd seen in this palace. It held an antique lantern, a colorful glasswork jar, a silver picture frame of a small painting, an incense burner and, finally, the reason I was here.

The lamp. As long as my forearm and shaped like a squat teapot with a snout-like spout. It felt strange to finally be so close to the reason my life had been turned inside out.

But why did Darius keep it by him the way people kept glasses of water? If he'd used it to banish Nariman, then he knew of the genie. Had he used it again since? Before? Did he use it to command ifrits that acted as a part of the kingdom's magical defenses? Was it his, his family's, or had she told the truth when she'd said it was hers, and he'd promised to marry her only to swindle her and use it against her?

None of my questions could have answers. Only these two knew the truth.

Picking it up, I examined it. It was heavy. I lifted its lid, but there was no inside. This lamp *was* made of pure, solid gold. On the surface, it served no further purpose. But I knew what was inside.

What if I too could use it against her? Genies fulfilled wishes, and I'd proved I could command one effectively. I had to try using that one. If I had two genies, maybe I could get the Fairborns back. I wouldn't even need to deal with Nariman. Her threat would be gone, and she'd remain in exile outside of Cahraman and unable to hurt anyone.

For the next ten minutes, I tried everything to get a response out of the lamp.

I'd shaken it, rubbed it, talked to it, hit it—and nothing.

I couldn't believe I had it in my hands after all this time and I could do *nothing* with it.

It couldn't need a witch to work it, since Darius wasn't one. So how did it work?

Frustrated, I examined it closely. The only mark on it was

a pattern around its lid. At closer inspection, it looked like calligraphic etchings that resembled ancient Cahramani, but not exactly.

I was starting to wonder if I'd gotten it all wrong. That there was no genie, and Dairus had banished Nariman with something else entirely.

I wished for answers from my ring, but it yielded none.

This meant it was on to the second plan. I'd always feared, and expected, it would come down to that, anyway.

So far, the only reliable power the ring had let me exercise had been over my own body and the wills of others.

That would have to do.

Tucking the lamp into my sack, I rushed out.

Passing by my room on the way to our old quarters and the trapdoor leading to the tunnels, I found an armored Ayman. He was nudging an unresponsive guard.

At my approach, Ayman whirled around, bumping into the column where the bust of Princess Zafira perched, nearly knocking it off its platform. "What happened?"

"I don't know," I wheezed, the lamp feeling as heavy as my guilt. Over what I'd done to him, to Cyrus. "Ayman, I know I don't have the right to ask anything of you, but can you tell me if the tunnel in our old dorm can lead out to the city?"

Instead of answering, he leveled me with a probing stare. "What happened with Cyrus then?"

"Please, don't ask," I begged him, the sound of Cyrus's name was enough to drive me to the verge of collapse. "Just answer me because I really must leave now. I'll understand if you won't."

I expected him to ask more questions, to argue, or worse, arrest me, but he just ran beside me. "It can lead out to different parts of the city, but the fastest way down is the train. If you take a right before the vault, then another, you can follow the tunnel right to its stop outside the palace."

Brimming with disbelief, I breathed raggedly. "Thank you!"

He made no response.

Upon arriving at my old quarters, I burst in and came to a stuttering halt.

Sitting on her old bed between her luggage, Cora wiggled her fingers at me. "Leaving without me?"

I shut the door in Ayman's face, flattening against it. "What are you doing here?"

"Figured you'd split after the king's tantrum. And I'm taking his behavior at lunch as my long-awaited dismissal. I had a feeling you'd escape through the trapdoor under Cherine's bed—before you ask, yes, I saw you use it—and I thought we could leave together." She stretched her neck. "What you got there? Loot?"

I showed her the inside of my bag.

Her face warped in an unimpressed scowl. "That's the infamous lamp? I expected better craftsmanship, maybe some opals and rubies."

"There's nothing in it either, I'm pretty sure I overthought the genie thing."

"It's better if you did." She jumped off the bed, heaving up her bags. "Let's go before they notice it's gone."

"Wait, are you just leaving or are you coming with me?"

"Coming with you *then* leaving. You need a hand with what you're dealing with."

Touched beyond words, my mouth wobbled. "Really?"

"Yes, really." She raised a balled fist. "Tell me I get to punch something today, *please*."

Though I could tell she was joking, her confidence helped put me at ease.

I was *really* going to miss her.

I gave her a thankful smile. "Let's go then."

Ayman barged into the room and behind him stood Fairuza, still in her white silk nightgown.

"She followed us here," he said, apologetic. "Do I let her pass?"

Swallowing, I waved her in.

Ducking under his arm, she rushed to me. "Are you leaving?"

When I nodded, she exclaimed, "Why?"

Facing her now, I remembered our test at the courthouse, with the two widows fighting over the child. One wanted him to maintain her way of life and the other let him go for his own safety and stability. But this was far more complicated. By letting Cyrus go, I let him keep his life and future, giving him a chance to keep her alive.

It would be like I'd never been here to upset their plans and expectations.

This was the best choice for both of them.

"Because you were right, you're the only option for Cyrus, and the king won't consider any others," I said, throat tight. "You have a chance now."

"But I really don't." Fairuza wrapped shaking arms around her middle, hair falling out of its loose bun, a dark, glossy frame for her pale, haunted face. "He won't ever love me. Even if it's possible, it won't be in time to break the curse."

"You can still try." My vision swam, blurring her before me. "You *have* to."

"Ada, I…" she trailed off, mouth agape as she came closer

and set her hands on my arms and her head on my shoulder in a light, tense embrace. "I'm sorry I was so horrible to you."

I sniffled, hugging her back. "It doesn't matter now."

Shaking her head against my shoulder with a sob, she pulled back.

As she walked to the door, she gave me a small, sad smile. "Goodbye, Ada."

Hearing her say my name for the first time was a foreign feeling. I didn't know what she meant by it or why it threw me off. Perhaps I was becoming a person worthy of remembering, someone I hoped she lived long enough to remember.

Ayman came up behind me. "I'll show you the way."

My jaw dropped as he went beneath what used to be Cherine's bed and removed the loose tile.

"Let's go." Ayman called out from beneath the bed.

Cora nudged me forwards. "How did you get one of them to help you out?"

The trade-off had been introducing him to Cherine, who had begun to fear him and dream of him on that bed. What Cora had witnessed going disastrously wrong.

And yet, he was still helping me.

Spiraling in my worsening guilt, I went in first, and then we slid down after him, out of the room and into the tunnels.

He looked as awful as I felt. I wanted to console him, or to tell him he'd chosen the worst possible candidate for his affections in Cherine, or that she might still come around after she calmed down. But in that acute time of hurt, it would be like pouring acid into his wounds.

When we went in deep enough to find the magical green-fire torches, I slowed down to look behind me, my heart squeezing so tightly it felt it was imploding.

I never got to say goodbye to Cyrus.

Just like I never had to my mother or Bonnie.

As the wave of desolation crashed on me, only one thing mitigated my misery.

That I was doing this so I wouldn't have to say goodbye to Bonnie. And so that Cyrus would one day become the best king Cahraman had ever known.

Cora pulled me behind her, snatching me out of my wretched thoughts as Ayman led us deeper inside the mountain, on a path that would finally take me out of the palace.

The palace that had been both a cage that fostered my sorrow and desperation and a trove of friendship and love.

A love I'd now lost forever.

CHAPTER THIRTY-EIGHT

My mind finally stalled when we boarded the train.

Silence, inside and out, reigned during its trip down the mountain.

Ayman, who'd discarded his armor at the tunnels, wore the hood of his cloak low to avoid attention and Cora had kicked off her shoes, bare toes finally free to wiggle among the bristles of the carpet. I was crumpled in the corner of my window seat, watching Sunstone Palace leave my sight and the distant, glittering details of the city below become larger and clearer as we spiraled towards it.

By the time the train reached its final station at the city walls, my eyes felt worn out and friable from the outpour of anguish. I rubbed at them, breaking off lashes, feeling as if my puffy lids might crumble and come off on my fingers, too.

The train stopped with a scraping screech of metal and aggravated puffs of steam. A horn brayed through the air, telling us to disembark.

Ayman moved first. He carried Cora's bags out as she

helped me up and we followed him down and out, wading through the growing crowd on the platform.

She squeezed me against her side in a one-armed hug. "It will be over soon."

Letting myself lean on her, I gathered all my remaining strength. I needed to be in control to face Nariman, and to enact my plan.

It would work. There was no reason for it not to. This time, I wouldn't even consider the worst. This time I was winning.

"It will," I said firmly, to myself more than to her.

"That's good then. You'll get your family, then we can both go home.

I caught her arm. "You can come with us for a visit on the way back if you'd like."

A look of affection lit her usually dispassionate face.

I impulsively hugged her, and after a moment of surprise, she hugged me back as fervently.

"Please do come, I don't want to lose you too now," I choked against her shoulder as Ayman came back to hurry us out.

We followed him across the threshold of the city gates.

Ayman pointed to a caravan, much like the one that had carried me into the city what felt like a lifetime ago.

"This is your way out of Cahraman."

I grabbed his arm, choking up again. "Thank you, really, you have no idea how much your help means to me."

He drew his cowl further down, so all I could see was his mouth twitching in a fake smile. "No problem."

"No, really. You didn't need to do all of this, especially after things went bad with Cherine."

"I didn't agree to help you because you could introduce me

to her." He crossed his arms under his cloak, looking offended.

"Then why did you?"

"You made Cyrus happy, even if it was just for a while," he admitted, further crushing my heart. "And you were nice to me when you had no reason to be."

I jumped up on my tiptoes and hugged him. He stumbled back, not knowing what to do with his arms until he steadied them by his sides, stiff and uncertain.

"Tell him I'm sorry," I sobbed against his chest. "And that I —that I loved him. With all I am. *Please.*"

"You should tell him yourself." One of his hands rose to my back, hovered there before patting me hesitantly. "But I suppose you have your reasons."

I hugged him tighter, squeezing my eyes shut to hold back tears. I failed.

"Here a day early, I see," said a cold, amused voice.

Nariman.

My breath hitched in my chest as I met her eyes from over Ayman's shoulder. Reflected in them was every harrowing moment of the past weeks.

Everything I'd been through, everything I'd done, had all been to reach this moment.

I'd started out as her prey. Then I'd become her instrument. Now—now I'd be her downfall.

Stepping away from Ayman, I faced her, blood burning, at what she'd done and with anticipation of what I had to do.

"I have to say I'm impressed you made it out intact," Nariman said as she advanced. She wore a wine-red velvet cloak, her dark hair held up in a chignon by a sparkling set of hair-sticks, her gold snake staff clutched in her ringed hand.

Ayman staggered back, scattering the sand of the firm dunes beneath us. "Lady Rostam?"

If she was surprised to see him, she didn't show it.

She stopped a foot away from him and examined his face from different angles. "I feel like I haven't seen you in ages, Ayman. You were always hiding in the shadows and under that ugly armor."

"What are you doing here?" he demanded, shock jostling his normally expressionless tone.

"I should be asking you the same question. Can't remember the last time you went this far out without being Cyrus's shadow," she said casually, circling us in long strides. "But now that you're out, you don't have to go back in. I could use someone like you for when everything is finally set right."

He gaped at her. "What are you talking about?"

She ignored his question as she circled back to her spot before him, leaning in to squint at his features. "Don't scowl, dear, it makes you look like your mother. You don't know how much restraint it took for me not to bash her royal skull in every time she made that sour face at me."

Royal…? Sour face…?

Loujaïne.

Loujaïne was Ayman's mother.

All the pieces suddenly crashed in place.

Ayman being from Almaskham. Loujaïne having been married and divorced by Azal, a prince of that nation. Her hostility towards Ayman.

It seemed, like everyone else, she saw his birth as a curse, his appearance grounds for her divorce and destruction of her marital life and future prospects.

I was still reeling with the realizations when Nariman

came before me and took my chin between her fingers, tilting my face up to hers. "Adelaide, it's so good to see you again."

After so long of being afraid of her, now I was no longer powerless, defiance flared within me fueling my angry sarcasm. "With you holding my friends hostage, I hope you don't expect me to reciprocate that statement."

She sighed dramatically. "I guess I shouldn't. But we did have a deal, the lamp in exchange for Bonnie and her father's lives."

I thumbed my ring as I stepped away from her. I put a dozen feet between us, before showing her the inside of my bag. "I want them back *now*."

Nariman let out a soft gasp at the sight of the lamp as it gleamed in the last rays of sunset.

I clenched my fist, feeling the metal band on my finger bite into my skin. I wanted to strike, to throw her into the ocean, to banish her to Faerie, but I had to wait. I couldn't jeopardize my rescue now that it was so close.

"This is what you wanted, isn't it?" I said through gritted teeth.

Excitement shook her features and voice as she gazed at it with reverent fascination. "It certainly is. "

"You got what you wanted. Congratulations. Now uphold your end of the deal. Hand them over and you get this."

She raised one hand and snapped her fingers. A circle of red light blasted out from around her and into the unseen distance. "There we go."

I held my breath, waiting for the Fairborns to appear.

They didn't.

I rounded on her, yelling, "Where are they? We had a deal!"

"And it has been fulfilled. Bonnie is not at risk of being eaten by the beast anymore."

She wasn't going to give them back. She was *never* going to give them back.

"Nariman, give them back and send us home!"

She paid me no mind, striding towards me, hands outstretched.

Anger exploded within me as I whispered to the ring, wishing for a trap.

Fire blasted across the sand around us. The flames met in a circle that trapped Nariman in a ring of blazing blue so hot it turned the sand to glass.

"What is this?" she gasped, her cool composure overrun by shock. "Whose magic is this?"

"Be quiet!" I raised the ring to my mouth, trembling with fury. "I wish Nariman would do as I say."

She stared at me through the flickering flames, amber eyes wide, caught in a processing silence like Cherine and Cyrus when I'd influenced their thoughts.

This was it. There would be no more of her tricks and everything would go back to the way it was.

Blood pumping with the thrill of the magic, and the power I held over her, I made my demand. "I wish for Nariman to send the Fairborns and I back to where she found us and for her to return to Almaskham and never leave it again."

Unblinking, Nariman raised her cane, pointing it ahead.

My excitement began to churn as a portal yawned into existence, a spiral of wind and light.

But this one was different from either her first portal or Marzeya's. It was ever-shifting, showing glimpses of two scenes. The first was of the Hornswoods, where Nariman had first snatched us, the trees pale and washed out in a wet twilight.

In the second I saw Bonnie!

And she wasn't in a dank, dark dungeon as I'd feared.

She was in a sunlit green-marble room with a mezzanine that encircled its walls. Between its high windows were massive bookshelves, with ladders propped against them, and colorful books crowding them from top to bottom.

Chattering excitedly, Bonnie stood on tiptoes in a blush-pink dress, her hair rolled in a bun, reaching for a book. The sound of clopping hooves echoed, drowning her words.

A man entered the scene, but not on horseback. This bespectacled, bearded man was half-goat from the waist-down, with horns protruding from his auburn curls!

The satyr brought the book down for her and said something that made her laugh.

As they turned to leave, Bonnie stopped dead, her wide-eyed stare pinned towards me.

She saw me!

Dropping the book on a piercing cry, she ran towards the growing portal.

Wracked with disbelief I rushed to the portal, calling her name and panting with relieved laughter.

It was all over, it was all—

Cold, hard metal struck the back of my head.

An explosion of pain and vertigo sent me crashing to the ground.

I clawed at the sand, trying to steady the world, to drag myself up. Pain and panic scattered whatever lucid thoughts remained as I saw Ayman and Cora fly off the ground, only to crash in opposite directions, impacting the hard dunes with nauseating thuds and agonized shouts. My scream came out a chafing whimper as I watched the portal shut down, dwindling as Bonnie rushed towards me, hand outstretched.

Then it was gone. *Gone!*

My worst nightmare only escalated as the flames entrapping Nariman were snuffed and she stepped over the hot glass left in their wake, shattering it as she howled with laughter.

"You almost had me for a minute there!"

No. How could she have denied me? The wish *had* worked! She'd done as I said!

Why had it stopped working?

"It was a passable attempt, Adelaide, but I thought you were smarter than this. I am the most powerful witch of my generation. I am the one who commands minds and fates. You cannot control me!"

With a flick of her wrist, my bag flew to her and she took out the lamp.

I watched her helplessly as she held it in delicate hands by the handle and spout, gazed at it in awe.

She turned in her hands, eyeing the lid, then she pulled her sleeve over her hand to polish its side.

Rubbing faster, Nariman stepped over me, saying the same strange words, over and over again. On the last chant, I understood their meaning, even when they themselves remained foreign.

"Come forth at my command and fulfill my demand!"

Sparking purple and indigo smoke flowed out of the lamp's spout in thick, curling clouds, turning red as they settled in the air around us.

"You were supposed to give them back!" I coughed, heavy smoke rushing into my lungs, the clouds now thick enough to block most of my sight.

Only Nariman remained clear in the middle of the billowing of noxious fumes, holding the smoking lamp overhead as it glowed and shook with a crackling noise that rose until it rivaled thunder.

"I never said you would get her back, I just promised she wouldn't be sacrificed to Rosemead's beast," Nariman shouted over the din, smug with power. "And you saw she won't. If you want her, you'll have to go get her yourself."

I whispered desperate wishes to the ring again, but this time nothing happened. Rage accumulated like steam within me as I staggered up, escaping me in a scream as I rushed at her.

Red flames shot out of the spout, burning through the smoke, singeing me as they knocked me back. The barrier of the terrible crackling broke, revealing it to be unbridled, manic laughter.

The lamp jumped from her hands levitating in the air as flames poured out of it, spiraling up in the air in an ever-widening tornado, taking the form of a fiery, humanoid creature.

It was the genie I had failed to summon.

The scene was straight out of my anthology's illustrations. A gigantic being of living fire rising from a blazing cyclone that poured out of a bottle. The only difference was that it now did out of a solid gold lamp.

The ring had misled me. When I'd asked it what it was, it had shown me a genie in a bottle, the one that had appeared to Esfandiar. It had me believe that with or without the one in the lamp, the one in my ring, with its unlimited wishes, would be superior.

But whatever lived in my ring was nothing like it.

The genie's blazing form settled before us as the lamp hit the ground, burning the dunes into glass. Its laughter turned the wind into a gale that spun its smoke and turned the dusky landscape into a moonless night.

Too bright to fully discern, its only clear features were its pointed ears and the golden shackles binding it to its lamp, the genie bowed to Nariman.

"Mistress, one who has set me free, wishes I shall grant thee but no more than three."

My hands flew to my ears as its rumbling voice shook apart the desert around us, and almost uprooted my heart and every bone in my body.

Nariman stepped up on the highest dune around us and raised her hands to the genie in silent praise, her hair falling out of its roll and flying in the hot wind, her eyes tearing up from the smoke but her mouth spreading in an ecstatic smile.

"Genie, I wish to be what I should have been all those years ago." Her voice rose with glee and command. "I wish to be the Queen of Cahraman!"

I fell to my knees as the genie's laughter exploded, quaking the whole world around us. The vortex of fire and smoke swatted me around as it reached hurricane strength.

Suddenly, everything died down.

I rose on trembling arms, mouth and eyes full of burning sand, looked around, desperately searching for Cora and Ayman. And what I saw froze every drop of blood in my veins.

In the background, the city walls crumbled to the desert like a house of cards, their demolition shaking the earth and tearing rifts in it that radiated like tentacles in every direction. The mushrooming cloud of destruction rose and hung in the air before it started settling, making way for a swarm of thundering clouds that further darkened the land as her wish distorted the architecture and lightning struck towers and temples, setting them aflame.

In place of all the luminous, gleaming structures that made

Cahraman a jewel of beauty and magic, towered dark, ominous structures that reeked of hatred and fear and evil.

Nariman had remade Cahraman in her image.

I remained on my knees, paralyzed as I watched everything I had feared come true.

I'd been forced to come here to save my friends from a horrible fate. I'd left for good to save Cyrus from the decisions that would have thrown his life and kingdom in chaos. I'd come to face her in a bid to fix everything.

But there'd been no point to any of it.

Bonnie was still thousands of miles away and Cyrus's kingdom was being irreversibly warped before my very eyes.

It hadn't mattered what choice I made, whether I left or stayed. From my first step past the city gates, my arrival had spelled doom for Cahraman.

I hope you've enjoyed PRINCE OF CAHRAMAN, the second installment in the Cahraman Trilogy as much as I enjoyed writing it!

Reviews and word of mouth are the life-blood of Indie Authors, so if you enjoyed the book, please help me spread the word!

Even a line on Amazon, Goodreads and Bookbub would be vital to my success and to the book's sales, and would be hugely appreciated.

If you haven't yet, please read where it all began in the #1 Amazon Bestsellers, THIEF OF CAHRAMAN and PRINCE OF CAHRAMAN and QUEEN OF CAHRAMAN and continue with Bonnie's arc BEAST OF ROSEMEAD & BEAUTY OF ROSEMEAD and the Cinderella/Snow Queen retelling PRINCESS OF MIDNIGHT!

We can expect DREAMER OF BRIARFELL, a Sleeping Beauty retelling in Spring 2020!

To find out when it's out, and other exclusive content,

news, updates and offers, please sign up to my VIP Mailing List.

I also love to hear from my readers, so please contact me at lucytempestauthor@gmail.com

Thank you for reading!

Lucy

PRONUNCIATION GUIDE

— People

Ariane: Aa-ree-ann

Cherine: Sheh-reen

Cyaxares: Sigh-ak-sa-reez

Esfandiar: Ess-fun-dee-yuhr

Fairuza: Fey-roo-zah

Farouk: Fah-rooq

Jumana: Zhoo-mah-nah

Loujaïne: Loo-zhaiy-enn

Marzeya: Mar-zey-yuh

Nariman: Nah-ree-maan

— Places:

Almaskham: Ul-maz-kham

Cahraman: Quh-rah-maahn

Campania: Kaam-pahn-yuh

Ericura: Air-ree-cue-ruh

Orestia: Au-ress-tee-ya

Tritonia: Try-tone-yaa

Zhadugar: Ja-doo-gaar

ABOUT THE AUTHOR

With one foot in reality and the other one lodged firmly in fantasy, Lucy Tempest has been spinning tales since she learned how to speak.

Now, as an author, people can experience the worlds she creates for themselves.

Lucy lives in Southern California with her family and two spoiled cats, who would make terrible familiars.

Her young adult fantasy series FAIRYTALES OF FOLK-SHORE is a collection of interconnected fairytale retellings, each with a unique twist on a beloved, timeless tale.

Sign up to her VIP mailing list at https://www.lucytempest.com/newsletter

And follow her on

facebook.com/LucyTempestAuthor

twitter.com/lucy_tempest

bookbub.com/authors/lucy-tempest

goodreads.com/lucy_tempest

pinterest.com/lucytempestauthor

Made in the USA
Coppell, TX
06 March 2022

74571655R00213